New York Times Bestselling Author

SHIRLEE McCOY

Her Christmas Guardian
&
Protective Instincts

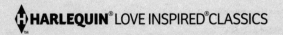

HARLEQUIN® LOVE INSPIRED®CLASSICS

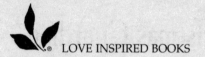

LOVE INSPIRED BOOKS

ISBN-13: 978-1-335-00674-5

Recycling programs
for this product may
not exist in your area.

Her Christmas Guardian & Protective Instincts

www.Harlequin.com

CONTENTS

Aside from her faith and her family, there's not much **Shirlee McCoy** enjoys more than a good book! When she's not teaching or chauffeuring her five kids, she can usually be found plotting her next Love Inspired Suspense story or wandering around the beautiful Inland Northwest in search of inspiration. Shirlee loves to hear from readers. If you have time, drop her a line at shirlee@shirleemccoy.com.

Visit the Author Profile page at Harlequin.com for more titles.

HER CHRISTMAS GUARDIAN

"Here is what I am commanding you to do. Be strong and brave. Do not be terrified. Do not lose hope. I am the LORD your God. I will be with you everywhere you go."
—*Joshua* 1:9

To Beth.
I miss going on long walks with you and your kids!

ONE

I've been found.

The thought shot through Scout Cramer's head, left her breathless, frantic. She veered the shopping cart toward the store exit, her heart pounding, her body vibrating with fear.

In her periphery, a man moved in. Casual in his dark slacks and sport coat, he looked like any other holiday shopper. She wanted so badly to believe he was.

Please, God. Please. Let me be wrong about who he is.

But she didn't think she was.

She thought she was right. Thought that somehow, after nearly three years, everything she'd tried to do for Amber, everything she'd tried to do for herself and Lucy had come to nothing. *If* she'd been found out, *if* he'd learned the truth, it was all for nothing. Every lie. Every broken friendship.

All of it.

For nothing.

"Please, God," she whispered as she unhooked Lucy's belt and lifted her from the cart. At just a little over twenty-four pounds, she was tiny for her age, her little arms wrapping snugly around Scout's neck.

"Mommy needs to find the restroom," Scout murmured, afraid to walk out into the parking lot. He'd follow her there. She was sure of it. After that...

What would he do?

Confront her?

Worse?

The store was filled with holiday shoppers, dozens of people crowding into Walmart's long lines, all of them desperate for Christmas bargains.

Would anyone notice if Scout was attacked?

Would anyone intervene?

Maybe, but she didn't plan to stick around long enough to find out.

She glanced at the man, hoping he didn't notice her sideways look. He was still, hovering at the head of an aisle, pretending to look at cans of asparagus.

She pivoted away, hurrying toward a restroom sign and the corridor beyond it. There had to be an emergency exit. She nearly ran to the end of the hall, stopping at double doors marked Employees Only.

What would happen if she walked in?

Would someone call the police? Set off an alarm?

Would she be arrested? If she was, what would happen to Lucy?

She looked at her little girl, smiling into dark brown eyes that were so much like Amber's it hurt to look in them.

"It's going to be okay," she whispered, and she hoped she was right. She'd made a lot of mistakes in her life. She'd done a lot of things she'd regretted, but she'd never regretted her friendship with Amber. She'd never regretted the promise she'd made to her.

Even if she did sometimes wonder if she'd been right to make it.

She glanced over her shoulder. No sign of the guy in the sport jacket. But her skin crawled, and her hair stood on end.

Something wasn't right, and that scared her more than anything else that had happened in the past couple of years.

She pushed the door open, took a step into what must have been an employee break room. No one there. Thank goodness. Just vending machines, a microwave, a refrigerator. Straight across from where she stood, an external door with a small window offered the hope of escape she'd been looking for.

"Everything okay, ma'am?" The voice was so unexpected, she jumped, whirling to face the speaker, her heart in her throat, her arms tightening around Lucy.

Tall.

That was the first impression she got.

Very tall, because she was eye to chest, staring straight at a black wool coat that hung open to reveal a dark purple dress shirt.

She looked up into ocean-blue eyes and a hard, handsome face, took in the black knit cap that almost covered deep red hair, the auburn stubble, the deep circles beneath the man's eyes. He smiled, and his face changed. Not hard any longer. Approachable. The kind of guy a woman might put her trust in.

If she ever put her trust in anyone.

"I'm fine," she managed to say.

"You're in the employee break room," he pointed out,

flashing an easy smile. There was nothing easy about the look in his eyes. She was being studied, assessed, filed away for future reference.

"Yes. Well." She glanced around, trying to think of a good excuse for being in a place she shouldn't be. "I was looking for the restroom."

"You passed it."

"I guess I did." Her cheeks heated, but she refused to look away. He hadn't hauled out handcuffs or threatened to arrest her yet, so he probably wasn't a security guard or police officer. She doubted he was working with the man who'd been following her. She'd have noticed him way before she'd noticed the other guy. That dark red hair and lanky height weren't easy to miss. "I'll just go find it."

She sidled past him, moving back into the hall, Lucy's arms still tight around her neck. She'd do anything for her daughter. *Anything.* Even run away from everything she knew. Give up a job she loved. Say goodbye to friends and never contact them again.

"Are you in some kind of trouble?" the guy asked, following her down the hall.

Was she?

She didn't know, wasn't made for intrigue and danger. She liked quiet predictability. No drama. No muss. Nothing that was even close to trouble. The one time she'd tried to break free, do something wild and reckless and completely different, she'd caused herself enough heartache to last a lifetime.

No more.

Never again.

Except that she *had* done it again. Gone out on a limb, done something completely out of character. For different reasons, but the results had been the same. Trouble. It was breathing down her neck. She felt it as surely as she felt Lucy's soft breath on her cheek.

"Ma'am?" The man touched her arm, and she jerked back, surprised and a little alarmed. She'd kept mostly to herself since moving to River Valley, Maryland, spent all her time with Lucy or at work. She didn't let people into their world, into the place she'd carved for them. The safe little house in the safe little neighborhood.

"*Are* you in trouble?" he asked again, shoving his hands in the pockets of his black slacks and taking a step back.

"No," she mumbled even though she wasn't sure. The guy in the sport jacket seemed to have disappeared, and she was beginning to think she'd let her imagination get the better of her. But if she hadn't…?

Then what?

Could she run again?

Did she need to?

"Sure looks like you are to me."

"I'm fine," she insisted, and he nodded solemnly, his blue eyes never leaving her face.

"I'm glad to hear it, ma'am, but just in case you decide you're not—" he pulled a wallet out of his pocket, took a business card from it "—take this. I can help. If you decide you need it."

She took the card. Plain white with black letters and a small blue heart in one corner. "'Daniel Boone Anderson. Hostage Rescue and Extraction Team,'" she read out loud.

He nodded. "That's right."

"I'm not a hostage." She tried to give the card back,

but he shoved his hands in his pockets, still eyeing her solemnly.

"That doesn't mean you don't need rescuing," he responded.

"I—"

"Take care of yourself and that baby." He nodded, one quick tilt of his head, and walked off, long legs eating up the ground so quickly he was out of the corridor and around the corner before she could blink.

She shoved the card in her coat pocket.

She wouldn't use it. Couldn't.

She'd promised Amber that she wouldn't tell anyone the truth about Lucy. She'd promised that no matter what happened, she'd keep it to herself. At the time, she'd expected Amber to be around, to help her navigate the world of subterfuge she'd agreed to. The fact that she wasn't didn't change the promise. Scout had an obligation to her friend. Even if she didn't, she had an obligation to herself and to Lucy. She couldn't cower in a store corridor, praying for rescue. She had to take action, do what needed to be done. Face her fear or call for help. One way or another, she needed to get moving.

"Mama! Go!" Lucy cried, impatient, it seemed, with staying in one spot.

"Okay, sweetie. I hear you." She put her shoulders back and her chin up, marched back to the break room as if she owned the place. Walked through the room as if she had every right to be there. Out the door and into the cold November evening. She'd parked close to the store entrance, and she had to walk around the side of the building to get there. Her heart tripped and jumped, the leaves rustling in the trees that lined the parking lot. A shadow moved in her periphery, and she took off, Lucy bouncing on her hip, giggling wildly as they rounded the side of the building.

The baby was giggling, but the woman looked scared out of her mind. Not that it was any of Daniel Boone Anderson's business. He should have gone back to hunting for the ingredients for pumpkin bread instead of leaving the store and waiting by the employee entrance. The problem was, he hadn't been too into the holidays during the past few years, and the entire store was decked out with tinsel and Christmas trees and wrapping paper. Every aisle had some reminder of the holiday he least liked to celebrate. The best Christmas had been the one right after Kendal's birth. Two months before Lana had walked out and taken their daughter with her.

Not Lana. He could almost hear his deceased wife's voice. *The Prophetess Sari. It has been ordained and it will be so.*

That had been her mantra when she'd finally contacted him. *Six months* after he'd returned from Iraq and found their empty apartment—and the note.

But he tried really hard not to think about that.

Four years was a long time to be missing a piece of your heart.

Which was probably why he spent so much time sticking his nose into other people's business and dealing with other people's problems.

He followed the woman around the side of the building, hanging back as she walked to an old station wagon. Nothing fancy, but she didn't seem like the fancy kind. Her jeans were a little too long, their scuffed cuffs dragging along the pavement as she buckled her daughter into a car seat. A long braid hung to the middle of her back. That had been what he'd noticed first—that long fall of golden-blond hair. Then he'd noticed the dark-haired little girl with her dimples and curls. Probably a couple of years younger than Kendal.

She'd turned five a couple of weeks ago.

He imagined her hair had grown long. It was probably straight as a stick, too.

But that was another direction he couldn't let himself go.

All the begging, all the searching, all the resources that were available, and he still hadn't been able to find Kendal. She'd been lost to someone in the cult. Probably someone who'd left it. Knowing Lana, she'd handed their daughter off without a second thought as to the child's welfare.

Boone never stopped thinking about it.

Even in his sleep, he dreamed about his daughter.

He clenched his fist, leaned his shoulder against a brick pillar that supported a narrow portico. Christmas shoppers moved past, hurrying into the store for whatever deal they thought Friday shopping would bring.

He noticed them, tracking their movements in the part of his brain that had been honed by years working long hours deep in enemy territory, but his focus was on the woman and her child. She opened the driver's door, tossed her purse into the vehicle, glanced around as if she was looking for someone.

Maybe whoever she was running from.

He was sure she was running. He'd seen it in her eyes when she'd lifted her daughter from the grocery cart and run toward the restroom—fear, desperation, all the things he saw in the gazes of the people he was hired to rescue.

The station wagon's headlights went on, and the woman backed out of the space. He'd have been wise to let her go and let the whole matter drop, but he'd never been all that wise when it came to things like this.

As a matter of fact, he often got himself in way deeper than he should be. Mostly because the one thing he wanted to accomplish, he hadn't been able to. He couldn't help himself, but he could help others.

Maybe he really did have an overinflated hero syndrome. That was what his coworker Stella said. She also said it was going to get him killed one day. She might be right about that, too, but he'd rather die trying to help someone than live knowing he hadn't.

He waited, watching as the woman drove to the edge of the parking lot. That should have been it—her driving out, Boone walking back into the store and retrieving the cart full of stuff that he'd left in aisle one.

Lights flashed near the edge of the parking lot. A hundred yards away, another set of headlights went on. A third followed, this one even closer to the exit the woman had used.

His heart jumped, adrenaline pumping through him, thoughts flooding in so quickly, he barely had time to process them before he was sprinting across the parking lot. Jumping into his SUV. All three cars were already exiting, and he had to wait for an elderly woman to make her way across the parking lot in front of him.

He made it to the exit as the last car turned east, its taillights disappearing from view. He followed, turning onto a narrow two-lane road that meandered through hilly farmland. A quiet road, nearly empty. Which wasn't good. His car would be easy enough to spot. Whether or not the guy in front of him realized he was being tailed depended on who was in the car.

They were making quite a line. His car, the one in front and two more just ahead of it. Taillights about a quarter mile ahead that he was sure belonged to the woman's station wagon. He wasn't sure where they were heading, but he pulled out his cell phone. One thing he'd learned a long time ago—only a fool headed into trouble without backup.

He never had a chance to call for it. One minute, he was keeping his distance, watching the procession of cars. The next, the car in front of him braked hard. He had a split second to realize what was happening before his windshield exploded, bits of glass flying into his face and dropping onto the dashboard.

He accelerated, adrenaline surging, every cell, every nerve alert.

The next shot took out a front tire. The SUV swerved, sideswiping a tree and nearly taking out a stop sign. He fought for control, yanking the vehicle back onto the road, the ruined tired thumping, the procession of cars pulling farther ahead.

"Not good!" he muttered, the SUV protesting as he tried to pick up speed again.

Not going to happen. The bumpy road and the flat tire weren't a good combination. He jumped out of the SUV, glad he was carrying. He'd been known to leave his Glock at home. Carrying it around made him feel safe, but it also reminded him of loss and heartache. Of a hundred things that he was better off forgetting.

He snagged his cell phone, dialing Jackson's number, hoping that his friend would pick up. In all the years he'd known the guy, there'd been only a handful of times when he hadn't been available.

But then, that was the way the entire team was. There wasn't a member of HEART who wouldn't be willing to drop anything, travel any distance, risk whatever was necessary to help a comrade.

Jackson answered on the second ring. "Hello?"

"It's Boone."

"Yeah. I saw the number," Jackson said drily. "What's up?"

"I need your help."

"With?"

"I've got a situation."

"What kind of situation?" Jackson's tone changed, his words hard-edged and sharp.

"The kind that involves guns and bullets. A woman. A kid. Three cars that are following her," he responded.

"You call the police yet?"

"Probably would have been a good idea, but I'm not used to having police to rely on." He was used to being deep in a foreign country, working in places where the only people he could count on were his team members.

"Where are you?"

"I didn't see the name of the road. It's the first right north of the Walmart you brought me to a few days ago."

"I'll be there in ten."

"Call the police before you leave. I think we're going to—"

The sound of screeching tires split the quiet, and he shoved the phone back into his pocket, racing toward the sound. He'd covered a hundred yards when light burst to life in the distance.

Fire!

His heart jumped, the new surge of adrenaline giving wings to his feet. He sprinted toward the soft glow and the velvety black of the eastern sky, the sound of sirens splitting the night.

TWO

Get out! Get out, get out!

The words raced through Scout's mind as she crawled over the bucket seat and unbuckled Lucy's car seat. Black smoke filled the car, filled her lungs. She grabbed the seat, relieved that Lucy was babbling away, more excited, it seemed, than frightened by the crash, the smoke, the crackling fire.

Get out!

She reached for the door handle, coughing, gagging on blood that rolled from a cut on her forehead to the corner of her mouth.

The door flew open, and hands reached in, dragged her out, Lucy in the car seat, singing in that baby language that only a mother ever really understood.

Scout jerked away, the car seat slamming against her legs as she ran. Straight toward the black car that had been following her. She veered to the left, saw him. Just standing there. Sport coat and slacks, hands in his pockets. He could have been anyone, but she knew he was death coming to call.

"Who are you?" she rasped, backing toward the tree her car had run into when the tire was shot out.

"It really doesn't matter," he responded, pulling a cigarette from his pocket and lighting it. The cold calculation in his eyes made her blood freeze in her veins. She wanted to scream and scream and scream, but there was no one around to hear. Nothing that she could do but try to find a way out, pray that the police came quickly. Keep Lucy safe.

Please, God. Help me keep her safe.

"I called the police," she said, her heart pounding in her throat, her eyes burning from smoke and fear. Every nightmare she'd ever had was coming true. All the fear she'd lived with since she'd left San Jose congealed in the pit of her stomach, filled her with stark hard-edged terror.

She needed to think, to run, to do something to save her daughter.

That was all she knew. All she cared about.

She lifted the car seat higher, pulling it to her chest, the heavy ungainly plastic filled with the only thing she cared about. "They'll be here any minute," she continued, because he was staring at her, the cigarette dangling from his mouth. He must think he had all the time in the world, must believe that there was no way help could come in time.

God, please! She begged silently, easing toward the line of trees that had stopped the wagon from careening down an embankment.

She just had to make it into the trees, find someplace to hide.

The faint sound of sirens drifted on the cold November air. Her heart jumped; hope surged. She could do this. Had to do this. She ran into the trees, blood still sliding down her face, Lucy giggling as the car seat bounced. She had no idea. None.

Scout's feet slipped on slick leaves, and she went down hard, her hip knocking an overturned tree. She bounced back up, the car seat locked in her arms, Lucy now crying in fear, sirens growing louder.

"Sorry, but this just isn't your night." The words whispered from behind her, the cold chill of them shooting up her spine.

And suddenly, she wasn't alone with the man and his cigarette. Two dark shadows moved in, and she was fighting off hands that were trying to rip Lucy away from her.

She screamed as something slammed into her cheek. Heard Lucy's desperate cries and the sirens endlessly blaring. Heard her own frantic breathing and hoarse shouts.

A car door slammed and someone called a warning. To her? To the men who were attacking her? The car seat was ripped from her arms and something smashed into her temple. Darkness edged in, sprinkled with a million glittering stars.

She fought it, fought the hands that were suddenly on her throat. Lucy! She tried to cry, but she had no air for the words, no air at all.

She twisted, kneeing her attacker in the thigh.

Something flashed in the air near her head.

A gun?

She had only a moment to realize it, and then the world exploded, all the stars fading until there was nothing but endless night and the sound of her daughter's cries.

"Go after the car!" Boone shouted as he jumped from Jackson's car. "I'll check to see if there are any injuries."

Too late.

Those were the words that were running through his head over and over again.

Too late. Just as he'd been the day he'd arrived home from Iraq, ready to confront Lana about her prescription-drug problem, willing to work on their marriage so that they could make a good life for their child.

Too late.

He heard Jackson's tires screech, knew he'd taken off, following the car they'd seen speeding away. Dark-colored. A Honda, maybe. Jackson knew more about cars than he did, and he'd know the model and make.

Good information for the police, but none of it would matter if the woman and her daughter were hurt. Or worse.

He ran to the station wagon, ignoring the flames that were lapping out from beneath the hood. The back door was open, and he glanced in. No car seat. No child. No woman.

He checked the third-row bucket seat, then peered into the front. A purse lay on the passenger seat, and he snagged it, backing away from the burning vehicle. He doubted it would explode, but getting himself blown up wasn't going to help the woman, her kid or him.

He broke every rule his boss, Chance Miller, had written in the fifty-page HEART team handbook and opened the purse, pulling out the ID and calling Jackson with information on the woman. Scout Cramer. Twenty-seven. Five foot two inches. One hundred pounds. Organ donor. Blond hair. Blue eyes.

Victim.

He hated that word.

In a perfect world, there would be no victims. No

losses. No hurting people praying desperately that their loved ones would return home.

Too bad it wasn't a perfect world.

He stepped away from the station wagon as a police cruiser pulled off the road. An officer ran to the back of the cruiser and dragged a fire extinguisher from the trunk.

Seconds later, the fire was out, the cold air filled with the harsh scent of chemicals and burning wires. Smoke and steam wafted from the hood of the car, but the night had gone quiet, the rustling leaves of nearby trees the only sound.

The officer approached, offering a hand and a quick nod. "Officer Jet Lamar. River Valley Police Department. Did you see what happened here?"

"I got here after the crash. I did see the woman and child who were in the car. They left the Walmart about fifteen minutes ago." And he didn't want to spend a whole lot of time discussing it. Scout and her daughter had disappeared. The more time that passed before they were found, the less likely it was that they ever would be.

Something else he had learned the hard way.

Every second counted when it came to tracking someone down.

"So, we've got two people missing?"

"Yes," Boone ground out. "And if we don't start looking, they may be missing for good."

"Other cars are responding. We have patrol cars heading in from the east. I just need to confirm that we're looking for a new-model Honda Accord. Dark blue."

Jackson must have provided that information, and Boone wasn't going to argue with it. He knew his friend well enough to know that he'd have to have been 100 percent sure before offering information. "That's right. It was pulling away as my friend and I arrived."

"I don't suppose you want to explain what you and your friend were doing on this road?" Officer Lamar looked up from a notepad he was scribbling in. The guy looked to be a few years older than Boone. Maybe closing in on forty. Haggard face. Dark eyes. Obviously suspicious.

"I followed the woman from Walmart. She looked like she might be in trouble."

"So, you just stepped in and ran to the rescue? Didn't think about calling the police?"

"I didn't want to call in the police over an assumption."

"Assumptions are just as often on target as they are off it. Next time," he said calmly, "call."

Boone didn't bother responding, just waited while Officer Lamar jotted a few notes, his gaze settling on the purse Boone still held.

"That belong to the victim?"

"Yes." Boone handed it over, shifting impatiently. "They could be across state lines by now."

"Not likely. We're about a hundred miles from the Penn state border. I'm going to take a look around. How about you wait in the cruiser?"

It wasn't a suggestion, but Boone didn't take orders from anyone but his boss or the team leader. He followed Lamar to the still-smoking station wagon, paced around the vehicle while Lamar looked in the front seat, turned on a flashlight and searched the ground near the car.

He didn't speak, but Boone could clearly see footprints in the moist earth near the car. Two sets. A woman's sneaker and a man's boot. "Looks like she survived the initial impact," Lamar murmured. He called something in on his radio, but Boone was focused on the prints—the deep imprint of the man's feet. The more shallow print of the woman's. There had to be more, and he was anxious to find them. For evidence, and for certainty that Scout and her child really were in the car that had driven away.

If not, they were somewhere else.

Somewhere closer.

He scanned the edge of the copse of trees that butted against the road. If he'd been scared for his life, he'd have run there, looked for a place to hide.

Protocol dictated that Boone back off, let the local P.D. do their job. It was what Chance would want him to do. It was what Boone probably would have done if he'd witnessed only the accident or even the kidnapping.

But Boone had spoken to Scout Cramer. He'd seen the fear in her eyes. He'd looked into her daughter's face and been reminded of what he'd lost. What he could only pray that he would one day get back.

He couldn't back off. Not yet.

A sound drifted through the quiet night. Soft. Like the mew of a kitten. Boone cocked his head to the side.

"Did you hear that?" he asked Lamar.

He knew the officer had. He'd stopped talking and was staring into the woods. "Could have been an animal," he said, but Boone doubted he believed it.

"Or a baby," Boone replied, heading for the trees.

"You think it's the missing child? How old did you say she was?"

"Two? Maybe three." *Cute as a button.* That was what his mother would have said. Probably what his dad would have said. They loved kids. Would have loved to know their first granddaughter.

Boone would have loved to know his only child.

In God's time...

He'd heard the words so many times, from so many well-meaning people, that he almost never talked about his marriage, about his daughter, about anything that had to do with his life before HEART.

"It's possible she was thrown from the car. I didn't see a car seat."

"She was in one."

Lamar raised a dark brow and scowled. "I'm not going to ask why you know so much about this lady and her child. You're sure the kid was in the car seat?"

"Positive."

"If the car seat was installed wrong, it still could have been thrown from the car. Wouldn't have gone far, but a child that age could undo the harness and get out. She's young to be out on a night like tonight, but I'd rather her be out in the woods than in a car with a monster." Lamar sighed. "Wait here. I'll go take a look around."

Wasn't going to happen.

Boone followed him into the thick copse of trees, his gaze on the beam of light that illuminated the leaf-strewn ground.

"Anyone out here?" Officer Lamar called.

No response. Just the quiet rustle of leaves and the muted sound of distant sirens.

"We should split up," Boone suggested. "The more area we cover, the better."

"I'll call in our K-9 team. That will help. In the meantime, you need to go back to the car. There's a ravine a couple of hundred feet from here. You fall into that and—"

"I'm a former army ranger, Officer Lamar. I think I can handle dark woods and a deep ravine." He said it casually and walked away. They were wasting time arguing. Time he'd rather spend searching.

If the little girl *had* been thrown from the car on impact, the sooner they got her to the hospital, the better. But he didn't think she'd been thrown. He'd seen Scout buckle her in. She'd been secure. Someone had taken her from the station wagon. That same person could have tossed her into the trees, thrown her down the embankment, disposed of her like so much trash.

He'd seen it before, in places where no child should ever be. He'd carried nearly dead little girls from hovels that had become their prisons.

Rage filled him, clawing at his gut and threatening to steal every bit of reason he had. He didn't give in to it. He'd learned a lot from his father. Watching him deal with the foster kids his parents had taken in had taught Boone everything he needed to know about keeping cool, working with clear vision, not allowing his emotions to rule.

"Baby?!" he called, because he didn't know the child's name, and because a scared little girl might respond to a stranger's voice.

Then again, she might not.

She might stay silent, waiting and hoping for her mother's return.

Was that how it had been for Kendal? Had she been dropped off and left somewhere with strangers? Had she cried for her mother?

He shuddered.

That was another place he wouldn't allow his mind to go. Ever.

"Hello?" he tried again, and this time he heard a faint response. Not a child's cry. More like an adult's groan.

He headed toward the sound, picking his way through narrow saplings and thick pine trees, the shadowy world swaying with the soft November wind.

He heard another groan. This one so close, he knew he could reach out and touch the injured person. He scanned the ground, saw what looked like a pile of cloth and leaves under a heavy-limbed oak and sprinted to it.

Scout lay on her stomach, pale braid dark with blood, her face pressed into leaves and dirt. For a moment, he thought she was dead, and his heart jerked with the thought and with the feeling that he was too late to make a difference. Again.

Then his training kicked in, and he knelt, brushing back the braid, feeling for a pulse. She shifted, moaning softly, jerking up as if she thought she could jump up and run.

"Don't move," he muttered, the amount of blood seeping into her hair, splattering the leaves, seeping into the earth alarming. He needed Stella. All her years of working as a navy nurse made her a crucial and important part of HEART. It wasn't just that, though. She had a way of moving beyond emotion, filtering everything external and unnecessary and focusing on what needed to be done. He coveted that during their most difficult missions.

Scout either didn't hear his demand or didn't want to follow it. She twisted from his hand, the movement sluggish and slow, her face pale and streaked with so much blood, he thought they might lose her before an ambulance arrived.

He needed to find the source of the blood, but when he moved toward her, she jerked back, struggling to her knees and then her feet, swaying, her eyes wide and blank. "Lucy," she said clearly, that one word, that name enunciated.

"Was she with you?" he asked, easing closer, afraid to move quickly and scare her again.

"She's gone," she whispered. "He took her."

That was it. Just those words, and all the strength seemed to leave her body. She crumpled, and he just managed to catch her before she hit the ground.

Footsteps crashed behind him, sirens blaring loudly. An ambulance, but he was terrified that it was too late.

He ripped off his coat, pressed the sleeve to an oozing wound on her temple, the long furrowed gash so deep he could see bone. He knew a bullet wound when he saw one, knew exactly how close she'd come to dying.

His blood ran cold, every hair on the back of his neck standing on end. Someone had come very close to killing Scout, and that someone had Lucy.

"Is this the woman?" Officer Lamar panted up behind him, the beam of his flashlight splashing on leaves wet with blood.

He knelt beside Boone, touched Scout's neck. "We need to get that ambulance in here. Now!" he shouted into his radio.

Voices carried on the night air, footsteps pounding on leaves and packed earth. Branches breaking, time ticking and a little girl was being carried farther and farther away from her mother, and if something didn't change, a mother was being carried farther and farther away from her daughter.

He pressed harder, praying desperately that the flow of blood would be stanched before every bit of Scout's life slipped away.

THREE

Lucy!

Scout tried to call for her daughter, but the words stuck in her throat, fell into the darkness that seemed to be consuming her. She tried to struggle up from it, to push away the heavy veil that blocked her vision, but her arms were lead weights, her body refusing to move.

She tried again, and nothing but a moan emerged.

"I think she's waking up," a woman said, the voice unfamiliar, but somehow comforting. She wasn't alone in the darkness.

"I hope you're right. Until she does, we've got nothing to go on," a man responded, his soft drawl reminding her of something. Someone. She searched through the darkness, trying to find the memory, but there was nothing but the quiet beep of a machine and the soft rasp of cloth as someone moved close.

"Scout?" the man said.

Someone touched her cheek, and that one moment of contact was enough to pull her through the darkness. She opened her eyes, looked into a face she thought she knew. Dark red hair, blue eyes, hard jaw covered with fiery stubble.

"Who are you?" she asked, her voice thick, her throat hot.

Where am I?

Where is Lucy?

That last was the question she needed answered most. It was the *only* question that mattered.

She shoved aside blankets and sheets, tried to sit up.

"Not a good idea," the woman said, moving in beside the man and frowning. She had paler red hair. Cropped short in a pixie cut.

"I need to find my daughter," Scout managed to say, the words pounding through her head and echoing in her ears. Sharp pain shot through her temple, and she felt dizzy and sick, but she wouldn't lie down until she knew where Lucy was.

"We're looking for her," the man said, his expression grim and hard, his eyes a deep dark blue that Scout knew she had seen before.

"*I* need to look for her," she murmured, but her thoughts were scattering like dry leaves on a windy day, dancing along through the darkness that seemed to want to steal her away again.

"You're not in any shape to look for anyone," the woman said, dragging a chair across the floor and sitting. "We're going to do this for you, and you're going to have to trust that we can handle it."

The words were probably meant to comfort her, but they only filled Scout with panic. Lucy was missing. That was the only clear thought she had. Everything else was a blur of feeling and pain, bits of memories and shadowy images that she couldn't quite hold on to. A store. A man. Flames and smoke.

"I don't know who you are," she responded absently,

her attention jumping from the woman to the man, then past them both. A hospital room with cream walls and an empty corkboard. A television mounted to a wall. A clock. In the background, Christmas music played, the carol as familiar as air.

"I'm Stella Silverstone. I work for HEART Incorporated." The woman took a card from her pocket and set it on a table near the bed. "Among other things, we help find the missing."

Missing. The word was like a dagger to the heart, and Scout had had enough. Enough listening. Enough talking. Enough sitting in a hospital room.

"I'm going to find my daughter." She scrambled from the bed, dizzy, sick, blankets puddling near her feet. "She's—"

"Been gone for three days," Stella said, the blunt words like hammers to the heart. "Running out of the hospital in some mad dash to find her isn't going to do any good."

"Stella," the man warned. "Let's take things slow."

"How slow do you want to take them, Boone? Because I'd say three days waiting to talk to the only witness is slow enough. I'm going to find Lamar. He's hanging around here somewhere."

She stalked from the room, closing the door firmly as she left. The sound reverberated through Scout's head, sent stars dancing in front of her eyes.

"You need to lie down." The man nudged her back to the bed, and she sat because she didn't think her legs could hold her.

"What happened?" she murmured to herself and to him, because she couldn't remember anything but those few images and the deep, deep fear for her daughter. It sat in her stomach, leaden and hard, the knot growing bigger with every passing moment.

"That's what we've been trying to find out." He sat in the chair his friend had abandoned, his elbows on his knees, his gaze direct.

"We've met before," she offered, the words ringing oddly in her ears.

"You remember." He smiled, but it didn't soften his expression. "I'm Boone Anderson."

The name was enough to bring a flood of memories—a trip to Walmart, Lucy in the cart. The man she'd been sure was following her. Boone handing her his business card.

And then…

What?

She pressed shaking fingers to her head, wanting to ease the deep throbbing pain. A thick bandage covered her temple, the edges folding as she ran her hand along them.

"Careful," Boone said, pulling her hand away and holding it lightly in his. "You're still stapled together."

"Tell me what happened," she responded, because she didn't care about the staples, the head injury, the IV line attached to her arm. All she cared about was getting up and going, but she didn't even know where to start, couldn't remember anything past the moment Boone had handed her his card. "Tell me where my daughter is," she added.

Please, God, let this be a nightmare. Please, let me wake up and see Lucy lying in her little toddler bed.

"We don't know much, Scout," he responded. "What we do know is that you were shopping. When you left the store, you were followed. The tire of your car was shot out, and you were in an accident."

She didn't care. Didn't want to know about the car or the accident or being followed. She needed to know about Lucy. "Just tell me what happened to my daughter."

"We don't know. You were alone when we found you."

"I need to go home." She jumped up, the room spinning. The knot in her stomach growing until it was all she could feel. "Maybe she's there."

She knew it was unreasonable, knew it couldn't be true, but she had to look, had to be sure.

"The police have already been to your house," he said gently. "She's not there."

"She could be hiding. She doesn't like strangers." Her voice trembled. Her body trembled, every fear she'd ever had, every nightmare, suddenly real and happening and completely outside of her control.

"Scout." He touched her shoulder, his fingers warm through thin cotton. She didn't want warmth, though. She wanted her child.

"Please," she begged. "I have to go home. I have to see for myself. I have to."

He eyed her for a moment, silent. Solemn. Something in his eyes that looked like the grief she was feeling, the horror she was living.

Finally, he nodded. "Okay. I'll take you."

Just like that. Simple and easy as if the request didn't go against logic. As if she weren't hooked to an IV, shaking from fear and sorrow and pain.

He grabbed a blanket from the foot of the bed and wrapped it around her shoulders, then texted someone. She didn't ask who—she was too busy trying to keep the darkness from taking her again. Too busy trying to remember the last moment she'd seen Lucy. Had she been scared? Crying?

Three days.

That was what Stella had said.

Three days that Lucy had been missing, and Scout had been lying in a hospital unaware. She closed her eyes, sick with the knowledge.

Please, God, let her be okay.

She was all Scout had. The only thing that really mattered to her. She had to be okay.

A tear slipped down her cheek. She didn't have the energy to wipe it away. Didn't have the strength to even open her eyes when Boone touched her cheek.

"It's going to be okay," he said quietly, and she wanted to believe him almost as much as she wanted to open her eyes and see her daughter.

"How can it be?"

"Because you ran into the right person the night your daughter was taken," he responded, and he sounded so confident, so certain of the outcome, she looked into his face, his eyes. Saw those things she'd seen before, but something else, too—faith, passion, belief.

"Who are you?"

"I already told you—Boone Anderson. I work for HEART. A hostage-rescue team based in Washington, D.C."

Someone knocked on the door, and Stella bustled in. Slim and athletic, she moved with a purposeful stride, her steps short and quick. "I'm not happy about this, Boone."

"I didn't think you would be," he responded, stepping aside.

"She's not ready to be released," she continued as she pulled on gloves and lifted Scout's arm. "You're not ready," she reiterated, looking straight into Scout's eyes. "You have a hairline fracture to your skull, staples in your forehead and a couple more days of recovery in the hospital before you should be going anywhere."

"I need to find—"

"Your daughter." Stella cut her off. "Yeah. I know. And she needs her mother's brain to be functioning well enough to help with our search." She pulled the IV from Scout's arm and pressed a cotton ball to the blood that bubbled up. "But I'm not going to waste time arguing with a parent's love. I've seen men and women do some crazy things for their kids."

She slapped a bandage over the cotton ball and straightened. "So, fine. We'll head over to your place. You can look around to your heart's content. Don't expect me to scrape you up off the ground, though. You fall, and I'm—"

"Stella..." Boone cut into her diatribe. Scout looked as if she was about to collapse, her face so pale he wasn't sure she'd make it into a wheelchair. "How about we just focus on the mission?"

"What mission?" she muttered. "This is pro bono, and I'm only helping because you saved my hide in Mexico City. If you remember correctly, I'm still supposed to be on medical leave."

"For the little scratch you got on the last mission? I'd have been back to work the next day," he scoffed, because he knew she wanted him to, knew that asking her if she was up to going back to work would only irritate her.

"If I remember correctly," she responded, her eyes

flashing, "you took two weeks off for that little concussion you got in Vietnam."

It had been a fractured skull, and he'd been forced to take a month off, but he didn't correct her. "True, but I'm not as pain tolerant as you are. I need a little more time to recover from my injuries."

She snorted. "We have some clothes around here for the lady? I don't think she wants to leave in a hospital gown."

"Just what she was admitted in." He pointed to a pile of belongings. He'd been through the purse, the pockets of the coat and jeans. He'd found nothing that might point him to a kidnapper.

"I'll help her get dressed. You wait in the hall."

"I don't need help," Scout murmured. "If you just call a cab for me, I'll get dressed and—"

"Not going to happen, sweetie," Stella said. "You go with us or you don't go at all."

"Says who?"

"Says the people who are looking for your daughter for free," Stella bit out.

"What Stella means," Boone cut in, "is that you're weak and you need to be careful."

"What I mean is that if we're going to do this, I want to get it done. Besides, if we don't go now, Lamar might show up and put a stop to our little party."

"We're not sneaking her out of here, Stella. It isn't that kind of mission."

"Whatever kind it is, Lamar isn't going to be happy that you're taking his only witness. He's been waiting three days to question her, and if he weren't following a lead that was called in—"

"What lead?" Scout asked, her eyes alive with hope.

He'd seen it many times before, watched hope flare and then die only to flare again. He knew the feeling, knew the quick grip of the heart when it seemed as if what was longed for would finally be had. Knew the despair when it wasn't.

"Don't know," Stella responded. If she noticed Scout's sudden excitement, she didn't let on. She wasn't one to give false hope, and she wasn't one to feed dreams. "I just know he left. Said he wouldn't be gone long. So, how about we get this show on the road?" She looked at Boone, pointed at the door. "Out."

He went because she was right. If they were going, now was the time. Lamar wouldn't be happy that they'd helped his lone witness walk out of the hospital. On the other hand, he had no reason to keep her there.

Except to protect her.

She'd nearly died and had lost so much blood, she'd been given five units her first night in the hospital. Whoever had taken her child hadn't planned on Scout surviving.

Why?

Who?

They were questions the police were desperately trying to answer with little to no success. They'd reviewed security footage from the store and parking lot, tried to ID the man who'd been following Scout. He'd been careful, though, his face always turned away from the cameras as if he'd known exactly where they were. No license plates had been visible on the cars that had followed her. No clear image of any of the drivers. The kidnapping had been planned by someone who knew exactly what he was doing. Lamar and his team weren't denying it, and they were doing everything in their power to find the people responsible.

The problem was, there were no good leads. No one who'd really seen anything. Most people had been caught up in preholiday daze and hadn't noticed Scout or Lucy. If they'd noticed her, they hadn't noticed the man who'd followed them around the store.

Three days on the phone with Chance, convincing him that using HEART resources was the only way to bring Lucy home, and Boone was just tired enough to feel as though he was biting off more than he could chew. He couldn't let the case go, though. He wouldn't, because he didn't want another parent to go through what he had. He didn't want anyone to ever have to spend every second, minute, hour of every day wondering where their loved one was.

Yeah. He was going to search for Lucy, and he was going to do everything in his power to bring her home safely. God willing, that would happen.

In the meantime, he'd promised Chance that he'd keep his nose clean, that he wouldn't overstep the boundaries or smash any local P.D. toes while he was working on the case.

He wasn't sure taking their sole witness from the hospital was the way to do it, but he'd seen the look in Scout's eyes before. Seen it in the gaze of every mother, father, uncle, aunt, brother, sister, loved one who'd lost someone. She'd do what she thought she had to in order to bring her daughter home. If that meant sneaking out of the hospital alone, she'd do it.

And sneaking out alone when someone had nearly killed her?

That wasn't such a great idea.

He pulled out his cell phone and dialed Lamar's number. The call went straight to voice mail. He left a message, figuring that was as good as asking permission.

Chance wouldn't see it that way, but Boone figured he was following the letter of the law. For now, that would have to be good enough.

FOUR

Please let me wake up from this nightmare.

The prayer flitted through Scout's throbbing head as Stella pushed her wheelchair outside. The full moon glowed from a pitch-black sky, the frigid November air slicing through her T-shirt and coat. Someone had washed all of her clothes, but she still thought she could smell the coppery scent of blood. Somewhere people were having a conversation, their voices drifting through the quiet night. A nightmare wouldn't be so full of details. A nightmare wouldn't let her feel the first drop of icy rain on her cheek or smell the frosty dampness of the air.

Lucy.

Gone.

The thought lodged in her head and stayed there. The only real thought she could hold on to.

An SUV pulled up to the curb and Stella opened the door, took Scout's arm and helped her in. "Seat belt," she barked, and Scout fumbled to snap it into place.

Her hands trembled, but somehow she managed. She wanted one thing. To find her daughter. Everything else—the throbbing pain in her head, the sick feeling

in her stomach, the fear that made her chest ache—
didn't matter.

Boone didn't ask for an address or directions to her
house. He just pulled away from the hospital, merg-
ing into light traffic on the main road that led through
River Valley.

Scout knew exactly what she'd see on her way home.
Dark trees stretching toward the moonlit sky, houses
dotting the landscape, a few cars meandering along.
She watched the landscape flying by, her eyes heavy
with fatigue. She felt weaker than she wanted to, and
she couldn't afford to be weak. Not with Lucy missing.

Boone turned into her neighborhood, bypassing the
bigger fancier houses and weaving his way through main
roads and side streets. He was familiar with the neighborhood and must have been to her house on several
occasions. It wasn't easy to find, tucked away from the
road, the driveway long and winding. In the next lot
over, Mrs. Geoffrey's house was dark, the porch light
off. She'd been planning to visit family for Thanksgiving and had asked Scout and Lucy to come along.

They should have gone.

Boone turned into the driveway, slowing as overgrown trees brushed the sides of the SUV. In the spring,
Scout would have them trimmed. Her rent-to-own lease
allowed her the luxury of doing whatever she wanted to
the tiny little rancher and the acre it sat on.

The lights were off at the house. She hadn't left them
that way. She always left the porch light burning and
the foyer light on. Too many dark shadows around the
house at night, and even with Mrs. Geoffrey just a few
hundred yards away, Scout always worried that someone might be waiting in the gloomy recesses of the yard.

Tonight, she had nothing to fear. She'd already lost everything. There was nothing more that could be done to hurt her. She opened the door as the car coasted to a stop, might have jumped out and run to the house if Stella hadn't grabbed her arm.

"Slow down, sister! You want to kill yourself before we find your kid?"

She didn't respond. The car had come to a full stop, and she wasn't waiting any longer. She stumbled out, nearly falling to her knees, her body refusing to cooperate with her brain's commands.

Just move! she thought. *It's easy.*

Only it wasn't. Her legs wobbled as she took a step toward the house, her purse thumping against her side. The keys were in it, and she needed to pull them out, but she wasn't sure how she was going to manage that and the walk.

"How about you not go rushing out of the SUV like that again?" Boone stepped into place beside her, his arm sliding around her waist. In another lifetime, she would have blushed at the zip of electricity that seemed to shoot through her at his touch. In this lifetime, she just wanted to get into the house, go into Lucy's room, make sure that her daughter wasn't waiting there for her.

"If I were rushing, I'd already be in the front door," she responded through gritted teeth.

"If you were *thinking,* you'd have realized that anyone could be waiting out here. It's a nice dark area. No streetlights. No neighbors around. You're an easy target. Might as well put a bull's-eye on your chest and stand out in the middle of Main Street," he drawled.

She hadn't been thinking about that.

Now she was, and she couldn't shake the feeling

that someone was watching. She shivered, fishing in her purse for keys that weren't there.

She dug deeper, found her wallet, cell phone, spare change. The little rag doll that Lucy loved. She pulled it out, her heart burning with tears that she wouldn't shed. Crying couldn't bring her daughter back.

"My keys," she began, but Boone had keys in his hand. Her keys—heart key chain with three keys: one for the front door, one for the back, one for the car.

"The police used them to access your place when they were looking for Lucy. They returned them last night."

And he'd taken them.

She didn't know how she felt about that, didn't think it really mattered.

The police *had* searched her house, just as Boone had said.

Lucy wasn't in there.

She felt defeated, sick to her stomach and ready to collapse, but she was going to look in the house anyway, because she didn't know what else to do.

The door swung open on creaky hinges. She'd been meaning to oil them, but time had got away from her—all the busyness of going to work and being a mother had made anything extra nearly impossible to do.

She walked into the dark living room, inhaling stale air and silence. No sound of Lucy giggling. No soft pad of little-girl feet on the floor. No squeals or cries. Nothing. The house felt empty and lonely and horrible.

Her foot caught on something, and she fell forward, would have hit the ground if Boone hadn't grabbed her arm.

"Careful," he said.

"There's something on the floor. I think it's the couch cushion."

"How about we turn on a light. Then you'll know for sure," Stella said drily.

The light went on, illuminating a room that had been taken apart. Couch cushions slashed and tossed on the floor, books torn and flung away. Photographs ripped from walls, their frames smashed. Lucy's little stuffed bear near the fireplace, its stuffing hanging out like entrails.

She started toward it, but Boone grabbed her arm. "Not yet."

"What—?"

"Take her outside." Boone cut her off, his face hard, his expression unreadable.

That was it. A quick sharp command, and Stella grabbed Scout's arm, started dragging her back toward the door.

Only she wasn't going, because this was her house, her daughter, her problem to solve. No matter how sick she felt, no matter how scared she was.

She yanked away. "I need to check Lucy's room," she mumbled, more to herself than to either of the people who'd brought her home.

"Not going to happen, sister." Stella tightened her grip, dragging Scout backward with enough force to nearly throw her off balance. She had a choice. Go or fight. Normally, she'd go, because she was a rule follower, the kind of person who'd never take a stroller on an escalator or park in a no-parking zone. She didn't try the grapes at the grocery store before she paid for them or take fifteen items into the twelve-items-or-less line.

But she had to find Lucy. Had to.

And if that meant fighting, that was what she was going to do.

She yanked her arm from Stella's, tried to run through the living room and into the hallway beyond. It should have been easy. She jogged nearly every day, sprinted after Lucy all the time, across the backyard, through the local park.

But her legs didn't want to move, and she stumbled forward, moving in what seemed like slow motion, the hallway so far away she wasn't sure she'd ever get to it.

"Not a good choice, Scout," Boone sighed.

Next thing she knew, she was in his arms, heading back the few feet she'd managed to go. Outside again, the cold November air stung her cheeks, and she wasn't even sure how she'd got there, where she was going, what she was looking for.

Lucy.

She zeroed in on the thought and held on to it, because she couldn't seem to hold on to anything else.

"Put me down!" She wiggled in his arms, trying to free herself. He just held on more tightly, striding to the SUV and opening the door. He set her in the backseat, leaned down so they were eye to eye.

"Do us both a favor," he growled, "and stay there."

He closed the door and walked away. She would have opened it and followed, but Stella was right there, hips against the door, back to Scout.

Scout slid across the bucket seat, reached for the handle on the other side, heard a soft click and a beep. She tried the handle. The door wouldn't open. She climbed over the seat and into the front, pushed the button to unlock the doors. Nothing.

Someone tapped on the window, and she looked out,

met Stella's eyes. "Not going to open, sister," Stella called through the glass. "We've got a special lock system for situations like this."

Like what? Scout wanted to ask, but Stella turned away, her attention focused on the edge of the property and the oversize trees that lined it.

Standing guard?

That was what it seemed as though she was doing— putting herself and her life on the line for Scout.

Why?

It was another question Scout wanted to ask.

Later.

First, she needed to find a way out of the SUV and back in the house. Lucy might not be there. *Wasn't there.* She admitted it to herself, because living in a fantasy world wouldn't help her get Lucy back. She had to be practical, had to be smart, had to trust that her daughter was okay and that they'd be reunited eventually.

If she didn't, she'd fall apart. That wouldn't do anyone any good.

She pressed a shaky finger to her temple, the bandage scratchy and thick, the throbbing pain of the wound it covered making her stomach churn.

"Concentrate," she muttered, looking around for some other method of opening the doors.

Maybe the hatchback?

Hadn't she seen something in a survival show about unlatching trunks from the inside? Was it possible to do the same with the hatchback opening of an SUV?

She crawled back over the seat, her stomach heaving as pain shot through her temple. Cold sweat beaded her brow, and her entire body seemed to be shaking, but she managed to get to the back section of the vehicle. She felt around for a mechanism that would open the door, found nothing.

Two police cars pulled into the driveway, lights flashing, sirens off. Scout stayed where she was as several police officers ran past. She didn't think they saw her lying on her side in the back of Boone's SUV. She doubted it would matter if they did. They weren't going to let her out of the vehicle, and Stella hadn't budged from her place near the passenger door.

Lights splashed out from the windows of the little rancher she'd lived in for three years. She knew each window, each light. Named them silently as they flashed on. Dining room at the side of the house. Her room in the front. Lucy's room. Behind the house, trees butted up against the night sky, the canopy of the forest illuminated by moonlight. She knew exactly how far the kitchen light would spill out from the window above the sink, knew just how much of the backyard would be painted gold by it.

Her heart thudded painfully as shadows moved in front of the window. Somewhere, her daughter was sleeping in a strange bed, in a strange house, with strangers all around.

Best-case scenario, she was.

Worst-case scenario…

Scout refused to put a name to it, refused to allow herself to imagine anything other than her daughter lying in bed crying for her.

She closed her eyes, trying to pray, wanting to pray. Her mind was empty of anything but fear and sorrow and the aching pain of her injury.

A car engine broke the silence of the night, and she managed to crawl back over the seat. She sat there as a small Toyota pulled up behind the police cars. Scout knew the car. It belonged to her landlady, Eleanor Finch. The police must have called to let her know there'd been a break-in at the property.

Eleanor got out of the car, but she didn't approach the house, just stood and stared at it. Maybe this was old hat for her. She owned a number of properties in River Valley. Most of them were a lot more impressive and lucrative than this one. Scout figured that was why she'd been willing to do a rent-to-own contract on the rancher. It didn't rent for enough to make it worth Eleanor's while to keep it.

She hadn't ever asked, though. Eleanor liked her privacy. She wasn't warm and fuzzy. Nor was she approachable. She'd insisted on three months' rent as a deposit and the contract read that she got to keep it if Scout decided to break her lease.

That had been fine with Scout. She hadn't intended to break the three-year lease, because she'd pictured living there forever with Lucy. A nice little place in a nice little town filled with lots of nice people. Good schools. Pretty little church. Everything clean and tidy.

Only it wasn't anymore, and maybe the house wasn't going to be a place for forever. Maybe it was just a stopgap on the way to somewhere else.

Eleanor pulled out her cell phone and made a call, her gaze still on the house. Scout wanted to get out of the SUV and talk to her, but the doors were still locked tight and Stella was still standing guard. There was nothing Scout could do but wait and wonder what was going on in the house and when someone was going to come out and tell her about it.

* * *

Boone had been hoping for a ransom note. There hadn't been one. No prints on the furniture, doors, pieces of broken frame. He watched as the local police processed the scene, staying out of their way because he didn't want to get kicked out. He needed information. The more the better. Unfortunately, there wasn't much to be had. Someone had torn the house apart.

Maybe more than someone.

Maybe several people.

Going through a house as thoroughly as this one had been gone through would have taken one person a few hours. A couple of people working together could have accomplished the job much more quickly.

He walked down the hall, bypassing a uniformed officer who was dusting the bathroom door for prints. Even that room had been torn apart, medicine cabinet emptied, a picture pulled off the wall and taken apart, the frame in pieces on the floor.

Lamar was two doors down, taking pictures of Lucy's room. Like the others, it was a wreck, the mattress on the toddler bed slashed, the stuffing strewn all over the floor. Stuffed animals had been dismembered, picture books thrown from shelves. It looked as if a hurricane had blown through.

"Find anything interesting?" he asked, and Lamar frowned.

"I should make you leave. This is a crime scene."

"I've been in more than a few of them. I'll be careful not to contaminate anything. Did you find anything?"

"Aside from a mess? No. Whoever did this was careful. No prints on the doorknobs or any other surface in the house. I pulled a couple of kid prints off the underside of the bed in here, but nothing else."

"Someone wiped things down?"

"Thoroughly." Lamar nearly spat the word out, the look on his face a mixture of disgust and frustration.

"Awfully knowledgeable petty thieves," Boone said, even though he didn't think the ransacking had anything to do with thievery. It had everything to do with the fact that Lucy was missing. He was sure of that; he just wasn't sure what the connection was.

"Neither of us believes that thieves did this," Lamar muttered.

"You have any leads on the kidnappers?"

"Nothing. I'm hoping I can get a description from Scout tonight. If she got a good look at our perp, we may finally have a lead." He eyed Boone for a moment. "Speaking of Scout, I don't suppose you want to explain why you brought her here."

"She wanted to come."

"Sometimes my son wants to come to work with me, but he's six, so I have to tell him it's not a good idea."

"Scout isn't six. She's a grown woman, and she was going to find a way here with or without my help. I figured it was better to give her my help and a little protection."

"Maybe next time, you can convince her to wait for the police instead."

"I'm hoping there won't be a next time."

"I wouldn't count on that, Anderson. Things aren't making sense, and in my experience that means there's a lot going on under the surface, a lot we don't know about, a lot that could cause Scout serious trouble."

"She's already *in* serious trouble." Boone pointed out the obvious, and Lamar frowned.

"Not your problem. I've been allowing your team to do some investigating, but that stops if you get in my way."

"Maybe you should explain what that entails so I can avoid it."

"Let's try this on for size," Lamar responded. "You don't take a witness out of the hospital without permission from me. You don't take her to undisclosed locations or hide her away somewhere for safekeeping, either."

"Seeing as how she's sitting in my SUV waiting for us to finish in here, I'd say she's not exactly hiding."

"I'm making it clear for future reference, because if she suddenly disappears, your entire team is going to be on the line for it."

"What's that supposed to mean?" It took a lot to get him riled up, but Boone was heading there. He stayed out of the way. He played nice. He'd followed Chance's rules of engagement with local police. What he wasn't going to do was stand there and take it while HEART was used as a scapegoat.

"It hasn't escaped my notice that you were the last person aside from Scout to see Lucy—"

"Don't go there, Lamar." He bit the words out. "Because if you do, I'll go here—you and your team need as much help as you can get on this. Turning away an organization that has made its name freeing hostages and bringing them home safely isn't the smart way to go."

"I know who you work for, and I know what HEART does. What I don't know is why you're wasting time on this case when there are bigger, more lucrative cases you could be tackling."

"Because it isn't about money. It's about family," he retorted, full-out riled, and he'd better not let it show. He'd made that mistake on one too many occasions, and local police hadn't much appreciated it. Neither had Chance. Boone didn't care all that much, but if he wanted to help Scout, he needed to play things smart.

"Everything is about money, Anderson. You work this job enough, and you start to realize it," Lamar said wearily as he used gloved hands to lift a photo from the floor. Nearly ripped in two, it was a close-up of Scout and Lucy taken when Lucy was a baby. Probably one of those Sears or Walmart portraits. It shouldn't have been beautiful. The background was a little too bright, the lighting a little harsh, but Scout looked soft and sweet, her expression so filled with love it made Boone's heart ache. He'd seen that look in Lana's eyes the day Kendal was born.

Had it been there after that?

He didn't remember. He'd been out of town a lot, working missions that he couldn't talk about in places he wasn't allowed to reveal. He'd missed out on weeks and months of memories. Some days that hurt worse than others. Today, looking at the photo of Scout smiling at a sleeping Lucy, it hurt a lot.

"I'll wait outside," he said abruptly, because he didn't want to stand in the doorway of the nursery any longer, thinking about his daughter, who was out in the world somewhere. Lost to him until he could find her again.

FIVE

Scout wanted to sleep.

She wanted it so badly she was trying to force herself into it. No amount of trying to slip away from reality worked, though. No matter how much she tried, she was still in the SUV watching police officers enter and exit her house.

She glanced at Eleanor. She was still standing near her car, but she wasn't alone. A police officer was beside her, jotting something in a notebook as she spoke.

Stella hadn't moved from her position. As a matter of fact, Scout wasn't sure she'd blinked in the time since they'd left the house.

She knocked on the window, and Stella glanced her way, then turned toward the yard again.

She knocked again.

Nothing. Not even a flinch or twitch.

"I know you can hear me," she yelled.

"I am ignoring you," Stella yelled back.

"You're going to have to acknowledge me eventually." She hoped.

Again. Nothing.

She settled back into the seat, closed her eyes, heard the quiet click of the locks.

Free?

She tried the door. It opened.

"Don't get out," Stella commanded without looking her way.

"I have to," she responded, opening the door wider, ready to hop out and go inside.

"You want your little girl to have to raise herself?" There was no emotion in Stella's voice. Nothing to indicate that she cared one way or another.

"My little girl is missing. Until I find her, that question is moot." She levered out of the car, swaying as the blood rushed from her head.

"Told you not to get out," Stella grumbled, grabbing her arm and holding her up when she might have fallen over. "You're still weak. The way I see it, you should be in the hospital. Since I'm not running the show, I guess you're going to be wherever Boone decides we're going to take you."

Wherever Boone decided?

She didn't think so, but he was walking toward them, his long legs eating up the ground between them, his dark red hair slightly ruffled as if he'd run his fingers through it a few dozen times.

"Did they find anything?" Scout asked. *Did they find her?*

She didn't ask the second question. She knew the answer.

"The place was wiped clean." He glanced at Stella and some secret message seemed to pass between them. She didn't like it. She didn't want to be left on the outside looking in.

"Professionals?" Stella's arms were folded across her chest, her stance wide. She looked larger-than-life but was probably only an inch taller than Scout.

"Looks that way."

"Guess we have a lot of questions that are going to need answering. Does Lamar want us to keep her here or take her back to the hospital to wait?"

"I'm right here, and I don't care what Lamar wants," Scout cut in. She sounded weaker than she wanted to, her voice faint.

"I was thinking the same." Boone smiled, his eyes crinkling at the corners. He looked a few years older than she was. Maybe in his early to mid-thirties, his body lean and muscular. The kind of guy who'd get attention wherever he went because of his good looks and his deep red hair. "Unfortunately, my boss does care, and he'll be mighty unhappy if we drive away without Officer Lamar's permission."

"Mighty?" Stella sighed. "Who says that?"

"Me and everyone I grew up with." He took Scout's arm. "How about we go inside and see if there's anything missing?"

"If the rest of the house is as torn apart as the living room, I'm not sure I'll be able to tell," she admitted. She was half hoping that he'd say it wasn't, half believing that it couldn't possibly be.

"It's pretty well messed up, but you'll know if there's any jewelry or valuables missing."

"I don't have much." A few pieces of jewelry of her mother's. Her parents' wedding rings. Some china that had belonged to her great-grandmother and that had been passed down to Scout. Her parents hadn't been wealthy, and they hadn't believed in collecting frivolities.

"That will make things even easier." He urged her inside, closing the door firmly behind them. Stella hadn't followed them. Was she still standing guard outside?

Did they really think it was necessary?

There were police cars and police officers and neighbors who'd gathered near at the edge of the driveway. It would take someone with a lot of guts to try anything with so many witnesses.

Then again, it had taken someone with a lot of guts to follow her through a grocery store, run her off the road and take her daughter.

Several police officers stood in the living room. They were silent as she followed Boone through into the hallway.

They knew who she was, knew she was the mother of the missing child. Knew how heavy her heart must be. She wanted to tell them that no matter what they were imagining, it couldn't compare to what she actually felt. There were no words to describe the thousand-ton weight pressing on her chest, no vocabulary that existed that could express the depth of her fear.

"Where do you keep your valuables?" Boone asked.

"In my room."

"Then how about we look there first?"

She didn't tell him where it was, but he didn't slow his pace or ask. Lucy's room was to the right. Hers was across the hall. There was a spare room, too. She'd put a futon and a small dresser in it to fill the space. Not because she had family or friends who might come for a visit. She had no family left and she'd cut ties with her friends in San Jose after she'd become pregnant with Lucy. Only Amber knew where she'd gone after she'd moved, and she'd been as anxious to keep that secret as Scout had been.

Had she taken the secret to the grave with her?

Scout had assumed that she had. They were best friends, more like sisters than anything else. She couldn't imagine that Amber would have betrayed her trust. Especially when she was the one who'd been so determined that Scout leave San Jose, so determined that she not tell anyone ever who Lucy's father was.

She followed Boone into her bedroom, her stomach sick with dread. The mattress had been slashed, the stuffing pulled out. The same for her pillow and the down comforter she'd spent a small fortune on. Every picture on her dresser had been tossed on the floor. All her clothes were emptied into a pile. The small jewelry box lay broken a few feet from the bed as if someone had tossed it there. She crouched beside it, head spinning from moving too quickly.

The rings and jewelry were there. Under the broken wood and the tiny ballerina that used to spin each time the box opened. Her mother had received the box for her tenth birthday, and Scout had inherited it after her death. She'd treasured it for nearly fifteen years. Now it was gone.

She grabbed the rings, her eyes burning and her chest tight.

"They didn't take them," she said, meeting Boone's dark blue eyes.

"Didn't take what?" A tall dark-haired man walked into the room before Boone responded. Dressed in a police uniform, his shoes shined, his gaze sharp, the officer glanced at the jewelry box, then met Scout's eyes. "Your jewelry?"

"Yes."

"Does it have any value?"

"I don't know. I never had it appraised."

He frowned, lifting one of the thin gold chains. "Looks like real gold. I'd say whoever was in your house wasn't looking for valuables. They didn't take the television. Didn't take your laptop. Is there anything else they might have been looking for?"

"Like what?"

"Don't know, but I'm figuring you might."

"I don't." He was trying to get somewhere with his questioning, but her sluggish brain wasn't following.

"Most kids aren't abducted by strangers. You know that, right?"

"I—"

"That being the case," he continued, not giving her a chance to speak, "it seems reasonable to assume that the person who took your daughter wasn't a stranger."

She didn't say anything, because she was afraid he was right. She was afraid that the secret she'd kept had been revealed and the people she'd feared had come for her daughter.

"Maybe you know the person? Maybe you've had some kind of interaction with him? Are you dating someone? Were you in a relationship in the last couple of months?"

"No." She shook her head, regretted it immediately. She felt light-headed and unsteady. She tried to stand, to put herself closer to eye level with the officer rather than having him tower over her.

Her muscles didn't want to cooperate.

Boone took her hand, tugging up in one easy motion. "You okay?" he asked.

"Should I be?" she responded.

"No," he admitted, glancing around the room.

The officer's attention was on Scout, and it never wavered. He didn't look as if he believed her story. "How about someone you work with? Someone in your circle of friends?" he pressed.

"I work at the library," she said, her mouth cottony and dry. "When I'm not working, I'm here with Lucy. I go to church on Sunday, but other than that, my life is pretty boring."

"Yet someone kidnapped your daughter and ransacked your house. There has to be a reason for that."

"I guess so." She rubbed her forehead, her fingers flitting over the bandage. It did nothing to clear her thoughts. She thought she knew where he was going with the questions. Thought he was implying that she'd brought all this on herself.

Maybe she had.

She'd made mistakes. Little ones. Big ones.

She'd thought that she'd moved beyond them, made a life that wouldn't be touched by what she'd done, the lies she'd told.

She should have known better.

There were always consequences. Maybe not right away, but eventually.

"Guessing isn't going to help us find your daughter," the officer said. There wasn't any kindness in his tone or in his eyes. Maybe he was assuming that she'd had some part in Lucy's kidnapping. Maybe he thought she'd brought it on herself. "How about you tell me what you have that someone is searching for? Money? Drugs?"

"What? No!" she protested, because there wasn't anything that anyone might want in the house. "I'm not into that kind of thing."

"Then what are you into? People don't get into this kind of trouble over nothing. Did you have a deal with someone? Did you get in over your head and not know where to turn for help?"

"I'm not the kind of person who gets into trouble, and I've never been into anything so much that I was over my head."

"This—" Lamar gestured to the slashed mattress, the picture frames smashed, the pile of clothes "—would prove otherwise. So, how about you be honest? Tell me what's going on?"

"How about you back off a little, Lamar?" Boone cut in, reaching down to grab the broken jewelry box from the floor and setting it on the dresser. He moved calmly, easily, no sign of tension. "She's still recovering from a serious injury."

"And her daughter is missing. Which is a more pressing matter?"

"Lucy is the most pressing," Scout cut in. She didn't want any time wasted. Not arguing or asking questions she had no answers to. "But I really don't have a boyfriend or an ex. I don't have a drug habit. I don't do anything illegal."

"Right." The officer pulled a business card from his wallet and handed it to her.

She glanced at it, read the name. Jet Lamar.

"Keep that with you," he continued. "If you remember anything, give me a call."

"There's nothing to remem—"

"And you!" He jabbed a finger at Boone. "Get her out of my crime scene and back to the hospital."

"Out of her house, you mean?" Boone responded.

"I want her out of here, and since you're the one who made her escape from the hospital happen, I figure you should be the one to make that happen, too."

He stalked out of the room.

Scout would have followed, but her ears were buzzing, the light dimming.

"You don't look so hot." Boone wrapped an arm around her waist. A good thing, because her legs were weak, her heart beating a strange uneven rhythm.

"Just what every woman wants to hear," she murmured, the words slipping away before they really formed.

He must have heard, because he smiled and shook his head. "It's good that you have a sense of humor, Scout. That's going to help a lot."

Help what? This time the words didn't come out at all. They got stuck in her throat and stayed there as blackness edged in and her vision went fuzzy.

Someone said her name, but she wasn't sure if it was Boone or someone else. Her knees buckled, and Boone scooped her into his arms, muttering something that she didn't hear or couldn't comprehend. She wanted to close her eyes and give in and just let herself slip away. It was what she'd wanted desperately while she was waiting in the SUV. Now she fought it because she didn't want to go back to the hospital.

"Put me down." She shoved at a chest that was sculpted and hard and had absolutely no give in it.

"So you can fall on the floor? I don't think so." Boone stepped outside, the cold air filling her lungs and clearing her head. "I think it's time to get you out of here."

"I'm okay now. I want to stay."

"Sorry, but Lamar doesn't want you here. I'm trying to stay on his good side." He set her in the backseat of the SUV, leaning in to grab the end of her seat belt. They were eye to eye, his scent filling the vehicle, a mixture of soap and spicy aftershave.

"I don't want to go back to the hospital."

"So, we won't go there." He closed the door, slid into the driver's seat while Stella climbed into the passenger seat beside him.

"Let me guess," she said. "We're going to Raina's."

"She has plenty of room." He backed up, maneuvering the SUV around parked police cars and Eleanor's car.

"So does a hotel."

"Not as easy to secure."

"Jackson isn't going to like it."

"Sure he is. Right now, he's staying in a hotel. I think he'll be happy to have an excuse to spend more time at his fiancée's house before he returns to D.C."

Scout had no idea what they were talking about. She didn't ask. She was too busy going over what Officer Lamar had said. He seemed to think she had something that someone wanted.

The only thing she'd had that anyone might want was Lucy, and the only people who might be interested in having her didn't even know she existed.

Did they?

Don't ever tell them, Scout. Swear to me that you won't. They'll take that baby from you and you'll never see it again. You try to fight them, and it'll get ugly. They'll find some reason to throw you in jail or make CPS think you're not going to be a good mother. They might even do worse. I wouldn't put anything past my family.

Scout could still hear the words, still see Amber's face as she said them—pale and gaunt, her eyes hollow. Nearly four years later, the conversation still haunted her.

Amber had said that if her family knew Scout was pregnant with her half brother Christopher's child, they'd do everything in their power to gain custody.

That had scared Scout enough to send her running. The Schoepflins had power and lots of it. They came from a long line of politicians and socialites. According to Amber, the money came from a great-great-grandfather who'd made it big during the California gold rush. Maybe it was true. Maybe it wasn't. Amber had had a vivid imagination and a way of twisting the truth to fit her mood. Whatever the case, the Schoepflins had money, political clout and plenty of friends in high places.

Scout had herself.

And right then, sitting in the SUV with two other people, she felt more alone than she'd ever been in her life.

SIX

Boone glanced in the review mirror as he drove down the dirt road that led to Raina Lowery's place. They hadn't been followed. He'd taken a few unnecessary turns and woven his way through a few quiet neighborhoods just to be sure.

Jackson had made it to the house ahead of them, and he wasn't happy. He'd made that known—loudly—during a phone conversation with Stella.

One night.

That was what he'd finally promised after Boone had grabbed the phone and called in about three dozen favors he'd done for Jackson over the years.

One night would work if Lamar cleared Scout's house as a crime scene and let her return the following day. Boone was hoping that would be the case. If not, he'd have to make other arrangements. He could bring Scout to his D.C. apartment, but he didn't think she'd like that idea.

He pulled into Raina's driveway and parked behind Jackson's car. Almost every light in the house was on, the porch light glowing invitingly. He'd had a porch at the house he and Lana had shared. A porch swing, too.

He tried not to think about those things, but when he got tired, the memories were always at the surface, tempting him to spend some time exploring them.

Not tonight. He had to get Scout in the house, get her settled. Then he was going to call Lamar. He'd hinted that Scout might be involved in something illegal, that maybe she'd got herself in too deep. Boone wanted to know if Lamar had found evidence to support that or if he was just making a conjecture. He suspected the latter. He'd done his own research. Scout had been in River Valley for three years. She'd been working as a librarian in San Jose before that. No criminal record. Not even a traffic ticket. Her neighbor said she was quiet and sweet. Her coworkers sang her praises. If she was involved in anything illegal, there wasn't a person around who suspected it.

He opened her door, offering a hand as she slid out. She took it, her palm dry and cool. She had thin fingers and delicate bones, her steps shuffling and slow as he helped her to Raina's door. It opened before they reached it, Jackson hovering on the threshold. He didn't look happy.

"Took you guys a while," he commented as he stepped aside and allowed them to enter. "I thought you'd be here half an hour ago."

"Boone insisted on taking fifty side trips," Stella growled. She didn't look any happier than Jackson. Perfect. The two of them together should be fun.

"I wanted to make sure we weren't being followed. I didn't want any trouble following us here."

"Maybe you should have thought about that before you decided to use Raina's place as a safe house. We've got property in D.C. if you need it." Jackson glanced at Scout, his expression easing. Boone had known it would. One thing about Jackson: he always rooted for the underdog, always wanted to help the helpless. Right at that moment, Scout looked about as helpless as anyone could be, her skin pale, the bandage on her forehead sliding down over her eyebrow. "You must be Scout," he said. "I'm Jackson Miller. I was sorry to hear about your daughter's kidnapping."

"Me, too," she said quietly.

"My fiancée has a room ready for you. If you want to follow me—"

"Samuel and I can bring her there." Raina Lowery stepped into the foyer, her blond hair pulled back with a headband. She'd been through a lot the past few years, first losing her husband and son in a car accident, then being kidnapped while on a mission trip to Africa. Boone had been on the mission to rescue her and had helped out when she'd faced more trouble after her return to the States. He liked and respected her. He also liked her cooking.

And she had been cooking. He could smell it in the air, something spicy and probably delicious. Hopefully, there were leftovers.

Samuel stood beside her, his face just a little less gaunt than it had been a few months ago, his prosthesis barely noticeable beneath the sweatpants he wore.

"Hey, Sammy," Boone said and was rewarded with a shy smile.

"Hello, Daniel Boone! You shoot any bears today?" The kid had been reading every book about Daniel Boone that he could get his hands on and loved to joke with Boone about his name. After everything he'd been through, it was good to see him loosening up and having fun. He'd been a child soldier in Sudan, but had risked his life to save Raina. Things had been easier for him since Raina had brought him to the U.S. Hopefully, bringing someone who was obviously injured and in trouble into his home wouldn't send the kid back into fear and anxiety.

Boone frowned. He should have thought about that before he'd talked Jackson into letting Scout stay there.

Raina stepped forward and took Scout's arm. "Come with me. I'll get you tucked into bed and then bring you a nice cup of tea."

"I don't want you to go to any bother." Scout met Boone's eyes, silently begging him to intervene.

Wasn't going to happen.

He smiled encouragingly and was rewarded by a deep scowl. That was fine. She could be mad as a wet hen. It wasn't going to change anything.

"I already have the water on to boil," Raina insisted. "Besides, I really don't think a cup of tea can be classified as a bother." She led Scout down the hall and out of sight, Samuel following along behind them.

There was a moment of complete silence. Not one word from Jackson or Stella. Not good. Neither of them was known for being quiet.

"Go ahead," he finally said. "Let it out before one of you explodes."

"The only thing I'm going to let out is a yawn," Stella responded. "You think Raina has an extra bed? I'll take the couch if she doesn't. I'll even take the floor if you've got an extra pillow and blanket."

"Upstairs. First door to the right. She made up the bed for you. I told her not to make it too comfortable.

You're not used to luxury." Jackson grinned, and Stella swatted him on the shoulder as she walked past.

"Good night, boys. Don't get into any trouble for the next six hours, because I plan on sleeping for at least that long." She walked up the stairs, moving a lot more slowly than usual. Her last mission had taken a toll on her. Physically and mentally.

She'd never admit it, but Boone saw it in her eyes, in the slope of her shoulders, the quick fatigue after minimal work.

He wouldn't say anything. Couldn't. Everyone who'd been on the team for any length of time had had missions that drained them. Stella would come out of it eventually. In the meantime, the team was rallying around her, making sure she didn't do anything stupid while she was recovering.

"Want some coffee?" Jackson asked, already walking down the hall and heading toward the kitchen.

"I'd rather have whatever it is Raina was cooking. It smells great."

"It's some kind of stew. Samuel requested it. Guess he ate it a lot before his parents died." Jackson grabbed a bowl, ladled thick stew out of a stockpot that was sitting on the stove and handed it to Boone. "Spoons are in the—"

"I know where they are." Boone had been in the house on a number of occasions. He'd even celebrated Thanksgiving there. He knew where the silverware was. He also knew where the soda was. He grabbed a can from the fridge and sat at the table.

"Make yourself comfortable," Jackson said drily.

"I have. Thanks."

"Smart aleck," Jackson grumbled as he dropped into the chair across from him.

"Were you expecting something different?"

"Sadly, no. Want to tell me why you decided HEART needed to be involved in this case?"

"For the same reason you got involved in Raina's. I realized someone needed help, and I decided I wanted to be the one to do the helping. HEART has all the resources necessary, and your brother wasn't opposed to using them to bring Lucy home."

"He wasn't enthusiastic about it, either."

"When is Chance ever enthusiastic about anything?" For as long as Boone had known the brothers, Chance had been the more serious one, the more practical. He didn't believe in doing anything based on emotion. He liked rules, and he followed them.

"Good point." Jackson rubbed the back of his neck and frowned. "You said someone ransacked Scout's place. Any idea what they were looking for?"

"None."

"Any idea why someone would go to so much effort to kidnap Scout's daughter?"

"No."

"Do you think *she* knows?"

"I don't know. She was unconscious for three days, and she's not in good enough shape to answer a lot of questions. I'm hoping when she is, she'll have some ideas."

"It might not be a bad idea to push her a little. There's a child missing. Time is of the essence. Scout didn't look great when she walked in here, but she was walking. That's better than a lot of witnesses we've interviewed."

"True."

"So? Why aren't you interviewing her?"

"I plan to. I want to run a couple of things past you first." He scooped up stew and ate it quickly, burning his mouth in the process. Didn't matter. The stuff was good. Lots of spices and chunky pieces of meat and vegetables. "This is good. You're one blessed man, Jackson."

"I'm blessed, but not because Raina can cook. I'm blessed because she's the woman she is and because she's bringing Samuel along with her when she marries me." The sincerity in his eyes was unmistakable. No matter how much Boone liked to jab at the guy, he was happy that Jackson had found someone to love and who loved him in return. That was a great thing, a powerful thing.

When it worked.

And when it didn't, it could cause more heartache than anyone should ever have to experience.

"You're a good guy, Jackson," he said, because it was true. "It pains me to have to say that, because most days I'm not all that fond of you," he added.

"The feeling is mutual. Now that we have that out of the way, how about you tell me what you've found out about Scout?"

"People at work like her. The neighbors like her. She attends church every Sunday and people there have nothing but praise for her. No criminal record. No outstanding warrants. She hasn't had a traffic ticket since she moved to town."

"How long ago?"

"Almost three years."

"Right before her daughter was born?"

"According to her neighbor, she had the baby four months after she moved in."

"Where'd she move from?"

"San Jose."

"That's a long way to come for—what? A job?"

"That's what she told people at her church."

Jackson raised an eyebrow. "You've got a lot of information in a short amount of time. You've obviously been busy."

"Not just me. Stella did a lot of the groundwork while I was at the hospital. The fact that Lucy is missing is opening a lot of mouths that might otherwise be sealed closed."

Jackson nodded. "Does she have family in San Jose?"

"Not that I've found."

"No ex-husband?"

"No record of a marriage or a divorce."

"Then who's the kid's father?"

"Good question. The birth certificate didn't list anyone."

"Interesting." Jackson drummed the tabletop, looking as though he had more to say.

Boone was too impatient to wait for him to think it through. "How so?"

"River Valley is a pretty conservative community. Small-town ideals, you know?"

"I've only been here twice, so I'm not all that familiar with it."

"You grew up in a small town. You know the way things are. People can be judgmental. They like to throw stones while they're living in their glass houses."

"That's a stereotyped view."

"No doubt, but it doesn't change my point."

"Which is?" Boone finished the stew, went back for another helping.

"There are plenty of people around here who would

probably be pretty judgmental of a single mother. They'd be watching carefully to see what kind of person she was. One mistake and gossip would fly, people would start murmuring. You haven't heard any murmurs."

"No," he responded, even though it wasn't a question.

"So, we can assume that Scout keeps her nose clean, that she's not out partying every night, probably doesn't have boyfriends who spend the night or druggie pals sleeping it off in her basement."

"What's your point, Jackson?"

"She's living a quiet life, minding her own business, not doing anything that anyone could remotely criticize her for. As far as I can see, there's no one in River Valley who would want to harm her, so we need to be looking a little more closely at her life in San Jose."

"That's what I've been thinking."

"Is that the direction the police are taking?"

"I think they're taking any direction they can find."

"Maybe Chance can put in a call. See what he can find out." Of everyone on the team, Chance was the most diplomatic. He knew how to get the team into areas no one else was allowed, knew how to get information that others would never be given access to, knew how to work the system so that it worked for him.

"You want to ask or should I?"

"Since you're already in the doghouse with him, I'd better do the asking." Jackson stood and stretched. He and Cyrus Mitchell had just returned from a mission to Colombia. The fact that they'd made it back before Thanksgiving was a minor success. The fact that the six teenagers who'd been held hostage at an international school there had been rescued and reunited with their families was a major one. Jackson seemed invigorated rather than worn-out from the trip, riding the high from a successful rescue.

Or maybe he was just riding the high of being reunited with the woman he loved.

Boone wasn't jealous, but he was a little tired of looking into his friend's contented face. He got up and washed his bowl, his back to Jackson. "You put in a call to him, and I'll talk to Scout, see what I can find out about Lucy's father."

"You think she's going to open up to you about it?"

"If she thinks it will reunite her with her daughter," he said as he walked out of the kitchen.

He followed the soft murmur of voices back through the living room and down a narrow hall. There were only two bedrooms there. Samuel's and Raina's. Light spilled out of Samuel's room, and he went there, peering into the open doorway.

Just as she'd promised, Raina had tucked Scout into bed. Or had tried. Scout was sitting on the edge of the mattress, her face pale, what looked like a flannel nightgown in her hand.

"Boone," she said as he stepped into the room, "I'm glad you're here. I was thinking that maybe I should just go back to my place."

"You mean the place that the police don't want you to be?"

"I can't stay here. I'm taking a ten-year-old child's bed." She smiled at Samuel as if she were afraid she'd offended him.

"Samuel is bunking with me," Raina cut in smoothly. "And he's really excited about it. We're going to read and eat popcorn before bed. It's all worked out."

"But—" She tried to protest, but Raina headed for the door.

"Come on, Samuel. I'm going to get Scout some tea, and you're going to finish your homework. Otherwise, we can't have our reading party."

Take me with you, Scout wanted to say, but they were already gone, their footsteps tapping on the hallway floor as they left her alone in the room with Boone.

He watched her intently, his eyes the deep blue of a midnight sky. He had something to say, and she was afraid of what it was. Had he heard from Officer Lamar? Had something been found? Had Lucy been found?

Her pulse jumped at the thought, and she stood on shaky legs. "Did you hear something from Officer Lamar?"

"No."

"So, they're no closer to finding her." She dropped back on the bed, the jarring movement sending pain shooting through her head. It hurt enough to bring tears to her eyes, but she wouldn't cry. If she did, she might never stop.

"I'm afraid not." He pulled over a child-sized chair and sat in it. He was so tall, they were still nearly eye to eye. "We need to talk, Scout, and I need you to be completely honest with me when we do. Can you do that?"

Could she?

She'd kept her secret for so long, she wasn't sure she could do anything else.

"You're hesitant, but it's the only way I can help you, Scout. If you're not honest, I may as well call my boss and tell him that HEART isn't needed."

"You *are* needed."

"Does that mean you're going to tell me what I want to know?" He didn't smile. As a matter of fact, he had no expression on his face or in his eyes. He could have been talking about taking a walk or going for a drive, could have had absolutely no vested interest in her answer at all.

Maybe he didn't.

Maybe this was just another job to him, and the fact that he was doing it for free made it less important than other jobs.

It was important to her, though.

She needed Lucy. She needed to hear her toddler giggles, listen to her singing in her little-girl voice. Christmas was coming. Scout had planned to put up the Christmas tree and let Lucy help decorate. She'd planned to take her to the live nativity at church, let her pick out gifts to put in a shoe box for Project Christmas Child. She'd had so many plans for this year.

"Scout," he prodded, and she cleared her throat of all the tears she wasn't going to cry.

"I'll tell you what you want to know." She managed to get the words out, and she knew there was no going back. She'd have to answer everything. She'd have to let him see into every dark corner of her life.

He nodded, his face relaxing. "Good. Then let's get started."

SEVEN

She knew what he was going to ask.

She braced herself for it, because she also knew she had to tell the truth, give the name, reveal what she'd never revealed to anyone but Amber.

"Don't look so scared, Scout. I'm not going to use any of the information you give me to hurt you. My only goal is to bring Lucy home."

"Right," she managed to say through a mouth that seemed filled with cotton.

"Then what are you afraid of?" he asked.

"Losing my daughter." That was the truth. It was the reason she'd kept Lucy's paternity to herself. All the other things Amber had warned her about had made her nervous, but losing her daughter? That had terrified her.

"She's already lost," he said gently.

"I know." She swallowed hard, her eyes burning, her heart beating hollowly in her chest. She wanted to go back in time, do something different, *anything* different, to keep Lucy safe.

"Tell me about her father."

"He's not in the picture. He doesn't even know Lucy exists."

"Are you sure?"

Was she? Not really. She didn't think Amber had told anyone about Lucy, but she couldn't be sure and she couldn't ask. "There was only one person who knew who Lucy's father is. She died last year."

His eyes narrowed and he leaned forward. "What happened to her?"

"She committed suicide."

"Did she leave a note?"

"I don't know. I heard about it on the news."

"Okay. Tell you what," he sighed. "How about we stop with the back and forth, and you just tell me the whole story? That'll probably save some time."

"Have you heard of Dale and Christopher Schoepflin?"

"Father and son, right? Both congressmen? I've heard the son might be in line for a presidential nomination."

"My best friend was Dale's daughter, Amber. Christopher is her half brother. He was ten years older than her." This was a lot harder to talk about than she wanted it to be. She hated the story, because it was her story, her mistake, her sin.

That was a hard truth to swallow and a harder truth to speak.

"Amber asphyxiated in her father's garage while he was in D.C. That was pretty big news," Boone said.

She nodded, because she still couldn't believe that her best friend had blocked the tailpipe of her Ford Mustang, turned on the engine and waited to die. The image didn't match with the happy, hyper person she'd grown up with. Amber had been the optimist, the ever-cheerful party girl. If she'd been hiding deep depression, she'd never let on.

"Did you attend the funeral?" Boone pressed for more.

"No, I…" She hesitated, then plunged forward with the information, because hiding it wasn't going to bring Lucy home. "Didn't want Lucy near the family. She's Christopher's daughter."

If Boone was surprised, he didn't let it show. "His wedding was a pretty big deal. I remember seeing pictures of it on magazine covers. When was it? Three years ago?"

"Yes. Two months before Lucy was born." He could figure out the timeline on that, because she wasn't going to go into details.

"He married Rachel Harris, right?"

"That's right." Rachel was a prominent talk-show hostess and an outspoken children's advocate. Scout had never met her in person, but she'd seen her on just about every magazine cover imaginable. The media loved her, because she was beautiful, smart and dedicated to the underprivileged. Her and Christopher's engagement and wedding had ranked right up there with British royalty, and for a while, it seemed it was all anyone had talked about.

"I guess Christopher wouldn't be happy if his wife knew he had a child with someone else," he murmured dispassionately, no judgment or heat in the words.

It didn't matter. Her cheeks were lava hot. She wanted to explain everything. The years she'd wasted on Darren, the way she'd felt when she'd finally realized that he wasn't who he'd claimed to be, the party Amber had invited her to, the secret crush that she'd had on Christopher for so many years it had almost defined who she was.

It seemed like a lifetime ago, and looking back, she could see how gauche she'd been, how naive and easily manipulated. She'd walked right into the perfect firestorm of temptation, and she'd given in to it, because she'd been tired of being the good girl, the good friend, the perfect companion.

"There's no need to be embarrassed," he said, which made her feel only more embarrassed. "This isn't confession time, and it's not about rehashing painful memories. What it's about is finding your daughter. Is it possible that Christopher found out about her?"

"I don't know."

"How about his wife?"

"I don't know that, either. The only one I told was Amber, and I don't know why she'd tell anyone else. She's the one who told me to leave town and warned me not to tell her family about the baby."

"Why?"

"Why what?"

"Why didn't she want you to tell them?"

"She was afraid they'd find a way to take Lucy from me. She was worried that I'd lose custody or that…" She hesitated. Amber's warning had seemed bizarre, her fear out of proportion with the situation. It had been contagious, though, and Scout had never shaken the anxiety her words had brought. "She didn't give me specifics. She just said she wouldn't put anything past them. She was worried that if they couldn't get me to relinquish custody, they might do something to force me into it."

"That could mean anything." Boone's words were light, but his expression was anything but. He looked tough and implacable, all his easy good looks lost in the hardness of his eyes, the toughness of his face.

"She was scared and that scared me. I started looking for a job out of town, and I managed to get an interview here. When they offered me the position, I took it."

"You ran a long way for such a vague threat."

"It didn't seem vague at the time. It seemed like I was doing what I needed to do to stay safe."

"Did you have any contact with Amber after you left? Phone calls? Emails? Texts? Anything that could have been traced?"

"Last year, she sent me two letters and a Christmas gift."

"Do you still have the letters?"

"I did. They were in my filing cabinet in my closet."

"I'll have Officer Lamar look for them. Did you respond?"

"She asked me not to. She said things were…weird." Those hadn't been Amber's exact words, but they were close. Scout closed her eyes, trying to force her brain to remember every detail of the short notes. One in the summer. One in the fall. Then the Christmas gift. Two weeks later, Amber was dead.

Had she planned to take her life when she sent the gift? Had it been some kind of cry for help?

"What are you thinking?" Boone touched her shoulder, and she opened her eyes, realized that he'd leaned closer. There was a faint scar on his cheek, the shadow of a red beard on his jaw. He had the longest lashes she'd ever seen on a man, thick and dark red like his hair. If she'd met him at church, she'd have found him attractive, and she'd have done everything in her power to avoid him.

"That Amber needed me, and I wasn't there for her?" she said honestly, because she'd already told him things she'd never told anyone else, and there didn't seem to be any reason to hide the truth.

He didn't tell her she was wrong, didn't say everything would be okay. "That's a tough thing," he said. "Knowing that you weren't there at the right moment to keep something from happening to someone you love. Me? I've been there. I know the weight of regret. I also know that it doesn't change anything, doesn't help anything."

"What—?"

"It's a story for another time, Scout. Right now, the best thing you can do is stay focused on the present, stay healthy and safe for your daughter's sake. You can make sure that when she comes home, you're able to care for her the way she's going to need to be cared for."

"I know."

"Good. So, you won't try to leave the house tonight? No climbing out the window and trying to get home? No heading off to the accident scene? You won't call anyone, won't ask for any outside help?"

"In other words, no doing anything?" She could have told him right then that wasn't going to happen.

"Exactly. Let us do what we do best and trust that it's going to be enough."

"What if it isn't?"

"I can't tell you that. I can only tell you that what HEART does will be the best anyone can offer, Scout. The rest is up to God." He stood, towering over her, his faded jeans clinging to muscular thighs and narrow hips, his T-shirt clinging to flat abs and broad shoulders. "I'm going to call Officer Lamar and give him the information you shared. He'll probably stop by later to ask more questions, but for now, I suggest you rest."

He walked into the hall before she could respond. Seconds later, Raina walked in. Scout was sure she'd been standing outside the door waiting, but she didn't mention it. Just bustled to the bedside table and set down a cup of tea and a glass of water beside it.

"I brought you some Tylenol." She handed Scout two tablets. "They're not going to do much for the headache, but they may take the edge off the pain. I called the hospital and asked for your discharge instructions. Your doctor wrote a script for pain medication, but you left too quickly to get it. I had the hospital fax it to the clinic where I work. We have a pharmacy there." She spoke almost nonstop as she helped Scout to her feet, pulled back the covers. "How about I help you into that nightgown? You'll be a lot more comfortable sleeping in that."

"I can manage."

"That doesn't mean you should. Did Boone tell you that I'm a nurse? I spent quite a few years working in the E.R."

"No. He didn't."

"I work at a medical clinic now, but I've seen plenty of head injuries. Yours was a serious one. Do too much too soon and you'll end up back in the hospital. I'm not going to push you to take my offer of help, but if you start feeling dizzy or off balance, don't fight through it. Sit down and wait or call for help. Okay?"

"Okay," she agreed, mostly because her legs were shaking and she wanted Raina to leave so that she could sit down again.

"Great. I'll check in on you later." She walked out, closing the door with a quiet click.

Scout dropped onto the bed, popping both Tylenol in her mouth and swallowing them with water. She didn't drink any of the tea. Her stomach was churning, and she wasn't sure she'd keep it down. She didn't bother changing. She wanted to be ready if Officer Lamar showed up. She also wanted to be ready to leave if she decided it was the best option. Right then, she felt too weak to even think about opening the window and doing any of the things Boone had warned her about.

She wanted to do them, though. She wanted to go home, wanted to go to the crash site, wanted to knock on every door in town and demand to look in every house, every room and every closet until she found her daughter.

How much time had passed between the moment she'd been shot and the moment Boone had arrived? Was it enough to have got Lucy out of town or had the kidnappers holed up somewhere to wait until the heat died down?

The police had been looking for three days and they'd found nothing.

She stretched out on the bed, her thoughts racing, her heart racing with them. Three days was a lot of time. Lucy could be anywhere.

If she was even alive.

The thought weaseled its way into her head and wouldn't leave. It pulsed there, screaming for her attention. She didn't want to give it any, because she didn't want to even imagine that she'd never see her daughter again.

She turned on her side, stared out the window, willing herself not to panic. If Amber had been right about her family, it was possible that Christopher had Lucy, that she was safe and being cared for by...

The people who'd tried to kill Scout?

She gagged and had to sit up to catch her breath.

Outside the gibbous moon cast gray-green light on shrubs and grass. It was a pretty yard, set off from any neighbors. On a bluff above it, a light shone through a thick stand of trees. She knew the building that light spilled from. She'd been there once when she'd first moved to River Valley, the little church on the bluff quaint and welcoming. In the end, she'd decided to attend a larger church. She'd wanted the anonymity that came from being in a larger congregation.

She grabbed the chair and dragged it over to the window, pulled the comforter around her shoulders and sat staring out at the night. She didn't want to lie in bed, didn't want to cuddle up under blankets when she wasn't sure if Lucy could do the same.

"Good night, sweet girl," she whispered, wishing those words could drift across the distance between them, settle into her daughter's heart, give her the comfort she needed.

They'd never been apart for more than a few hours. They'd never spent a night without each other. Lucy had to be scared, and thinking about it broke whatever was left whole in Scout's heart.

The house settled around her, the sound of voices slowly dying. The floor creaked above her head. Boone and Jackson settling down for the night? She imagined it must be. Imagined that the doors opening and closing in the hall were Samuel and Raina.

Mother and son?

They looked nothing alike, but the bond between them had been obvious, the young boy's eyes constantly tracking Raina as she moved around the room.

She wanted to know their story, but she wanted Lucy more.

The Tylenol had done little to dull the throbbing in her head, but the aching pain there was nothing compared to the pain in her heart. She had a ten-ton weight on her chest, and if she didn't get up and *do* something, it would crush her.

She crept across the room, opened the door. It didn't creak or groan, but the floorboards gave a little under her feet, the quiet sounds like a soft moan in the darkness.

She didn't know where she was going, but she made her way into the living room and then into the kitchen. Someone had left a light on above the stove, its mellow glow barely illuminating the room. She didn't turn on another light, had no idea what she thought she'd accomplish by being there rather than in the bedroom. She just knew she couldn't sit and wait.

She'd had her purse with her earlier, but she didn't know where it had gone. Her cell phone was in it, and if it still had some charge left in the battery, she could do an online search for Christopher. It had been a while since she'd looked him up. The one night they'd spent together had cured her of the childish crush she'd had. When she'd left the Schoepflin mansion early the next morning, she'd wanted nothing more than to forget what had happened and move on with her life—a little smarter and a whole lot wiser.

She liked to think that she had, but burying her head in the sand, hiding the truth, doing everything in her power to keep Lucy safe hadn't been enough.

She walked back into the living room, looked around for her purse and didn't find it. She'd probably left it in the SUV. She doubted Boone had left it unlocked, but she was just restless enough, just desperate enough to check.

She began easing the bolt open, going slow to avoid unnecessary noise.

"Going somewhere?" Boone said from behind her.

She screamed, whirling to face him.

"What in the world are you doing there?" she gasped.

"What I'm doing is being really unhappy," he muttered, taking her arm and leading her to the couch. "Sit."

She dropped down a little too quickly, her legs weak, her head spinning. "I was looking for my purse."

"I told you to stay inside," he ground out, towering over her. Again. She wanted to tell him to sit down so she wouldn't strain her neck looking up at him, but it would have taken too much effort, so she didn't say anything at all. "You're not going to save your daughter by getting yourself killed," he continued a little more gently.

"Who's going to kill me? You said yourself that no one followed us from my place."

"That's not the point."

"Then what is?"

"You didn't follow the first rule for working with HEART."

"I didn't realize there were rules I had to follow." She squeezed the bridge of her nose. It did nothing to ease her headache. "The fact is," she continued, because he didn't respond, "I couldn't lie in a warm cozy bed while my daughter is missing. I can't close my eyes and sleep when I don't know if she's okay. I don't expect you to understand that, but it is what it is. Until she's home, I have to be working to find her."

Boone eyed Scout, knowing what he needed to say, but not liking it. He didn't talk about Kendal much. Not to friends or family or even fellow members of HEART.

He kept his daughter tucked away in a sacred place in his heart that no one was allowed to touch. It was tough, tougher than he'd ever have imagined that it could be, to have a child out in the world somewhere, to be constantly wondering if she was loved, cared for, safe. It ate at a person, and if Boone let himself, he could tumble down deep into depression at the thought of what he'd lost.

That was why he worked so hard, why he kept busy and focused. It was that or lose himself to grief.

"I do understand," he said quietly, and she frowned, her eyes dark with fatigue, the bandage on her head slipping a little to reveal one of many staples that had closed the wound. The bullet had grazed her head, fractured her skull. A millimeter was all that had stood between her and death. If the gunman had adjusted his aim just that fraction of an inch, she wouldn't have survived.

"I doubt it. You think you know. You're trying to understand, but until your daughter is the one missing—"

"My daughter *is* missing," he cut in. "She was taken from me four years ago, and I haven't seen her since."

The words were out, bitter and ugly, but a truth that he hoped would forge a bond between him and Scout. Without her trust, he'd be fighting an uphill battle to keep her safe while he searched for Lucy.

She looked as if she was trying to wrap her head around the words, figure out what they meant in the grand scheme of what was happening to her. "Who took her?" she finally asked. "A stranger? Someone you knew?"

"My wife. I was serving in Iraq, and she left with our daughter. She died of a drug overdose a year later. My daughter wasn't with her."

"Where—?"

"I don't know. I've been all over the country trying to find her, but she's still not home. All I can do is keep looking and pray she's safe, pray she's with someone who loves her and cares for her. *That's* why I joined HEART. It's why I've devoted my life to reuniting families. It's the only reason I do what I do, Scout, because I *do* understand. I've lived it."

"I'm sorry," she said, touching his arm. He felt it like the spring thaw after a harsh winter, the warmth seeping through him, the surprise of it making him look a little more deeply into her eyes.

Her hand dropped away, and she stood. Maybe she'd felt what he had, and maybe she was just as uncomfortable with it as he was.

"I didn't tell you to make you sorry, Scout." He stood, too, stretching a kink out of his lower back and walking to the front door. "I told you because I want you to know that I know what it's like to want to do something even when there is absolutely nothing that can be done. I'll get your purse. You stay in the house. Next time you need something, ask."

He left it at that, walking outside and letting the crisp fall air fill his lungs, clear his head and chase away the memories that were never far from his mind.

EIGHT

Scout didn't sleep. She couldn't. Every time she drifted off, she heard Lucy crying and woke again. Just dreams. She knew that, but her heart jumped every time, her body demanding that she leap out of bed, run from the dream, from the house, from the horrible knowledge that her daughter was gone. By dawn, her eyes were gritty and hot, her body cold and achy. She wanted coffee. Black. She didn't think it would do much to wake her up, but it might chase some of the ice from her veins.

She paced across the room, but didn't open the door. She didn't dare leave the room. She was too afraid she'd run into Boone again. The story he'd told her would have broken her heart if it hadn't already been shattered. She'd wanted to tell him that, but he'd got her purse, handed it to her and escorted her back to the bedroom.

He'd said good-night, and she'd bitten her tongue to keep from asking a dozen questions about his wife, his daughter, the years that he'd spent searching. They were two people who had one terrible thing in common. It didn't make her feel any better to know that someone else had lived through her nightmare, but it did help her understand why Boone was so determined to find Lucy.

Someone knocked on the door, and she hurried to open it, glad for the distraction.

Raina stood in the hallway, a stack of clothes and towels in her hand, her hair pulled back with a pretty blue headband. She wore scrubs and sturdy shoes, and somehow she still managed to look chic and stylish.

"I heard you moving around in here, so I thought I'd peek in before I left for work," she said with a smile. "I brought you some towels and clean clothes."

"I don't want to put you out."

She laughed lightly and thrust the stack into Scout's arms. "Please! Some clothes and towels aren't putting me out any more than the tea I made you last night was. How are you feeling this morning?"

"Like I got run over by a train," she responded honestly.

"I don't doubt it. I want to change that bandage and take a look at the wound, if you don't mind."

"That's not necessary."

"Actually, it is. You don't want an infection to take hold. That can take a person down pretty quickly." She pulled small scissors and gauze from one pocket of her scrubs and rubbing alcohol and cotton balls from the other. "Go ahead and sit down. This will only take a minute. Then you can take a shower and freshen up. There's a new shower cap in the bathroom. I put it on the counter near the sink. It should work to cover your head, but try not to submerse your head." Just like she had the night before, she kept up a running commentary.

Scout gave in and sat, listening to Raina's chatter as the old bandage was eased off her head.

"Hmm," Raina said, dabbing at the skin with an alcohol-soaked cotton ball.

"Hmm what?" Scout glanced in the mirror above the dresser. Did a double take. Sallow skinned with dark circles under her eyes, she had at least two dozen staples from midforehead to her temple. "Good grief! I look like Frankenstein's monster!"

"Not quite." Raina tossed the cotton ball into the trash can and soaked another one.

"Lucy would scream if she got a look at me now."

"Your daughter is three, right?"

"She will be soon. Her birthday is right after Christmas. We were going to have so much fun putting up the Christmas tree and going to the live nativity."

"You'll still be able to do those things."

"They won't be the same if she's not with me."

Raina pressed gauze to Scout's forehead, gently covering the wound. "They won't be, but you'll survive it. You'll learn to get along without, and then when she comes home, you'll be all that much happier to have her with you."

"If she comes home."

"Have a little faith, Scout," she murmured.

"I have plenty of faith."

"Then stop doubting what God can do." She tossed dirty gauze into the trash can, put the rubbing alcohol and extra cotton balls back into her pocket. "I hate to clean wounds and run, but I need to get out of here. Work won't wait. Samuel is still asleep. Hopefully he'll stay that way for a while. If you want coffee, I already started a pot. There's cream in the fridge and sugar in a bowl on the table."

"Thanks," Scout said.

"No problem. If you want some, you should probably get it now rather than later. All bets are off when the boys get back."

"Boys?"

"Men," she laughed. "Boone and Jackson took off about an hour ago."

"I didn't hear them." And she'd been up, pacing the room and listening to the silence.

"They didn't want you to. Boone said they had a meeting with the local police. He probably wanted to weed through the information before giving it to you."

"I'm not sure I like that." As a matter of fact, she was sure she *didn't* like it.

"It is what it is," Raina said calmly. "You're here. You might as well make the best of it. Get a shower. Drink some coffee. Have some breakfast. It could be a busy day today, and you want to be ready for it."

"Of course I do," Scout muttered.

When she saw Boone, she was going to tell him exactly how she felt about being left behind while he went to the police. It wasn't Raina's fault, though, and she didn't want to take her frustration out on her. She tried to smile. "Thanks for the clothes and towels, and thanks for letting me stay here for the night."

"You don't have to thank me, Scout. I was happy to do it. Now, I really do have to get out of here. If you need anything, Stella is upstairs."

She walked into the hall, stood right outside the room. "By the way, I tucked a phone charger in with the clothes and towels. Kind of felt like putting a handsaw in a cake and delivering it to prison, since I'm pretty sure Boone would rather you not have one."

Another thing she didn't like. "He doesn't want me to use my phone?"

"He wants to keep you safe. Cutting you off from the world is the easiest way to do it." She shrugged. "The way I see things, you'll be more likely to stay put if you have some access to the things you want. I'll see you this afternoon." She bustled out of the room, and Scout grabbed the pile of clothes and towels, rifled through them until she found the charger. She plugged in her phone, took a quick shower and dressed in the borrowed jeans and sweater. The jeans were a little loose and a little long. The sweater hung to midthigh. She didn't feel like herself in them. Or maybe she just didn't feel like herself period.

Without Lucy, she didn't know who she was.

Without her, she wasn't sure what to do with her time, how to spend her morning, her afternoon, her evening.

She took the phone and the charger into the kitchen, plugged them in, poured a cup of coffee, went through the motions of a normal day even though nothing about it was normal. She didn't usually take sugar with her coffee, but she scooped in a couple of teaspoonfuls. She hadn't eaten in hours and didn't think she *could* eat, but she needed energy for...

What?

Waiting?

Her phone rang, the sound so unexpected, she jumped.

It rang again, and she scrambled to lift it from the charger, fumbling to hit the right button and answer.

She thought it was Boone, calling to check up on her. "Where are you?" she demanded.

"Shut up and listen," someone hissed, the words chilling Scout's blood. "You want your daughter—you do exactly what I say. Hear me?"

"Yes," she tried to say, but the word caught in her

throat and came out as a breath of air. "Yes," she repeated.

Footsteps pounded behind her and she thought someone had walked into the room, but she didn't turn. She was afraid she'd drop the phone, break the connection, lose her one shot at getting Lucy back.

"Good. You have information I want. I have your kid. We'll do an exchange. What I want for what you want."

"I don't have—"

"I said *listen*," the caller snapped. A man. She was sure of that. "You have something I want, and if I don't get it, your daughter is mine."

Stella appeared at her side, her red hair wet, her face makeup free. She had freckles—lots of them—and a deep scowl that creased her forehead.

She pulled a chair over and sat, leaning in so that her ear was pressed close to the phone, then grabbed Scout's hand, angling the phone so she could hear.

"You're going to bring me what I want," the caller continued. "And then you're going to get what you want. A nice easy exchange. No drama. No fuss. Understand?"

"Yes, but I don't know what you're talking about. I don't have anything of yours," Scout said, her throat dry, her hand shaking so hard, she almost dropped the phone. Stella tightened her grip on Scout's hand and held it steady, but didn't say a word.

"Don't waste my time, lady. You have it. I want it. You don't know what it is—you'd better figure it out. You've got until midnight tonight. You bring it to the little park near your house. You know the one? You and your kid like to play there."

The fact that he knew that made her numb with fear. "I know it."

"Good. No police. Anyone but you shows up and you'll never see your kid again. Understand?"

"I understand, but I want to talk to Lucy. I want to know she's okay."

The man hesitated, then muttered something that she couldn't hear. She thought she heard a woman's voice, braced herself for the connection to be lost, for any chance she had of speaking to her daughter being lost with it.

"Sixty seconds," the man said abruptly.

She heard shuffling movement, a whimper that made the hair on her arms stand on end. "Lucy?" she said, her voice trembling, her entire body shaking. "Is that you?"

"Mommy!" Lucy wailed, the cry spearing straight through Scout's heart.

"Don't cry, sweetie," she said, tears streaming down her face. She didn't wipe them away. She had sixty seconds, and she couldn't waste even one of them. "Are you okay? Are you hurt?"

"Get me, Mommy." Lucy continued to cry, and Scout wanted to climb through the phone, put her arms around her and hold her close.

"I am. I will. It's just going to take a little more time." Her chest ached, her heart pounding so hard she thought it would fly out. "It's okay. You're okay."

"Get me!"

"I love you, sweetie. I'll be there as soon as I—"

"Time's up," the man cut in, Lucy's cries fading into the background, mixing with the faint sound of a woman's voice. "Tonight at midnight. The park. You bring what I want. I'll deliver what you want. Simple. Easy."

He disconnected.

Scout didn't move, didn't think she was breathing.

Her chest was too tight, her lungs unable to expand. She'd suspected the Schoepflins had something to do with Lucy's kidnapping, but this was worse. A stranger had taken her, wanted to exchange her for something that Scout was sure she didn't have.

"You are not going to panic," Stella growled, taking the phone from her hand and disconnecting the call. "You are not going to fall apart."

Yes, I am, she wanted to say, but Stella glared at her, her eyes hot and angry.

"I texted Boone while you were on the phone. The police are already on this," she continued, every word enunciated and clear as if she didn't think Scout was going to be able to comprehend anything else.

"She was crying." It was all Scout could think of saying. Right at that moment, it was the only thing that seemed to matter. Lucy had needed her, and for the first time in her daughter's life, Scout had failed to bring her comfort.

"I know. I heard," Stella said more gently. "Move past it, okay? You need to focus. The guy said you had something that he wanted. What is it?"

"I don't know." That terrified her, made her breath come faster, her heart race.

"You think you don't. *He* thinks you do. Since he has your kid, I think you'd better figure this out. Think back. Were you given an unexpected gift recently?"

"No."

"Did you bring any books home from the library? Maybe something that had just been reshelved?"

"I brought a bunch of books home last week, but I'm not sure if any of them had just been returned."

"We need to find those and look through them. It's

possible someone tucked information into one of them and you grabbed it before the intended recipient." She was texting as she spoke.

Sending information to Boone?

Scout didn't ask. She felt hollow and empty, Lucy's cries still ringing in her ears.

"Go get your purse," Stella barked. "Grab your coat. Boone will be here in two minutes, and he's taking you over to your place. The police will meet you there."

She tried to jump up, but her body refused anything more than a slow unfolding. She ached. Every bone, every muscle. She hurried to her room, heard the front door open as she grabbed her purse and coat. Boone was there. He'd take her to her house; he'd help her search for the information.

If they didn't find it, what then?

She shrugged into her coat, stumbled back out into the hall, walking right into Boone.

He grabbed her arms, holding her steady. "It's okay," he said.

"No. It's not." But Stella was right. She wasn't going to panic. She wasn't going to fall apart. She was going to search through every inch of her house; she was going to hunt through every book, lift every broken picture frame. She was going to find what she needed, and she had only until midnight to do it.

She hitched her purse up on her shoulder, eased out from Boone's hands. "We need to go. I have no idea what he wants, and I only have a few hours to figure it out."

She walked past him, down the hall, past Stella and Jackson and Samuel, who must have heard the commotion and woken up. She didn't say anything to any of

them. Just walked out the door and headed for the SUV
that was still idling in the driveway.

They had something to go on. Finally. And Boone had
every intention of following up on it. Lamar wouldn't
be happy about it. Neither would the FBI agent who'd
been at their meeting. They hadn't told him to back off,
but they'd made it very clear they could handle the situation themselves.

They could. No doubt about it.

They weren't going to have to.

HEART had plenty of resources and those could be
accessed quickly. No bureaucracy, no hoops to jump
through. The team decided what needed to be done, and
they found a way to do it. Cyrus Mitchell was already
working his magic. Lucy's kidnapper had used a cell
phone, and Cyrus thought he could follow the signal
and pinpoint a location.

If so, they could have Lucy well before the midnight
deadline.

He didn't tell Scout that. He didn't want to get her
hopes up, and he didn't want her to have any less urgency
in the search for whatever it was the kidnapper wanted.

He glanced in the rearview mirror.

Scout sat silently, her body so tense he thought she
might snap in two. She hadn't spoken since they'd left
Raina's place. Hadn't asked any questions, hadn't mentioned hearing her daughter's voice.

He let her keep her silence. Asking a bunch of questions she couldn't answer wasn't going to help the situation. Stella had filled him in on the conversation and
the demands. That was all he needed to know. For now.

He took a straight shot to Scout's place. No side roads.

No worries about being followed. The kidnapper had made his demands known, and the goal was to make him believe those demands were going to be met. Let him see Scout return to her house, let him watch the police and FBI combing the area. The fact that the guy had made his demands by phone just proved that he didn't think he could be caught.

Or maybe he just thought that having a hostage would keep him from being pursued.

It didn't matter.

He'd be caught. HEART had worked cases like this dozens of times. While the FBI and local P.D. went through the proper channels, HEART worked like a well-oiled machine.

He pulled into Scout's driveway, parking behind a squad car. There were several unmarked vehicles, as well, and a uniformed officer stood at the door.

"This should be interesting," he murmured as he offered Scout a hand out.

She didn't take it. Just sat where she was, her face pale, her eyes glassy. She'd been crying, but she'd stopped before he'd arrived at Raina's house.

"Scout," he prodded, touching her fisted hand. "You can't stay here."

"I don't know what he wants." She met his eyes, her gaze hollow and filled with the kind of pain most people would never know. "What am I going to do?"

"You're going to get out of the car." He pulled her to her feet, his hands settling on her waist. "You're going to go inside, and you're going to search the house until you find whatever it is he wants."

"I have never," she whispered, "been so scared of failing in my life."

"You're not going to fail."

"I already did. She was crying for me. She wanted me to come for her, and I couldn't." Her voice broke, but she didn't let any more tears escape.

"That wasn't a failure."

"To Lucy it was. There has never been a time when she's needed me that I haven't been able to be there for her. Until today."

"You'll be with her soon, and she'll forget that you ever weren't."

"You hope."

"I *believe*. There's a difference. Come on." He wrapped an arm around her waist, was surprised when she leaned into him. The subtle shift, the easing of her muscles, the slow melting toward him—it took him by surprise. Since Lana's death, he hadn't had much interest in dating. After experiencing married life, having a child, seeing the beauty of family, he hadn't been interested in playing games. He hadn't wanted short-term, and he'd been sure that he didn't want long-term, either. His life was full of work, of friendships, of a passion for something that most people couldn't understand. He'd dated a few women in the past few years, but he'd known it wouldn't be fair to offer more than one or two dinners, maybe a trip to the movies. He didn't just love his job. He was compelled by it, driven by it. He couldn't *not* do it. Even if he'd wanted to. That left little time for relationships.

That had always been fine by him.

But maybe it wasn't fine anymore.

Maybe he wanted more than his empty apartment and his potted plants. Maybe he wanted someone to go home to.

NINE

She was slogging through mud.

At least, that was how it felt to Scout. She tried to match pace with Boone's long-legged stride, but no matter how much she willed herself to move more quickly, she just couldn't seem to do it.

He must have realized it. He slowed his pace, keeping his arm firmly around her waist as he led her toward a uniformed police officer. If she'd felt stronger, she'd have told Boone she could manage just fine on her own. She didn't. She felt weak and scared. Despite what Boone said, she wasn't sure she'd find what Lucy's kidnapper had demanded. She was hoping that it was in one of the library books she'd brought home. If it wasn't, she had no idea where to look. And if she didn't find it, what would happen? Would she ever see her daughter again?

She gritted her teeth to keep from asking the questions. She knew Boone couldn't give her a definitive answer. He'd said she would be with Lucy soon, said he was believing it rather than hoping it. All the belief in the world couldn't make something true. She'd learned that the hard way.

"Good morning, Ms. Cramer," the officer said, his

gaze jumping from Scout to Boone and back again. "Officer Lamar is waiting for you inside. Your friend is going to have to wait out here."

The muscles in Boone's arm tensed, his fingers pressing a little more firmly into her side. He didn't speak, though, didn't argue. She could have walked inside and left him where he was. It should have been the easy thing to do. She'd been going it alone for so many years that she'd forgotten what it was like to have someone in her corner.

Until Boone had come along, and suddenly she remembered how it felt to stand shoulder to shoulder with another person, to know there was someone to hold her up when she wanted to fall down. She didn't want to give that up.

"I'd rather he come with me," she said, and his fingers caressed her waist, smoothing along the edges of her waistband in a subtle sign of approval.

"Sorry. That's not possible."

"Why not?" Boone asked without heat or aggression. He might have been asking the time of day or commenting on the weather, for all the emotion in his voice.

"The house is a crime scene. We're still processing it."

"I don't think so," Boone said with a smile that looked more feral than polite. "I was in Officer Lamar's office earlier this morning. He made it very clear that Scout could return home. Would he have done that if he was still processing the scene?"

"I don't—"

"We both know that he wouldn't," Boone continued. "So, what's the problem?"

"The FBI is already working with the River Valley P.D. We don't need a third party involved."

"I'm here as Scout's friend. Are you going to deny a crime victim the support she needs?"

"We're doing everything in our power to make this as easy on Ms. Cramer as we can."

"You didn't answer my question," Boone pointed out.

The officer scowled. "Stay here. I'll check with Lamar. If he says you're in, you're in. If he says you stay out, you're out."

He walked inside, closing the door just a little too firmly behind him.

"Nice guy," Boone said easily.

"He probably is. Most days."

"Just not today?" Boone asked with a half smile. He seemed distracted, his eyes scanning the yard, the driveway, the copse of trees across the road.

"What are you looking for?" she asked, and his ocean-blue gaze landed right smack-dab on her face. She'd thought he was handsome the day they'd met, but she hadn't realized how handsome. The angle of his jaw and cheekbones, the firm curve of his lips, the day's growth of beard on his chin created a picture that nearly stole her breath.

"Someone affiliated with the guy who took your daughter. He wasn't working alone. More than one car followed you from the store the night Lucy was taken. I'd say that he's got someone watching the house, making sure you're looking for whatever it is he wants."

She tensed, the thought of someone watching her, stalking her while she searched, making her skin crawl. "We should tell the police."

"They know. The FBI knows. This is something we've all done dozens of times. Every kidnapper thinks he's unique, but most of them are working under the same premise. They want something. They make sure they have something valuable to barter with. In this case, Lucy. Once they have that, they aren't content to sit and wait. Most of the time, they're actively keeping tabs on the victim's family."

"Nice." She shivered, and he shrugged out of his jacket, draped it around her shoulders. It smelled like soap and aftershave, and she burrowed in, letting his warmth seep into her.

"*Predictable* is a better word," he responded. "See the guy in your living room window?" He eased her around so she was facing the house.

Sure enough, someone was standing in front of the window. "Yes."

"He's doing the same thing I am—looking for someone who's hanging around watching you."

"I'm not sure I like the idea of someone skulking around keeping tabs on me."

"The guy who called you is going to want to know that you're following orders. He'll be happy to see that things are going exactly the way he wants. It's nothing to worry about."

"I'm not worried about him watching me. I'm worried that I won't be able to find what he wants by the midnight deadline. I have limited time, and I'm standing outside my house waiting."

"It's your house, Scout. If you want to be inside, go inside."

"The officer—"

"Can't keep you from your property. Lamar cleared it as a crime scene last night. That being the case, he can't keep you outside."

"I've never been much of a rebel, Boone. I can't imagine doing something a police officer told me not to do."

"There's a first time for everything." He reached past her, turned the doorknob. The door swung open, revealing her still-trashed living room and a group of men and women who seemed to be in the midst of a heated discussion. They went silent as Boone nudged her across the threshold.

"Sorry to break up the party," he said. "But we're on a time crunch here, and Scout is feeling a little stressed about it."

"The last thing I want," Officer Lamar said as he separated himself from the group, "is to cause you any more stress than you've already had, Scout. But we really need to conduct this search in an organized manner. The best way to do that is to limit the number of people in the house." He sent a pointed look in Boone's direction.

She ignored it.

"I'll make sure not to invite anyone else. If you don't mind, I'm going to look at the library books I checked out last week." She grabbed Boone's hand without thinking, tugging him past the group and into the narrow hall. They made it all the way to her bedroom before he pulled her to a stop.

"What?" She met his eyes, her cheeks heating when he smiled.

"I'm impressed, Scout," he said, his Southern drawl deep and rich. If she heard it every day for the rest of her life, she didn't think she'd get tired of it. "I can't say I've ever seen a conformist rebel quite so well."

"I never said I was a conformist." She tugged away, because heat was shooting up her arm, swirling in her belly, and she didn't have time to think about what that meant or to decide if she wanted to explore it more.

"Seems to me that you probably are. You live a quiet life, doing quiet things that don't bother anyone. I talked to your neighbors, your coworkers, your church family. Not one person had a bad thing to say about you."

"First, you make that sound like a bad thing. Second, I'm not all that happy about the fact that you were talking to people I know."

"You were unconscious and your daughter was missing. Would you rather I waited until you came to to figure out if you might have had someone in your life who was capable of taking Lucy?"

"I'd rather none of this had happened," she responded, stepping into her room.

It looked the same as it had the day before, the mess somehow magnified in the watery light that streamed through the window. She walked to the bookshelf that usually housed the library books she brought home for the week. All ten of the books were on the floor, jackets torn off, spines broken. She'd have to pay for them, but that didn't matter. What mattered was that they'd already been searched. She could see that. Should have thought of it before.

Deflated, she knelt beside them, lifting the one closest to her. The pages were bent, the cover torn off and ripped apart. "The books have already been searched."

"Did you hang your hat on the idea that you'd find something in one of them?" Boone picked up another book, flipped through the pages several times.

"Stella thought maybe that's how I'd got whatever it is the kidnapper wanted. She said I might have brought it home in a library book."

"It was a good idea," he said gently, taking the book from her hand and setting both on the shelf. "But sometimes even the best ideas don't work out."

"I…" *…just wanted to think that it would.* She lifted another book, shook it out and set it with the others, her heart too heavy to continue. She hadn't hung her hat on the idea, but she'd wanted so badly to walk in and find what she'd been looking for. "Don't know where else to look."

"Did you buy anything recently? Furniture? Computer? Something used that someone might have hidden something in?"

"No. I was waiting until after Christmas to do my shopping. Lucy has grown so much this year, and she needs new everything." Her voice wobbled and she knew that if she didn't do something, she was going to cry again. She stood, walked to her closet and the file cabinet. It had been emptied, of course, and she sifted through the tax documents and receipts, looking for the letters Amber had sent. They weren't there.

She frowned, lifting the cabinet and looking under it.

"Are you looking for Amber's letters?" Boone asked as he grabbed the mattress and tossed it back on the bed.

"They aren't here."

"You're sure?" He stopped, both of her pillows under his arms. It looked as if he was trying to make up the bed, and for some reason, that touched her heart.

"They're not with the rest of the things that were in here, but there's stuff strewn all over the room, so maybe I just haven't found them yet."

He frowned, tossing the slashed pillows on top of the mattress. "I need to know for sure. If those letters were taken, that provides a direct link to the Schoepflin family."

"What does?" Officer Lamar walked in, a woman in a dark suit following him.

"I got some letters from Amber Schoepflin before she died. They're missing."

"Interesting," the woman said. "I'm Special Agent Lynette Rodriguez. My team and I are working with Officer Lamar to bring Lucy home. We've already sent an agent to talk to Christopher Schoepflin. He's denied any involvement in this but will be flying in from California tomorrow to meet with us."

She nodded, because she didn't know what to say.

There was nothing *to* say. When Christopher arrived, she'd have to explain to him. At that moment, she couldn't make herself care. All she wanted was to have Lucy back. Everything else could be worked out after that. Whatever mistakes she'd made, she could rectify them. Whatever wrongs she'd committed, she could apologize for. She couldn't go back in time and change her decision, but she could make better ones in the future.

If she had the chance. If Christopher hadn't been involved in kidnapping Lucy.

"What we'd like to do today," Agent Rodriguez continued, "is look for two things. The letters you've said are missing and whatever it is the kidnapper wants."

"I have no idea what that is," she admitted, and the agent nodded.

"Let's go sit in the kitchen. We'll make a list of possibilities."

She didn't like the idea, especially because Officer Lamar had pulled Boone aside and was speaking quietly to him. She couldn't hear what he was saying, and that bothered her. It was as if they had a secret they were trying to keep from her.

Boone must have sensed her hesitation. He met her eyes. "Go ahead. I'll be there as soon as I can, and I'll fill you in on what we discuss."

She didn't normally take someone's word on blind faith. Not anymore. Darren had told her that they'd get married, have a family and build a life together. He'd ended up running off with his sister's best friend. Christopher had whispered a thousand sweet promises in her ear. He'd told her that she was beautiful and sweet and that he'd never realized just how much he was missing out on. He'd promised that they wouldn't just have one night, that every night would be special. By the next day, he'd decided that he'd made a mistake, that Rachel really was the woman he wanted.

Scout had been devastated. Again.

She didn't plan to repeat the mistake. She wasn't going to put her trust in someone who wasn't trustworthy.

But Boone? She believed him. Maybe she even believed *in* him, because she trusted that he'd do everything he could, spend every hour he had available trying to bring Lucy home.

"Scout," the agent urged. "We really do need to get this list made. In cases like yours, time is of the essence."

"Right," she said, turning away from Boone and following Agent Rodriguez into the kitchen.

Three hours, fifteen minutes and thirty seconds.

That was how long Boone and Officer Lamar spent searching the house for the letters Amber had written.

They looked in every closet, looked under every piece of furniture. They checked under throw rugs and in the trash can. No sign of the letters.

"Someone took them," Lamar growled as he dropped a basket full of clothes on the floor of Scout's tiny laundry room. There was just enough space in the room for one adult, but somehow Lamar had maneuvered his way in. Boone wanted to tell him to back out, but he didn't want to butt heads with the guy. Not when they were working toward the same goal.

"It looks that way. Although, with the mess the perps left, it's possible we missed it."

"We didn't miss it." Lamar smoothed his hair and grimaced. "First time in my career as a police officer that I wish I'd been wrong about something."

"Wrong about what?"

"The Schoepflins. I was hoping we wouldn't find a connection between them and the kidnapping. Too much hassle involved in pretending diplomacy to appease their high-class sensitivities. I'd much rather forget about them and look in another direction."

"What direction would that be? Drugs? Money?"

"Who knows?" Lamar shrugged. "Scout could have walked into any number of scenarios. She could have seen something, heard something. Plenty of innocent people get pulled into trouble that way. Not that it matters. At this point, with those letters missing, I'd say the Schoepflins are the direction we need to look. I just hope it leads us to the kid. I have a daughter of my own, and I don't like the idea of a toddler out there in the world with a stranger."

"Any luck tracking the cell phone that was used to call Scout?"

"Not yet. The FBI is working on it." He paused. "How about your team? And don't tell me they're not trying."

"As far as I know, we've come up empty." Though he was pretty sure Cyrus was getting close. He expected to get a call at any moment, and when he did, he was moving out. Nothing was going to keep him from going wherever that cell phone signal had come from.

"I'm expecting that the FBI will locate the signal before your people do. Don't mess things up for them, Anderson. Don't try to go maverick and save the kid on your own. We don't need a hero—we need a live child to bring home to her mother."

"Your assumptions are insulting. I may work in the private sector, but I'm not doing it for the glory. Fact is," he said, keeping his tone neutral, because Lamar looked as though he was pushing for a fight and Boone wasn't in the mood to take him up on it, "there isn't any glory involved in what I do. You ever see any of our team members talking to the press, building up HEART to get more clients?"

Lamar scowled and didn't respond.

"Of course you don't, because that's not why we do what we do. Now, if you'll excuse me—" he brushed by Lamar "—Scout's probably wondering where I am."

"Hold on a minute," Lamar called.

Boone ignored him.

He'd done his part. He'd played nice. He'd followed the rules and walked around the house looking for something he'd known they weren't going to find. He was done. Time to get things moving along.

He walked into the kitchen, saw Scout sitting at the kitchen table alone. She had deep shadows under her eyes and hollows beneath her cheekbones, but she smiled when she saw him, and his heart jumped in response.

"Hey," she said. "I was wondering when you were going to show up."

"Sorry it took so long. I got sidetracked." He sat beside her. "Where's Agent Rodriguez?"

"She got a call a few minutes ago and walked out back. I don't want to get my hopes up, but I've been sitting here wondering if maybe they've found Lucy. I've even been thinking about what I'm going to do when I finally get my hands on her again. Thinking about all the hugs and kisses that I'm going to give her." She scraped at a little spot on the table and frowned. "That's probably stupid, isn't it? I should probably be preparing for the worst."

"No." He covered her hand with his, waited until she met his eyes. "Stupid would be giving up hope."

"What is hope except the belief in something that you desperately want but aren't sure is going to happen?" She stood and paced to the window above the sink, her slim body nearly shrouded by jeans and an oversize sweater. "It seems useless. Like sitting at a kitchen table answering dozens of questions about things that probably have nothing to do with my daughter's disappearance."

"What kind of questions are we talking about?" he asked, curious about the direction the FBI was heading. More than likely, they were trying to rule Christopher out. Or rule him in.

"We went over every delivery I've received in the past year. We talked about my friends, my work. She wanted to know about Amber, too. I told her about the letters. Funny, I'd put them out of my mind until all this happened."

"Yeah?" He moved up behind her, turned her so that they were facing each other. She looked tired, weary, discouraged—all the things he'd seen in all the faces of the waiting and wondering. He wanted to tell her that everything would be fine, that Lucy would come home to her and that they'd go on the way they had before. He couldn't. Not if he were going to be honest.

"Were you friends for long?" he asked instead.

"Forever. She was like a sister to me. I hadn't thought about that in a while, either." She smiled, but the sadness in her eyes was unmistakable. "You know how it is when you meet someone and you just know you're going to be friends forever? That's how it was with me and Amber. We were completely opposite of each other and completely the same."

"I've never had someone like that in my life," he said honestly.

"I'm almost as sorry for you as I am for myself, then." She walked past him, filled a kettle and set it on the stove to boil. "I don't suppose you're a tea drinker? All my coffee got dumped. I guess whoever ransacked my house thought I might be hiding something in with it."

"No tea, but if you've got anything to eat around here, I'd be grateful."

She laughed a little and pulled a box of animal crackers from the cupboard. "They didn't dump these. I guess because the box was sealed, they didn't think I'd hidden anything in it."

"Perfect." He tore open the box and took a handful. He imagined they were what she gave Lucy as a treat, but he didn't mention it. She looked wounded enough, and he didn't want to add to that. "Did you give Agent Rodriguez the gift Amber sent you?"

"She didn't ask for it. It was just a Christmas-tree ornament. A glittery pink frame with a photo of us when we were kids in it. I kept it in the living room for a while, but Lucy loved it and always tried to get her hands on it. I finally just put it in a box with the rest of the Christmas stuff."

"Where's that?" he asked, snagging another handful of crackers and handing one to her.

"My landlady has a storage unit. She let me keep a few things there."

"Do you have access to the unit?"

"Yes. I have a key to the lock and the combination to the front gate."

"Agent Rodriguez didn't ask for it?"

"She did, but she seemed more interested in the letters. She asked me what Amber said, if there was anything unusual in them. There wasn't."

He nodded, but his mind was circling back to the picture frame. "I was thinking that maybe you want to decorate for Christmas before Lucy gets home." He took a few more crackers. "I can send Jackson out to get that box for you, and he can bring it over here."

"I'm not in a holiday mood," she said wearily, putting the cracker he'd handed her back in the box and taking a tea bag from a small box in the cupboard. She poured water over it even though he doubted it was much more than lukewarm.

"I don't need you to be in the mood for it. I just need you to give me the information so that I can send Jackson to get the box."

"If that's what you want, go for it." She grabbed a scrap of paper from a pile on the counter, found a pen in a drawer and jotted the information down for him. He figured the FBI was already checking things out, but he made the call to Jackson anyway. He was just finishing the call when Agent Rodriguez walked in.

She didn't look happy.

"I've got some unpleasant news," she said without preamble.

"Is it Lucy?" Scout asked, her face losing every bit of color. He slipped an arm around her waist, felt her whole body shaking. Was surprised when her hand settled on his side, her fingers clutching the fabric of his shirt.

"No. Sorry. I should have made that clear from the beginning." Rodriguez frowned.

"Yeah, you should have," Boone retorted, not happy with how pale Scout looked, how weak she seemed to be. He knew what it was like to wait, knew the helpless feeling, the desperation. Knew how easy it was to forget things like sleep and food. She hadn't eaten the animal cracker. Had she eaten anything since she'd left the hospital?

"We all make mistakes, Mr. Anderson. I've made my apology, so how about we get back to business? I spoke with the medical examiner who autopsied Amber Schoepflin's body. He ruled suicide because of the circumstances Amber was found in, but he noted some bruising on her arms and a needle mark that was consistent with an injection. Toxicology reports showed that she had a high level of heroin in her body."

"Amber didn't take drugs." Scout frowned. "She didn't even like taking Tylenol."

"That's what her family said, but the circumstances were indicative of suicide and the M.E. ruled accordingly. With everything that's happened, I've asked for her case to be opened again. I want the San Jose police to take a closer look at what she was doing before she died, because I don't think she committed suicide. I think she was murdered."

TEN

A million questions. That was what Agent Rodriguez was asking. Scout wasn't able to answer many of them. She knew that Amber had been working as a reporter for the local paper, that she'd loved to party but never drank to excess. She knew that she'd broken up with her boyfriend and had been dating someone new in the months before her death, but she couldn't remember the guy's name and wasn't even sure Amber had ever mentioned it.

"How many times did you speak to Amber after you left San Jose?" Agent Rodriguez didn't seem to be wearing down, but Scout sure was.

She rubbed the back of her neck, trying to ease the tension there. "Not many. She was always afraid her family was listening in on the conversation."

"Why would they do that?"

"Because they were crazy that way? That's what Amber always said. I don't know what she meant. I didn't spend all that much time at her father's place."

"Did she—?"

"You know what?" Boone interrupted. "I think you've asked enough questions. Scout is still recovering, and she needs her rest."

"Which does she need more? Rest or her daughter's return?"

"If answering your questions could bring her daughter back, she'd be standing in this room right now."

"This is all part of the process," Agent Rodriguez argued. "By gathering the facts, we can narrow down our search area."

"Is there a search area?" Scout asked, because it seemed as if nothing was being done. It seemed as if they were spending all their time in the kitchen, discussing something that had happened a year ago while her daughter got ready to spend another night without her.

"Yes," Agent Rodriguez assured her, but she doubted it was true. How could it be? Not only did they not know who had Lucy, but they had no idea where to look to find her.

"I'm supposed to meet with the kidnapper at midnight. I need to—"

"You may as well know up front that that meeting is not going to happen." Agent Rodriguez cut her off. "It would be too dangerous, and the likelihood that your daughter will be at the park tonight is slim to none."

"You can't keep me from going," she responded, standing so quickly, her head spun.

"Actually, I can. It may be your daughter who's missing, but this is my case, and I can't have you interfering. You try to go, and I'll have my officers detain you."

"So, I'm just supposed to sit here and wait for the deadline to pass?"

"Unfortunately," Agent Rodriguez said, "yes."

The room seemed to close in around her, and Scout's chest hurt so badly, she thought she might be having a heart attack. She wanted to scream, to rant, to rage against everyone and everything that was keeping her from her daughter. She couldn't. She didn't have Amber's strength or Boone's courage. She was just herself, a little meek, a little quiet. Darren had called her mousy, and she hadn't been all that offended, because mousy was how she usually felt.

Right then, she just felt suffocated. "I need some air," she muttered.

She didn't wait for permission, just ran out the back door, raced across the little yard that she and Lucy had spent so much time in. She'd made it to the edge of the trees at the back of the property when Boone caught up. He pulled her to a stop, his hand wrapped around hers, his palm warm and just a little rough.

"Next time, wait for me," he said.

"I couldn't breathe," she responded. "I really couldn't." Her voice broke, and all the tears she'd been holding back, all the fear and anxiety and anger burst out. She cried as if the world had ended, because she thought that maybe it had.

"Shh," he said, pulling her into his arms. He smelled like fresh air and sunshine mixed with something masculine and just a little dark, and she wanted to burrow into him, stay there until the nightmare ended and Lucy was home. "You're okay."

"No. It's not," she sobbed. "Lucy is missing, and all I'm doing is sitting at my kitchen table, having tea and answering questions."

"I didn't say *it* was okay. I said *you* were." He eased back, cupping her face in his hands, his eyes dark blue and filled with compassion. "There's a big difference, Scout. One you have no control over. The other you do."

"I don't have any control over any of it—that's the problem." She stepped away, swiping at the tears.

"You know what I've realized during the years my daughter's been missing?" he asked quietly, his hair gleaming in the afternoon sunlight, his eyes deeply shadowed. "We don't always have to be in control to be content. We don't always have to know every outcome to have peace. Sometimes we've just got to trust that the things we can't control are in God's hands, that He's working His good through the worst of circumstances."

Coming from anyone else, it would have sounded clichéd and trite, but Boone had lived her nightmare. He knew every ache of her heart. "I wish I had your faith. I wish that I could believe something good was going to come out of this."

"I wish I had my daughter," he responded. "But I don't, and because I don't, I'm helping you find yours."

"It's not a fair trade. Not for you."

"Nothing about life is fair." He smoothed loose strands of hair from her cheek, his hand settling at her nape, kneading muscles that were taut from nerves and fear. "But I think you already know that."

She nodded, her heart pounding in her ears, butterflies dancing in her stomach. His hand felt warm and wonderful, and that scared her more than she wanted to admit. She'd made a big mistake with Christopher, her silly childhood crush allowing her to believe all the sweet lies he'd whispered to her. She'd given up everything she'd believed in so she could believe in him.

She wouldn't make that mistake again.

She moved away, cold air cooling her heated cheeks.

"What I know is that you didn't have to help me the night of the accident, and you did. You've been helping me ever since, and I don't know how I'm ever going to repay you." That was the truth. Everything else—the butterflies in her stomach, the connection that seemed to arc between them when she looked in his eyes— didn't matter.

"I'm not doing this for payment. I'm doing this to bring your daughter home." He raked a hand through his hair and sighed. "So, do me a favor. No more running outside when the mood strikes, okay?"

She couldn't promise that. If she thought it would bring Lucy home, she'd run straight toward a firing squad. "I don't—"

Something snapped in the woods behind them, the sound echoing on the still air and chilling Scout's blood.

One minute, she was standing, and the next, she was on the ground, Boone lying on top of her, the weight of his body pressing her into the loamy earth. She twisted, trying to see if something was coming. If some*one* was coming.

"Don't move," he whispered, his breath tickling the hair near her ear.

The world had gone still, the day silent. No birds chirping in the trees. No animals scurrying in the underbrush. Nothing but her quick panting breaths. "What—?"

"Shh," he murmured. "Listen."

She did. Silence. Then the soft crunch of leaves, barely audible, but there. Someone was coming, and her muscles tightened with the need to run. She wanted to spring from the ground, race back to the house, hide under a bed or in a closet, but Boone had her pinned to the ground, his weight crushing the breath from her lungs. Or maybe it was fear that was doing that.

She could feel the thud of his heart through her shirt,

feel his muscles contract as the footsteps stopped. "Listen to me," he breathed. "We've got a line of underbrush separating us from whoever is there. As long as you stay low, you're gold. Understand?"

She nodded, because she couldn't catch enough air to breathe, and because anything she might have wanted to say was trapped in the lump of terror that clogged her throat.

"Good. I'm going to check things out. Stay here until I get back or until Lamar or Rodriguez comes to escort you to the house."

His weight lifted, and she could breathe again, think again, and what she was thinking was that they should both stay right where they were and let the FBI or the police find whoever was skulking through the woods.

"Boone, wait!" she whispered as he eased into the foliage.

He looked back, his ocean-blue eyes blazing in the afternoon sun. He didn't look like the man who'd held her when she'd cried. He didn't look like the guy who'd eaten handfuls of animal crackers from the box. He didn't look like the grieving father still searching for his daughter. He looked…dangerous, deadly.

"Stay here and stay down and stay silent." The words were clipped, his tone dead of all emotions. He turned away, slid into the thick undergrowth, barely rustling the leaves as he moved.

She lay where she was, counting silently in her head. Sixty seconds. One hundred and twenty. No one exited the house. Nothing moved in the woods, but the birds were silent, the afternoon eerily quiet. Thick bushes and brambles butted up against her yard, dead fall leaves covering the ground. She'd hear someone coming, wouldn't she?

And if she did, then what?

Would she lie still like Boone had said?

Run for the house?

Fight?

The police were in her house; the FBI was there. Someone had to be aware of what was happening. Didn't they?

She reached in her pocket, pulling out the cell phone she'd stuck there. She'd been carrying it everywhere, because she hadn't wanted to miss a call from the kidnapper.

Stay here and stay down and stay silent!

That was what Boone had demanded she do, but what if there was more than one person in the woods? What if Boone was ambushed because she'd stayed silent and complacent? She couldn't live with that. She had to call 911, make sure that the men and women in the house knew what was happening outside.

The phone buzzed, and she nearly dropped it in surprise. She glanced at the caller ID. Anonymous.

She knew who it was.

Knew that the man who had her daughter was calling her again. She had to answer. She didn't care if someone heard her talking or took a shot at her because of it.

"Hello?" she said, her voice trembling, her body stiff and tense. She expected a gunshot, expected to feel the pain of a bullet piercing her flesh.

"Tell your friend to back off."

"I don't know what you're talking about," she lied, because she wanted to buy time, give Boone a chance to catch up to whoever it was he was hunting.

"You tell him he's in my crosshairs. Tell him he keeps coming and he's not going to live to see another day. Maybe he won't care so much about that, but he's not the only one on the wrong end of the barrel. First him. Then your kid."

Then the phone went dead.

It was a trap. She was almost certain of it, but she couldn't *not* go after Boone. Not just for Lucy's sake. For his, because he'd done so much and asked so little, and because he deserved more than to die in a cold forest on the outskirts of River Valley.

She jumped up, plunged into the woods, branches breaking, twigs snapping. Behind her, someone shouted, but she didn't stop. She could lose Boone and Lucy, and the fear of that was greater than the fear of being kidnapped, wounded or killed.

Branches snapped, twigs broke, the sounds reverberating through the forest as Boone stepped across a small creek and climbed the steep embankment on the other side. He paused at the top, crouched low as he listened. Someone was coming, and he wasn't being quiet about it.

Not the guy Boone was tracking. That was for sure.

He was up ahead. Close enough that Boone had caught a glimpse of him scrambling over the embankment.

Running scared, and he should be. The Feds had already set up a roadblock to keep anyone from entering or exiting the country road that wound through the sixty-acre park that Scout's property backed onto.

If the perp had parked there, he'd be caught before he made it to the main road.

If he hadn't, he'd be traveling a long way by foot

before he could get to his vehicle. Stella was on that, checking parking areas and neighborhoods that butted up against the park. No doubt the local P.D. and Feds were doing the same.

He stepped behind a tall spruce, the boughs shielding him from whoever was following. More twigs snapped; feet splashed through water. Feet and hands scrambled on dirt, and Boone could hear rocky earth falling into the creek. Finally, his pursuer made it up the embankment.

Boone didn't wait. Didn't even hesitate. He had limited time to get this job done, to dispatch his pursuer and get back to hunting the guy he was pursuing.

He lunged from his cover, saw dark blond hair a moment before he made contact.

Scout!

He rolled onto his back to keep from crushing her as they fell, grabbed her arms as she tried to fight him off.

"Cool it!" he hissed, so angry he could barely get the words out.

"Boone?" She stopped struggling, looked up into his face with such abject relief that some of his anger faded away.

"Lucky for you," he spat, all his frustration seeping out in the words. "Didn't I tell you to stay put?"

"I got a call from Lucy's kidnapper. He said he had you in his crosshairs and that if you didn't back off, he was going to shoot you. He said Lucy was next." She was out of breath, the bandage that had covered her wound gone, exposing staples from the middle of her forehead to her temple.

"You could have been first." He pulled her to her feet. "Did you think of that before you came tearing out into the woods?"

"Yes." She raised her chin a notch, her eyes blazing. "And I decided you and Lucy were worth the risk."

What could he say to that?

It made sense, and he knew that if he'd been in her position, he'd have done the same.

"Here's the thing," he said, trying to tamp down the frustration that was hammering away at his chest. "I was an army ranger before I joined HEART. I know how to track someone without becoming his victim. I know how to bring someone down without making a sound. You—" he shook his head, because he still couldn't wrap his mind around what she'd done "—are a librarian."

"What does that have to do with anything?" she demanded.

"You aren't trained for this. You know nothing about it. You came running through the trees making enough noise to wake the dead. In a situation like this, that's a surefire way to get yourself killed!"

"I did that on purpose," she protested. "To distract the kidnapper."

If the situation hadn't been so serious, he would have laughed. "Did you really think he was going to be distracted?"

"What I thought," she said quietly, all her defensiveness gone, nothing left in her eyes but emptiness and loss, "was that you and my daughter were in danger and if I had to sacrifice myself to save you both, I would."

That hit him harder than it should have. He'd worked with plenty of men and women in the military who'd have given their lives for a comrade. He'd found the same in his buddies at HEART. But out in the great wide world where ordinary men and women lived ordinary lives doing ordinary things, it wasn't often he ran into someone willing to risk everything for those she loved.

"That's admirable," he said gently, taking her arm and leading her back toward the embankment. "But you being dead won't keep me or your daughter from dying. Remember, the guy who kidnapped Lucy believes you have something he wants. Since it wasn't in your house, he's going to need you to find it. More than likely, he was trying to flush you out, get you away from the safety of the people who are trying to protect you."

"And I was walking right into his trap?"

"You were running," he corrected. "Loudly."

She smiled at that, but there was still a hint of sadness in her eyes and a whole bucketload of loss. "And with purpose. For the record, I knew that I was probably heading into a trap, Boone. I just didn't care. I figured if I was kidnapped, maybe they'd bring me to Lucy. If I was killed…" She shrugged. "Anyway, I may just be a mousy little librarian, but I'm not stupid."

"Mousy? I don't recall saying anything about that," he said as he walked along the edge of the embankment.

"You didn't have to," she responded, following so closely behind him, they might as well have been one person. "I know what I am."

"I don't think you do," he responded. "Because from where I'm standing, you are beautiful, interesting, kind. That's a pretty heady combination for a guy like me," he said honestly, because he'd never been the kind of guy to beat around the bush. When he wanted something, he went after it. When he thought something, he said it. When a woman intrigued him, he didn't see any reason to hide it.

And Scout *did* intrigue him.

"What kind of guy is that?" she asked.

"One who is just trying to make the best of the hand he's been dealt."

"You do more than that," she said softly, and he glanced over his shoulder, met her eyes.

"Some days I think I do. Some days, I'm not sure. This spot looks good. I'm going to climb down. Then I'll give you a hand."

"I can—"

"Scout," he interrupted. "You may intrigue me, but you also irritate the living daylights out of me. Please, can we just skip the argument so I can get you back to the house and get back to my search?"

"You're not going to keep chasing the guy, are you?" she asked, and he sighed, dropping down over the side of the embankment. He landed on soft moist earth, then reached up to help Scout down when something moved in his periphery. Not something. A man. Slipping out from between the trees.

"Get down, Scout!" Boone yelled, pivoting and pulling his gun in one smooth motion.

ELEVEN

Scout dropped to the ground, expecting the world to explode in a barrage of gunfire, expecting that everything she'd been hoping to avoid by running into the woods was about to happen.

"Hold your fire!" a man called, and she lifted her head, looked down into the creek bed.

"Are you nuts, Mitchell?" Boone growled. "You about near got your head blown off."

"When have you ever fired a gun without knowing exactly what you were going to hit?" the man asked, stepping out from the shadow of the trees.

"Good to know you've got so much confidence in me, but I'd have rather you let me know you were out here." Boone reholstered his gun.

"Kind of hard to do when you said you wanted radio silence." Mitchell looked up, his dark eyes settling on Scout. "You must be Scout."

"Yes."

"Cyrus Mitchell. With HEART."

"Nice to meet you," she said, scrambling to her feet and wondering how she was going to get into the creek bed without tumbling onto her butt.

"Just shimmy over the edge," Boone said as if he knew exactly what she was thinking. "It's only ten feet. I'll help you to the ground."

"Okay. Sure." Except that ten feet looked a whole lot more like twenty when you were standing on the top of it.

"Are you really going to start doubting me now?" Boone sighed. "I'll come up and lower you down to Cyrus."

"No!" No way ever was she going to let him lower her down anywhere. "I'm coming."

She slid over the edge, pressed her feet to rocky soil, her fingers slipping in dry leaves.

"I've got you," Boone said, grabbing her waist.

"Are you sure?"

"Scout, you weigh less than my grandmother's prized turkey. Just let go!"

"Fine, but if you break your back, it's on your head." She let go, and he lowered her to the ground.

"See," he whispered in her ear, his hands still on her waist. "Piece of cake. Which, by the way, I love. If you ever happen to have a need to bake one, and you're looking for someone to eat it, I'm your man."

"I'll keep that in mind." She could have stepped away, but she liked the way it felt to be near him. Liked how secure and safe she felt when he was close. She liked the way his eyes softened when he looked at her, the way he smiled just a little, even though there really wasn't anything to smile about.

"Hate to interrupt this cozy moment," Cyrus said drily. "But I came in here to bring Scout back to the house. Jackson's orders."

If Boone was bothered by his comment, he didn't show it. "Did he bring the box?"

"With the Christmas stuff? Said it wasn't there."

"It has to be there." Scout had put the frame in it a few months after Christmas. She'd brought that and Lucy's playpen. They didn't use it anymore, but Scout hadn't had the heart to sell it. Like the frame, it had been a gift from Amber. One she'd given to Scout before the move.

"If it was, he couldn't find it."

"It should have been easy to find. I marked the box, and it was sitting right near the door."

"Maybe so, but Jackson is a pretty savvy guy. If he didn't see them, I'd guess it was because they're gone." He shrugged, his shoulders broad beneath a fitted coat. A white button-down shirt peeked out from beneath it, and his pants looked more suited for a board meeting than hostage rescue, but somehow he gave off an air of danger, his eyes so dark she couldn't see the pupils, his face hard and just a little too handsome. "He wants to bring you over there anyway. Maybe you can find the stuff. Ready?"

"Sure."

"Let's get out of here, then. I'm not an outdoorsy kind of person."

Boone snorted. "You grew up outdoors, Mitchell."

"Doesn't mean I want to grow old there. You coming back to the house or heading off to find the perp? Jackson says they've got a half dozen officers and agents combing the woods, so I'm thinking your time might be better spent somewhere else."

"You have an idea where that might be?" All the softness was gone from Boone's eyes as he glanced at Cyrus,

and Scout had the distinct impression that they were ex-
changing an unspoken message.

"I do. I think you might be really interested, but
if you want to stay out here, suit yourself. Come on,
Scout. Let's get you back home." Cyrus took her arm
and started leading her away.

She didn't want to go.

Not without Boone.

Which felt strange.

She'd been just fine before he'd appeared in her life.
She'd known what she needed to do, and she'd always
got it done. She'd had only herself to rely on, and she'd
never expected anyone to come running to the rescue.

She hadn't *needed* anyone to run to the rescue.

The fact that she needed help finding Lucy didn't
change that. But she was still relieved when Boone
stepped into place beside her.

They walked to the house silently, the distant sound
of voices filling the quiet afternoon. Cyrus had said
there were a half a dozen people searching the woods,
but Scout thought there might be more. It should have
comforted her to know that they were trying to track
down whoever had been in the woods. All she could
think about was Lucy and what her kidnapper had said.
He hadn't hurt Boone, but he hadn't had the opportunity. Would he hurt Lucy?

"What are you worried about?" Boone asked as he
opened the back door and ushered her inside. "Aside
from the obvious."

"He said he was going to hurt Lucy if you didn't
back off."

"I backed off."

"And dozens of other people went after him."

"Would you rather they waited here and did nothing?" Cyrus asked bluntly. "At least if they catch him, they might be able to get the information they need to find your daughter. They let him go and he could be gone for good. Your kid with him."

"How about you lay off a little, Mitchell? Your mean is starting to show," Boone cut in.

"I'm being honest, and I'm pretty sure Scout would rather that than a pat on the back and an 'it's going to be okay.'"

He was right, but she didn't say it. Her tea was sitting on the counter where she'd left it. Cold now, but she didn't bother heating it up. She couldn't drink it.

"Are we going to the storage unit?" she asked. It was so much easier to think about that than about Lucy being carried off to someplace where she would never be found.

"Jackson's in the living room. Why don't you go ask him?" Cyrus suggested, glancing at Boone with that same look she'd seen in the woods.

She didn't like it, and she wasn't going to ignore it. Not this time. "What's going on?"

"I already told you. We can't find the box with the Christmas stuff in it. We're going to need you to look for it." Cyrus smiled, but there was no warmth in his eyes, and Scout didn't believe a word he was saying.

"There's something else. If it has anything to do with my daughter, I want to know it."

"Scout?" Jackson appeared in the kitchen doorway. "I'm glad you're back. I've called your landlady. She's going to meet us at the storage unit to give us a hand looking for your things."

They'd planned this all out, choreographed everything, thinking that she'd just go blindly along with the plan. She wasn't going to. Not this time.

"You can meet with her yourself. I'm staying here." She dropped down into a chair, her head aching, her pulse racing. They knew something about Lucy. She was certain of it. "Or you can tell me what's going on, and then I'll be happy to do whatever you want me to."

"You're not being reasonable," Cyrus responded. "And that's not going to help us locate your daughter."

"She's being plenty reasonable," Boone said. "And I guess if there's something that needs to be said, it may as well be said in front of her." He dropped down beside her, his thigh brushing hers, his arms crossed over his chest.

"You know the rules," Cyrus responded. "We keep things quiet until we're sure of what we're looking at."

"Sometimes rules are meant to be broken. I think this is one of those times." Boone snatched the box of animal crackers from the table, dug into it. "The way I see things, if I were in Scout's place, I'd be wanting to know every detail of the investigation."

"The way I see things," Cyrus replied, "we follow the rules, because they're there for a reason."

"You know what?" Jackson grabbed the box of animal crackers from Boone's hand. "You need to stop with the sugar, and you both need to stop bickering like a couple of old fishwives. The fact is, Scout, we got a ping on the cell phone that called yours. The police and FBI are already in the area, and we've got permission to be part of the search team."

"You think you've found her?" She jumped up, hope soaring. "I need to clean up her room, buy a new mattress for her bed."

"Hold on now." Boone grabbed her arm. "You're getting ahead of yourself. That's one of the reasons we don't usually share this kind of information. Clients get their hopes up and sometimes those hopes are dashed."

"But you may know where she is." And that was a lot. That was more than they'd had that morning.

"We've got a general area," Cyrus responded. "But we're talking miles and miles of forest. She could be anywhere in it. The best thing you can do is go with Jackson, look for the missing box. If we don't find your daughter today, that might help us find her tomorrow."

For the first time since she'd met him, he actually sounded…kind.

"He's right. For a change." Boone nudged her toward Jackson. "Go on and find the box. I'll call you if *we* find anything."

"I'd rather go with you. If you find Lucy, she's going to need me."

Boone shook his head. "That's a rule we're not going to break."

"We'd better go. Your landlady is going to be waiting." Jackson had her arm and was leading her to the door before she could think to protest.

They walked out into late-afternoon sunlight, a cold breeze scattering leaves across the driveway. In the distance, steel-gray clouds dotted the horizon. They'd have rain before sundown. Lucy loved the rain. She loved the way it pattered on the roof, and she loved jumping in puddles on the driveway.

Scout wanted to believe that her daughter would be home before the first drop fell. She wanted to believe that she'd be able to tuck Lucy into bed tonight, but she felt hollow, her faith shriveled up and useless.

Jackson opened the door of a blue SUV, and she climbed in. She thought he'd shut the door, but he stepped back and Boone appeared, leaning in so that they were close enough for her to see the hints of green in his eyes, the tiny scar on his cheek.

"You didn't say goodbye," he said.

"No one gave me a chance."

"You know that this is the way that it has to be, right?"

She wasn't sure she did, but she was too tired to say it. Her head ached; her body ached. She wanted to go to bed and wake up and find her daughter safe in her bed.

"Scout?" He touched her cheek, his fingers warm and light against her skin. "If it could be any other way—"

"You don't have to explain."

"Yeah," he said. "I think I do. You feel helpless and hopeless, like all your power has been taken away. That's not what I want for you. What I want is for you to have your daughter back. I want you to wake up to her giggles and go to sleep knowing she's safe in her bed. I don't want you to spend the next week or month or year wondering if she's okay, wondering if she's being fed, if she's warm, if she's even alive."

Her heart jerked at the words, because she heard the pain in them, saw it on his face and in his eyes.

"I'm so sorry, Boone," she whispered, and she knew he understood, because he smiled that easy smile that was becoming as familiar as sunrise.

"So am I, but it doesn't change anything. I still wake up every morning wondering and go to bed every night wondering and live every day of my life hoping and praying that my daughter is alive. If I can keep that from happening to you, I'm going to. If that means leaving you behind while I go search, that's what I need to do."

"I understand." More than she had in the house, more than she'd have thought she could. This wasn't a power play; it wasn't Boone making decisions because he could. It was him caring deeply, wanting things to work out almost as badly as she wanted them to.

"Good, because I don't want you running off to try to find Lucy yourself. Stay with Jackson. Do what he says. I need to be fully focused on finding your daughter, and I can't waste any energy worrying that you're heading into danger."

"I won't."

"Promise me," he urged. "Because I really can't stomach the thought of you being on your own. Not after everything that's happened."

She didn't like making promises. They were difficult to keep and way too easy to break, but she couldn't deny Boone. Not when he was watching her so intently, not when he'd shared so much of his heart. "I promise," she said.

"Good." He lifted her hand, kissed her palm, folded her fingers over the spot. "I'll see you later."

He closed the door and walked away, and she sat exactly where she was, her hand fisted over his kiss, while Jackson backed out of the driveway and headed toward town.

Boone waited until the SUV disappeared from sight, then turned to face Cyrus. "Let's head out. You have the gear in your truck or do we need to try to get our hands on some?"

"Do you even need to ask?" Cyrus led the way to his Chevy Silverado.

"Would I be me if I didn't?" Boone responded as he climbed into the passenger seat of the truck.

"Would I be me if I wasn't prepared for anything?"

"I don't suppose you would be." If there was one thing Boone knew about Cyrus, the guy thought things through, planned them out. He didn't act before he knew exactly what he was going to do and how he was going to do it.

"Lucky for you. Otherwise, we'd be wasting more time trying to come up with what we need. Some of my equipment is state-of-the-art. It's not all that easy to find."

"And some of it is so old-school, they probably had it during colonial days."

"Hey, man, don't knock the old ways," Cyrus retorted, shoving a key into the ignition and starting the car. "They worked for my grandfather and great-grandfather, and they work for me."

"I wasn't knocking them. I was just pointing out that you work as well without all the fancy stuff as you do with it."

"Was that a compliment?" Cyrus asked as he pulled away from the house. "Because if it is, you must want something from me."

"Lunch would be nice." All he'd eaten in the past twenty-four hours were a few handfuls of animal crackers. If he weren't going on a search, he could have made it on that, but he was, and he knew his body enough to know what it needed to keep fueled.

"Is there ever a time when you're not thinking about your stomach, Anderson?" Cyrus grumbled, but he pulled into a fast-food parking lot and into the drive-through line.

"Generally speaking? No. Practically speaking? Yes. When we're deep in a mission, I don't think about it at all. Which is why I'd like a double cheeseburger, large fries and a soda."

Cyrus mumbled something but made the order.

Unlike Boone, he didn't eat fast food or sweets. He preferred nice meals in fancy restaurants, bottled water and lots of fruits and vegetables.

When the order was ready, he thrust the greasy bag into Boone's hands and took off again. "Happy now?"

"Ecstatic," he mumbled through a mouthful of fries. "So, how about you tell me where we're headed?"

"Twenty miles east. The signal came from somewhere around an abandoned ski resort there. The place closed down in the 1980s. Plenty of places for our perp to hide with a little girl."

"How many buildings are we talking about?"

"Fifty and a lodge spread across five thousand acres of pretty rugged terrain. The property got scooped up a couple of years ago, and the owner rents cabins during hunting season."

"Is he renting any now?"

"Six. The renters checked out. No criminal records. No connections with San Jose or the Schoepflins. At least none that Charity could find. She's still looking."

Another member of HEART, Charity was Jackson and Chance Miller's sister. Though she had specific training in search and rescue, the brothers didn't like to use her for anything more than computer research and general office help.

She wasn't happy about it, and she'd made it known.

"She's going to be upset when she hears we ran this search without her."

"She already knows, and she's already upset. I'm just hoping she doesn't show up at the search location. The Feds are running their own K-9 team, and if she shows up with Tank, they might renege on the invitation to join the search."

"We were invited?" Boone doubted it, but he knew Chance. His boss could convince just about anyone to do anything.

"Or they were coerced." Cyrus shrugged. "Either way, we're in. I've already pinpointed the most likely location on a map. We'll check in with the local P.D. and then track in on foot. There are three cabins near a small tributary of some sort. Might be a creek or stream. Not as big as a river."

"Did you get that from Charity or look it up yourself?"

"I did a little research before I left D.C."

"You do know it's her job to provide information about locations, right?"

"She was working as fast as she could, getting me as much as she could, but up until we located the cell phone signal, her focus has been on digging into the Schoepflins' past."

"She find anything interesting?"

"Nothing that is going to help. Senator Dale Schoepflin is well liked and a shoo-in for the next election. He's been married three times. The third time seems to be the charm. He's been with Alaina Morris Schoepflin for fifteen years. No kids of her own. She pretty much raised Amber. People in their community like them. America likes them." In typical Cyrus fashion, he was spouting out facts and lots of them. The guy had a mind like a steel trap. He never forgot a detail, never missed an important piece of information.

"What about the son?"

"Christopher is even more well-known. Married to Rachel Harris. They make the rest of us look bad."

"That's it?" Boone prodded because it wasn't like Cyrus to be short on details.

"There's plenty more, but none of it is pejorative. Jackson asked Stella to head to the airport. Christopher's plane is supposed to arrive this afternoon. She's going to see if she can get a little face-to-face time with him."

"Knowing Stella, she'll manage it. Does anyone in the Schoepflin family own land out here?"

"Wouldn't that make things easy?" Cyrus asked with a cynical smile.

"What would be easy is getting to the ski resort and finding out that Lucy has already been found."

"Easy and nice," Cyrus responded. "But this is the real world, and as far as I've seen, there's not a whole lot of either of those things in it."

Boone had lived long enough to know he was right. The world was filled with things that were difficult and harsh, ugly and mean.

He'd seen the worst of the world and the people in it, but he'd also seen the best. In the midst of the darkest times, he tried to remember that.

He reached for the radio and flicked it on, filling the silence with some bluesy tune that he knew Cyrus would hate. The guy was a great team member and, most of the time, a good friend, but he didn't have much to offer in the way of positivity and optimism.

Up ahead, the road curved toward distant mountains,

the afternoon sun shining gold against the fading fall foliage.

Somewhere, in the middle of that vast wilderness, Lucy was waiting to be found. He had to believe they'd find her, had to believe that God would bring them to exactly the place they needed to be at exactly the time they needed to be there in order to save her.

TWELVE

They were late, and Eleanor wasn't happy.

Scout couldn't find it in herself to care. She wanted to be with Boone, searching the woods for Lucy, not standing in a cold storage unit while her landlady shifted boxes around from one area to another.

"Are you sure it was here?" Eleanor asked, her dark eyes narrowed with irritation. "Because I don't recall seeing it when I was here last."

"I'm positive," Scout responded. "It was right next to the chair you said I could store here." She pointed to the old rocker that used to be in Lucy's room. She'd spent countless nights sitting in it, rocking her daughter to sleep. In those early days, there'd been times when she'd wanted nothing more than to fast-forward to a time when Lucy wouldn't need her so much, when getting a full night's sleep wasn't just a pipe dream.

Now Lucy almost never woke in the middle of the night. Up until the past few days, Scout had had plenty of sleep. She wanted to go back in time, though. She wanted to sit in that rocking chair in Lucy's room, inhale the sweet baby scent of shampoo and baby lotion. She wanted to enjoy every moment of looking into her daughter's face and not waste a moment wishing for something different than what was.

She blinked back tears, rubbed the knotted muscles at the back of her neck. The headache she'd had since she'd woken in the hospital was still pounding behind her eyes, but she forced herself to focus. "Someone must have moved it."

"Who?" Eleanor sighed heavily. "No one has access to the unit but my renters, and they are all upright and honest people."

"You *think* they are." Jackson lifted a tarp that had been thrown over several items. A couple of old bicycles and a jogging stroller appeared. A dresser. A lamp. A futon. No box, though.

"I did credit checks on everyone. They all pay rent on time. Never had issues with neighbors reporting loud noise or partying. No police being called to the house." She glanced at Scout. "Until recently."

"I'm really sorry about that." Scout rushed to apologize. The last thing she needed was to be kicked out of her house, and she had no doubt that Eleanor was the kind of landlord who'd be more than willing to toss someone out on the street if she thought she had a good enough reason.

"No need to apologize. I'm sure you didn't bring these troubles on yourself," Eleanor assured her, but she didn't look as if she believed it. She looked as if she was annoyed, her dark gaze scanning the storage unit, her fingers tapping a quick tattoo on her oversize leather purse.

"How many other renters use this unit?" Jackson asked. He didn't seem to be bothered by Eleanor's mood.

"Three. I already gave the FBI the list, so I don't know why we've got to go over it again." She glanced at a fancy gold watch that had probably cost more than Scout's car and frowned. "I have an appointment in thirty minutes, which means I need to leave in five. As sorry as I am for your loss, Scout—"

"She's not dead," she broke in, because she couldn't stomach Eleanor's word choice, couldn't bear to hear it.

"I meant 'lost' in a very literal sense. She is lost to you. For now. I'm sure the police and FBI will be able to track her down."

"I hope you're right." Scout pressed a hand to her stomach, trying to still its wild churning.

"They're doing everything they can to find her. These things take time and a lot of patience. I know it's hard, but you just have to keep holding on to that hope you've got. Keep cooperating. Keep working with the men and women who are searching for your daughter," Jackson said, patting her shoulder awkwardly. He meant well, but having him around wasn't anything like having Boone there. She felt cut off from the investigation, separated from the one person who'd been keeping her informed.

"I know." She didn't tell him that she was worried that no amount of work would be enough to bring her daughter home. She didn't say that she could feel every tick of the clock as the day wore on and midnight drew nearer. She didn't tell him how scared she was that when midnight came and went, her daughter really would be lost to her.

She didn't say any of those things because she didn't think Jackson would understand the way Boone did. "I just want to do my part to help the investigation move forward. The box was here. If it's not here, someone took it. There must be security cameras in a storage facility like this, right?"

"I saw them on our way in," Jackson replied. "I've already put in a call to the local police. They're trying to get hold of the owner so the security footage can be released. For now, let's take one more look around. I didn't look inside any of the boxes when I was here earlier. Maybe that's our next step." He walked to a pile of neatly stacked boxes near the far wall.

"It's not there," Eleanor said. "Those are my things. I keep them separated from my renters'. See the blue tape on the floor? Anything within that is not to be touched by anyone but me."

"Just because something isn't supposed to be touched doesn't mean it hasn't been," Jackson pointed out.

Eleanor shrugged. "If you feel the need to check in that area, go ahead, but the boxes are sealed with packing tape. Unless they look like they've been tampered with, I'd rather you not open them."

"No problem," Jackson responded, lifting a box from the top of a stack. "Was your stuff in a white box, Scout?" he asked.

"No. Brown. With the word *Christmas* written on both sides in black marker." She eyed the pile of boxes. There were a lot. More than she remembered from her last visit. But then, she hadn't been paying any attention to Eleanor's things.

The boxes were stacked three deep and four tall, all of them white and clean and clearly marked—silverware, linens, photographs.

Scout dragged an entire stack away, looked at the stack behind it. All white.

"I do have everything alphabetized," Eleanor huffed. "I'd like it to be put back that way."

"Sure thing," Jackson responded, dragging more boxes out of the way.

And there it was, the brown box, *Christmas* emblazoned on the side.

Scout's pulse jumped, and she lifted it from the spot. "This is it."

It felt heavier than she remembered, and she set it down, lifted the lid, her breath catching as she saw the glittery Christmas balls and strands of lights. Lucy had been too young to understand the meaning of Christmas, but she'd loved the decorations. Last year, she'd been fascinated by the tree, the lights, the tiny nativity that Scout put on the coffee table.

"See anything?" Jackson asked, his words pulling her back to the moment and the task. She needed to concentrate, because the key to Lucy's disappearance could be right in front of her.

"It should be on the top. That's where I left it." She frowned, lifting several strands of lights and boxes of glass Christmas balls.

"It probably got shifted when the box was moved. What I'm interested in knowing is who moved it. But," Eleanor said, glancing at her watch again, "I really do need to get out of here. Would you mind taking the box with you so I can lock up?"

"No problem." Jackson lifted the box, turned away.

And Eleanor moved. Not in the quick short steps Scout was used to seeing. In a flurry of movement that didn't register until it was over. A quick shift of her hand. A wide arching motion of something that Scout couldn't quite see.

Jackson must have sensed it. He pivoted, the box falling from his hands, glass shattering as he lunged toward Eleanor.

She lunged, too, a wild look in her eyes and on her face as she smashed something into his stomach, then hit him in the head with her purse.

He went down hard, his body crashing onto the concrete floor.

Scout reacted a second too late, barreling into Eleanor with enough force to send them both flying. They landed with a thud, and Scout was up again, running toward the door, escape just seconds away.

But could she leave Jackson?

What would happen if she did?

Would he be killed?

She couldn't live with that, and she stopped just outside the unit, rain pouring down on her head and soaking into her clothes.

"You can run," Eleanor said, already on her feet, the wild look gone from her eyes. "That's your choice, but I have instructions to bring you and whatever your friend sent you with me to the cabin where your daughter is being held. If you don't show up, you may never see Lucy again."

"Jackson—" She looked past Eleanor, thought she saw Jackson's hand move.

"He's fine. I didn't use enough juice to do more than knock him down for a few minutes. The brick in my purse was my employer's idea. It worked a little better than I thought it would, but I doubt he'll have more than a headache from it." She tucked a Taser in her purse, brushing a hand down her black slacks. "We leave here together, and he'll be up and moving before we pull out of the parking lot. So, how about you grab that box and everything in it, and we get going? Your daughter has been crying for you nonstop since they took her. Seems to me you'd want to get to her quick."

"Why did you take her?" Scout righted the box and started tossing things inside. Broken Christmas balls stabbed her hands, but she didn't care. "What do you want from me?"

"*I* didn't take her, and I don't want anything from you. I've seen your financial information, remember?" she said with a cold smile. "You're not worth much. Besides, I've got nothing against you. It's my employer who wants what you have. I don't know what it is, and I don't care."

"Then why are you doing this?" She lifted the last strand of lights, realized that Jackson had shifted subtly.

Was he conscious?

"Because I was offered a boatload of cash and a ticket out of the country. After today, I'm going to be living the high life in a country where the American dollar is worth a lot more than it is here. Come on." She gestured impatiently. "If I don't have you there by four, I'm out of luck and you might be, too."

"Where are we going?"

"Enough chitchat!" Eleanor barked. "You want to see your kid again?"

"Yes."

"Then let's go." She took a step, and Jackson was up, moving so quickly Scout wondered if he'd ever actually been unconscious.

One fast surge of muscle and strength, and Eleanor was facedown on the ground, her arm hiked up behind her back.

"Good job, Scout," he said, not even breathless from the effort.

"Doing what?"

"Getting a little more information than we had before." He dragged Eleanor to her feet. "Now, how about we all head out together? Because I really hate to be left out of the party."

"You're going to have to figure out where we're going first," Eleanor spat. "And I'm not telling you. I do that and I may as well shoot myself in the head right now."

"Let's not be dramatic, Eleanor," Jackson said drily. "You're here, you're safe, and as long as you cooperate, I'm going to make sure you stay that way. We're going to take your car. I hope you don't mind."

"I do," she growled, tugging against his hold.

"Too bad. I wouldn't want your boss to realize your mission wasn't successful. I'm sure he's got someone watching the facility to make sure your car leaves with you in it. Scout, want to get her keys out of her purse?"

Scout picked up Eleanor's oversize bag, pulled out the brick and dropped it onto the ground. Found a wallet, a cell phone, the Taser and, finally, the keys.

"Got them," she said, her voice shakier than she wanted it to be.

"Good." Jackson took them from her hand. "So, here's how it's going to be, Eleanor. You get to drive, and you'd better drive well, because the amount of time you spend in jail is going to depend on it."

"You're assuming that there's going to be jail time."

He laughed. "Come on, lady. You hit me over the head with a brick. You zapped me with a Taser. There are two witnesses who heard you confess to being paid by a little girl's kidnapper. You're in deep. You cooperate and you can dig yourself out a little."

Eleanor pressed her lips together, but didn't respond.

"I'll take your silence for assent. Let's go. Scout, if you can manage the box, we'll be set." He dragged Eleanor outside, and Scout followed with the box.

The day had grown darker, rain pouring from the sky in sheets.

If the temperature dropped, there would be ice in the mountains. Would they call off the search for Lucy if that happened?

Jackson opened the trunk, had Scout put the box in it and then urged her into the passenger seat. As soon as she was in, he walked Eleanor to the driver's side of the car. "I'm riding in the back. I've got a feeling Eleanor's boss has someone stationed outside the storage facility and I don't want to be seen driving this car. Play nice," he ordered as he opened the driver's-side door. "I've got a headache, and I'm not going to be happy if you don't."

He climbed in the backseat, then handed Eleanor the keys.

She shoved one of them in the ignition and started the engine, her jaw tight, her gaze focused straight ahead. "Where do you want me to take you?"

"Same place you were going before I decided not to cooperate with your plans," Jackson responded.

"I'm not going to do it."

"Then just drive yourself to jail, because that's where you're headed."

"I'll be out on bond before you can sign your name on the complaint."

"How much do you think that's going to be for someone who's been arrested for kidnapping, attempted murder—?"

"I wasn't trying to kill you!" Eleanor protested.

"I'm not talking about me. I'm talking about Scout."

"I had nothing to do with what happened to her."

"But you knew she was going to be attacked, and you did nothing about it."

"I didn't! All I knew was that Lucy was going to be held as collateral. No one was supposed to get hurt."

"Held as collateral?" Jackson snorted. "That's a pretty way of saying she was being held for ransom. Kidnapping is kidnapping. No matter the name you put on it. Murder is murder, too."

"No one was murdered," she snapped.

"What do you think is going to happen to Lucy when your boss realizes you weren't successful? You think he's going to try to run with her?" Jackson said, his words like knives to Scout's heart. "If so, you're a fool."

Eleanor didn't speak. Not a word as she drove down Main Street and made her way through River Valley.

Scout wanted to fill the silence. She wanted to beg for the information, demand it, offer anything to have it.

She knew it wouldn't do any good. Eleanor had never been warm or friendly. She'd never been unkind, either. All Scout could do was pray that she'd be reasonable, that in the deepest part of whoever she was, she'd understand the value of Lucy's life and agree to do what it would take to save it.

Finally, Eleanor sighed. "I'll take you there, but only for the kid's sake. She's a sweet little thing, and I don't want anything to happen to her."

"Thank you," Scout breathed, and Eleanor scowled.

"I already said that this is for Lucy. Not for you. Now, how about both of you just shut up and let me drive. Otherwise, I might change my mind."

"I have to make a few phone calls," Jackson replied. "But I'll try to keep the talking to a minimum."

Scout wanted to ask if he was calling Boone, but she was so afraid that she'd annoy Eleanor, she kept her mouth shut as River Valley disappeared behind them and the mountains loomed ever closer up ahead.

THIRTEEN

Boone's phone rang as he and Cyrus geared up.

He answered quickly, his mind on the mission ahead. "Anderson here. What's up?"

"I'm heading in your direction with Scout and her landlady," Jackson responded.

"I'm assuming you have a good reason for that?" Boone shrugged into his pack and slipped a parka on over it. The temperature was going to drop as the sun went down, and he needed to stay as dry as possible.

"Eleanor was planning to take Scout to visit her daughter. She thought she'd do it without me, but things didn't work out that way."

Boone stilled, rain pouring down around him, Cyrus mumbling something about getting a move on because the sun set early in November. "She knows where Lucy is?"

Cyrus looked up from the GPS he was programming. "Who knows?" he asked.

Boone raised a hand, silencing him as he tried to hear above the pounding rain.

"Says she was paid to take care of the kid while her

boss looked for whatever it is he thinks Scout has," Jackson said.

"Who's her boss?"

"Who is *she*?" Cyrus moved closer, his dark eyes flashing with impatience. A hundred yards behind him, a three-story building jutted up against low-hanging clouds, the windows and doors boarded up, graffiti marring the dingy white facade. The place had probably been beautiful at its peak. Now the neglected lodge was nothing but an eyesore in the midst of stunning wilderness.

"She says she doesn't know." Jackson answered Boone's question. "He contacted her a month ago, asking questions about Scout and Lucy. Offered her a few thousand dollars to snoop around the house."

"I was *not* snooping," a woman called. "It's my property. It is within my legal right to inspect it."

"Save it for the police," Jackson growled.

"I take it that's Eleanor? Did she say how she got involved in all this?"

"Long story short, the guy who hired her to *inspect* Scout's things asked if she'd like to earn a nice chunk of change and a plane ticket out of the country. All she had to do for it was babysit Lucy for a few days while he found the thing he was looking for."

"She have any idea what that thing is?"

"Not that she's admitting to. We've got the box with the picture frame in it. Haven't found the frame yet, though. We got a little sidetracked. The good news is, Eleanor has the exact coordinates of the cabin where they're keeping Lucy. It's a tough three-mile hike through the woods, but we shouldn't have any trouble finding it."

"Go ahead and give me the location. I'll—"

"I don't think so, Boone. We're going to have to think this through. We go in there half-cocked and someone is liable to get hurt."

"Since when do I do things half-cocked?"

"Since the day I met you."

Boone couldn't argue with that.

He did go with his gut a lot, move into situations on a hunch. He never did it without knowing exactly what he was getting into, though. He didn't this time. He had no idea if there was one person or ten or none at the cabin with Lucy.

"Okay. Fine. What's the plan?" he asked, glancing over his shoulder at the police and FBI agents who were gathered beneath a canvas awning in the ski resort's parking lot. They'd already drawn a grid of the area, divided it into quadrants. Search dogs were sniffing at the ground, but no one had moved into the woods yet. No one would until the perimeter of the area had been secured. That required man power and coordination from local police in two counties. Those things took time. Which was one of the reasons Boone preferred to work outside of local law-enforcement channels.

"We're almost there. Hold off until we arrive. I already put in calls to Rodriguez and Lamar. They've given me permission to send Scout and Eleanor in ahead of the search teams."

"No." He said it definitively, because there was no way he was letting it happen. Scout was too fragile, too wounded. Sending her out into the wilderness with a woman who'd already admitted to working with Lucy's kidnapper was a surefire way to get her killed.

"That's not your decision to make," Jackson responded.

"It's not yours, either."

"Right. It's Scout's, and she's already decided."

"Probably because she doesn't know what she's getting into."

"She knows. I explained everything."

"I think I should explain it again."

"We're pulling into the parking area now," Jackson responded. "Knock yourself out."

Boone glanced at the entrance to the parking lot, saw a dark sedan rolling in. It pulled up beside Cyrus's truck, the front passenger's door opening almost before it came to a full stop.

Scout climbed out, her skin pallid, the staples a dark stain against the paleness. Her hair hung around her shoulders, the strands tangled and matted from rain. She shouldn't have been beautiful, but she met his eyes and smiled, and there was absolutely nothing about her that wasn't lovely.

He took her hand, pulled her away from Cyrus, the truck, the sedan. "You okay?" he asked, and she nodded.

"I'm not the one who's been standing out in the rain, so I guess I'm fine." She swiped her hand across his cheek and frowned. "You, on the other hand, are soaked."

"Not even close, but *you* will be if you head out into those woods. You don't have the gear for it. No parka. No hiking boots. You'll be frozen before you get a hundred yards in."

"Do you really think I care?" She glanced at the building that had once served as the ski resort's lodge, eyed the forest that stretched out beyond it. "I would walk a thousand miles in the snow to get to my daughter, and I know you would do the same for yours. Don't make this be about discomfort or hardship. All it's about is love. I have enough of that to get me through anything."

There were a lot of things he could have said. He could have told her how dangerous it might be. He could have said that she might get to the location and find that Lucy had already been moved. He could have told her the harsh truth of the matter—that love wasn't always enough. He could have formulated a dozen arguments against her going with Eleanor, but she was right. He'd have walked over burning coals to get to Kendal. "Tell you what," he said. "I won't make it about anything but doing everything I can to help you."

She smiled at that. "Thanks, Boone. When this is all over, I'm going to make you that cake you want."

"Is that a promise? Because I take promises about food very seriously."

"It's a promise."

"Are we talking chocolate? Yellow? Angel food?"

"We're talking whatever you like best."

"What I like best," he said quietly, "are blond-haired librarians with staples in their foreheads."

That surprised a laugh out of her. "Thank you. I think."

"You two done over there?" Jackson called, his tone just shy of being amused. "Because we've got some planning to do before the ladies head to the cabin. They don't get there by five and our guy might get suspicious."

"Four," a dour-looking woman with dark hair and pale green eyes said. Eleanor Finch. He'd seen her at Scout's house, but he hadn't thought much of it because she'd had plenty of reason to be there. "He was very specific about that. If I'm not there by then, he's not going to wait around."

"Okay, then," Jackson responded. "We have even less time, and we have a lot to talk through. How about we get under the tarp and hash things out with the rest of the team?"

"How about we pretend we did and just come up with our own plan?" Cyrus responded.

"Great idea except for two things," Jackson said, rubbing at a lump on the side of his forehead. It was blue and red with a few hints of green and yellow mixed in. Obviously, he'd left a few things out during their phone conversation. "First, I'm not in the frame of mind that's required to irritate the local police and the FBI all at one time. Second, I'm not in the mood to irritate my brother."

"Your brother is always irritated," Boone pointed out. He liked Chance Miller, enjoyed working for him, had even gone on a couple of hunting trips with the guy. But facts were facts, and the fact was, Chance spent a good portion of his life trying to micromanage the world. It made for a well-run, successful business, but it didn't do much for the happiness quotient.

"Yeah, well, seeing as how I got beaned on the head with a brick today, I'm not feeling all that happy, either. So, how about we follow the rules on this? We've got a two-year-old child to think about. The more heads we put together to plan the rescue, the better."

"Then let's get to planning."

"I'd prefer we not stand out in the rain to do it," Eleanor grumbled.

"Not that I care all that much what you prefer," Jackson said, "but there's probably room for us under the tarp. Rodriguez and Lamar should be here soon, and we can get this show on the road."

"I'd like to get it on the road now," Scout murmured, but she didn't protest when Boone pressed a hand to her lower back and urged her across the parking lot. She stayed close as Rodriguez and Lamar arrived, hovering near his elbow as the team formulated a plan, went over every detail again and again and again. He could sense her impatience to get moving, but she didn't voice it, didn't try to rush the process.

That impressed him.

She impressed him.

Rather than panic, she focused, and that was going to serve them all well in the next few hours. If they'd been alone, he would have told her that, but they were surrounded by a dozen agents and officers.

"That's it," Special Agent Rodriguez said, her dark gaze settling on Scout. "Are you sure you're up to this? If you don't think you can do it, we'll have an agent step in for you."

"I don't think any of your agents are going to be able to pass for me," Scout responded.

"We can find someone," Rodriguez assured her, but Scout shook her head.

"I'll be fine."

Rodriguez eyed her for a moment and nodded. "Just make sure you do exactly what we've discussed. Don't veer from the plan. If you do, things could go bad really quickly."

"I won't," Scout assured her.

Boone wondered if she meant it. She probably *thought* she meant it.

The problem was, when it came to love, the heart worked a lot faster than the head.

"Do we have the frame Amber sent you?" Officer Lamar asked, and Scout shook her head.

"I haven't had a chance to look for it yet."

"You have the box?"

"In Eleanor's car."

"Let's get it. If you're going to pull this off, you need to have something to bargain with."

If.

Scout didn't much like the word.

There was too much room in it for error, too much of a chance that the thing she didn't want would come true. Everything had been explained to her in excruciating detail. Every word she needed to say, every move she needed to make. *If* she did those things, she might get her daughter back. But she might not, and that was the thing that was killing her.

She followed Officer Lamar to Eleanor's car, waiting while Jackson opened the trunk. She felt sick, her head pounding, the cold wind spearing through her coat. Boone had been right about her not being prepared for the weather. She'd been standing outside for an hour, and she felt cold to the bone.

"There it is," Jackson said, pointing at the box. The contents were a jumbled mess, strands of lights and shards of colored glass mixed up together.

"Is the frame in there?" Boone leaned over Scout's shoulder, his breath ruffling her hair, his warmth seeping through her coat and chasing away some of the chill.

"I don't know. We didn't get a chance to look." She shoved some of the lights aside, lifting out boxes of broken glass balls. The frame had been on the top of the pile before, but if Eleanor had gone through the box, it could be at the bottom.

"It's in there," Eleanor said.

"And you know this how?" Officer Lamar asked.

"Here's the deal," Eleanor huffed. "I'm cold. I'm wet. And I'm already in more trouble than I want to be. I want to get this over with sooner rather than later. So, I'm just tossing the information out there. I went through the box a couple of weeks ago. I was told to look for journals or letters. There weren't any in there, but I did see a picture frame."

Scout plunged in deeper, nearly falling over in her effort to get to the bottom of the box.

"Careful," Boone murmured, his hands settling on her waist. He left them there as she pushed aside several ornaments, spotted something pink and glittery near the bottom of the box.

"Here!" She pulled it out, the picture a colored photo that must have been taken during one of her first playdates with Amber. They'd been young. Maybe eight or nine years old, their hair in pigtails. Even then, Amber had been a rebel, the ends of her ponytails died purple with grape juice. If Scout remembered correctly, Amber's parents hadn't been happy about it.

"Glitzy," Boone said, touching the edge of the frame.

"That's how Amber was. She liked showy things, glittery things. The more it sparkled, the happier she was." She smiled at the memory.

"Much as I'm enjoying your trip down memory lane," Eleanor griped, "I'd like to get this over with. The hike is difficult on the best of days. It's going to be atrocious today."

"Mind if I take a look at that?" Special Agent Rodriguez asked, ignoring Eleanor's comment.

Scout handed it to her reluctantly, waited impatiently as she studied the photo and then flipped over the frame.

"Ever opened it?" she asked.

"No. I never had a reason to. Amber wrote me a note saying I should switch out the photo and put one of me and Lucy in there, but I loved the one she put in it, so I didn't bother."

"She said you should or could?" Boone asked, his brow furrowed.

"Should. She mentioned it three or four times in the Christmas card that came with it."

"Mind if I open the back?" Special Agent Rodriguez asked, her fingers already working at the tiny clasp on the back. She opened it up. Scout didn't know what she expected, but there was nothing there but the photo, a few numbers and letters scrawled on the back. "This mean anything to you?" She handed the photo to Scout.

Don't forget to visit.
J.A.C. 6/02/97
M.E.C. 11/15/04

"I don't…" …*think so* was what she was going to say, but then it hit her like a ton of bricks. The letters. The numbers. "My parents," she said, so surprised the picture almost fell from her hands.

Boone took it, eyeing it as if it had more secrets to reveal. "Those are their initials?"

"And the day each of them died. Amber was at both of their funerals. It was just the three of us in my family. No uncles or aunts or grandparents. She stood in as family."

"She says you shouldn't forget to visit," he pointed out. "Is she speaking about their grave sites?"

"Probably. They were buried in the family crypt in San Jose. Once a month, Amber and I would place flowers there. When I left San Jose, she promised to continue doing it."

"Interesting," Special Agent Rodriguez said. "I think I'll send an agent out to check out the grave sites. Can you give me an address?"

She did as she was asked, feeling almost as if Amber were there, trying to convey some secret message. If only she knew what that message was. "I wish I'd seen that sooner. Maybe…"

"What?" Boone asked, handing the photo back to her.

"Maybe it was a cry for help. Maybe she was telling me that I shouldn't forget to visit her grave site after she died."

"I doubt such a flamboyant person would send such a subtle message," Boone said. "Based on what I've read and what you've told me, I'd say that if Amber knew she was going to die, she'd have been more likely to send you a bouquet of balloons with her epitaph written on them than a cryptic message."

"You're probably right. Amber always did things in a big way." Scout's heart ached as she thought about her friend and the message she'd tried to send. Had she expected Scout to find it before she'd died?

"It's possible there is more to the message. She might have left something at the grave site. My people will check things out in San Jose," Special Agent Rodriguez cut in. "For now, though, we need to focus on Lucy. Let's put the photo back in the frame and get moving."

Scout would have been happy to do it, but her hands

were shaking from cold or, maybe, from nerves. No matter how many times she told herself and everyone else that she was prepared to go after Lucy, she wasn't sure it was true.

She was terrified that she'd forget what she'd been told, walk into a situation that was nothing like what she was expecting and somehow do something that would cause Lucy to be hurt—or worse. She *wanted* to make the long trek through the forest and come out an hour or two later with her daughter. She just wasn't sure she had it in her. She'd spent her entire life playing it safe. The one night she'd done something different, gone out of her comfort zone, played the game by different rules, she'd ended up pregnant and alone, starting her life all over again in a town far away from everything she'd ever known.

That hadn't proved anything about her adventurous spirit or her ability to buck the system and play by her own rules. All it had done was prove that she had the ability to make a stupid decision, disappoint herself and disappoint God.

"Let me," Boone said, brushing her hands away from the frame and sliding the photo back in. "There you go."

"Thanks," she said, tucking the frame into her coat pocket, her fingers and nose cold, her heart a leaden weight in her chest. She felt sick, her head aching, her stomach churning. She didn't know how much of that was from her head wound and how much was from nerves, but she really hoped she wouldn't lose her breakfast in front of a dozen law-enforcement officials.

"You don't have to do this, Scout. There are other options." He cupped her cheek, looked into her eyes. For a moment it was just the two of them, standing in the rain, a thousand promises dancing in the air between them, a thousand dreams just out of reach. She wanted to step into his arms, rest her aching head against his chest, but they weren't alone, and her daughter was waiting in a cabin just a few miles away.

"None of them are as good," she said, because it was true. They'd discussed every option during the hour-long planning session. None of them made as much sense as the one she'd agreed to—she and Eleanor walking to the cabin escorted by Boone until they were a quarter mile away. The remainder of the team spreading out in the woods, surrounding the cabin before Scout and Eleanor arrived. Everyone moving silently and stealthily, giving Lucy's kidnapper no indication that they were there. If everything went as planned, Scout and Eleanor would be allowed to leave with Lucy once the frame was delivered.

Barring that, Scout would take Lucy into one of the cabin bedrooms, signal by opening a window that they were away from the kidnapper and wait for their rescue.

Everyone involved in the planning had admitted that it wasn't a perfect plan, but it was their best option for a good outcome for Lucy.

That was all Scout cared about.

"No," Boone admitted, his hand dropping to her nape, his fingers warm and a little rough against her skin. "But there are good-enough options."

"Would good enough work for you if this were Kendal?"

His eyes darkened, and he shook his head. "No, and that's the only reason why I'm not fighting tooth and nail against this plan."

"You could fight it with more than that and it would

still be what it is," Cyrus cut in, impatience in his voice and on his face. He didn't look like the kind of guy who liked to wait around, and he'd been pacing the edges of the group almost from the moment the planning had begun. "So, how about we get going? Four o'clock will be here soon, and if Lucy is moved, we're going to have to spend a long night hunting these woods for her."

The thought was enough to get Scout going.

She moved away from Boone, shrugging into a black parka someone offered, the vinyl-like material doing nothing to warm her chilled skin. Her feet were soaked through her tennis shoes, her jeans clinging to her legs.

It didn't matter.

Nothing did.

Except finding Lucy and bringing her home.

FOURTEEN

The storm whipped itself into a wild frenzy as Boone led Scout and Eleanor into the woods. Marked paths had once shown the way from the lodge to the rental cabins and ski areas. Time and neglect had hidden them. Aside from a few painted arrows on tree trunks, there was no indication that large groups of people had once vacationed in the area.

"Which way?" he asked Eleanor. He had the coordinates she'd provided, and his GPS was pointing the way. He wanted to test her, though. See how helpful she planned to be.

"South. Just keep heading in that direction until we hit the creek. Then we turn east. It's about a half mile from there. It usually takes me a little over an hour. It's going to take longer today." She pulled her hood up over her hair, buttoned her coat. She'd worn thin-looking black slacks and black hiking boots. She'd have been better off in jeans. She'd been offered a parka and refused, claiming that her boss would get suspicious if she and Scout showed up wearing the same thing.

She had a point.

She also had more explaining to do. No one believed

her claim that she didn't know the man who had hired her. He was someone within her sphere of influence, and that relationship had led to her involvement. Eventually, the truth would come out. For now, he'd pretend he believed every word Eleanor said if that meant accomplishing the goal and completing the mission.

The wind picked up, the rain mixing with sleet as they climbed a steep hill and headed down the other side. Already, they were cut off from civilization, the view of the lodge hidden by the slope they were descending.

Scout slipped, and he caught her arm just in time to keep her from sliding down the last hundred yards of the slope.

"Careful," he said, keeping his hand on her elbow as they picked their way down the last several yards. "You break an ankle and we're in trouble."

"I'm sure if that happened, your friends would find a solution to the problem," Eleanor muttered, holding on to sapling trees as she made her way down ahead of them. "Must be nice to have so many people fighting for you. Me? I've got no one. My no-good husband dumped me the day I turned forty. Left me with a mortgage and a debt that I didn't think I was ever going to pay off. No kids. Thank goodness! The last thing I need are a few of his brats trying to spend every bit of the money I've managed to scrape together over the past ten years."

"She's just a little bitter," Scout whispered, slipping again, her fingers grasping on to his shirt as she tried to maintain her balance. "And I am really regretting my decision to wear tennis shoes this morning."

"There isn't enough tread in the world to keep someone from slipping on this stuff," he responded, keeping his gaze on Eleanor. She was increasing her pace, and he had a feeling she was going to make a break for it.

Maybe she thought she could get to the cabin, convince her boss to give her the plane ticket and money she really seemed to believe he had for her, before the dragnet they'd created closed in.

It wasn't going to happen.

Boone didn't bother telling her that.

She wouldn't have believed it.

He kept an eye on her progress as he helped Scout over a fallen log. "Looks like your landlady is trying to ditch us."

"You can run up ahead and stop her, if you want. I'll catch up as quickly as I can."

"There's no point. She gets too far ahead and someone will grab her and hold her for us."

"What if they don't?" she asked, picking up her pace so that she was nearly jogging.

"Do you really think they're going to let her get to the cabin before you?" He ducked under a low-hanging pine bough, tugging her under behind him.

"I don't know anything anymore, Boone," she replied, her words so quiet he could barely hear them over the storm. "One day, everything was great. I had a job and a daughter and a life that was exactly what I wanted. The next, everything was ripped away from me, and now..."

"What?"

"I just want Lucy home. Then I can figure out the rest of it."

"Like what we're going to be when this is over?" he asked, tracking Eleanor as she trudged up another hill.

"We? As in us?" Scout asked, and he didn't think she was surprised by the thought, didn't think she hadn't thought about it before. There was something between them, a connection that had been building since the moment he'd seen her in the grocery store. Where that would lead, what it would bring them to, was something that he was ready and willing to explore.

"Why not? We're both single and unattached," he responded. Life was too short to beat around the bush.

"I'm not unattached. I have Lucy."

"There are plenty of people in relationships who have a child or two," he pointed out, and she frowned, rainwater and ice sliding off her parka hood and dripping onto her cheeks.

"I know, but if I get Lucy back, I can go back to what I had before she was taken. My job, my church family, my friends. Every day just kind of the same as the one before. That's the way I like it, Boone."

"Safe?"

"Yes."

"That's a problem for us, then. It's never going to be safe if I'm in your life. There's always going to be the risk that I won't come back from a mission, that the next time I get on a plane will be the last time you see me."

"I know."

"So, maybe the two of us together isn't such a good thing." He offered her an easy out, because he didn't want her to live with regrets, didn't want her heart broken the way his had been when Lana walked away.

"Maybe it's not," she responded, and there was so much sadness in her voice, he wanted to pull her into his arms, tell her that sometimes the reward outweighed the risk.

There wasn't time.

Eleanor crested the rise, paused at the top, turning to look back at them and waving impatiently.

"I guess she decided not to leave us," Scout said, sprinting forward as if the most important thing in the world was catching up to her landlady.

He'd scared her with talk of a future together. He knew it.

He didn't regret his words, though.

Life was finite. In a fraction of a second it could end. A bullet, an explosion, a knife attack. Or the more mundane: car accident, heart attack, falling tree. He glanced at the heavy-laden spruce trees that were bowing with the force of the wind. He was always on guard, always watching, and that made him more than a little aware of just how little time there was. He never wanted to waste any of it, never wanted to miss an opportunity to go where God was leading.

If He was leading to Scout, if He had brought Boone there, that was where Boone wanted to stay. No matter the risk. No matter the potential for heartache.

All he needed to know was that Scout wanted to be there, too.

The thought was better left for another time, though.

Time was ticking away, the afternoon wearing on, the sun already sinking behind dark clouds. Darkness came early in the mountains. Even without the four o'clock deadline that Eleanor had been given, they'd have had to hurry. Already, the woods were shrouded with shadows, the icy rain and wind limiting visibility. Things were only going to get worse as the day wore on, and every bit of Boone's focus had to be on getting to the cabin and getting Lucy out.

He caught up with Scout easily, taking her arm as she

trudged the last few steps to Eleanor. She didn't meet his eyes, refused to glance his way, and he thought that maybe the moisture sliding down her cheeks wasn't just icy rain. Maybe there were tears mixed in, as well.

"It's about time," Eleanor snapped. "Do you know what time it is? We'll never make it to the cabin at the rate we're going."

"We'll make it," Boone assured her.

"It was all that planning," she continued as if he hadn't spoken. "A huge waste of valuable time. For all any of us knows, Gaige decided to go back to leave with the kid and without me. He cleaned out the San Jose bank accounts, so he's got plenty of money to do it. He and Lucy could be miles away by now, while we try to execute some stupid plan come up with by a bunch of nincompoop federal agents and foolhardy local—"

"What do you mean *cleaned out the bank accounts in San Jose?*" He cut her off midtirade. "I thought you said you didn't know anything about the guy."

"I don't."

"Then how do you know he has bank accounts in San Jose?"

"He must have mentioned it to me when we were making arrangements for payments," she responded, her face suddenly devoid of color. She was afraid. That was something she hadn't shown before, and that made Boone a lot more nervous than he'd already been.

"I don't think so," Boone said. "I think you know him well. I think you've probably known him for years."

"And I think you're full of it," she scoffed, but the fear was still there, her dark eyes hollow.

"You're scared of him, aren't you?" he asked, and she

pressed her lips together, trudging on as if she hadn't heard him.

"What? Is he a boyfriend? Some guy who abuses you?" He offered her an explanation, curious to see if she latched on to it.

"Of course not! Gaige would never lay a hand on me. Not in that way! He's...a friend. Someone I met a couple of years ago."

"You're in a relationship with him," Boone said. He didn't make it a question, because he already knew the answer, had heard the same sorry story play out too many times to count. "And he already has a wife and a couple of kids, right?"

"It's none of your business," she snapped.

"Which means he does. Have you met her?"

"Who?"

"The wife? The one he's left behind so that he can run off with you? How about the kids? How many does he have? Two? Three? Is he missing their ball games and school plays to spend time with you?" He poked at her, hoping to get her riled up enough to let a little more information slip.

"His kids are grown, and his wife is cold as a dead fish. He says—"

"I'm sure he says a lot." He cut her off. Not really interested in the details. "Did he promise to leave them if you helped him with this? Did he say you two would run off together once he got what he wanted?"

"You know nothing about anything!"

"I know plenty. I've seen this over and over again. Do you know how many women I've met who are just like you? So desperate, they'll believe any lie to have the thing they think they need."

"I'm not desperate, and the only thing I need is for you to shut up!" she shouted, her eyes blazing, her hands fisted.

"And I need you to realize you're being used. Once you do, then you can be useful to yourself and to us."

"I'm not interested in being useful to you, and I'm *not* being used."

"Right," Boone said, snorting for good measure.

"It's true! He showed me the tickets and the passports last night. Everything is set. As soon as I get to the cabin, we're supposed to leave for the airport. He decided we shouldn't fly out of any nearby airports, so he's got us booked on a flight leaving from New York. He laid the whole itinerary out for me last night. First New York, then L.A. After that—" She stopped short of finishing, but it was too late. She'd already said more than she'd intended.

He knew it.

She knew it.

"You really think that's what was going to happen?" Boone said, wanting to push her even harder, make her even angrier, keep her talking about Gaige's plans. "I've been doing my job for a long time, Eleanor, and I can tell you for sure that if he'd wanted to run off with you, he'd have been waiting for you outside that storage unit. You'd have gone to the airport from there, climbed on board a plane and been at some romantic getaway before the sun rose tomorrow morning."

"He didn't want to be seen."

"I don't see why not. We don't know who he is. We don't know what he looks like. He could be standing five feet from me, and I wouldn't know it."

"He couldn't leave Lucy alone, and if he'd taken her with him, someone might have recognized her."

"He's good—I'll give him that. The argument would almost be convincing if I didn't know he has accomplices. Aside from you, there have to be at least three or four people working with him. I saw them following Scout the night Lucy was kidnapped. One of them could have stayed with Lucy while you two took off."

"They're gone. He paid them and sent them away, because he was afraid too many strangers in such a small town would draw people's attention. He's smart that way." She turned away, started walking again, picking her way over fallen logs and through ankle-deep puddles. She was obviously finished with the conversation. That was fine. He could let it go. He'd got more information than he'd thought he would.

Apparently Scout didn't feel the same.

"Did you see the tickets?" she asked, her breath panting out, hot and raspy. She looked worn-out and ready to collapse, but he knew she'd keep going until she found her daughter. That was another thing he'd seen too many times to count. There was no limit to a parent's love, no way to measure just how far someone would go, how hard she'd push herself for the sake of her child.

"Of course I did," Eleanor huffed. "All three of them."

She must not have realized what she'd said, but Scout did. She grabbed her arm, pulled her to a stop. "How many tickets did he have, Eleanor?"

Eleanor stood silently for so long Boone wondered if she'd answer.

Finally, she looked straight at Scout. There was no color in her face, no emotion. The words, when they came, were as dead as her expression. "Three. One was for Lucy. He said we'd be a family. The three of us."

"You were planning to take her out of the country and never come back?" Scout sounded horrified, her eyes wide with shock.

"We were going to give her what you couldn't."

"There is nothing that she needs that I can't give," Scout replied, her voice pulsing with all the emotions that were absent from Eleanor.

"You're too young to realize how limited your life is, how little you really have to offer Lucy."

"That is one of the most insulting things anyone has ever said to me!" Scout protested, but Eleanor started walking again, stepping over a fallen tree and ducking under a low-hanging branch.

"I didn't mean it as an insult. You're a nice young woman. You work hard. You pay your bills on time. But there are plenty of things that you can't provide your daughter—culture, wealth, an opportunity to be something more than a small-town kid living a small-town life."

"I think she'd rather have her mother than those things," Boone cut in, and Eleanor sent a hard look in his direction.

"Lucy isn't even three yet. Her mother is whoever happens to be taking care of her."

"That's not true!" Scout sputtered.

"Maybe not, but in a few months, she'd have almost forgotten you. In a year, you wouldn't even be a memory. Same for you. Eventually, you'd have had other children and forgotten all about Lucy."

"I would never ever have forgotten Lucy." Scout bit out every word, the weight of them hanging in the air.

"Like I said, you're young," Eleanor replied blithely. "You have no idea how fleeting and fragile love is. You have it one minute. The next it's gone and you move on to someone else."

Something inside Scout must have snapped.

She lunged forward, rage seeping from every pore, pulsing from every muscle.

Boone just managed to grab her before she made contact, pulling her up short and wrapping both arms around her waist.

"Cool it," he said quietly. "She's not worth your anger."

"I am not angry. I'm infuriated!" She shoved at his arms. "How dare she say that I would forget my daughter!"

"I meant it in a benign way," Eleanor tried to explain, but Scout wasn't having any of it.

She wiggled out of Boone's grip and pointed her finger in Eleanor's face. "You are nuts if you think that anything you just said to me was benign!"

"She's nuts," Boone cut in, pulling Scout back into his arms, because he wasn't sure he could trust her to *not* tear into Eleanor, "if she thinks Gaige was actually going to take her on that plane. I'd venture a guess that the passport and ticket weren't for her. Did you get a look at the photo in the passport, Eleanor? Did he give you a good close look at it?"

She lifted her chin. "I didn't have to. I trust him."

"Trust in men is often unfounded," Boone responded.

"Not in this case. Gaige has always been trustworthy."

"Except when it comes to his wife and kids?" Scout asked, and Eleanor frowned.

"They didn't earn his trust. I have. Not that it matters," Eleanor responded. "I won't be going anywhere. Except jail. The way I see it, if I have to be there, he may as well be, too. The problem is, if we don't get to the cabin by four, he's going to leave. His flight takes off at one tomorrow morning, and he warned me that if I didn't make it back to the cabin in time, he'd go without me. He'll do it, too. I can tell you that right now. He'll take Lucy and he'll leave the country, and no one will ever see either of them again."

She marched away, chin tilted so high Boone was surprised she didn't drown.

"Wow!" Scout breathed, sagging against Boone, her slim weight pressing against his chest and abdomen. He had a moment of pure insanity, a moment when all he could think about was how good she felt in his arms, how right it was to be standing there with her.

"Wow what?" he asked, stepping back, giving himself a little breathing room.

"Does she really believe he was going to take her to some exotic location? Did she really think that the two of them could travel with my daughter and not get noticed?"

"You said it yourself—she's crazy."

"There's crazy, and then there is *crazy*," Scout sighed. "She's both."

He nearly laughed at that, but they had a job to do, and standing around chatting about things wasn't getting it done. "At least we have some information to go on. Airport. Time. Connecting flight."

"It's great to have, but if he leaves the cabin with Lucy—"

"Don't borrow trouble, Scout." He pressed his hand to her back, urging her in the direction Eleanor had gone.

"How is it borrowing trouble to think through the possibilities?"

"It steals energy away from dealing with the realities. Right now, the reality is that we don't know what we're going to find at the cabin. Until we get there, there's nothing we can do but keep running with plan A."

"Is there a plan B?"

"If we need one."

"Are you going to tell me what it is?"

"Once I come up with it, sure."

She laughed shakily. "You're a funny guy, Boone."

"I'm also a hungry guy, so how about we get this show on the road and bring your daughter home so you can make me that cake we were discussing?"

"You make me believe," she responded, "that those things are really going to happen."

"Believing is half the battle."

"What's the other half?" Scout asked.

"Knowing that whatever happens, God is in control of it, and that it really will be okay." He took her hand as they headed up another steep hill, Eleanor marching a few yards ahead, her shoulders slumped as if the reality of what she'd done was finally settling in.

She was smart to feel defeated. By the time they reached the cabin, it would be surrounded by law-enforcement officials. There was no way Gaige would ever make it past the blockades that were being set or the armed men and women who were lying in wait. If he tried, he'd be stopped.

FIFTEEN

Lucy's prison was nicer than Scout had imagined.

Or maybe it was the distance that was making it appear that way. From a quarter mile back, the log cabin looked to be in pristine condition, its tin roof sparkling with millions of tiny ice pellets.

Scout squinted as she looked through the binoculars Boone had handed her, focusing on the windows, trying desperately to catch some glimpse of Lucy while he texted their location to the team, made sure everyone was in place.

Eleanor stood under the canopy of an old oak, head down, a layer of ice coating her hood and coat. She hadn't spoken a word since she'd admitted that they'd planned to leave the country with Lucy.

Was she regretting the confession?

Realizing what a fool she'd been?

Or was she as exhausted as Scout, the grueling three-mile hike taking its toll?

Scout didn't ask. She was afraid to strike up a conversation, afraid of what Eleanor might say and of her response. She didn't get angry often. She didn't ever have much to get angry about, but she'd seen red when Eleanor had said she'd have forgotten Lucy. Every thought in her head had flown out, and all she could feel was rage.

"We're ready," Boone said quietly.

She turned to face him, her pulse jumping with nerves and fear.

"You know what to do, right?" he asked, his hand on her shoulder. "There's no chance he's going to let you leave with Lucy. You're going to have to find a way to get your daughter into another room."

"I'll help," Eleanor said. "I'm sure I can distract him for a few minutes. There's a bathroom at the back of the cabin with a window in it. It's tiny, but I'm sure you and Lucy can squeeze through. The only other window on that side of the house has shades that Gaige keeps closed. He won't be able to see anyone approaching from the back unless he opens them. If you can get into the bathroom, maybe someone can be waiting under the window to grab Lucy."

"What about you?" Scout asked. The woman was a criminal, a kidnapper and a fool, but Scout didn't want her left in the cabin alone with Gaige. Regardless of what Eleanor thought, the man was dangerous. He'd nearly killed Scout, and she doubted he'd hesitated to hurt anyone who got in his way.

"Why do you care?" Eleanor asked.

"Because you're a human being, and I don't want you hurt," Boone said.

"Whatever!" She turned, stalked back to her little shelter under the tree.

Boone ignored her. His gaze was on Scout, his expression soft and unguarded. She could see the worry in his eyes, the anxiety on his face.

"I'll be okay," she said, as much to convince herself as him.

He nodded. "I know."

"Then why do you look worried?"

"Because I care, and because I want to go in there for you, and I can't. Gaige sees me coming and there's no telling what he'll do to Lucy."

"I know."

"Then I guess you know how dangerous this situation is, and I guess you know just how helpless I feel right now." He ground the words out, his eyes flashing with frustration.

He didn't look angry, though. He looked like a man who knew how to love and who deserved to *be* loved, and in that moment, Scout wished she had been brave enough to do more than promise him cake. She wished that she'd been confident enough, strong enough, sure enough of herself to tell him that she wanted there to be an *us* once Lucy was home.

"Boone," she said, wanting to get the words out, because she was afraid there might not be another opportunity to say them.

"Just focus on the mission, Scout," he said quietly, brushing strands of hair from her cheeks, tucking them under her hood. "We'll work everything else out afterward."

"But—"

"Focus. Stay calm. Find a way to get Lucy into that bathroom, and find a way out the window. Okay?" he urged.

She nodded, because her throat was tight with fear and hope and something she wasn't sure she'd ever felt before. Not attraction. Not infatuation. Something deeper, more lasting.

She touched his jaw, her hand sliding over several days' worth of stubble. It felt soft beneath her fingers, and she levered up, her lips brushing his.

He pulled her close, his hands sliding down her arms, his fingers linking with hers. Palm to palm, warmth to warmth, and she knew that if she had a thousand years to stand in Boone's arms, it would never be enough.

He broke away, his forehead pressed to hers.

"That," he rasped, "was the most fun I have ever had breaking a rule. Now go. The longer we put this off, the more antsy Gaige is going to be." He nudged her toward the cabin, and she went, her lips still warm from their kiss.

Eleanor stepped into place beside her. They didn't speak as they approached the cabin. There was nothing to say. The plans had been set; everything had been worked out. In the forest surrounding them, a dozen men and women were watching. Scout should have felt comforted by that, but all she felt was terror.

What if Lucy wasn't in the cabin?

What if Gaige had already left for the airport?

Was it possible he'd got wind of Eleanor's capture?

Did he know he was about to be betrayed?

The questions pounded through her head as they stepped from the canopy of the trees and into an overgrown clearing. The cabin sat in the center of it, a small porch at the front with an old hanging swing worn with age.

Up close, the place had an abandoned feel, and she wondered if he really had left.

The front door swung open, but no one appeared on the threshold.

Did he know that the cabin was being watched?

Eleanor grabbed her arm, long fingernails digging through the parka and her coat. "Remember," she hissed. "The bathroom in the back of the cabin. Take Lucy there. It's the only room with a lock on the door."

"Okay."

"One more thing." She slowed her steps, looked straight into Scout's eyes. "I'm sorry. For all of this. I was played a fool before, and I didn't think I'd ever be played a fool again. Pride goeth before the fall." She laughed, the sound sending chills up Scout's spine.

"What—?"

"Shh." Eleanor cut her off as they stepped onto the porch. Sure enough, a man was standing just beyond the doorway, the shadowy interior of the cabin hiding his face. It couldn't hide the child he was holding, though. Not a dark-haired little girl. A blonde.

For a moment, Scout's heart stopped, every fear she'd had about Lucy not being at the cabin stealing her breath and making her feel dizzy and faint. Or maybe it was the scent of gasoline that was making her feel that way.

Gasoline?

It couldn't be.

Could it? She inhaled, nearly gagging on the fumes. They stung her nose, made her lungs hurt.

She backed up, fear crawling along her nerves, settling like a hard knot in her chest.

Something wasn't right.

She wanted to signal to Boone, let him know that things weren't working out the way they'd planned.

Then she heard something that she'd been afraid she'd

never hear again, the sound as sweet as the first bird-song of spring.

"Mommy! Mommy, let's go home!" Lucy cried, her voice hoarse, her hand reaching out.

Scout didn't hesitate, didn't think another thought about the acrid scent. She ran into the cabin and snatched Lucy from the man's arms.

They were in, the cabin door closing behind Eleanor.

That was Boone's signal to move, and he did, winding his way along the edges of the trees, staying low and hidden by the overgrowth of vegetation until he was at the back of the cabin.

He eyed the building, scanning the one-story log exterior. The window Eleanor had mentioned was there, a small rectangle cut into the wood, its glass wet from the storm. Higher than he'd anticipated, probably close to seven feet up, it barely looked big enough for a child to fit through.

Would Scout be able to squeeze through the opening? She was small, but the opening looked tiny.

The only other window on the back of the building was triple the size. Just as Eleanor had said, the shades were drawn.

Leaves rustled behind him. He didn't bother looking to see who it was. Cyrus had been assigned to the back quadrant of the cabin, and Boone had no doubt he was about to make an appearance.

"You're usually quieter than that." He tossed the words over his shoulder, his attention completely focused on the cabin.

"You usually don't show up in my quadrant." Cyrus slid from the shadow of an elm tree, his movements so smooth that it almost seemed that he wasn't moving at all. "You're supposed to be at the front of the house. Since you're not, I'm assuming something has come up."

"You're assuming right." Boone filled him in quickly, his gaze riveted to the small window. Nothing yet. Not a hint of movement from beyond it.

"Might have been a good idea to fill everyone else in," Cyrus said when Boone finished speaking. There was no heat in his words and no judgment. They trusted each other implicitly, had worked together enough to know that every move was made deliberately, every decision thought through carefully.

"It *would* have been a good idea," Boone corrected. "But I wasn't sure Eleanor was being honest about the window until I got here, and I didn't want to waste time on a last-minute scramble to get back into position."

"The window's there," Cyrus pointed out. "Want me to make the call?"

"Yeah. Thanks. Tell the team that if Scout signals me, we'll need a distraction at the front of the house. I don't want Gaige looking out the window as I'm approaching. I'm not sure how he'll react if he sees me."

"Does he have a weapon?" Cyrus asked, gathering all the facts the way he normally did. He'd spout them back when he radioed the team, and Boone had no doubt he'd get every last detail right.

"Eleanor didn't mention one, but Scout was nearly killed with a .45. I'd say there's a good possibility that he does."

"Got it. So, she signals and we provide a distraction at the front of the building. What if she doesn't signal?"

"Then we move to plan B," Boone responded.

Cyrus didn't ask what that plan was. He'd worked with Boone for too many years to think there was one.

Instead, he slipped deeper into the trees, murmuring something into his radio. They tried to maintain radio silence on missions like these, but with so many entities working together on this rescue, it wasn't possible. That suited Boone fine. He wanted quick communication. If the bathroom window opened, he needed a way to keep Gaige from figuring out that his prisoners were escaping.

Cyrus returned a few seconds later, binoculars in hand, his attention on the back of the cabin. "Any movement at the window?"

"Not yet."

"We've got some stuff going on off scene. FBI found a Gaige Thompson from San Jose. He's a divorce lawyer. Wife says he's on a business trip and won't be home for a couple of weeks."

"She give any indication of where he went?"

"Washington, D.C." Cyrus lowered the binoculars. "Guy is licensed to practice law there and in California. He's pretty well-known in political circles, has helped a lot of high-level people avoid messy divorce battles."

"Nice," Boone said, his gaze still on the cabin. No movement there. Nothing to indicate that Scout had made it into the bathroom.

"Not if he's in that cabin with the kid."

Bam!

Fire exploded from the front of the building, flames leaping into the sky.

Boone sprinted forward, racing to the back of the cabin, praying that the bathroom window would open and Scout would appear. It stayed closed, the glass just above head level.

Too late, his brain shouted. *You're too late. Again.*

His radio buzzed, people calling for ambulance crews and fire trucks. Others yelling for flanking to the left and right of the house. Someone called for a bomb unit, and someone else was calling his name over and over again. Fire blazed and crackled at the front of the cabin. Men and women streamed out of the woods, racing toward the burning building.

He ignored it all.

His focus was on the window and the chance that Scout and Lucy might have made it into the room beyond it.

He dropped his pack onto the ground, stood on it, looking into a room filled with swirling smoke. Nothing. No sign of anyone or anything, but he wasn't ready to give up hope, wasn't ready to stop believing that God would bring Lucy and Scout out of this alive.

No way could he fit through the bathroom window, so he used the pack as a battering ram, slamming it against the other window, glass shattering into a million pieces, smoke billowing out, everything moving in slow motion except for the fire. It crawled up the roof of the cabin with warp speed, consuming wood, melting metal and destroying everything in its path.

SIXTEEN

Lucy was crying.

Scout heard it through a fog of pain.

She opened her eyes, coughing as smoke filled her lungs. "It's okay, Lucy," she tried to say, but a fit of coughing stole the words.

No sound from Lucy, and she almost closed her eyes again, let herself drift away from the pain. Above her, thick black smoke swirled near the ceiling, but she felt no sense of urgency, no need to get up and find a way out.

Somewhere close by, a child coughed, the sound just enough to make Scout turn her head. Lucy lay beside her, limp as a rag doll. At least, she thought it was Lucy. The hair was blond, not brown.

It didn't matter. Whoever the little girl was, she was in trouble, and Scout had to help her.

She managed to get to her knees, blood dripping from her head, memories flooding back. Short, stocky Gaige with his bright blue eyes and cocky smile. Eleanor. Their argument over whether or not Lucy was going to go to the airport with them. Eleanor meeting Scout's eyes, something in her gaze warning her that she needed to find a way out.

Lucy had already been in Scout's arms, clinging to her and begging to go home. Scout had backed down a hall and found her way into a tiny bathroom, closing and locking the door. She set Lucy in the shower stall and climbed on the toilet seat.

And... What?

She couldn't remember anything else, but somehow she'd ended up on the floor with smoke everywhere.

She coughed again, lifting Lucy into her arms. She didn't have time to grab a towel and soak it. The door was intact, but hot to the touch. There was no escape that way. She climbed onto the toilet, the window within reach. Her fingers were clumsy as she tried to unlock it one-handed. The latch moved, but the window wouldn't open.

She needed to put Lucy down, but she was afraid that if she did, she'd never find her again.

Please, God, she prayed. *Please help me save my daughter.*

She slammed her hand against the glass, but her movements were sluggish, the smoke stealing every bit of oxygen in the room. She tried again, her muscles so weak she could barely slap the glass.

Something banged on the other side of her hand, and the glass shattered, falling like rain all around her, the smoke pouring up and out into gray daylight.

Hands reached in, and a voice shouted for her to hand Lucy out. She struggled to do as she'd been asked, the fire lapping at the door, crawling toward her across the floor.

And suddenly, Lucy was out, and Scout was alone in the room, the heat of the flames searing her skin, her head swimming with the need to give in, let go, allow herself to give up.

"Don't you dare give up now!" Boone shouted, reaching into the window, his hand brushing her face. "Come on, Scout! You've got to help me. This window is too narrow. My shoulders won't fit through. I can't come in. You've got to come to me," he said, and there was so much desperation in his voice, she made herself grab the windowsill, broken glass slicing into her palms as she tried to lever into the opening.

He grabbed her arms, yanked her through, icy rain falling on her heated skin, cold air filling her lungs as Boone carried her to the edge of the clearing. He stopped there, lowered her onto the ground, pulling off his coat and covering her with it.

A few feet away, a man held Lucy, her body so limp and fragile Scout's heart shattered into a million pieces.

"Is she dead?" she wanted to say, but all she could do was cough, her lungs burning and heaving, her mind screaming as Cyrus laid Lucy on the ground, his palm pressing against her chest as he tried to force her heart to beat again.

No! She wanted to shout, because they'd come so far, worked so hard to bring her baby home. She tried to sit up, tried to run to her little girl, but Boone pressed her back down, said something to someone she couldn't see.

Jackson edged in next to him, kneeling beside Scout, blocking her view of Cyrus. She saw Boone's red hair and his shoulders behind Jackson, knew he had gone to help.

"Move!" she rasped, shoving against Jackson without any force, because she had no strength.

"You're injured. You can't help your daughter if you

don't help yourself." Jackson pressed something to her head, and she brushed it away and sat up, pushing at his hands with every bit of power she had left.

She was on her knees, then her feet, ignoring his command to stay down, stumbling to her daughter's side.

"Lucy," she croaked, dropping down beside Boone, darkness clouding the edges of her vision as she watched him breathe for her daughter.

SEVENTEEN

"Come on! Breathe!" Boone muttered, every bit of the desperation he felt seeping into the words.

"Breathe!" he said again as Cyrus compressed her chest.

"Thirty!" he called, and Boone breathed into her mouth.

Once. Twice.

Lucy coughed, her eyes fluttering open, deep brown and filled with confusion. She tried to cry, her mouth opening, nothing but gasping coughs escaping.

He touched her head, smoothed her soot-stained hair, his heart beating frantically. They'd almost lost her.

Had lost her.

He'd felt the limpness of her body as he'd lifted her from Scout's arms, and he'd known that she was gone, had prayed as he'd handed her to Cyrus, begged God to give her back to Scout. "It's okay, sweetie. You're okay."

She wasn't.

Her respiration was shallow, her heartbeat thready. They needed to get her to a hospital. The sooner the better.

"We need an oxygen mask," Cyrus hollered, the relief on his face raw and real. He'd been through this before, years ago, and as far as Boone knew, he'd never got over it.

Lucy coughed again and again, and Boone rubbed her chest and stomach, terrified she'd stop breathing.

"Lucy!" Scout leaned in, trying to lift her daughter from the ground, tears streaming down her face. He wasn't sure if they were tears of relief or fear, but they left streaks in the soot that covered her cheeks.

"Shh," Boone said. "You're going to scare her more than she already is."

She nodded, but the tears kept rolling down her face, and Lucy's harsh, raspy coughs continued.

He lifted the little girl, set her in Scout's lap, his heart beating hollowly in his chest. Both were covered in soot and breathing rapidly, their respirations shallow. A few more minutes and they would have succumbed to smoke inhalation. He'd almost lost them, and he couldn't shake the thought that he still could.

An ATV pulled up beside them, an EMT jumping off and running to Scout's side. Five minutes later, she and Lucy were en route to the lodge, where an ambulance was waiting to transport them to the hospital. The cabin fire had nearly been doused by a team of forest rangers, and Boone was staring at the smoldering ruin, his heart still beating too hard and fast in his chest, his mind going back to that moment when he'd realized how futile his rescue attempt was. Flames had been shooting out the bedroom window, and he'd been trying desperately to get past them.

If Cyrus hadn't pulled him away, he'd have probably found a way. And then what?

Would he have made it into the bathroom?

"You're a mess, Anderson," Jackson said, his tone much more solemn than usual. "Maybe Lucy and Scout aren't the only ones who need a trip to the hospital."

"I'm fine," he growled.

"You're angry," Jackson retorted. "You think you could have done something different, affected a different outcome."

"I could have broken the bathroom window before I tried to get in another way. I could have got them both out sooner. Then maybe they wouldn't be in such bad shape."

"You're giving yourself way too much credit," Jackson cut in.

"What's that supposed to mean?"

"You think that you get to decide who lives and dies. That by your actions a life is saved or not."

"No," he argued. "I don't. I think that I have a responsibility to do my best. I think that if I have an opportunity to help, I'm obligated to do it."

"If that's really what you think, then why are you beating yourself up over this? Scout and Lucy are both alive, and they're both going to be fine. What more can you ask of yourself?"

"A lot," he ground out. "That little girl was dead, Jackson. When I took her from Scout, she was gone." His voice broke, and he had to swallow hard to keep tears from falling. "If I'd been there a few minutes sooner—"

"If you'd been there a few minutes *later,* there wouldn't have been any chance of resuscitating her. Much as I hate to make your big head any bigger—" Jackson ran a hand over his hair and sighed "—you did good. Don't play the what-if game on this one, Boone.

Just be thankful that things worked out the way they did."

"I am thankful. I just wish—"

"Right. Wish. Hope. Want. So, here you are, standing there regretting something that didn't even happen while Scout and Lucy are heading to the hospital without you."

"Was I supposed to hang off the back of the ATV?"

"No, but you could be walking out of here instead of feeling sorry for yourself."

"I am not," he growled, "feeling sorry for myself. There are things to do around here. Lamar and Rodriguez are going to want a rundown of everything Eleanor said and did on the way here." He glanced at the burned-out shell of the cabin. The entire front was gone, the eaves of the porch caved in. "It doesn't look like she had any chance of escaping. I didn't much like the lady, but she didn't deserve that."

"I don't guess she did," Jackson agreed. "Something accelerated the blaze. Makes me wonder if that was the kidnapper's plan all along. Get rid of everyone and leave town. Go back to his family and pretend nothing had ever happened."

"In other words, all he wanted was the information written on the photo."

"Seems to me that might be the case," Jackson responded. "Stella called in a few minutes ago. She met Christopher Schoepflin at the airport, and she asked him if he knew Gaige Thompson."

"Let me guess. Thompson represented his father during his divorces."

"Exactly."

"What a mess," Boone muttered.

"Yeah. It is, and it's going to take a while to sort out.

I'm thinking that you might want to head to the hospital before you're dragged downtown to answer a bunch of questions."

"Are you telling me to leave the scene?"

"That's exactly what I'm telling you. Get Cyrus and take off. Go to the hospital, because I can guarantee you that when Scout looks for someone who will tell her that her daughter is going to be okay, it's you she's going to be looking for. If you get dragged to the sheriff's office, it's going to be hours before you can be there for her."

"You're being awfully accommodating, Jackson," Boone said, but he grabbed his backpack, shook shards of glass off of it and put it on.

"Aren't I always?"

"No."

Jackson shrugged. "Hey, if you're not interested in the job, I'm sure Cyrus would be willing to hold Scout's hand while she waits for news. Of course, you know how bad his bedside manners are."

Boone knew. Cyrus had sat vigil at the hospital when Boone had been recovering from his fractured skull. It hadn't been pleasant for either of them.

"You'll call me when you have any news? Scout will want to be updated."

"I'll call or stop by the hospital. I don't know how much more they can do here. They won't be able to recover Eleanor's or Gaige's body until what's left of the structure is stabilized. It could be days before they know how the fire started. Like I said, there's no sense in waiting around while they do their job. I'm going to talk to Lamar, and then I'm heading back to town. Since you'll have good cell phone reception, why don't you give Chance a call when you get back to town? Let him know what's going on."

There it was. The reason Jackson was pushing Boone to leave. "I should have known you had ulterior motives. You don't want to be the one to tell your brother that we were around this much chaos, so you're passing the job on to me."

"I don't mind telling him. I just prefer not to listen to his response," Jackson said with a smile. "I'm going to find Lamar. You get Cyrus and get out of here." He gave him a none-too-gentle shove in the right direction and walked away.

Boone didn't need to be told twice. Not when doing what he was told meant being near Scout.

Scout needed to see her daughter. She didn't care what the doctor said about needing to rest, didn't care what the nurses told her about being weak and unsteady on her feet, didn't care about anything but making sure Lucy was okay.

She struggled out of the bed they'd put her in, tossed the blanket around her shoulders and dragged her IV pole into the hall. There was an elevator sign to the left, and she headed in that direction.

Lucy was in the pediatric ICU, and she was stable.

That was the extent of the information Scout had received, and it didn't touch on whether or not Lucy was awake, unconscious, crying, calm. Scout needed to know those things with a desperation that pounded through her aching head, refused to allow her to close her eyes or rest.

She punched the elevator button, waiting impatiently

for it to open. As soon as it did, she walked on, bumping into a man who was heading out.

"Sorry," she began, looking up into a face that made her heart melt and her legs go weak.

"Boone," she managed to say as he opened his arms.

She stepped into his embrace, her arms winding around his waist, her head settling against his chest.

He smelled like smoke and rain, and she burrowed closer, her hands fisting in his shirt. It didn't matter that Cyrus was watching or that a nurse had made her way to the elevator and was loudly explaining why Scout couldn't leave the floor.

Boone was there, and she felt down deep in her soul that everything was going to be okay.

"Going somewhere?" he asked, smoothing her hair back, frowning at the fresh bandage on her forehead. "Because from the look of things, you should probably be in bed."

"I want to see Lucy."

"And you *will* see her, Scout," the nurse said, holding the elevator doors open. "After you're both feeling a little better."

"I think," Boone said, "that it would be difficult for any mother to feel good when her child is injured. If you want them both to heal and get better, you should have them together."

"We're doing this in the best interest of both of them," the nurse responded sincerely. "We understand the extenuating circumstances and that the two have been separated for several days, but the doctor is worried that too much excitement might contribute to respiratory distress. Especially in Lucy. The next thirty-six hours are critical."

"I can see the doctor's point," Cyrus cut in. "How about we all just be reasonable about this?"

"What are you talking about?" Scout demanded, because she wasn't in the mood to be reasonable.

"Let him do his thing," Boone whispered in her ear, his breath tickling against her skin and lodging somewhere deep in her heart.

"What I'm talking about," Cyrus responded, stepping off the elevator and walking a few feet away, "is all of us being where we need to be and doing what we need to do. We wouldn't want to break any hospital rules."

"It's not about rules." The nurse turned to face him, her hand slipping from the elevator door. "It's about doing what is best for our—"

The door slid closed, cutting off whatever she was going to say.

"There," Boone said with a half smile. "Cyrus at his finest. Now, I don't suppose you have any idea where they're keeping Lucy?"

"Pediatric ICU," she responded. "But I have no idea where that is."

"Fortunately for you, I do. Samuel had a pretty bad infection a few months ago, and they kept him in the ICU overnight." He punched a button, his free arm around her waist, his fingers warm through the cotton hospital gown. She could feel his palm through the fabric, feel his breath ruffling her hair, feel the heat of his body seeping through the blanket and gown, and she wanted to lean into him, close her eyes, just let herself relax against his strength.

She shivered with emotions she hadn't expected to feel, and he tucked the blanket closer around her, his fingers sliding along her neck, brushing against the tender skin there. "Cold?"

"Scared," she admitted.

"Lucy is going to be okay."

"I'm worried for her, but that's not why I'm scared."

"Then what?" he asked as the elevator door opened.

"You. Us. The things you were talking about at the ski resort," she admitted. She couldn't hide things from Boone. Not after what he'd done for her and for Lucy. Not after she'd looked deep into his eyes, tasted his lips, spent days knowing that he was the one person who understood her grief and pain.

"That," he said, his hand cupping her elbow as he led her to the pediatric ICU, "is not something to be afraid of."

"That's easy for you to say. You haven't made the mistakes I have."

"Maybe not, but I've made plenty of other ones. I've trusted and loved someone who wasn't trustworthy. I've spent too much time away from people I cared about and lost my daughter because of it. I've failed again and again, Scout." He stopped, turned so they were facing each other. "And every single time, God has picked me up and brushed me off and let me have another chance. This is your chance. *I'm* your chance. And you know what? You're mine."

"Boone…" She had a dozen things she wanted to say, but none of them seemed right, because not one of them could match the pure and simple honesty of his words. "I don't know what to say to that."

"You don't have to say anything. You just have to tell me the truth. Are you going to walk away from us because you might fail again? If you are, I need to know it now rather than a year from now."

"I'm not," she said. Simply. Honestly. Because he deserved it.

A slow smile spread across his face, tension easing from his jaw and his shoulders. "You're sure? Because I've got a crazy life, Scout, and I can't give it up. I'm away for days and weeks at a time. When I'm home, I'm tired and—"

"Hungry?" she suggested, and he chuckled.

"I am always hungry," he said. "But when I get back from a mission, I'm tired and worn, and sometimes, I'm a little quiet and a lot grumpy. That's not going to be easy to deal with."

"But it's going to be worth it," she assured him. "Because you are everything I didn't know I needed—everything I never knew I wanted. You really are my second chance, Boone. And I'm not going to turn my back on that—or you."

"We'll see if you're still saying that in twenty years," he quipped, pushing open double-wide doors that led into the ICU reception area.

"At the end of a lifetime, I will still be saying it," she assured him.

"I hope so," he said.

"I *believe* so," she responded. "There's a difference."

He shook his head, that easy smile that she loved so much curving the edges of his mouth. "You're throwing my words back in my face. Do you plan to do that often?"

"Yes."

He laughed, dropping a quick kiss to her lips, a lifetime of promises in his eyes, in the gentleness of his touch.

"Glad to hear it, Scout, because I'm planning to say a lot of really wonderful things to you in the future. Come on. Let's go see your daughter."

He took her hand and they walked to Lucy's side together.

EIGHTEEN

Apparently, children recovered from nearly dying much more quickly than adults did.

The thought flitted through Scout's mind as she watched Lucy twirl around the living room, her nightgown swirling around her legs. Nearly four weeks after the fire and she didn't seem any worse for wear. Cheeks pink, newly cropped hair bouncing in short brown ringlets around her head, she giggled and danced and acted for all the world as if they'd never been apart.

If it hadn't been one in the morning, that would have been great, but it was, and Scout was exhausted.

The past few weeks had been…challenging.

She'd had to face Christopher and Rachel, explain the circumstances of Lucy's birth, ask for forgiveness for the secret she'd kept. They'd been gracious and kind, but it had still been hard. She'd kept Christopher from his daughter for nearly three years, and no matter how much she'd justified it in her mind, no matter how scared she'd been, she hadn't had the right to do it.

Somehow, Christopher had understood. He'd listened as she'd explained Amber's words and her warning, and he'd said that he'd have made the same decision she had.

She wasn't sure it was true, but she'd been grateful. When he'd asked for twice-yearly visits with Lucy, Scout had been happy to comply.

For now, things were going the way they had before the kidnapping. Aside from a quick visit while Lucy was in the hospital, Christopher had stayed away. He and his father were dealing with a firestorm of media attention as the FBI investigated Christopher and Amber's stepmother, Alaina.

Special Agent Rodriguez had confirmed that the FBI had found information hidden at the crypt where Scout's parents were buried. Rolled up and wrapped in cellophane, the three small pieces of paper had been hidden in a vase attached to the wall. Scrawled on each was the name of a bank and the number of a safe-deposit box. Each box had been filled with photos of women, interviews with them, long pages of stories about how they'd been tricked into traveling to the United States for job opportunities, sold to the highest bidder and made to work for nearly nothing.

If the FBI was right, Amber had been working on an exposé that would reveal her stepmother's involvement in what amounted to a modern-day slave trade.

It didn't surprise Scout. As much as Amber loved to party, she also loved social justice. She always rooted for the underdog and cheered for the dark horse.

She'd have been excited to expose Alaina's illegal business and reroute the millions of dollars that she claimed Alaina made from it into social reform. Maybe she'd got in too deep, or maybe she'd found something even more incendiary than what had been found in the safe-deposit boxes. Whatever the case, the FBI believed she'd been worried about how deep she was digging, that she'd been afraid for her life.

Rather than going to the authorities, she'd done what Amber always did—pushed harder, dug deeper, done everything she could to keep the party going for as long as she could. Special Agent Rodriguez speculated that Amber had told her stepmother about the hidden information in a last-ditch effort to stay alive.

It hadn't worked. Alaina had murdered Amber or hired someone to do it. According to Agent Rodriguez, a small storage unit that Amber had secretly rented had been auctioned off at the beginning of November, and a box of her personal belongings had been discovered and returned to the Schoepflin family. Several diaries were in the box. Most of the information in them was mundane, but there was mention of the letters and gifts Amber had sent to Scout highlighted in pink. Agent Rodriguez believed that had been enough to worry Alaina.

Alaina wasn't admitting to it, and with Gaige Thompson dead, they couldn't question him, but it seemed that had been the catalyst to everything else that had happened.

The two had been friends for years. Such close friends that they'd traveled together with their spouses, had Christmas and Thanksgiving meals together. Dale Schoepflin was cooperating fully with the investigation, and he claimed that both he and his wife had known about Gaige's relationship with Eleanor. He said that it had begun shortly before Scout left San Jose.

Unlike his son, he'd known about Scout's pregnancy. He'd overheard Amber discussing it with her, knew that Amber had told Scout to leave town. He and Alaina had both suspected that the child was Christopher's, and they'd decided to make moving away easy for Scout. They'd asked Gaige to find her a job opportunity and an inexpensive rental in a nice neighborhood. Gaige had met Eleanor while he was in River Valley, opening doors that probably would have stayed closed for Scout if not for the Schoepflin family.

She shivered.

She'd spent years afraid of being found, and she'd never really been hidden.

Scout walked to the Christmas tree she'd set up in the corner of the living room. With Eleanor dead, the fate of her little house was up in the air. Next year, Scout and Lucy might be somewhere else. Maybe it would be for the best. Even with the little tree decorated with tinsel and Christmas lights, the house didn't feel like home. Not like it used to.

Funny how that didn't matter as much as it used to.

Lucy zipped past, reaching for the sparkly pink frame that hung from the tree.

"Pretty, Mommy," she said.

"It is," she responded, her throat tight with hundreds of memories of Amber as a child and a teenager and an adult. She missed her friend, but she saw hints of her in Lucy's face.

Lucy reached for another frame. Hand carved from pinewood, it held a photo of Scout, Boone and Lucy, sitting at a booth in a diner on Main Street. Scout had just got her staples out, and Boone had taken them to lunch to celebrate. He'd asked the waitress to snap the photo, and Scout's cheeks had been pink with embarrassment. In the photo, she'd been looking at him, and he'd been looking at Lucy, and the love they all had for each other nearly jumped out of the frame.

She missed Boone more than she wanted to let herself admit.

He'd been on a mission for a week, gone somewhere that he couldn't talk about, doing things he couldn't explain. He'd given her the frame the night before he'd left, told her to put another picture inside. One that didn't have his ugly mug in it.

He must have known that she wouldn't do it.

He must have known that she would walk to the frame every other minute of every day just to see him smiling that soft easy smile of his.

"Boone! I want Boone," Lucy cried.

"He'll visit as soon as he finishes his job."

"When?" Lucy asked, her little hands on her hips, her lower lip out. She hadn't been sleeping well since the kidnapping. She did well at day care and fine while the sun was out, but as soon as bedtime rolled around, she tossed and turned, woke crying, sobbed about things living under the bed and in the closet. The sleepless nights were taking a toll on both of them, but with Christmas just around the corner, Scout was trying to be cheerful.

"I don't know when he'll be back, but I'm hoping it will be soon." Boone hadn't been able to give her anything more than a vague time frame. A week. Maybe two. If he was going to be longer, he'd promised that someone from HEART would contact her.

"I want Boone!" Lucy insisted, and Scout picked her up, snuggling her close, inhaling the sweet smell of baby shampoo and lotion.

"Me, too, but he's not here."

"Tomorrow?"

"Maybe."

"Mommy," Lucy said, pressing her palms to Scout's cheeks. "I want cake."

The request made Scout chuckle. "Not at this time of the morning."

"We have cake for Boone."

True. She'd made a different flavor cake every day that Boone was in town. Thinking about how much he'd enjoyed each flavor and each kind of frosting made her smile.

"Tell you what," she said, glancing out the window at the dark morning and gray-blue clouds that drifted lazily across the moon. Somewhere, it was full light, and somewhere Boone was working hard to reunite another family. "Let's make cake."

"Cake!" Lucy squealed with glee, running into the kitchen ahead of her.

They took out the bowls and the hand mixer, the eggs and the flour. Scout had never made a coconut cake for Boone, but she thought he'd like her grandmother's recipe.

It didn't take long to mix the batter, and soon the scent of vanilla and coconut filled the air. They spent two hours baking and frosting the cake. It was still dark when they finished. Outside, the first snowflakes of the season drifted lazily from the sky.

"Look," Scout said, lifting Lucy so she could see out the window over the sink. "It's snowing."

"Let's go play," Lucy mumbled, half-asleep, the adventure of being awake and baking cake before the sun came up finally wearing her down.

"Not yet. We'll wait until the sun rises."

"And Boone comes?"

"Sure," she said, because she had to trust that he

would come. That wherever he was, God would bring him back to them.

She carried Lucy into the living room, laying her down on the new love seat and covering her with a throw. She turned off the lamp, plugged in the Christmas-tree lights so that they twinkled multicolored in the darkness.

She thought about turning on some Christmas music, letting the quiet sounds of it soothe her to sleep, but she didn't bother, just lay on the couch watching the snow fall on the front yard, praying that wherever Boone was, he was safe.

Headlights flashed on the newly fallen snow, splashing over her driveway and across the shrubs and trees that lined it.

Surprised, she stood, walking to the window and watching as a car rolled along the driveway.

No. Not a car.

She pressed her face close to the glass, her heart jumping. An SUV.

Boone!

She was out the door and across the yard before he parked, throwing herself into his arms as he stepped out of the vehicle.

"You're back," she cried, and he kissed the sound from her lips, kissed her forehead, her cheek.

"You smell like cake," he whispered in her ear, and she laughed through tears that shouldn't have been falling.

"Lucy and I were awake. She insisted we have cake."

"Is there any left?" he asked, his arm sliding around her waist, his hands strumming along her sides. He seemed thinner, his face shadowed by a beard that hadn't been there when he left.

"Plenty."

"Good, because Stella and Cyrus are with me, and they're not happy."

"And cake isn't going to make us happy," Stella grumbled as she climbed out of the SUV. "You don't shanghai someone and then think they're going to be pleasant."

"I don't mind being shanghaied as long as there's a bed on the other end of the trip." Cyrus got out and stretched, his body leaner than it had been the last time she'd seen him.

Had he been ill?

She didn't ask, just led the way into the house while Stella mumbled about bringing her own car to the airport the next time they went on a mission together.

"Shh," Cyrus said as he walked into the house. "The kid is asleep, and that's exactly what I want to be, too. You got a place I can bed down, Scout?"

"Lucy's room. It's down the hall. The first room on the ri—"

He was already gone, Stella following along behind him, shooting Boone a hard look as she went.

"She's not happy," Scout said, and Boone shrugged.

"She'll get over it."

"What'd you do?"

"Refused to bring her home. She wanted me to bring her into D.C. I wanted to come here. Since it was snowing, I was afraid I might not make it if I took a side trip."

"I would have been here when you *did* make it."

"I don't know if I would have survived that long."

"Without cake?" she joked, and he shook his head.

"Without you and Lucy. I missed you, babe. More than I can say. There was a moment when I was gone that all I could do was pray that God was going to bring me home to you."

"He did." She led him into the kitchen, pressed him down into a chair. "He will. Always. I have to believe that or I won't be able to live my life while you're gone."

He smiled, taking a cup of coffee that she handed him and setting it on the table.

She put a slice of coconut cake down in front of him, but he didn't touch it, just grabbed her hand, pulling her close. "How is Lucy?"

"Ornery. She doesn't sleep well. It shows."

"Time will heal that." He stood and they were inches apart. She could see the dark circles under his eyes, the pale cast to his skin. He looked tired and a little sad, and her heart ached for him.

She wrapped her arms around his waist, hugging him tight because she didn't know what else to do. "Are you okay?"

"I will be. After a few long walks in the snow with the woman I love. Did you put a new photo in the frame?"

"And miss out on seeing your ugly mug every day?" she joked, wanting to ease some of the sadness from his eyes.

He didn't laugh, just studied her face intently. "Then you missed out."

"On what?"

"My secret message." He led her into the living room, handed her the frame. "Go ahead. Open it up."

Her fingers shook as she slid the back clasps open and lifted the back of the frame. There, on the back of the photo, were letters and numbers.

D.B.A.

S.C.

L.C.

Together 4 ever?

She met his eyes, her heart pounding wildly.

"Boone—"

"I love you, Scout. I love your daughter. I don't want to come home from a mission, go back to my empty apartment and wait until a decent hour to visit or call you. I don't want to barge in on your life at four in the morning and have to leave a few hours later, because I have no right to stay."

"You have every right to stay." She touched his cheeks, slid her hands to his shoulders, feeling all the tension that he'd carried on his trip and wanting desperately to take it away. "I can always make space for you and your team."

"I am not my team," he responded. "Not when I'm here. Here, I am just me, and I want to come home to you and to Lucy. I want to know, when I'm crawling through mud and blood and searching for people that I don't know and have never met, that when I come home, I'm returning to my family."

"And I want to know when you're gone," she responded softly, "that family is exactly what you'll be returning to."

He smiled then, leaning down, kissing her so gently, her heart ached with it.

"My world is right again," he said quietly, and it was as if those words freed something in him, some of the old Boone peeking out from the depth of his eyes.

"Mine, too," Scout whispered, kissing him again, holding him tight, trying to will the peace that he deserved into his tired body.

He broke away, his eyes dark with longing, his lips

curving in that sweet, sweet smile. "Better stop, Scout, because I don't think there's a preacher who'd be willing to marry us at this time of the morning. Seeing as how that's the case, there's only one thing to do."

"What's that?" she asked, and he grabbed her hand, smiled into her eyes.

"Dig into that cake you made," he responded, and she laughed as he tugged her back into the kitchen.

* * * * *

PROTECTIVE INSTINCTS

"For I know the plans I have for you," declares the Lord, "plans to prosper you and not to harm you, plans to give you hope and a future."
—*Jeremiah 29:10–12*

To Glenda Winters,
because she knows how to hold on and how to let go.
Blessings to you, my friend. And prayers that
God will give you comfort and courage and peace.

PROLOGUE

Sudan
Six months ago

Dying felt like summer heat and dusty earth. It sounded like flies and buzzards, humming and flapping in Raina Lowery's ears as she lay on the hot, hard ground of the African savanna.

Please, God, just let it end soon. The prayer flitted through her mind. There and gone so quickly she couldn't quite grab hold of it.

Close by, someone groaned, the sound drifting on waves of scorching heat. Twenty days traveling rugged terrain with little water, five days lying in cages in the blazing sun. They'd all die soon. Some of them already had.

Of the ten-member missionary team, seven had survived the initial attack against the small village where they'd been staying. Only five of the remaining had completed the forced journey to the rebel encampment.

Raina didn't know how many more had died since they'd arrived. If any of them lived, it would be a miracle, and she'd given up believing in those years ago.

A fraud trying to live a faith that she'd professed when she was a child; that's what she'd felt like when she'd agreed to travel with the medical mission. She'd die a fraud, because she hadn't found what she'd been looking for when she'd left Pine Bluff, Washington, and flown to Africa.

Dear God, please...

Something rustled beside her, and she opened her eyes, squinting against the late-afternoon sun. A gun strapped to his shoulder, his eyes hollow and old, a boy soldier peered through the cage bars. Young. Six or seven. A year or two younger than Joseph would have been. His close-cropped hair was coated with dirt, his cheeks covered with grime. He wore a baggy shirt and faded red shorts. His feet were bare.

Raina thought that he'd spit on her the way others had, but he pulled an old water bottle from beneath his baggy black T-shirt and slid it through the bars.

"Drink," he whispered, his English thick and heavily accented.

She wanted to thank him, but her tongue stuck to the roof of her mouth, and she couldn't get the words out. She lifted the murky water and drank greedily, gulping it down so quickly she almost choked.

She passed the bottle back through the bars, desperate for more. But the boy shoved it back under his shirt and ran off.

Alone again, she curled into a fetal position, the hot earth burning her cheek, the water roiling in her stomach. The buzzards flapped their wings, the droning sounds of the flies growing so loud they were almost deafening.

The air hung still and heavy, the heat so thick she

could taste it on the back of her tongue, feel it in the sluggish pulse of her blood. It dragged at her, pulling her down into a darkness she wasn't sure she'd ever escape.

Someone shouted and gunfire blasted through the encampment, the explosive power of machine-gun rounds vibrating through the hard ground. Raina pushed to her knees, couldn't make it to her feet. Fire blazed from the roof of one of the rebel's huts, the shimmering heat dancing against the afternoon sky. A black helicopter hovered above, blowing the smoke and flames into a frenzy of motion. Men ran toward the tall savanna grasses, weapons slapping against narrow backs, boots thudding on drought-dry earth.

A small figure darted through the chaos, running straight toward Raina's prison. Black T-shirt and old red shorts, skinny legs pumping hard. No gun this time. Just wild fear in his ancient eyes.

He crouched near the cage door, his hand shaking as he shoved a key into the padlock.

"You have to run and hide!" Raina tried to shout, but her voice caught in her parched throat, and all that came out was a croak.

The door swung open, and the boy held out his hand. "You are free."

Their gazes locked, and she reached for him, her fingers brushing the warm, dry tips of his.

Another explosion, and his eyes went wide as he fell into the cage.

"No!" Raina rasped, not caring about the open door that he'd fallen through, the war raging behind him. A rebel soldier lay a dozen yards away, blood pooling beneath him, the gun he'd used to bring down the boy lying near his outstretched hand. All Raina cared about was the boy. She touched his neck, felt his thready rapid pulse.

Her training kicked in then. All the years of being an emergency room nurse drove her to action. Blood spurted from the boy's leg. The injury to his thigh was so severe, she didn't think the limb could be saved. She ripped off a piece of her shirt, tied it around the top of his leg to cut off blood flow. It was that or watch him die.

He couldn't have weighed more than fifty pounds, but Raina struggled to lift him and stagger out of the cage. Dizzy, disoriented, she aimed for the tall grass, stumbling past the rebel's body. Heat blazed from the raging fire and the endless sun. Her arms and legs trembled, but she couldn't stop, couldn't put the boy down.

Please, God...

Please...

Her legs gave out, and she tumbled backward, her arms still wrapped around the boy. He groaned, his dark eyes staring into hers, blank but still lit with life and hope.

Please.

"It's okay. You're safe now. We're going to get you home," a man said, crouching beside her, his tan pants and long-sleeved shirt crisp and clean, his accent the deep drawl of a true Southerner. Deep blue eyes and an unyielding face. Hard edges and sharp angles and a scar that split one dark eyebrow.

Who are you? she thought, the words trapped in her head, unable to escape the fiery heat in her throat, the dryness of her mouth.

"Let's get out of here." He tried to pull her from the boy, but she tightened her grip.

"No."

"We can't bring him with us. There's no room on the chopper." His voice was as gentle as sunrise, and Raina wanted to close her eyes, release her grip, let herself fall into the care he seemed to be offering.

She couldn't leave the boy, though.

Wouldn't.

"Take *him,* then." She thrust the boy into his arms, her muscles trembling, blackness edging at the corner of her mind. Maybe this was where she was meant to die. Maybe four years of searching for the faith she'd lost had led her straight into God's arms.

She swayed, so ready to give in that her knees buckled.

"Don't give up now," he growled, his free arm snaking around her waist. He pulled her upright, and she had no choice but to run beside him. It was that or drag all three of them down.

"Jackson! Hurry it up. We've got heat coming in from the west." A woman raced toward them, her blond hair pulled into a ponytail, a gun strapped to her chest. She wore the same uniform as the man. A blue heart was stitched on one shoulder.

"Everyone is accounted for?"

"If this is Raina, then yes." The woman offered Raina a kind smile that didn't quite fit the hard angles and edges of her face. Her gaze dropped to the boy, and she frowned. "We can't take him. You know that, right?"

"Rules are meant to be broken, Stella. Isn't that your philosophy of life?"

"True." She took the boy from his arms. "Let's get out of here."

She ran toward a waiting helicopter, dust and debris swirling, her blond ponytail flying. Raina wanted to run, too, but she couldn't feel her feet, her legs, her body. Didn't know if she was standing or lying down. Hazy sky and yellow sun and midnight-blue eyes. The endless flap of buzzard wings.

"You're going to be okay, Raina," someone whispered as she slid into darkness.

ONE

Help me, Mommy. Please! Help me!

The cries drifted into Raina's consciousness, weaving their way through vivid dreams: Africa. A young boy who wasn't Joseph, but who could have been. Hot sun. Desperate thirst. Fear.

And that cry!

Help me, Mommy! Please! Help me!

She jerked awake, her heart thundering so loudly, she thought she was still hearing the cries.

She *was* still hearing the cries.

Wasn't she?

She scrambled out of bed, the sheets and blanket dropping onto the floor, her flannel pajamas tangled around her waist and legs. Wind rattled the windows, the darkness beyond the single-pane glass complete. She cocked her head to the side, heard the house creaking, ice pattering on the roof. Other than that, there was nothing. Her hand shook as she brushed bangs from her forehead and tried to take a few deep breaths. Tried, but her lungs wouldn't fill.

"Calm down!" she muttered. "It was just a dream, and you're still waking up from it."

It wasn't as if she hadn't had the dream many times in the six months since she'd returned from the mission trip, and it wasn't as if she hadn't learned how to deal with it.

She paced to the window then back to the bed, inhaling, exhaling, forcing herself to relax.

She'd spent the past thirty hours wondering how the young boy who'd given her a drink of water and unlocked her cage was faring. Was it any wonder that she'd had such a vivid nightmare? After fighting red tape and bureaucracy, petitioning, begging, pleading and pulling every string she could think of, Raina had finally managed to get him to the United States on a medical visa. He'd stepped onto U.S. soil the previous morning. The flight from L.A. to Atlanta had gone off without a hitch, but the flight from Atlanta to D.C. had been canceled.

Good thing Raina had hired an escort to bring Samuel to the United States. One she trusted implicitly. Stella Silverstone worked for HEART, the hostage rescue team that had risked everything to save her and the rest of the mission team. Stella had been brusque and to the point when she'd called to tell Raina about the delay. They were stuck in Atlanta, their flight canceled because of the storms. Samuel was fine. Stella would call again when they got a flight out.

That had been more than twelve hours ago.

Raina hadn't heard a word since. She was worried about Samuel. His leg had been amputated above the knee, and he'd suffered reoccurring infections in the stump. He'd been hospitalized for a few weeks before his trip to the United States, and the doctors hadn't been hopeful for his recovery. No wonder Raina was having nightmares.

"But now you're awake, so do something productive instead of standing around panicking." Her words echoed in the room she'd once shared with Matt. Like everything else since the accident that had taken her husband and son, the room seemed to be nothing more than a shadow of its former self. Wedding pictures hung crooked on the wall. Family photos lined the dresser, their frames covered with dust. The pretty yellow bedspread that had been a wedding gift was faded to a muted ivory.

Destiny had tried to get her to redecorate, but Raina hadn't seen the point, so she'd ignored her best friend's suggestions. Now that Matt was gone, the room was just a place to sleep. Half the time, she lay on the couch, watching TV until she finally drifted off.

Matt wasn't around to gently shake her shoulder and laugh while she grumbled about not wanting to get up. He wasn't there to usher her into their room and nuzzle her neck while she pulled down the covers.

It had been years, and she should be used to that, but she wasn't.

She left the room that suddenly seemed too full of memories, and walked down the short hall into the great room. That had been Matt's name for it. It was really nothing more than an oversize living room that had been created when the former owner had combined a formal living and dining area. Matt had lots of big ideas, lots of beautiful ways of looking at the ordinary. She missed his optimistic perspective, but she'd been trying to move on, to create something for herself that didn't include all the dreams that had died when Matt and Joseph had been taken away from her.

She pulled back the curtains and stared out into the

tiny front yard. The property butted up against a dirt road that dead-ended a half mile to the west. A century ago, the area had been dotted with farms and orchards, the nearby town of Middletown, Maryland, a bustling community of businessmen and farmers. The Great Depression had hit it hard, but it had rebounded in the 1980s when yuppies willing to take on a long commute had moved there from the Baltimore and Washington suburbs. Farther west, though, where farms had once been the livelihood of the town, abandoned properties and fallow acreage had proven a deterrent to the area's revitalization. Matt had seen it as a blessing, but that was the way he'd always been. Focused on the positive. Willing to work hard to make dreams a reality. He'd seen the old farmhouse and twenty acres of overgrown orchards as an answer to prayer.

Raina had gone along for the ride. Just as she always had, because she'd loved Matt, and she'd wanted what he'd wanted. Now, of course, she was stuck on twenty acres in the middle of nowhere. No close neighbors to visit on the weekends or children playing basketball or hockey on the street. Just Larry, and he stuck close to his house and his property.

Something moved in the early-morning darkness, and she leaned closer to the glass. Probably just a deer. This far out, she saw plenty of them. There were coyotes, too. An occasional bear that wandered in from the deep woodland and hill country. The thing crossed the yard, heading toward Larry's property. No streetlights illuminated the shape, but she was sure it was a biped. Too small to be a bear. A man?

She flicked on the outside light. The shadow darted across the street, disappearing into heavy shrub.

Larry?

She hoped not. Two days ago, he'd been outside barefoot, walking up the road. She'd spotted him on her way home from work at the medical clinic. He'd said he'd been heading to his mailbox at the head of their road, but that hadn't explained the bare feet in fifty-degree weather.

She grabbed the phone and dialed his number, knowing that he wouldn't answer. He never did. That was the thing about Larry. He wanted to be left alone, but if he was outside, he could freeze to death before anyone ever realized he was in trouble.

She yanked on jeans, pulled a coat over her flannel nightie and shoved her feet into boots.

The flashlight was still where Matt had always left it—tucked on the top shelf of the closet with a first-aid kit, a box of candles and matches and a stack of blankets. If Matt had been an outdoorsman, she might have a shotgun to take, too, but he'd been more of an academic, country living more a dream than a reality he'd been prepared to deal with.

She'd been the practical one in their relationship, the one who thought of things like bears and bobcats, who'd built the chicken coop that now stood empty. She'd taught Matt how to camp, fish and even hunt. Not that they'd ever been successful at any of those things. Matt's idea of camping was staying in a hotel near hiking trails, and his vision of hunting had never included actually shooting anything.

She smiled at the memories, touching the bear spray she kept in her coat pocket. Better safe than sorry. It was cold for early November, the temperature well below freezing, ice coating the grass and trees. It took five long strides to cross the front yard, the wind snatching her breath and chilling her cheeks. Across the street, Larry McDermott's house stood shadowy and dark. Shrouded by overgrown trees and a hedge that had probably been planted in the 1950s, it was a Gothic monstrosity that looked as worn and mean as its seventy-year-old owner.

Not mean, she could almost hear Matt whisper. *Lonely.*

Maybe. In the years since Matt's and Joseph's deaths, Raina had tried to be kind to her neighbor. For Matt's sake, she'd baked him bread, invited him for Thanksgiving and Christmas. She'd shoveled his driveway after snowstorms and checked in on him when she hadn't seen him for a few days. No matter what she did, he never seemed to warm up to her.

She walked to the edge of his property and made her way along his driveway. Her flashlight beam bounced over cracks in the pavement and illuminated the three stairs that led to Larry's front door. She jiggled the door-knob, knocked twice, wondering if Larry would hear if he were asleep. Her fingers were freezing, but she wanted to check the back door, too. She swept the flashlight across the front yard, her pulse jumping as it passed over what looked like footprints in the icy grass. Instead of thick ice, a thin layer of slush coated the grass there. She scanned the area, found another set of prints near the edge of the house.

"Larry!" she screamed, her voice carried away by the wind. "Larry! Are you out here?" She rounded the side of the house, following the footprints to a gate that banged against the fence with every gust of wind.

"Larry!" She tried one last time, her flashlight track-ing footprints to the edge of the woods that separated

Larry's yard from the church his grandfather had pastored. The church Matt had pastored for five years before his death. Their home away from home. The only church Joseph had ever known. She knew the path that cut through the woods so well she wouldn't have needed her flashlight to follow it. She used it anyway, making sure that the footprints didn't veer off into the woods.

Larry couldn't be too far ahead.

If it was Larry.

She glanced back, could see nothing but white-crusted trees.

She walked another half mile. She'd reach the church parking lot soon, and then what would she do? The place was closed for the night. She was already near frozen. She'd be all the way frozen by the time she walked to the church.

This was a stupid idea. A colossally stupid one. She needed to go back to the house and call the police. If Larry was out in the cold, they'd find him. The problem was, she couldn't stand the thought of her crotchety old neighbor freezing to death while she cowered in her house. She couldn't stomach the idea of one more person dying because she hadn't been able to offer the help he needed.

"Larry!" she shrieked, her words seeming to echo through the woods. The trees grew sparser as she neared the church, and she flashed her lights toward the end of the trail, hoping to catch sight of the older man. Suddenly, a figure stepped out from behind a tree. Not stooped and old like Larry. Tall and lean. Her light flashed on thick ski pants. It glanced off a heavy black parka, landed straight on a black ski mask and glittering eyes that could have been any color.

"Who are you?" she said, her voice wobbling. "What are you doing out here?"

"Go home!" he hissed, pulling something from his pocket.

No. Not something. A handgun. He lifted it, pointed it straight at her head.

"Go!" he repeated, shifting the barrel a fraction of an inch and pulling the trigger.

The night exploded, a bullet whizzing past her head and slamming into a tree. She dodged to the left, dashing into trees as another bullet slammed into the ground behind her.

She tumbled down a small hill, pushed through a thicket. Behind her, branches cracked and feet slapped against frozen earth. He was following her!

She didn't know where she was, where she was heading. She knew only that she had to run. If she didn't, the death she'd avoided in Africa was going to find her.

"This wasn't one of your better ideas, Stel," Jackson Miller muttered as he maneuvered the SUV along an icy dirt road that led to Raina Lowery's house.

"Shh!" Stella responded. "You're going to wake the kid."

"Avoiding the comment doesn't negate it," he replied without lowering his voice. "Besides, Samuel slept through your rendition of 'Take Me Home, Country Roads.' I think he can probably sleep through anything."

"You could be right. My mom once told me that my voice could wake the dead."

"Did she also tell you that driving down icy country roads in the middle of the night could *turn* you into one of the dead?"

Stella laughed. "My mother was all about the thrill. She would have loved this, and you would have loved her. She was crazier than I am."

He doubted it. Stella had a reputation at HEART— hard-core, tough, determined and absolutely fearless. A former army nurse, she handled stress well, and in the four years he'd known her, she'd never caved under pressure. "Most of the time, I like your kind of crazy, Stella, but the next time you want to go for a country ride in the middle of an ice storm, call my brother."

The silence that ensued told Jackson everything he needed to know. Stella and Chance hadn't worked things out.

He hadn't expected them to. They were both as stubborn as mules. The fact that they'd dated at all still surprised him. The fact that his brother, a consummate bachelor, had bought an engagement ring had shocked him. Stella and Chance's breakup four weeks ago? Not surprising at all.

"I didn't call you," Stella finally said. "I stopped by your place. I wouldn't have done that if Samuel hadn't had to use the bathroom."

"Sure. Go ahead and blame it on the kid who's asleep in the backseat," he responded, and Stella laughed again.

"Okay. So I didn't want to come all the way out to Podunk Town alone. Country roads are creepy."

"You've been to some of the most dangerous cities in the world, and you think *this* is creepy?"

"Every ghost story I've ever heard has taken place on a country r—"

Someone darted out of the woods, and Jackson slammed on the brakes. The tires lost traction, and the SUV spun. Jackson managed to turn into the spin, get the vehicle back under control. It coasted to a stop an inch from a giant oak tree.

"What was that?" Stella yelled into the sudden stillness.

"A person." He unbuckled his seat belt, praying for all he was worth that he hadn't hit whoever it was.

"Where'd he go?"

"I don't—"

A woman appeared beside the car. Hair cropped short and plastered to her head, black coat hanging open to reveal what looked like a flannel pajama top. Jeans. Plastic rain boots. A face that was so familiar his breath caught.

Raina.

It had been over six months since he'd seen her, but her image had been carved into his memories so deeply that it seemed like yesterday. He'd been on dozens of rescues, brought plenty of people to safety. He hadn't forgotten any of them, but Raina had been different. He hadn't just remembered her; he hadn't been able to get her out of his mind.

"Help me!" she begged, glancing over her shoulder, her eyes wild with fear. "There's someone chasing me."

He opened the door, scanning the woods behind her. "Who?"

"I don't know. He had a gun. He tried to shoot me." Her teeth were chattering, and he dropped his coat around her shoulders and bundled her into the car.

She grabbed his wrist before he could turn away, her hands cold against his skin. "We need to call the police."

"Okay," he responded, meeting Stella's eyes. Raina didn't seem to know who either of them was. Her lips were pale from cold, rivulets of water streaming down her cheeks and neck. She'd been outside for a while, and she seemed to be suffering the effects of it. "Tell me what's going on."

"I told you. Someone was chasing me through the woods." She glanced at the trees, her eyes widening. "There, look!"

He whirled in the direction she'd indicated, his hand resting on the gun strapped to his chest. All he saw were trees and deep shadows. "I don't…"

His voice trailed off. Something *did* seem to be moving through the forest. Stella must have seen it, too. She leaned toward him. "You want to check it out, or you want me to?"

"I'll go." He grabbed a flashlight from the glove compartment and headed toward the trees, moving quickly and quietly, the patter of icy rain enveloping him as he entered the woods. It had been years since he'd been hunting, but he knew what to look for. Tracks in the ice, broken branches. He could clearly see the path Raina had taken, the slippery progress she'd made. She'd run haphazardly, zigzagging through foliage.

He moved deeper into the trees, the stillness of the woods broken only by the murmur of leaves and the soft whistling of the wind. The storm seemed to be dying down, the ice turning to a gentle rain. He pushed through a thicket and found himself on a dirt path that ran east and west. West led to the road and the SUV, so he headed east, his light illuminating the slushy path. He could make out footprints, all of them indistinct. Other than that, the dirt yielded nothing.

The path opened into a parking lot, a small church at the far end of it glowing grayish-white in the gloom. A Jeep sat near the tree line a hundred yards away. Dark-colored, the windows tinted, it had a thin layer of ice covering the roof and so much dirt on the license plate it couldn't be read.

He moved toward it, the hair on the back of his neck standing on end. He knew the feeling of impending danger. What six years as a U.S. marine hadn't taught him about it, five years working for HEART had.

Someone was in the car.

He was as sure of it as he was of his own name.

He kept his firearm loose in his right hand, tucked the flashlight into his coat pocket and pulled out his cell. He snapped two pictures of the Jeep and was getting ready to take a third when the engine coughed. Black exhaust poured from the muffler, but instead of speeding out of the parking lot, the driver backed up and pointed the Jeep straight at Jackson.

He dove for cover, tree branches snagging his coat and ripping into his face as the Jeep slammed into the trees behind him. Leaves and water rained down on his head, blurring his vision as he dropped the cell phone, pivoted and fired his Glock.

TWO

If the perp escapes, Chance isn't going to let me live this down. I'm *not going to let myself live it down.*

Those were Jackson's first thoughts as he fired a second shot at the tires of the fleeing vehicle. The tire blew, the Jeep swerving and righting itself as the driver stepped on the gas and raced away.

He wouldn't get far.

Not in the Jeep.

He might get somewhere on foot. Jackson didn't know the area well, and he wasn't sure how far they were from a main thoroughfare. He ran out into the street, watching as the Jeep's taillights dipped and swerved along the country road. No streetlights to speak of, but Jackson could see a small town in the distance.

If the Jeep was heading in that direction, it should be easy enough to track down. Jackson jogged back to the tree line, flashing his light on the giant oak the Jeep had hit. Bits of bark had sheared off and specks of dark blue paint stuck to the wood. Evidence for the police to collect. Jackson left it alone, careful not to step on tread marks deeply engraved in the muck at the edge of the blacktop. The last thing he needed was to get in deep with the local P.D. The fact that he'd fired his Glock was going to cause problems enough.

Problems that Jackson wanted to handle without any help from Chance.

Not that he didn't appreciate his older brother's input and advice, but Chance got a little too involved sometimes. He worried a little too much. Since they'd lost Charity, everyone in the family did.

His cell phone rang, the sound muffled. He followed it to a pile of ice and leaves, dug through the dirty mess and pulled out the phone.

"Hello?"

"Where are you, Jackson?" Chance's shout cut through the quiet.

"In a church parking lot just outside of a little town called—"

"River Valley," Chance cut him off. "Where's the church? Stella said—"

"You two are finally on speaking terms again?" He tried to change the subject, because he wasn't in the mood for one of his brother's lectures, and because a police car was pulling into the parking lot. Sirens off, lights on, it moved toward him slowly.

"We're always on speaking terms when it comes to work. Delivering Samuel Niag to Raina is work. Chasing people through the woods in unfamiliar territory is not."

"Maybe not," Jackson responded lightly. No sense in getting into it with Chance. Not when he was pretty certain he was about to get into it with River Valley law enforcement.

The officer got out of the car, face shrouded by the rim of his uniform hat. "Keep your hands where I can see them," he growled.

Jackson obliged, lifting both hands in the air, his brother's voice still audible.

"You have any weapons on you?" The officer asked, his gaze on Jackson's shoulder holster and the gun that was visible in it.

"Just my Glock," he responded.

"You have a permit?"

"In my SUV."

"Which is where?" The officer stayed neutral, but he was moving in closer, and Jackson could sense the tension in his shoulders and back, the nervous energy that wafted through the darkness.

Jackson rattled off Raina's address, and the officer nodded. "I'm going to have to take your firearm until your permit can be verified."

Apparently the officer also had to handcuff Jackson and stick him in the back of the police cruiser while he looked around, because that's exactly where Jackson found himself. Sitting on a cold leather seat, the smell of urine and vomit filling his nose. He'd been in worse situations, been in a lot more danger, but he still didn't like it. Not when the guy who'd tried to run him down was making his escape.

He would have been happy to tell the police officer that, but the guy was a few feet away from the cruiser, speaking into his radio as he scanned the parking lot.

An SUV pulled in. Not just any SUV. The brand-new one Jackson had purchased to replace his old Chevy truck. Chance must have called Stella. She got out of the vehicle and stalked to the police officer's side, her close-cropped hair barely moving in the wind. Used to be, she'd had shoulder-length hair. That was before she and Chance had called it quits. Seconds later, Raina exited the SUV and opened the back door. Samuel slid out, an old wooden crutch under one arm, a giant coat wrapped around his shoulders.

He was tiny for ten, his cheeks gaunt from illness, his jeans hanging loosely, one pant leg rolled up and pinned beneath his stump. Seeing him after so many months had only made Jackson regret leaving him in Kenya more than he had the day he'd flown home. He'd left hundreds of dollars for the young boy's care, and he'd planned on keeping tabs on Samuel, making sure that he got what he needed to survive and thrive.

Raina had stepped in first, making phone calls from her hospital room, transferring money, doing everything a mother might do for a child stuck in a foreign land. Jackson had heard all about it, had followed the news stories about Raina's fight to get a medical visa for Samuel, about the offers from medical experts in D.C. who'd promised surgery and state-of-the-art prostheses for the child if he could be brought to the United States.

Raina put a hand under Samuel's elbow, but the boy shrugged away, determined, it seemed, to make his way across the still-slick parking lot himself. The police officer moved toward them, said a few words that Jackson was really desperate to hear.

Raina nodded, then gestured to the church.

Seconds later, she and Samuel were moving toward the building. She opened the church door, allowed Samuel to walk in front of her. The door closed, and they were gone, lights spilling out from tall windows and splashing across the parking lot.

Jackson wanted to follow. It was impossible to know if the church was empty. If it was always left unlocked, anyone could be inside, sleeping in the sanctuary on a pew, hiding in a restroom until dawn. Lying in wait for a victim.

The cruiser door opened, and Stella peered in, her eyes gleaming with amusement. "I see you've found your way into trouble again."

"I didn't find it. It found me." He glanced at the officer standing behind her. The guy seemed more focused on the notebook he was writing in than on the crime scene.

"That's always your story, Jack." Stella sighed, grabbing his arm and tugging him from the car. "Hear you lost your Glock."

"I had it confiscated, and I wouldn't mind having it back."

"I wouldn't mind knowing exactly why you decided to fire it," the officer responded without looking up. "I found two bullet casings. You forgot to mention that you'd fired shots."

"You didn't give me a chance."

"You've got one now." He finally met Jackson's eyes. "Want to explain what happened?"

"Someone tried to run me down. I tried to stop him."

"By putting a bullet in him?"

"By putting a bullet in his tire. Which I managed to do. You should find a late model Jeep with a blown tire somewhere nearby. There's a photo of it on my cell phone."

The officer nodded, but didn't look as though he was any closer to letting Jackson out of handcuffs.

"I don't suppose that it occurred to you to do what the pastor of this church did when he heard gunfire— call for help?"

"It occurred to me, but I was occupied with trying to keep myself from being crushed by a Jeep."

That got a smile out of the guy. "Fair enough. I'll call in an APB on the Jeep, see if we can find it and our guy. Want to show me that photo?"

"Want to get me out of these cuffs?"

"Sure, but don't get the idea you're going anywhere. I have some more questions for you." Jackson nodded his agreement and stood still while the handcuffs were being removed. What he really wanted to do was go into the church and make sure Raina and Samuel were okay.

As he handed the officer his cell phone, he glanced at the building. Its pretty white siding and colorful stained glass gleamed in the darkness. A beautiful little building that had probably been standing for generations, but that didn't mean it was safe. One thing Jackson had learned in his time in the military and with HEART— the places that should be safest were often the most dangerous of all.

It had been nearly four years since Raina had last stepped foot in River Valley Community Church. She hadn't stopped attending because her faith had been shaken after Matt and Joseph died. She hadn't stopped because her best friend had invited her to a new church in town. One that had lots of young people and plenty of upbeat music and was designed to make people feel good about their lives and their faith.

She'd stopped attending because it had been too hard to keep going.

Too hard to sit in a pew and listen while Pastor William Myer preached. Too hard to listen to his wife play the piano Raina had once played. Too hard to be there and not remember the years she and Matt had served together.

Too hard, and she'd been too weak, too sad, too *destroyed* by what had happened. Too overwhelmed by her guilt and her inability to forgive God and herself.

She touched the vestibule wall, remembering the way she and Matt had laughed as they'd painted sunny yellow over the mud-brown that had been there since the 1960s. They'd wanted to see the old church shine again, and they had. Matt would say that was a blessing. To Raina it was just another memory that she'd rather forget.

Water ran in the sink, the door to the church's only bathroom still firmly closed. She wanted to knock and make sure that Samuel was okay, but she didn't think he'd appreciate it. He hadn't seemed to want her help, hadn't wanted to talk. He'd been traveling for thirty-six hours, and he was tired and ill. Stella had said he'd been running a 103-degree fever, and that the wound on his stump was seeping and infected. All those things needed to be dealt with, but first Raina had to get him home.

That's where she'd wanted to go.

Straight back to the house. But Stella had had to make a call, then she'd asked if there was anything on the other side of the woods. The next thing Raina had known, they'd been heading for the old church.

She touched the wall again, a million memories flooding her mind and her eyes. It had been a while since she'd cried over what she'd lost, and she didn't plan to cry now, but she couldn't stop thinking about the dream that had woken her. The hot African sun and the little boy crying for help.

The vestibule door opened, cold fall air drifting in and carrying the scent of wood fires and wet leaves. Her favorite time of year, but it seemed as if she'd missed every moment of every fall for the past four years. As if she'd just drifted through the seasons without even noticing the leaves changing color, the snow dusting the ground, the first tulips of spring.

She turned, letting the cold moist air kiss her cheeks and ruffle her hair. She expected Stella to walk through the open door, but the figure that moved into the vestibule was tall and masculine. Her heart jumped as she met Jackson Miller's eyes. Even in the midst of her terror, even half-frozen and desperate, she'd known who he was. She'd recognized the sharp angles of his face, the scar that sliced through his eyebrow, the broadness of his shoulders. She'd dreamed about him dozens of times, relived her captivity and her rescue every day for months.

Yes. She'd have known Jackson anywhere, anytime, in any situation.

"Everything okay in here?" he asked, his Southern drawl as warm as sunlight on a summer morning. It had been months since she'd heard it, but she hadn't forgotten the thick twang, or the way it reminded her of home and safety and freedom.

"Yes." She looked away from his searching gaze. "I'm just waiting for Samuel."

"You've been waiting a long time."

"He's sick and exhausted. Everything takes longer under those circumstances."

"I guess so." He knocked on the door. "Hey, Sammy! You about done in there?"

"He doesn't—" She was going to say *speak much English,* but Samuel poked his head out of the bathroom, his face and hair wet.

"I am finished."

"What'd you do, kid? Take a bath?" Jackson stepped into the bathroom and came back out with a handful of paper towels. He dabbed at Samuel's head and his face, swiped water off the back of his neck, pausing for just a moment at a ridge of scars just below Samuel's hairline. When the young boy tensed, Jackson moved on, finishing the job with quick, efficient movements that Raina envied.

She could have been the one helping. She probably should have been the one. After all, she'd be Samuel's caregiver for the next year. She felt awkward, though. As if losing Joseph had caused her to lose every bit of maternal instinct she had.

"Good enough!" Jackson proclaimed with a smile that eased the hardness from his face. "We have to stay here a few more minutes while the police officer collects some evidence. You want to sit down?"

He didn't wait for Samuel to reply, just scooped him up with his crutch and placed him on a pew at the front of the sanctuary. The young boy looked surprised, but didn't protest. Maybe he was more used to men than women. Or maybe he just sensed the difference between Jackson and Raina—one was relaxed and open, the other tense and closed in and scared.

She had to get over it.

No one had twisted her arm or begged her to help Samuel. She'd come up with the idea all on her own, because she owed him her life. She hadn't been able to forget that, hadn't wanted to. The problem was, she didn't know how to care for a young boy. Not anymore. She knew it, and Samuel seemed to know it.

That was a shame, because she'd really wanted to

hit it off with him, to make him feel comfortable and at home.

What she hadn't wanted was to think about Joseph every time she looked into Samuel's face, but she couldn't seem to help herself. They looked nothing alike, but when she looked into Samuel's eyes, she was reminded of Joseph. When she touched his arm, she thought of her son.

"You should probably sit down, too," Jackson said quietly. "You're looking a little pale."

"I'm fine." She met his eyes, felt something in her heart spring to attention. He was as handsome as she'd remembered. As tall. As muscular. He was exactly what she'd have imagined if someone had told her there was a team of people who'd devoted their lives to rescuing the kidnapped, the lost, the wounded from dangerous situations.

"Fine doesn't mean you're not going to fall over faster than Grandma Ruth during a summer revival meeting."

"Your grandmother faints during revival meetings?" she asked, plopping down next to Samuel because her legs were feeling a little weak. She wanted to blame it on fear and stress, but it had more to do with that little ping in her heart when she'd met Jackson's gaze.

"Only when it's hot and she hasn't had enough water."

"You're making that up," she accused, and he smiled, dropping onto the pew beside her.

"Not even a little. The fact is Grandma Ruth has fainted once or twice during revival meetings, and we have to take care to keep her hydrated. The other fact is you look pale as paper, and you really did need to sit down."

"At least I'm not beaten up and bruised," she responded, touching a bump that had formed on his cheekbone. His skin felt warm and just a little rough, and she had the absurd urge to linger there.

She let her hand drop away, and he touched the bruise. "Guess I ran into something while I was avoiding the Jeep that tried to run me down."

"What Jeep?"

"Parked in the church lot." He watched her steadily as he spoke, his eyes dark blue with thick, long lashes surrounding them. Women would pay to have lashes like that, and they'd probably swoon to see them on Jackson. "You know anyone with a blue Jeep?" he prodded.

"No."

"That was a quick, decisive response."

"Because I don't know anyone who owns a Jeep."

"Have you ever known anyone who did?"

"Probably, but I can't think…" Actually, she could think of someone with a blue Jeep. She and Destiny had gone to D.C. for a girls' weekend, and Destiny had borrowed her boyfriend's Jeep. "Lucas Raymond has one, but he lives in D.C."

"Lucas Raymond," he repeated. "Who's that?"

"My friend's boyfriend. I've only seen the vehicle once. I think it's newer."

"Do you have any reason to believe this guy would—"

"Raymond is a great guy. A psychiatrist. He's gotten awards for his work at the hospital and in the community."

"That doesn't mean he doesn't have an ax to grind with you." He stood and stretched, his T-shirt riding up along a firm abdomen.

She looked away, because she felt guilty noticing.

"Say we rule out Raymond," Jackson continued. "Who would want to hurt you, Raina?"

"No one," she replied, her mind working frantically, going through faces and names and situations.

"And yet, someone chased you through the woods and fired a shot at you. That same person nearly ran me down. Doesn't sound like someone who feels all warm and fuzzy when he thinks of you."

"Maybe he was a vagrant, and I scared him."

"Maybe." He didn't sound as if he believed it, and she wasn't sure she did, either.

She'd heard something that had woken her from the nightmare.

A child crying? Larry wandering around? An intruder trying to get in the house?

The last made her shudder, and she pulled her coat a little closer. "I think I'd know it if someone had a bone to pick with me."

"That's usually the case, but not always. Could be you upset a coworker or said no to a guy who wanted you to say yes."

She snorted at that, and Jackson frowned. "You've been a widow for four years, it's not that far-fetched an idea."

"If you got a good look at my social life, you wouldn't be saying that."

Samuel yawned loudly and slid down on the pew, his arms crossed over his chest, his eyelids drooping. He looked cold and tired, and she wanted to get him home, tuck him into bed, spend a little time trying to decide how best to proceed with him.

She couldn't keep being as uncomfortable as she was, couldn't continue with her stiff and stilted approach.

"Samuel needs some medicine, and he needs some sleep," she said, taking off her coat and draping it over him.

He opened his eyes, but didn't smile.

He had the solemn look of someone much older than ten and the scars of a soldier who'd fought too many wars.

"I'll go talk to Officer Wallace," Jackson responded. "See if he's ready to let us leave."

"He's going to have to be. Samuel—"

A door slammed, the sound so startling Raina jumped.

Samuel scrambled to his feet, clutching her coat in one hand and the crutch in the other. She grabbed his shoulder, pulled him into the shelter of her arms.

"Is someone else in the church?" Jackson demanded, his gaze on the door that led from the sanctuary into the office wing.

"There shouldn't be."

"Which means whoever slammed that door doesn't belong here. Stay put. I'm going to check things out."

He strode away, and she wanted to call out and tell him to be careful. The church was cut off from the rest of River Valley, the land a couple of miles outside of town. There'd been a few break-ins during the years Matt had been pastor and several more since then.

She pressed her lips together, held in the words she knew she didn't need to say. Jackson could take care of himself. She'd seen him in action, knew just how smart and careful he was."

"I will go, too," Samuel asserted, pulling away and hopping after Jackson.

She grabbed his arm. "No, Samuel. It's not safe."

"There is nothing that is safe," he responded, and her throat burned with the reality of what he'd survived.

"You have to stay here. Let Jackson and the police take care of this. Here in the U.S., kids don't take care of adult problems." It sounded lame, but it was all she could think of.

She thought he might yank away and keep walking, but he handed her the coat. "We will go outside, then."

"It's too cold."

"But in here it is dangerous for you. Outside, it is safe."

Maybe. Maybe not.

At this point, she didn't know, and all she could do was stay where she was and hope Jackson or Officer Andrew Wallace would figure out who was in the church or outside of it, who had been in the Jeep.

"It's safe here, Samuel. Let's just sit and wait."

He nodded but perched on the edge of the pew as if he were sure that at any moment, they'd have to run.

She waited beside him, tense, anxious, wanting to pray but unable to find the words that would spiral from her soul to God's ears.

Her faith, like so many other things in her life, was a shadow of what it had once been.

Her own fault.

After Matt and Joseph died, she'd stopped reading her Bible, stopped praying, stopped believing that God really cared. Somehow, though, He'd still rescued her from almost certain death in Africa.

There had to be a reason for that.

She'd thought it was so that she could help Samuel, but Samuel seemed perfectly capable of helping himself.

Sick as he was, hurt as he was, he was ready to face the world and whatever trouble it brought him.

She wished she could say the same for herself, but the best thing she could say, the only thing that she could say, was that she was there, ready to do what God wanted.

If only she knew what that was.

THREE

This wasn't a good time to be without a weapon, but since Officer Wallace hadn't seen fit to return Jackson's Glock, that was the situation he found himself in. He eased through the dark hall, allowing his eyes to adjust to the darkness. Straight ahead, an exit sign hung above a door. Two other doors led off the short hallway. He turned the handle of the closest one and walked into a spacious office, running his hand along the wall until he found a light switch.

A large desk took up one corner of the room, a high-back rolling chair behind it. Two other chairs stood near a wall lined with shelves and books. Another wall was blank, but for several portrait photos that must have been of former pastors and their families.

His heart did a little pause and jerk when he recognized Raina's blond hair and violet eyes. Her face had been fuller then, her cheekbones not as sharp, the area beneath less gaunt. She sat beside a dark-haired man whose smile looked genuine, and she held a little boy who looked just like his father.

Her family.

He filed the information away, turned off the light and left the room.

The next door opened just as easily, and he walked into a large choir room. Piano in one corner, racks of long blue choir robes in another. Chairs were arranged in a semicircle in front of a music stand. He stood still, listening to silence that seemed too thick and heavy to be natural.

Someone was there.

"You may as well show yourself," he said, moving toward the choir robes. "I know you're here."

Nothing, but he thought he saw a robe sway. Not much. Just a hint of movement. Enough to get his heart pumping and adrenaline coursing through him.

"I said—"

Someone lunged from the robes, darting out so quickly Jackson barely had time to respond. He dove toward the scurrying figuring, bringing the person down to the ground in a hail of fists and kicking feet. The music stand fell, clanging onto the ground with enough noise to wake the dead.

Jackson grabbed a skinny arm, tried to grab another, a man's hoarse cries filling his ears.

"Cool it!" he said as he finally managed to snag the guy's flailing hand. He looked down into a grizzled face and hot black eyes.

"Let me go, worthless VC!" the guy shouted.

"You're not in Vietnam, man," Jackson tried to assure him, still holding his arms in a tight grip. "You're in the States. In Maryland. In a church."

He was rewarded with spit in the face.

He didn't bother wiping it off.

He'd experienced worse, heard worse than the stream of curses coming from the man's mouth.

"Tell you what, buddy," he suggested, hauling the guy to his feet. "How about you put a sock in it?"

"Give me a sock and I'll—"

"What's going on?" Raina peered in the open door, her face pale. She looked like a dim reflection of the happy young woman in the photo he'd seen, and he felt exactly the way he had when he'd seen her in Africa. Worried. Determined. Willing to do whatever it took to get her home safely.

Only they weren't in Africa. They weren't even in danger. Unless a hundred-pound sixty-something-year-old man who smelled like the inside of a beer keg could be considered a threat.

"I found this guy hiding in the choir robes," he responded, turning his attention back to his prisoner, because he didn't want to look in Raina's face. He didn't want to see the loss written so clearly there, didn't want to know that her pain was the same pain he felt when he remembered Charity. Because there was nothing that could be done about that kind of pain. No magic pill that could be taken, no barrier that could be put up. Nothing but time could ease it, and even that only dulled the sharp edge of grief.

"I wasn't hiding!"

"Butch," Raina said. "You know you're not supposed to be in here without permission."

She stepped farther into the room. "Did you ask Pastor Myer if you could sleep here?"

"It's God's house. I asked *Him*," Butch said with a sly smile.

"How about you show a little respect for the lady,

Butch?" Jackson asked, giving the guy a little shake. Not too hard, though. He didn't want to rattle fragile bones.

Raina ignored his comment.

So did Butch.

As a matter of fact, Jackson thought they'd done this whole thing before—many times—and that they were just letting things play out the way they always had before.

"You've been drinking again." Raina walked to the choir robes and dug through them, pulling out an empty bottle of beer.

"Nah. I'm just collecting old bottles for the money," Butch replied. "Gotta make a living somehow."

"You could try getting a job," Jackson muttered, releasing the guy's arms.

"Who's going to hire me? I got PTSD, a bum back, wrecked knees. Got no hearing in one ear and barely any in the other. Thank you, Uncle Sam, for taking care of your veterans." Butch grabbed a backpack from behind the clothes, not nearly as drunk as Jackson thought.

"If you need work, I have some jobs around the house that I can't do myself," Raina said casually.

Jackson doubted there was anything casual about the offer.

As a matter of fact, tension lines were etched across her forehead, her skin pulled taut along her cheekbones.

He also doubted it was a good idea to have a guy like Butch hanging around her place. He'd steal her blind and not feel a bit of guilt about it.

"What kind of jobs? 'Cause I already told you, my back is bad and my knees are gone."

"The fence needs whitewashing, and the lawn needs one more mowing before winter."

"You still got that riding lawn mower? The one Matt loved so much?"

At his question, Raina tensed, her hands fisting. "Yes."

"I'll come by day after tomorrow and get that done for you. The fence might be a little harder. Probably will take me a week or more. Gotta take lots of breaks."

Raina nodded, but didn't speak.

Jackson wasn't sure if it was the mention of her husband that had thrown her or if it was the fact that Butch had taken her up on her offer of work.

"See you then, Raina." Butch waved and would have walked out into the hall, but Jackson wasn't done with the guy.

"How long were you in here, Butch?" he asked, and the old vet paused on the threshold, his gray hair falling in a ratty braid down the middle of his back.

"Awhile," he finally muttered.

"You must have heard the gunshots earlier."

"Could be that I did." Butch turned slowly, his black eyes blazing in his gnarled face. He looked older than he probably was. Seventy or more when Jackson suspected he was in his early sixties. Life hadn't been kind to him, but then, Jackson doubted the guy had been very kind to life.

"Did you hear anything before that?" Jackson pressed.

"Who wants to know?"

"Me. Probably the police. Raina."

"Here's the deal, soldier," Butch responded. "I don't deal with the police, and I don't like you. For Raina's sake, I'll tell you this—I heard a car pull into the parking lot a couple of hours ago. You tell the police that, and I'll tell them you're lying."

"Butch—" Raina started to say, but the guy raised a hand, cutting her off.

"You've always been good to me, but I'm not getting pulled into trouble. Been there too many times to count, and I'm starting to realize I'm getting too old for it."

"You didn't just hide in the choir robes and let whoever was in the parking lot do what he wanted to the church, Butch," Jackson said. "You went and looked out a window, right? This is your space. You were ready to protect it. You looked out the window, and you saw something. It wouldn't hurt to tell the police what that was."

"Wouldn't hurt. Wouldn't help. I'm an old, drunk vet who's been wandering around these parts sleeping in churches and abandoned railroad cars and under overpasses for more years than either of you have been alive. I've got a rap sheet a mile long. You think the police would listen to a word I said? Even if they did, my word is worth squat."

"It's worth something to me," Raina cut in, and Butch frowned.

"Could be I looked. Could be I saw an old Jeep. Could even be that I saw someone get out of that Jeep and walk into the woods, but even if all those things are really what happened, ain't one person around here who's going to believe me."

"You need to tell the police what you saw," Raina suggested, and Butch scowled.

"I owe you, Raina, and I owe your husband. I even owe your little boy, but I'm not talking to the police." He hitched the pack onto his back and walked out into the hall.

Jackson could have stopped him, could have forced

him outside and brought him to Officer Wallace. He didn't. Butch was obviously a well-known figure in the community. If Wallace wanted to interview him, he could track him down easily enough.

He followed Butch into the hall, watching as the guy limped to the exit, opened the door and disappeared outside. Cold air wafted in, the scent of rain and wet leaves hanging in the hallway after the door closed.

"Poor Butch," Raina murmured, her arm brushing his as she stepped past. She smelled like flowers, the scent feminine and alluring. She'd chopped her hair short, the thick strands just reaching her nape. On some women, the style would have been harsh, but on Raina it worked.

Everything about her worked.

The faded jeans and flannel nightgown. The unadorned fingernails and scuffed boots. She looked natural, and he found that beautiful, but he didn't think she saw Butch for who he was—a guy who'd take what he could, use who he could and never feel a bit of guilt over it.

"He's made his choices," Jackson responded. "Those choices brought him to the place he is."

"Maybe if he'd had a family who cared about him, he would have made different choices." She ran her fingers through her hair and sighed. "I'd better get back to Samuel. I really do want to get him home."

"Let's go, then." He cupped her elbow, as ready as she was to leave the church and get on with things. "We need to talk to Officer Wallace. Let him know what Butch saw."

"Unfortunately, he didn't see much."

"Not much that he's telling us, but he may be more

open to providing details when the police bring him in for questioning."

"I really hope Andrew doesn't do that to him. He'll probably resist and end up being arrested for it."

"Andrew?"

"Officer Wallace."

He nodded, leading her back down the hall into the sanctuary and telling himself that it wasn't his business that Raina was on a first name basis with Wallace.

Pull away! Raina's brain shouted as she and Jackson stepped into the quiet sanctuary, but her body refused to obey.

There was something…nice about having his hand cupped around her elbow, his fingers curved along her inner arm.

She let herself be ushered to the pew where Samuel still sat. She'd given him a pen and an old church bulletin that she'd found, and she'd told him to stay put.

He'd listened.

Thank the Lord.

She didn't think she could take any more drama. After six months of living quietly, of going to work and returning home, of going to church and returning home, of quiet dinners with friends and quiet evenings trying to forget just how alone she was, she'd stepped into a world of chaos.

All she wanted to do was step out of it again.

And not with Jackson's hand around her arm, his fingers a warm reminder of what she'd lost when Matt and Joseph had been taken away from her.

"Ready to get out of here, buddy?" Jackson asked, releasing her elbow as he took Samuel's hand and helped him to his feet.

Samuel nodded, but he seemed too tired to speak, his eyes glassy from fever.

"We'll go to the house, get some medicine in you. Maybe a little something to eat," Raina told him, her voice tighter than she wanted it to be.

"I'm not hungry," he protested weakly, but she still planned to make him some soup, maybe a piece of toast.

"You'll be hungry once that fever goes down," Jackson commented, holding the door open so they could walk outside. "You'll probably eat half the house."

"I can't eat a house," Samuel sounded more confused than amused, but he edged away from Raina and moved closer to Jackson.

She felt like a third wheel as the two discussed how much a healthy kid could eat. She tried not to let it bother her.

Rays of sunlight streamed over distant mountains and gleamed on the hood of Andrew's squad car. He waved, motioning them over. "I'm about done here. Anything else you want to add to what you told me?"

He eyed Jackson, looking as if he thought there might be more information to be had. That was the way Andrew had been for as long as Raina had known him—driven, serious and devoted to the law.

"Actually," Jackson replied, "there was someone in the church who might have seen the Jeep and its driver."

He explained briefly while Raina and Stella helped Samuel back into the SUV. Raina was about to slide in beside him when Andrew touched her shoulder.

"Hold on a second, Rain," he said quietly, and she paused, her hand on the hood of the vehicle, her back to Andrew. "I found something in the woods. I think you need to see it."

A crisp breeze blew dead leaves across the pavement. She watched as they skittered toward the SUV, refusing to turn, because she was afraid of what she'd see in Andrew's eyes.

"Rain?" he said again, and she knew she couldn't avoid it.

She turned, cold air bathing cheeks that suddenly felt too hot and too tight. "What is it?"

He hesitated. A sure sign that whatever he had to show her was as horrible as she'd thought it would be. She knew Andrew well, knew him enough to know that hesitation meant worry and worry meant things were bad.

Destiny's brother had spent most of the time Raina was growing up teasing her. After she'd married Matt, he'd stayed close, forming as strong a bond with him as he had with Raina. He'd responded to the accident that killed Matt and Joseph, and he'd been the one to tell Raina that Matt had died at the scene. He'd been at her side when the doctors declared Joseph brain-dead. He knew what she'd been through, and he'd never have wanted to add to it.

She had a feeling he was going to.

"Whatever it is, just show me," she demanded, her voice hoarse with fear.

She hated that, hated that Stella was standing on the other side of the SUV, watching with curiosity. Hated that Jackson's eyes were filled with pity.

"I left it where it was until I could bring in an evidence team, but I have a picture. I want to get your take on it." He was all business, his tone brusque just the way it usually was when he was working.

But he watched her with that steady gaze, that sorrowful look that she'd only ever seen one other time.

She didn't want to see the picture.

She didn't want to know what he'd found.

Because she was afraid that whatever it was would change everything, that it would turn her life upside down, make her question everything she believed, make her want to turn the hands of time back.

Just like four years ago.

Just like the day she'd lost everything.

Andrew reached into his pocket and pulled out a camera. He scrolled through a couple of photos and frowned. "Here it is."

She took the camera, her hands steady despite the fact that her entire body seemed to be shaking. The image on the screen was clear. Wet ground, bright-colored leaves strewn around. That wasn't the focus of the picture, though. A stuffed dog was. Fluffy and blue. About twelve inches high. Muddy and wet, but obviously well loved by a child, its ears ratty, its fur threadbare in a few places. She knew that if she could lift the dog out of the camera and study it closely, she'd be able to see that one eye was missing and that its tail had almost no fur. She thought that if she could hold it close to her nose, she'd still be able to smell baby powder and shampoo on it.

Her eyes burned, her chest so tight and heavy she didn't think she'd ever breathe again.

"It looks like the dog I gave Joseph that day we all went to the county fair together. Remember?" Andrew prodded.

Remember?

She couldn't forget. Not any second of any minute of the short time she'd had with her son. If she let herself, she'd lie in bed at night, remembering his laughter, his chubby toddler belly and happy blue eyes.

She *never* let herself.

And she didn't want this…*reminder*.

She thrust the camera back into Andrew's hands and turned on her heels, walking away from him and from Jackson. Walking past the SUV and Stella, leaving Samuel right where he was. Walking faster and faster until her feet were flying and her breath was heaving, and she was running so fast her legs ached and her lungs hurt, and the tears were streaming down her face.

And still, she couldn't outrun her sorrow.

FOUR

Footsteps pounded behind her, but she didn't stop. She knew the way home. Just a mile to the main road, a half mile from there to the dirt road and another mile to the house. She'd run it many times in the past few years, so many times she thought she might have worn potholes into the pavement.

"You can't run forever," Jackson said, his voice and breath so even he might have been walking.

Her breathing was frantic, her lungs burning from cold air, from anger, from sorrow, from all the emotions that stuffed dog had made her feel.

It couldn't be Joseph's.

Could it?

Jackson grabbed her hand, forcing her to slow down to a walk. She could have pulled away. His grip was loose, his touch light.

She let her hand lie where it was, the warmth of his palm seeping into her cold skin. He didn't speak again, and she didn't.

Ahead, the sun peeked over the trees, bright gold rimmed with pink. The beginning of a new day, and she had another little boy to take care of. One who hadn't ever had a blue stuffed dog won at a local fair. Her breath caught, the tears that had been sliding down her face pooling in her throat and chest and heart.

An SUV pulled up beside them, and Jackson opened the back door. Raina slid into place beside Samuel, turning her face away because she didn't want him to know she'd been crying. He'd seen too much sorrow in his life. She didn't want to bring any more into it. She'd brought him to the United States because he'd needed more medical help than he'd been getting. She didn't want to add to his burdens or create more trouble for him.

To her surprise, he reached for her hand, his fingers hot from fever as he patted her knuckles. He didn't speak, and she couldn't speak.

"Officer Wallace said he's going to stop by your place after the evidence team arrives at the scene." Stella broke the silence, not a hint of sympathy in her voice. "I told him I'd give you the message. Here's one from me. The next time you want to go running off, don't."

"I apologize. I shouldn't have left you with Samuel," she managed to say.

"You think that's what this is about?" Stella glared into the rearview mirror. "Me not wanting to babysit the kid? I've got news for you, sister. Someone was in the woods with you this morning. That person fired a shot that could have taken you out like that." She snapped her fingers.

"He's long gone," Raina pointed out, tears drying on her cheeks, some of the shock of seeing the stuffed dog fading away.

Maybe that's what Stella had hoped for.

"You can't know that. The woods are pretty dense,

and it would be easy for someone to hide in them," Stella pointed out.

"Jackson saw him drive away." And Raina couldn't imagine that the guy would have wanted to hang around. Not with the police there.

"In a Jeep with a flat tire," Jackson broke in. "He might have pulled off the road and run into the woods. Anything is possible, Raina, and Stella is right, you need to be more careful."

If she hadn't seen the photo of the stuffed dog, she might have argued that the man in the woods had been a random stranger, someone who'd been as surprised by her as she had been by him, but the dog…

Thinking about it made her stomach churn and her throat ache. Had the dog been left there for her to find?

If so, by whom?

And why?

"The dog was your son's," Jackson said. Not a question, but she nodded anyway. "When was the last time you saw it?"

"A few weeks ago." Destiny had helped her clean out Joseph's room. They'd packed up all the things that had been sitting in the closet and the toy chest—little boy things that needed to be replaced with things a ten-year-old would enjoy.

She'd felt ready to let go of the clothes and all the stuffed animals Joseph had loved so much, but it had still been difficult. Without Destiny's prodding, she wasn't sure she could have done it. "My friend and I cleaned out Joseph's room. The dog was with the things we packed up."

"What did you do with it?"

"My friend took it to Goodwill. I had to work." And

she hadn't had the heart to put the boxes of Joseph's things in her car and drive away with them.

"You're sure she took the dog to Goodwill?" Stella asked as they turned onto the dirt road that led to Raina's house.

"Yes. There were several boxes, and she took them all."

"Do you think it's possible your friend took the dog? Maybe as a keepsake? Something to remember your son by?"

"I don't know why she would have. If she did, she wouldn't have left it in the woods."

"You're sure about that?" Stella pulled into the driveway and turned to look over the seat. "People often do unexpected things."

"Not Destiny. She's as dependable as sunrise."

"That's what everyone says right around the time they find out their best friend or sister or husband—"

"Stella," Jackson interrupted. "How about we let the police figure things out?"

"Because your brother won't like it if we butt our noses in?"

"Because you're tired, and it's starting to show."

"What are you talking about? Since when do I ever act tired?" she demanded.

Raina got out of the SUV. Let the two of them argue about what the police should handle or not. She needed to get Samuel inside, give him something for his fever, feed him.

"Come on, Samuel," she said, offering her hand. "We're home."

"This is not home," he responded, but he allowed himself to be helped out of the car. She handed him his crutch, would have ushered him into the house, but Jackson got out of the SUV.

"I'll get his bag and walk the two of you in. I want to check the house. Make sure it's clear before we leave."

"There's no need."

"I think there is, Raina," he responded, his eyes the deep dark blue of the evening sky. She could lose herself in eyes like his, so she looked away, concentrating on the ground, on Samuel's threadbare shoes, on her own scuffed boots.

"You don't really think someone is waiting in my house, do you?" she asked.

"Probably not." Stella got out of the SUV and stretched. There were dark shadows beneath her eyes, and her clothes hung limp and wrinkled from her thin frame. She'd been traveling for nearly two days, and it showed. "But better safe than sorry. Besides, I'm in desperate need of a cup of coffee. I drove all the way from Atlanta. Much as I hate to admit that Jackson is right, I'm wrung out. A little caffeine before we head back to D.C. wouldn't be a bad thing."

"I should have thought of that," Raina admitted. "Come on in. I'll start coffee and make everyone some breakfast."

"What kind of breakfast?" Stella asked.

"Bacon? Eggs? Pancakes?"

"You're speaking my language, sister. Let's go." She hooked her arm through Raina's and dragged her toward the house.

Jackson watched them go.

He had to give Stella credit. She knew how to get what the team wanted. Whether it was a helicopter in a third world country, last minute hotel accommodations in Paris or an invitation into the home of a woman who didn't seem to think she needed protection, she managed it.

He grabbed Samuel's beat-up backpack from the SUV. No suitcase. No electronic devices. No toys. Just the one bag that probably contained everything Samuel had ever owned.

The morning had gone quiet, the sun cresting the trees and shimmering in the pristine sky. Across the street, an old house jutted up from a sparse brown yard. There were no other neighbors. Whoever had been stalking Raina through the woods would have little to deter him if he decided to break into her house.

He carried Samuel's backpack up the porch steps, scanning the front yard as he went. It was a nice piece of property set on a pretty lot. He imagined Raina and her husband had been thinking that when they'd bought it, and he couldn't help wondering what Raina thought about it now.

Jackson had read the newspaper articles. He knew that Pastor Matt Lowery had been driving his son to get ice cream when he'd plunged over an embankment. He'd been killed instantly. Raina's son had survived for three days before succumbing to his injuries.

It couldn't be easy to live in the house they'd all shared.

He knocked, then opened the door and stepped inside. The place was homey, the living room furnished with a sturdy couch and love seat, two end tables and a coffee table. A large fireplace took up most of one wall, a watercolor painting hanging above it.

Someone had painted the walls a cheery yellow and hung flowery curtains from the windows. The place wasn't cheery, though. It had the empty stagnant feel of museum air. He knew how that happened, knew what it was like when a member of a family suddenly wasn't there. His parents had tried to fill the space Charity had left, but they'd never been able to. Eventually, they'd sold the house Jackson had been raised in, downsizing to a little cottage on a couple of acres.

He followed the sound of voices through the living room and into a dining room. A doorway opened from there into the kitchen. Spacious and gleaming, it felt warmer than the other rooms. A small square table stood against one wall, the Formica top nicked with age and use. Stella sat in a chair there, a cup of coffee in her hands, exhaustion etching fine lines near the corners of her eyes. Samuel leaned against the counter, his crutch forgotten on the floor beside him. Like Stella, he looked exhausted, his eyes tracking Raina's movements as she cracked eggs into a skillet.

"There's coffee in the pot. Mugs in the cupboard next to the sink. Go ahead and pour yourself some," Raina said, glancing over her shoulder and offering a smile. "If you take cream, it's in the fridge. Sugar in that little jar on the table."

"Thanks." He grabbed a mug, poured the coffee. No cream or sugar. Just black. He needed it as much as Stella seemed to. He'd been pushing hard for the past few months, running mission after mission. If he hadn't nearly gotten himself killed in Egypt, he'd probably still be running.

"Want some help with the food?" he asked.

"No. Thanks." She turned back to the eggs, her shoulders tense, her hand shaking as she cracked another one into the skillet.

"I'm thinking you do." He leaned over her shoulder, picked a piece of shell from the pan. "Otherwise, we'll all be eating crunchy scrambled eggs."

"You cook it, and we'll be eating burnt eggs," Stella muttered.

"I don't burn food," he protested, the scent of flowers and sunshine filling his nose. At first he thought the window was open and a spring breeze was wafting in. But it wasn't spring, and the air outside was cool and moist.

Raina shifted, her hair brushing his chin, and the scents floated in the air again. Flowers. Sunshine.

"Nice shampoo," he murmured without thinking, and Raina's cheeks went three shades of red.

She ducked away, hurrying to a bright yellow refrigerator that looked as if it had been there since the 1940s. "I have bacon and sausage. Which do you prefer?"

He wasn't sure who she was asking, but Stella shook her head. "No bacon. No sausage. Not for me, anyway. And I don't think for Samuel. He looks like he's about to fall over."

"He needs to get some sleep, but I want him to eat first." Raina spooned eggs onto a plate, dropped a slice of toast onto it and set it on the table. "There you go, Samuel."

"I'm not hungry." But Samuel sat down anyway, accepting the fork that Raina handed him and digging into the food.

Hungry or not, it seemed he was going to eat.

Stella, on the other hand, shook her head when Raina offered her a plate. "I'm too tired to eat. I don't even think the coffee is going to wake me up."

"I have a couple of spare rooms," Raina said as she

scooped more eggs onto the plate. "You're welcome to use one."

"If the room in question has a bed, I'm there."

"It does." Raina buttered a second piece of toast, spread jam on top of it and set it next to the eggs. She handed the plate to Jackson, and unlike Stella, he wasn't too tired to eat.

"Thanks."

"There's no need for thanks," Raina said. "A couple of eggs and two slices of toast doesn't even come close to repaying you for what you did in Africa."

"We got paid well for that gig. You don't have to feed the guy to thank him." Stella scowled.

"Hey," Jackson protested, digging into the eggs. "If she wants to cook, let her cook."

"She doesn't. She's just doing it because she feels sorry for you."

"Why," Jackson asked, knowing he was going to regret it, "would she feel sorry for me?"

"Because you're scrawny and look like a stiff breeze could blow you over. Your own fault. If you hadn't gone and gotten yourself—"

"How about you be quiet and let me enjoy my food," he growled. The last thing he wanted to do was discuss Egypt and the mistake he'd made there. It had nearly cost him his life. Something that Chance had mentioned dozens of times since Jackson had returned home with thirty stitches in his side.

"Why? Because you don't want me to embarrass you in front of a pretty young woman?" Stella smirked.

"This isn't junior high, Stel," he said mildly. "I'm not worried about being embarrassed in front of a beautiful woman."

"I said pretty. Guess you get an upgrade, Raina," Stella quipped.

Raina didn't look amused.

She looked appalled, her cheeks blazing. "I...think I'll go change the sheets on the beds in the spare rooms."

She sprinted into a small alcove and up stairs that creaked and groaned beneath her feet.

"Not cool, Stella," he chided.

Stella didn't look at all contrite. "Sure it was. I wanted her out of here, and I got my way."

"You could have just asked for privacy."

"Probably, but I'm used to working in more subtle ways." She rubbed the back of her neck and yawned. "What do you think, Jack? Are we going to be here more than a few hours?"

"Why are you asking?"

"Nothing that needs immediate discussion."

"Then why ask at all?"

"Because a girl likes to know what she's got on her agenda. If we're staying until we take a nap and regain some pep, that's one thing. If we stay for a couple of days—" she shrugged "—I need to rearrange my schedule."

"You don't have any missions. Not for the next week or two." Like Jackson, Stella was going on a forced vacation. Chance's idea. He'd insisted they both needed time to renew.

He was probably right, but it wasn't something Jackson planned to admit. Not to his brother, anyway.

"What's your point, Jack?"

"That your schedule is probably as empty as mine is."

"You're assuming that I don't have a social life, and you're assuming wrong." She tossed nonexistent locks of hair over her shoulder and probably would have made a show of marching from the room, but her gaze dropped to Samuel.

He'd managed to eat half the eggs and a few bites of toast, but his head was drooping. His eyes closed.

"He's about to face-plant in the eggs," she commented. "You keep him from doing that, and I'll go ask Raina where he's going to be sleeping."

She left the room but didn't head upstairs.

Apparently, she had something else to do. A phone call to make? He could hear her talking to someone, and he was curious to know who. Every member of HEART was family, and in his family, one person's business was every person's business.

He'd have followed her, gotten close enough to eavesdrop, if he hadn't had Samuel to contend with. The kid was drifting off again, his head dropping closer to the plate and the eggs that were still on it.

He eased the boy up, pressed the fork back into his hand.

"You need to eat more," he encouraged, his head cocked to the side as he strained to hear what Stella was saying.

No luck with that. The walls of the old house were thick and he couldn't hear anything but faint mumblings and the soft creak of the floor above his head.

"I've been had, Samuel," he said, dropping into the chair beside the young boy.

Samuel nodded, his eyes glassy and vague.

"Stella is a wily one," he continued, hoping to keep Samuel awake.

"What is wily?" Samuel mumbled through a mouthful of eggs.

"Smart. Sneaky."

Samuel shrugged, his eyelids drooping as he shoved another bite of eggs into his mouth. "I like Stella."

"Everyone likes Stella, but that doesn't mean she's not a manipulative piece of work."

"Mmm-hmm," Samuel responded, and then the fork dropped from his hand, his eyes closed and Jackson just managed to catch him before the face-plant Stella had predicted came true.

FIVE

An hour later, and everyone had been tucked away into his or her own bedroom. Jackson knew he should try to sleep, but he felt wound-up and on edge. Too much coffee and too many eggs. Not to mention the third piece of toast Raina had made him after she'd gotten Samuel into bed.

Homemade bread and homemade raspberry jam. Breakfast had been the best he'd eaten in months. Maybe even years. That didn't say much about the quality of Jackson's culinary skills. Not that he spent all that much time in his D.C. apartment. When he was there, he didn't cook. He ate out. Sometimes alone, sometimes with one of his siblings. Sometimes with a date.

Dates had been few and far between lately. He'd been too busy. Always busy. That's what his sister Trinity said. Of course, she'd been trying to get him to take some time off work so that she could step into the company as a search-and-rescue team member, rather than as office help.

Wasn't going to happen. Not in Jackson's lifetime, anyway. He'd already lost his older sister. He had no intention of losing his younger one.

He rubbed the back of his neck and glanced around the small room Raina had escorted him to. Stella's was across a narrow hall. She'd closed the door the minute she'd stepped inside it. Unless he missed his guess, she was already in bed.

His cell phone rang, but he ignored it. Chance was the only one who'd be calling at six in the morning, and Jackson wasn't in the mood for another lecture. He kicked off his shoes and stretched out on the narrow twin bed. Not the most comfortable sleeping arrangement for a six-two, one-hundred-ninety-pound guy, but he'd slept on a lot worse.

The house settled around him, sunlight glimmering at the edges of the thick shade that covered the room's lone window. A few creaks and groans of old wood joists and Raina's house drifted into silence. He tried to let himself drift along with it, but he was wound up tight, thoughts of his run through the woods filling his head. He could picture the Jeep clearly, but he couldn't change the fact that he hadn't seen the driver.

He wanted another chance at it, but he had a feeling the cops were going to find the Jeep abandoned somewhere, the driver long gone. If they were fortunate, there'd be evidence to lead them to the perpetrator. If not, the guy who'd stalked Raina through the woods might return to continue whatever game he'd been playing.

And Jackson had no doubt it had been a game.

The woods were thick enough and far enough from help that Raina had made an easy target. If the perp had wanted to kill her, he could have done so. Easily. The thought didn't sit well, and Jackson got up, walking to the window and opening the shade.

He had a perfect view of the front yard and the road that wound close to the property. Beyond it was the neighbor's house and beyond that thick woods stretched along a bluff. The church had to be at the top of the rise. He couldn't see it from the house, but he figured it was an easy mile and a half walk through the woods. Probably on the path he'd found.

A noise drifted into the quiet—water running, the soft clank of dishes. He didn't think about what he was doing or why, just opened the door and walked to what had probably once been servants' stairs. The walls were covered with peeling flowered paper. Raina had apologized as she'd led the way to the attic, but Jackson had seen nothing worth apologizing for. The old house had character and charm. Unlike his modern D.C. apartment, it was filled with the stories that had been lived out in it. A little dust, a little peeling wallpaper, those things were to be expected.

He walked down the stairs, wincing as they creaked. The water was still running as he walked into the kitchen. Raina stood with her back to the stairwell, her hands deep in a suds-filled sink.

"Want some help?" he asked.

She jumped and spun toward him, suds flying across the room and splattering his shirt and face.

"Oh, my gosh! I'm so sorry!" She hurried toward him, swiping at his face and shirt with a dish towel. "I didn't hear you coming."

The scent of flowers and sunshine drifted in the air, her soft hair tickling his chin the same way it had done before. His stomach clenched, every nerve in his body jumping to life. Maybe Trinity was right. Maybe his life had become too busy, his schedule too limited by endless missions. Based on his reaction to Raina, he'd say he needed to get out more, spend a few pleasant evenings with a pleasant woman.

One who did not look as though she was going to break if Jackson wasn't careful with her.

"It's okay," he muttered, taking the cloth from Raina's hand and putting a few feet of distance between them. "I've been covered with worse."

"Still...dirty dish water?" She shook her head, her cheeks pink, a smile hovering at the corner of her lips. It changed her face, turned all the angles soft, filled in the hollows beneath her cheeks. Made her look like the woman he'd seen in the photo at the church. Young and happy and filled with enthusiasm for life.

She was beautiful. More so than she probably knew.

And he probably shouldn't be noticing, but he was.

"It's better than mud. Or spit." He handed back the dishcloth. "I've had those and a few other things that I won't mention splattered on my face."

"Maybe I should send you home with a backpack full of dishcloths," she joked, turning back to the sink and plunging her hands back into the water. She'd changed into a soft black T-shirt and faded blue sweatpants that were baggy enough and long enough to have been her husband's.

"And, maybe, *you* should sit down and take a breather. I'll take over."

"Washing dishes isn't the kind of job a person needs a breather from, but if you want..." She dug a clean cloth from a drawer and handed it to him. "You can dry. The plates go in the cupboard to the left of the stove. Utensils—"

"In the drawer beneath it?"

"Yes." She didn't look up from the pan she was scrubbing. Jackson had the distinct impression that she wasn't comfortable having him beside her, but she didn't comment further as he lifted a bright yellow plate from the drainer and dried it.

If she'd had her way, they probably would have finished the job in silence, but Jackson had some questions he wanted to ask, some things he needed to know. In a few hours, he and Stella would head back to D.C., and Raina and Samuel would be on their own, sitting ducks in Raina's little house in the middle of the woods.

He frowned, sliding the plate into the cupboard and grabbing another. "You've got a pretty piece of property out here, Raina," he commented, hoping to open up the line of communication, maybe make her a little more comfortable.

"You mean secluded?" She met his eyes. "That's what Matt liked about it."

"Matt was your husband?"

"I think you know he was."

He didn't deny it, and she sighed, grabbing a couple of mugs from a cupboard and filling both with coffee. She didn't offer, just handed him the cup and then sat at the table. "We're probably both going to need more caffeine for this conversation."

"I'm already pretty wired, but thanks." He set the cup on the counter and dried a small handful of utensils.

"Do you like the seclusion?" he asked, eying the backyard beyond the kitchen window. He could imagine living in a place like this one. Set apart from the hectic pace of D.C., it seemed like exactly the sort of place he'd want to raise a family in. If he were going to have a family.

Right now, that was off the table.

He didn't have the time. His relationship with Amanda had proven that. If she hadn't broken things off three months before their wedding, they'd be living unhappily ever after, her constant frustration with his travel stealing any joy they might have found when he was home.

"Sometimes," she responded. "Other times, it's lonely."

"Have you considered moving?"

"Yes. Hundreds of times."

"But you're still here," he pointed out, carrying his mug to the table and taking the seat beside her.

"Selling a property that's out in the middle of nowhere isn't as easy as buying one. Even if it were, I'm still not sure I'm ready to leave. There are a lot of memories here." She fingered a scratch in the Formica. "I'd feel like I was letting those go if I walked away." She dug at the scratch, her short fingernail bending. In another minute, it would rip, but she didn't seem to care.

He covered her hand, gently stopping its movements.

She stiffened, looked straight into his eyes. "What?" she asked as if he had said something.

"The memories aren't in the place."

"That's easy to say, Jackson. If you've never lost someone you loved."

"You're making assumptions, Raina. That's never a good thing."

"I'm just stating a fact. Unless a person has experienced what I have—"

"My sister was kidnapped in Cambodia eight years ago," he cut her off. "She hasn't been recovered. My folks sold the house we all grew up in because they couldn't stand to live in it after she was gone. That didn't help ease their grief. Every Christmas they buy her a gift and put it in their spare bedroom. They do the same on her birthday. You can't walk in that room without seeing what was lost or feeling every memory they have of her."

"I'm sorry," Raina said, turning her hand so that she could squeeze Jackson's. She'd been washing dishes, feeling sorry for herself, and she'd allowed that to color their conversation.

"For what?" he asked, his fingers twining through hers, his skin rough and warm. Her heart ached at the contact, all the memories she'd been reliving as she'd stared out into the backyard fading as she looked into his dark blue eyes.

"For what happened to your sister. And for making assumptions. You're right. That's never a good idea." She eased her hand from his, grabbed cream from the fridge. She didn't need it, but she poured some into her coffee. Anything to keep from looking into his eyes again.

"You're forgiven," he responded, that deep Southern drawl as warm as his hand had been.

She shivered, staring into the coffee cup as if it could offer some answer to the reason why her heart was galloping in her chest.

"Cold?" he asked.

Scared, she wanted to respond.

Of you and the way you make me feel.

"No. Just…tired. It was a long night."

"A long six months, I'd say," he commented. "It was quite a fight to get Samuel here."

"That's true, but it will be worth it if he regains his health. This is the best place for him to do that."

"I'm glad you think so. There are plenty of people

who would have sent money for his care and left him right where he was."

"He'd have died there, Jackson. I couldn't live with that. Although, right at this moment, I think he'd be happier if I could have."

Much happier.

Samuel hadn't said a word to her when she'd brought him to his room, had seemed angry when she'd tried to help him into cotton pajamas. He'd brushed her hands away, turned his back to her. She'd been too tired to respond with anything other than "Sleep well."

"He's sick and exhausted and probably a good bit of scared. Don't base your judgment of how this year is going to play out on today or even tomorrow."

"I'm not," she said. "I won't."

But she couldn't say it hadn't bothered her.

She'd given him Joseph's room, and she'd wanted him to feel at home in it. Otherwise, what was the point of cleaning out the drawers and the closet, packing up the boxes, moving out all of the things that had once belonged to her son?

"Andrew never showed up," she commented, wanting to change the subject and her focus. "I wonder if the evidence team found something else."

"I was wondering the same. I'm hoping they've got the Jeep. That seems to be the key to finding our perpetrator." He took a sip of coffee, eying her over the rim of the mug. "Have you spent any time thinking about what I said?"

"You've said a lot, Jackson. Exactly what should I be thinking about?"

He chuckled, setting the mug on the counter and unwrapping the loaf of bread she'd made the previous day.

She'd cut it into thin slices, and he took one, opened the fridge and grabbed the raspberry jam. "I guess I need to be more clear," he responded as he slathered the bread with jam. "Have you thought of anyone who might have a bone to pick with you? Anyone who might think it's funny to scare you?"

"Like I told you, there's no one."

"There's someone, Raina, and he definitely wanted you to know about him.

"I know." How could she not? She'd seen the guy standing in the trees, his face hidden, his eyes glittering. She shuddered, swiping sweaty palms across the sweats she'd saved when she'd cleaned out Matt's drawers and given away his clothes. They were old and worn, the fabric soft with time. She should have thrown them out, but she just kept washing them and shoving them back in her pajama drawer.

"Then maybe you can spend a little more time trying to figure out who it might be," he suggested. He bit into the bread, closed his eyes. "This is the best jam I've ever had, but if you tell Grandma Ruth I said it, I'll deny every word."

"Are you afraid she'll disown you?"

"I'm afraid she'll smack me upside the head with her frypan."

The comment surprised a laugh out of her.

"That's better," he said, running a knuckle along her cheek.

Her breath caught, her heart jerking hard. "What?"

"You laughing. You should do it more often, Raina. It's good for the soul."

"What I should probably do is get some rest," she responded, moving away because standing close to Jackson wasn't conducive to clear thinking. "As soon as Samuel wakes up, I'm taking him to the clinic. He has an infection that needs to be treated."

"That's what Stella said," he replied before she could make an excuse and leave the kitchen. She wanted to go, because the last time she'd been in the kitchen alone with a man, the man had been Matt.

"She's a nurse, right?" That's what Raina had been told when she'd contacted HEART and asked if someone there would be willing to escort Samuel to the United States. Two days later, she'd gotten a call from the owner and CEO, Chance Miller. He'd said they'd be happy to help and that they had a nurse on staff who'd be perfect for the job.

Raina hadn't realized the nurse was the woman she'd met in Africa until a few weeks later.

Not that it would have mattered.

She hadn't wanted Samuel to travel alone. Even if she had, the airline wouldn't allow it. He was still sick, still fragile, and *she* was too much of a chicken to step foot on African soil again. Hiring someone was the only option, and the people at HEART already knew the situation, knew Samuel, knew what he'd been through and what he needed.

"She was a navy nurse for a few years before she joined the team." Jackson replied. "You two probably have a lot in common."

"I doubt it. I've spent most of my life in River Valley." Except for college and the mission trip to Kenya, she'd never considered going anywhere else.

"You were an emergency room nurse here," he pointed out.

"I was. Now I work at Moreland Medical Center."

"Owned by Dr. Kent Moreland, right? He spearheaded the mission team you were part of in Kenya."

"You know a lot more about my life than I know about yours. I'm not very comfortable with that." She leaned her hip against the counter, looked straight into his face. He needed to shave. Or maybe not. The stubble on his jaw added to his rugged good looks.

She blushed, but didn't shift her gaze.

"Ask me any question you want to about my life, and I'll answer," he offered, not even a hint of humor in his eyes.

"Why are you here? I thought Stella was escorting Samuel alone," she asked, because she didn't want to ask him anything personal. She didn't want to know if he had a wife, kids, a family that was waiting for him when he returned home.

Or maybe she did and just didn't want to admit it to herself.

He raised an eyebrow. "Playing chicken, Raina?"

"What's that supposed to mean?"

"That you could have asked me anything, and that's a pretty lame choice."

"Okay. Fine. What is your family like?"

"Big. I have three brothers and two sisters. One of them is missing, but I already told you about that."

"Is that why you and your brother founded HEART?"

"That would be exactly why." He moved close, his broad shoulders blocking her view of the room, his gaze steady. "Now it's my turn."

"I didn't know we were taking turns."

"You do now." He tucked a strand of hair behind her ear, his fingers trailing along her jaw. "It's been four years since your husband died. Why are you still wearing his sweats?"

The question jolted her from the moment, from whatever strange spell Jackson was weaving. "That's a really personal question."

"I thought the rule was that we could ask anything."

"No rules, because this isn't a game," she snapped, more embarrassed than angry. It had been four years, and that did seem like a long time to be wearing her deceased husband's sweats. "But I'll answer your question, and then I'm going to my room to get some rest. I'm wearing the sweats because they're comfortable and because they remind me of Matt. If that's a crime—"

"I don't recall saying that it was," he cut in gently. "I was just curious."

"Why?"

"Because I want to know just how in love with your husband you still are, Raina."

"I—"

The doorbell rang, cutting off whatever response she might have given. It was for the best. She had no idea what she would have said, no answer that really made sense. She loved Matt, but she wasn't in love with him. Not anymore. She was more in love with the idea of what they'd still have if he hadn't been taken from her.

She ran to the door, her heart pounding hollowly in her chest. She shouldn't care about Jackson's reasons for asking such a personal question. She shouldn't wonder why he had.

Somehow, though, she did.

SIX

Jackson followed Raina from the kitchen, sticking close as she hurried to the front door. It was early for a visitor. At least in Jackson's world it was. Raina didn't seem bothered by it. She peered through the peephole, her husband's sweats skimming over narrow hips and thin legs. He shouldn't have asked about the pants, but he'd wanted to know. He'd spent the past six months trying to get Raina out of his head. He'd failed. He was still trying to figure out why. He'd blame that on his lapse of judgment and forget about the way his heart softened every time he looked into her violet eyes.

"Kent!" Raina exclaimed, unlocking the door and pulling it open. "What are you doing here?"

"Since you wouldn't let me come to the airport with you, I spent half the night awake, worrying about Samuel." A tall, lanky man stepped into the house, his dark slacks and white dress shirt perfectly pressed, his shoes polished to a high gleam. Jackson had seen him before in much worse circumstances—a few weeks' worth of beard on his emaciated face, his eyes burning bright with fever. Dr. Kent Moreland had recovered well from his time in the Sudanese insurgent camp, his face filling out, his smooth-shaven jaw and cheeks nicely tanned. He looked as though he spent a fair amount of time in the gym and probably even more on the golf course. Not that it was any of Jackson's business or concern.

"I didn't go to the airport, either, so you didn't miss out on much," Raina responded, brushing a hand over her T-shirt and sweats.

"No?" Kent's gaze jumped to Jackson, and he frowned. "I didn't realize you had a guest. I guess that's his SUV parked in your driveway?"

"I have guests. This is Jackson Miller from HEART. He and his coworker brought Samuel here. The ice storm delayed the flight, so they drove," Raina offered. If she felt uncomfortable, it didn't show.

The doctor, on the other hand, looked fit to be tied, his dark eyes flashing with what could have been irritation, judgment or both.

"I see," Kent said. "I wish I would have known that. I'd have come by earlier."

"It's already pretty early," Jackson pointed out.

Kent eyed him for a moment, his gaze hard. Jackson thought he'd say something sarcastic. Instead, his expression changed, the irritation in his eyes fading away.

"True." He smiled. "I was on my way to work. Sometimes I forget the rest of the world isn't filled with morning people. I'm Dr. Kent Moreland."

He offered a hand, and Jackson clasped it, not convinced that the change in attitude was sincere. "I remember. We met on a helicopter about six months ago."

Kent stilled, his dark brown eyes settling more intently on Jackson's face. "You were in Africa?"

"Yes."

"I wish I could say *I* remember *you*. When it comes

to my time in Africa, things are a little fuzzy around the edges." He sat on the couch, his legs stretched out and crossed at the ankles, his muscles relaxed. From the look of things, he'd been there dozens of times before. Something about that bothered Jackson, but he refused to acknowledge the reason.

"I'm not surprised. You were out of it when we found you," he offered, and Kent nodded.

"I'd say I was within twenty-four hours of dying when your team arrived. I owe you guys a lot."

"We were paid for what we did," he responded. It sounded cold. He didn't mean it to.

The fact was, HEART took on clients who could pay and those who could not. Cases were decided on an individual basis, discussed as a team and agreed on as a team. Money was never the biggest factor to consider. Family was. If HEART could bring someone home, reunite loved ones, make one less person suffer loss… they'd do it. No matter what the cost.

"I know, but I'm still grateful. If not for HEART, Raina and I would have ended up like the rest of the mission team."

Dead, you mean? Jackson wanted to ask, because Kent seemed almost too nonchalant about what had happened to the other doctors and nurses.

Eight people gone, their lives ended by men who valued nothing but their own agenda. Did the doctor feel any sorrow over that or was he just relieved to be one of the survivors?

That was a question Jackson would never ask, but he was thinking it as Raina settled onto the edge of the love seat and smiled in his direction.

That smile did something to him. Made his heart jerk

to attention, reminded him that being a bachelor hadn't always been part of his life plan.

"Kent is right. I think with all the excitement of last night, I forgot to tell you and Stella how thankful I am for what HEART did," she said quietly. There was no mistaking the sincerity in her voice or the sorrow in her eyes. She felt the loss. Even if Kent didn't.

Jackson felt it, too. HEART had hoped to bring everyone out of the insurgent camp alive. They hadn't been able to, but at least the families who'd been waiting and praying and hoping had closure. He tried to take comfort in that.

"I wish we could have done more," he responded honestly.

"From the reports I've read, everyone else on the team had been dead for at least twenty-four hours before you arrived. There was nothing you could have done for them," Kent said, his eyes on Raina, a frown line carved deep between his brows. "What kind of excitement did you have last night?"

"Excitement might have been an overstatement. It was just a little…drama."

"With Samuel? I was worried that would happen. He lived most of his life as a child soldier, and there's no way—"

"No, not with Samuel," Raina cut him off. "Someone was hanging around outside my house before Samuel got here. I had to call the police."

She didn't mention her run through the woods or the shots that had been fired at her.

"Who was it?" Kent demanded.

"I don't know, but the police are going to try to find out."

"They better find out soon," Kent muttered. "I've never liked the idea of you being out here alone. Now I like it even less. Maybe you should move into town. I have that rental property on Main Street. You and Samuel could stay there."

"I appreciate the offer, Kent, but I'll be fine."

"It's not just you anymore, Raina. It's a ten-year-old boy who's been through the wringer. He needs stability and security. Not excitement and danger."

"He needs to get well, and he will," Raina responded.

"Not if some creep breaks into your place and—"

"No one is going to break in," Raina assured him. "The police have a witness and they should be able to find the guy quickly. In the meantime, I'll keep the windows locked and the door bolted."

"A witness? Your neighbor, you mean? Because you said Luke's memory seems to be going. I doubt he'll be able to give the police many details."

"His name is Larry. Not Luke," Raina said. "And he's not the witness. Bu—"

"Raina." Jackson put a hand on her shoulder. "I'm not sure the police would want that information to be public."

Kent frowned. "No worries, Jackson. I'm not going to tell anyone."

"I'm sure you won't, but I think we should let the police decide whether or not the information should be given out." Besides, he was getting a little tired of the doctor, and he was ready to send him on his way.

"I can probably guess," Kent persisted. "There's only one person I know of who wanders around near here. Butch Hendricks? Seeing as how he's usually drunk as a skunk, I don't think his testimony will hold much weight."

"Maybe not. You can ask Andrew Wallace about it, if you want to. He was the responding officer."

"I think I will. I saw him on my way here. He and a couple of other officers were taking photos of an old Jeep that was stuck on the side of the road."

Jackson's pulse leaped at the words. "What color was the Jeep?"

"Blue? Black? I think it had been in an accident. One of the tires was flat as a pancake and the front was dented."

"Where did you see them?" Raina asked, her gaze on Jackson. He could see hope blazing from the depth of her gaze, and he wanted to tell her not to get too excited. Finding the Jeep didn't mean finding the perpetrator. It was a start, though, and that was something to be thankful for.

"Three miles away from here. On Highway 6."

"That's the local road that runs between here and town," Raina explained, and Jackson nodded.

"What?" Kent glanced from one to the other, his gaze settling on Jackson. "Is there something I should know?"

"Ask Officer Wallace. He'll give you whatever information he thinks is necessary." From Jackson's past experience dealing with law enforcement, he'd guess that would be next to nothing.

He kept that thought to himself as Raina stood, smoothing her T-shirt. "You'd probably better do that after your workday ends, Kent. Speaking of which, if you don't leave now, you'll be late."

"Are you kicking me out, Raina?" Kent teased. "Because something like that could really hurt a guy's feelings."

"I'm not kicking you out. I'm kicking you to your office, because I have to get some rest before I bring Samuel to see you," she responded lightly, pulling the door open and ushering Kent outside.

Jackson followed. Mostly because he was curious about the two of them. Were they a couple? Raina didn't seem to think so, but Jackson had the distinct impression that the doctor felt differently.

"My schedule is full, but I'll clear a spot for him. Just call when you're on your way."

"I appreciate it, Kent."

"It's my pleasure." He dropped a hand to her shoulder and smiled. "We made it through worse together. We'll make it through this."

Together?

Obviously, the doctor had a major thing for Raina.

Did she know it?

Jackson watched as she slid away from Kent's hand, crossed her arms over her chest. Not the body language of someone who felt comfortable and at ease with a situation. "Samuel will be fine. Thanks for stopping by, Kent. I'll see you in a couple of hours."

"See you in a few hours," Kent called as he walked down the porch steps.

Raina wanted to walk back inside and close the door, but she didn't want to be rude. Good manners had been bred into her, and she waited on the porch, waving as Kent got into his Corvette.

Jackson stood beside her, and she tried not to notice the warmth of his arm pressed close to hers or the way the sunlight added fiery strands to his dark hair. She tried not to think about the question he'd asked or about the way he'd looked when he'd said he wanted to know if she was still in love with Matt.

"So," he asked as Kent pulled away, "want to tell me about you and the good doctor?"

"There's nothing to tell," she responded truthfully.

"Does he know that?" Jackson slid an arm around her waist and led her back into the house.

"Of course he does," she responded, stepping away from his warmth and almost wishing that she didn't have to. It had been a long time since a man had put his arm around her waist. A long time since she'd wanted one to.

She wasn't sure what to think about that, and she was too tired to figure it out.

"You're sure?"

"I work for him, Jackson. There's no way we could have a relationship. Even if one of us wanted to. Which we don't."

"*You* don't."

"Neither of us do," she reiterated. Although, she wasn't quite sure that was true. The fact was, Kent had asked her out a couple of times in the past few years. She'd figured that he was bored and that he'd thought she was, too. She'd said no every time, and he hadn't seemed at all heartbroken.

"I think he might say something different, if I asked him," Jackson commented casually, but there was nothing casual about the look in his eyes.

"Why would you?"

"Because someone is stalking you, and stalkers are generally not strangers. If he has a thing for you, maybe he's not willing to accept that you don't return his feelings."

She laughed. She couldn't help it.

Kent? A stalker?

He had dozens of women begging for his time and attention. He certainly didn't need her.

"What's so funny?" Jackson asked, crossing his arms over his chest, his biceps bulging beneath the sleeves of his dark T-shirt.

Was it her fault if she noticed?

She glanced away, surprised and a little appalled by just how attracted she was to him.

"The idea that Kent would be desperate enough to stalk someone," she mumbled, hoping Jackson didn't notice how red her cheeks had gotten. "He's out with a different woman every weekend."

"That means just about nothing, Raina. Stalkers are mentally ill. They don't act like typical, healthy individuals."

He had a point. A good one.

"Kent is a doctor."

"Meaning?"

"He's not mentally ill."

"One thing does not preclude the other, Raina."

"You're right, but I'm too tired to discuss it, so I think I'll go tuck myself into bed for a couple of hours. You should probably do the same."

She took a step away, but he snagged her hand. "You forgot something."

"I did?" Her heart thundered, her mouth went dry and every thought in her head flitted away. Because he was there, so close she could see the fine lines at the corners of his eyes, the ridged edges of the scar on his temple.

"The door?" He gestured to it, turning the lock and

then the bolt. "You did tell Kent you were going to keep things locked up tight."

"Right. I forgot."

"Forgetting isn't an option, Raina. Not until the police have a suspect in custody."

She nodded, because a hard lump had formed in her throat, and she couldn't speak past it.

Matt had never bothered with locks.

But, then, Matt had never worried that things would go wrong. He'd had the kind of trust in God that Raina had never quite been able to achieve—an all-encompassing belief that God was in control and that He would make things work out the way they should. Raina had been a Christian for so many years she didn't remember what it felt like to not be one, but compared to the deep, rich hues of Matt's faith, hers was a pencil drawing—all soft lines and gray tones.

Maybe she hadn't needed it to be more.

Until the accident, she'd been able to tackle just about any problem, handle just about any trouble. Matt had been a wonderful husband, but he'd spent a lot of time with his head bent over books and commentaries. He'd had more scripture memorized than any person Raina had ever known, but he could never seem to remember what day the car payment was due.

She'd loved him despite those things and probably because of them, but she'd been the one to hold down the fort, take care of the problems, put out the fires.

"Raina." Jackson touched her wrist, his fingers warm and just a little rough. "Are you okay?"

"Fine. Great," she lied, because she wasn't going to tell him that having him in her living room was reminding her of all the things she used to have, all the things she'd dreamed of when she'd been young and sure that she could make life work out just the way she wanted it to.

He eyed her for a moment and shook his head. "You don't look fine. As a matter of fact, you look like you've been rode hard and put up wet."

The comment surprised a laugh out of her. "I look like a tired horse?"

"You look like a beautiful woman who may need to be taken care of a little better," he responded, so sincerely her heart jerked. The hard, quick beat reminded her of shy first glances and giddy first words, of nerve-racking first dates and tender first kisses. It reminded her of dreams and hopes and yearnings.

"I take good care of myself, Jackson." She moved past him, walking to the fireplace and the oversize flower painting that Matt had hung there the first night they'd slept in the house.

"I'm sure you do," he said quietly. "Sometimes I open my mouth before I use my brain. Sorry if I offended you."

"Since when is calling a woman beautiful offensive?" She turned around, and he was still standing near the door, his arms relaxed, his expression open. She'd seen more than one side of Jackson. The tough protector, and now the easygoing boy next door. She wondered which one was really him. Wondered if maybe they both were.

He studied her for a moment, his gaze touching her hair, her cheeks, her lips.

"Never," he finally said. "But from the look on your face, I'd say I stuck my foot in something, and it wasn't anything pleasant."

That made her smile. "Not really. I'm just tired. Like

I said, I need to tuck myself into bed and get some sleep. See you in a few hours, Jackson."

She walked out of the room even though she wanted to run. Walked to her bedroom even though she wanted to race there.

She closed the door quietly, her hands shaking. She didn't turn the lock. Jackson wouldn't open the door. He wouldn't even knock on it unless there was an emergency. She should have found that comforting, but she felt empty and old as she lay down on the bed.

Above her head, floorboards creaked as Jackson returned to his room. She tried not to think about him up there as she closed her eyes and willed herself to sleep.

SEVEN

"Mommy? Where are you? Mommy!"

Joseph called to her from the darkness, and Raina tried to run toward him, but thick trees surrounded her, the branches catching at her clothes. She couldn't move, couldn't free herself.

"I'm coming!" she tried to yell, but the words came out a whisper, the sound fading away before it even had time to form.

"Mommy!" he called again, and she jerked against the tree branches, realized they weren't branches at all.

A man held her, his arms viselike and hard, his grip unyielding. She struggled against his hold, twisting until she could see a featureless face and deep holes where eyes should be.

Raina woke with a start, a scream dying on her lips.

She shoved the comforter from the bed and stood on shaky legs, her heart still thudding loudly in her ears. She thought about Joseph every day, but she hadn't had a nightmare about him in months. Now she'd woken to the sound of his voice twice in—she glanced at the clock—less than twenty-four hours.

She walked to the window, cracking it open and taking a few deep breaths of cold air.

"Just a nightmare. That's all it was," she murmured, willing her frantic heartbeat to quiet. Her words scared a couple of birds from the trees, and she watched them fly to the fence and land on one of the posts. They sat in the sunlight, enjoying the afternoon warmth. She wanted to shut the window, close the curtains and go back to bed, but Samuel was sick, and she had to get him in to see Kent. Otherwise, she might end up making a trip to the emergency room with him.

She changed quickly, sliding into jeans that were a little loose and a warm sweater that was more cozy than stylish. She wasn't out to impress anyone, but she ran a brush through her hair, applied a little blush and mascara. She didn't bother with foundation. It would take a boatload to cover the circles under her eyes or to give her complexion a healthy glow.

The house was still silent as she slipped into the hall, the quiet creak of floorboards as familiar as sunrise. She'd been hearing it for so many years, the sound barely registered. Samuel must have heard. His door opened, and he peered out, his face drawn, his eyes glassy with what looked like fear.

"Hello," Raina greeted him. "Did you sleep well?"

He nodded, his gaze jumping to a spot just beyond her shoulder and settling there. She knew what he was looking at. The family photo that hung on the wall. There'd been plenty of times when she'd thought about taking it down, but that had felt like too much of a betrayal, so she'd left it hanging.

"My family. I'm the only one left," she said.

"We are both left," he responded, his English thickly

accented but very clear. He looked so young hovering in the doorway, a crutch tucked under one arm. She wanted to touch his forehead, see if he was still hot, but she was afraid of moving too quickly and too soon, of pushing herself into his life when he'd rather be left on his own. She was afraid of trying too hard and of failing, of proving to herself and to Samuel that she really had lost her ability to mother a young boy.

"We are together now," she pointed out. "So I guess neither of us are left anymore."

He nodded solemnly, but she wasn't sure that meant he agreed.

She ran a hand over her hair, feeling unsure of herself and hating it. "So how about we go have something to eat and then I'm going to bring you to the doctor."

"No," he replied.

"No to food or no to the doctor?"

"No doctor."

"I'm sorry, Samuel, but you are going to the doctor. You have an infection, and if we don't get it healed, you won't be able to be fitted for your new leg."

"No doctor," he repeated as if he really thought he was the one who'd be making the decision about it. She supposed that made sense. He'd told hospital workers that his mother and father had been killed when he was six. He'd been making decisions for himself for a long time, surviving what most children wouldn't have.

"Samuel—"

The doorbell rang, and Samuel grabbed her hand, his eyes wide with fear.

"What it is?" he asked, and she could hear the slight tremor in his voice, feel his muscles trembling. Something in her heart went soft, the feeling similar to the one she'd had when she'd seen Joseph for the first time, his newborn baby face red from his frantic cries.

"Just the doorbell," she reassured him, gently squeezing his hand. "Someone is here for a visit. I need to go see who it is."

"I will come, too," he said stoically, and she wondered if he thought he would need to protect her from whoever stood on the other side of the door.

"It's okay. I'll be fine. You get ready for our doctor's visit."

"No doctor!" Samuel muttered under his breath, but he hopped back into his room and closed the door.

Gently.

Thank goodness.

The doorbell rang again, and she ran down the hall, peering through the peephole. Andrew stood on the front porch, uniform hat pulled low over his eyes, hands shoved in his coat pockets. He didn't look happy.

She opened the door, her stomach churning with nerves. "Andrew! What are you doing here?"

"Freezing," he replied drily. "Mind if I come in?"

"No. Of course not." She gestured for him to enter. "Is everything okay?"

"You want me to beat around the bush or just give it to you straight?"

She wanted him to tell her that nothing was wrong, that he was just checking in, making sure that she was okay. That wasn't going to happen, though. She could see it in his eyes—bad news and sorrow. "Give it to me straight."

"Butch is dead."

The words were so blunt and so unexpected she couldn't quite process them. "What?"

"Butch Hendricks. He's dead."

"I just saw him a few hours ago. He was fine." Even though he'd repeated it, she could barely comprehend that the man who'd been part of the community, who'd stood on Main and Third asking for handouts for as long as she could remember, was gone. "Are you sure it's him? Maybe—"

"Raina," Andrew interrupted. "Do you really think I'd be here telling you this if I wasn't sure?"

"I… No. What happened?" She dropped onto the couch, and he took a seat across from her.

"The medical examiner will determine that." He rested his elbows on his knees, his hands clasped together. He looked exhausted, his eyes deeply shadowed, his jaw scruffy with the beginning of a beard. He hadn't shaved, probably hadn't been home.

"You must have some idea, Andrew," she pressed. "Or you wouldn't be here."

"There was no sign of foul play, but I don't like the way this is shaping up."

"The way what is shaping up?" Jackson walked into the room, still dressed in the jeans and black T-shirt he'd been wearing the night before. Just like Andrew, he was sporting a day's worth of beard growth. It didn't make *him* look tired or worn. It made him look…masculine, rugged. Sexy.

"Miller," Andrew acknowledged with a slight nod in Jackson's direction. "We were discussing Butch Hendricks. Specifically, his death."

"What happened?" Jackson walked farther into the room, his movements lithe and powerful. Even without trying, he looked strong. Even when there was no danger, he looked like the kind of guy who could face down just about anything or anyone and come out on top.

"He died sometime early this morning. That's all I know."

"He was right as rain when he left the church. That was only six hours ago."

"A lot can happen in six hours, Miller. I think you know that. The medical examiner is working on cause of death. I'll let you know his findings once I have them."

"You don't think it was a coincidence and you don't think he died of natural causes, do you?" Jackson asked, dropping onto the sofa next to Raina.

"I'm not going to speculate."

"Sure you are. You're just not going to do it on the record."

"You want off the record?" Andrew scowled. "I'll give it to you. He either died of an overdose or was murdered."

Murdered?

Raina tensed at the word, every muscle balled up so tight she thought she'd shatter if she tried to move.

"Relax," Jackson whispered, his breath ruffling the hair near her ear. "Everything is going to be fine." He smoothed a hand up her arm, his fingers kneading the muscles in her neck.

Andrew noticed.

Of course he did.

Raina should have cared, but she didn't.

"Were you the one who found Butch?" Jackson asked, his palm resting against the corded muscles in Raina's shoulders. She was wound up tight, her eyes shadowed, her face drawn. If she'd slept at all, it hadn't been much.

"No. Another officer found him while the evidence

team was processing an abandoned blue Jeep that fit the description and photo you provided."

"Kent mentioned that you'd found the Jeep," Raina said quietly.

"I saw him drive past in that fancy sports car of his. Didn't realize he was on his way here."

"He wanted to check on Samuel," Raina said, and Andrew laughed.

"Right."

"He did," Raina protested, her hands fisting in her lap. In Jackson's opinion, she needed some of the chamomile tea Grandma Ruth was always drinking. According to Jackson's mother, it was great for calming nerves.

"Maybe, but he also came to see you. He's a good guy, Raina, and there's nothing wrong with spending some time with him."

It was Jackson's turn to tense up.

He didn't like the idea of Raina and Kent getting together. He didn't like it at all.

"Except that I don't want to spend time with him, so how about we get back to what you came here for."

"Right." Andrew sighed. "We pulled a couple of prints from the Jeep. We'll try to run them, but it was reported stolen from D.C. about a month ago. It could have been in any number of hands since then."

"D.C.?" Jackson's pulse jumped and he met Raina's eyes. "Isn't that where your friend's boyfriend lives?"

"Are you talking about Lucas Raymond?" Andrew asked, and Raina nodded.

"He's the only one I know who owns a blue Jeep."

"I hadn't thought of that, but you're right. He's been driving that thing for years." Andrew pulled a notebook from his pocket and jotted something in it.

"You're not actually going to question him? If he were going to do something like this, don't you think he'd use a different car?" Raina sounded horrified.

"Maybe. Maybe not. Criminals make mistakes all the time. This might have been his."

"Destiny will have your hide if you call him."

"Why would she?" Andrew shrugged. "They broke up two weeks ago."

"What?" Raina jumped up, and Jackson stood with her. "Why didn't she tell me?"

"You were getting ready for Samuel's arrival. She didn't want to add more to your burden."

"She's my best friend!"

"And she was trying to protect you." Andrew stood, tucked the notebook back into his pocket.

"I don't need protecting."

"Tell her, then. I'm going to the office. I want to make a few phone calls, see if Lucas was home last night. I've never really liked the guy, and I wouldn't put it past him to pull something like this in order to force himself back into Destiny's life."

"How would chasing me through the woods accomplish that?" Raina asked.

"He's a psychiatrist. Maybe he's hoping to be called in for help with the case."

"Sounds like a stretch," Jackson said, and Andrew shrugged.

"Stranger things have happened, Miller, and as far as I'm concerned everyone is a suspect until I can prove they aren't."

"Are you including me in that?" Jackson asked, following him to the front door, Raina just a few steps behind.

"According to my sources, you've been here since six this morning. Butch died sometime after that, and since you obviously weren't the one driving the Jeep that almost ran you down—" he stepped out onto the porch "—I think I can remove you from my list."

"Thanks," Jackson responded drily. "Glad to hear it."

"Now that we've gotten that cleared up, I've got to head out."

He jogged down the porch steps and got in his squad car. Jackson wanted to get in his SUV and follow. He had more questions to ask. About Butch's death, about Lucas Raymond, about the stuffed dog that had been left in the woods.

"You know what I need?" Raina asked so quietly he almost didn't hear her.

"What?" He looked into her eyes, saw the fear and anxiety there, wanted nothing more at that moment than to chase it away. "Name it, and I'll get it for you."

She cracked a smile, her eyes crinkling at the corner, a tiny dimple appearing at the corner of her mouth. "You're tempting me to ask for the moon."

"If I could, I'd wrap it in a bow and put your name on it."

"Don't be so charming, Jackson," she responded, the smile faltering but not quite disappearing. "It could get us both in trouble."

"I love trouble. Ask Stella. She'll tell you all about it."

She shook her head and sighed, hooking her arm through his and tugging him into the kitchen. "Then I guess it's a good thing for you that all I want is a cup of black coffee and three minutes with absolutely no drama."

"That," he said, taking her hand and kissing her knuckles, "can absolutely be arranged."

EIGHT

Raina got her coffee.

She even got her three minutes without any drama.

Things went downhill from there.

It started with Samuel having a major meltdown about the doctor visit and ended with an endless battle with Jackson about whether or not she needed an escort.

"I don't need you to come with me," she said for the fiftieth time as she grabbed her coat from the closet. "I don't," she repeated.

"Okay," he responded, finally conceding the point.

"I'm glad you're finally seeing it my way," she responded, but she didn't feel glad, she felt anxious and antsy.

"Why wouldn't I?" he responded, helping her into her coat and pulling the collar up around her neck, his fingers sliding against the tender flesh behind her ear. "If you want to go off unprotected with a vulnerable young boy, that's your business, and it's on your head if something happens to him."

"You're playing dirty," she accused, but he had a point, and she knew it. Samuel was her responsibility, and she couldn't risk his life because she needed a little…breathing room.

"I'll play any way I have to to keep you and Samuel safe."

"Fine. You can come," she agreed, and she didn't feel nearly as irritated about it as she probably should have.

"I'm glad you're finally seeing things my way," he said with a grin. "I'm going to check in with Stella. You get Samuel. I'll meet you back here in five."

He bounded up the stairs, and she headed down the hall, not realizing she was smiling until she reached Samuel's door.

She shook her head, exasperated with herself.

If she wasn't careful, Jackson would charm his way deeper into her life than he already had.

She shouldn't want that to happen, but there was a tiny part of her heart that didn't think she'd mind much if it did.

She knocked gently on Samuel's door. "Ready to go, Samuel?" she called.

He didn't answer, and she turned the knob, frowning when she realized it was locked. She knocked again, cold air tickling her bare toes.

Had he opened the window? "Samuel?"

Still no answer, but she could definitely feel cold air drifting under the door.

She ran back to the kitchen and out the door, rounding the corner of the house at breakneck speed, her breath catching as her worst fears were confirmed. The window was open, the room beyond empty.

"Samuel!" she shouted at the top of her lungs, pivoting to the left and right, trying to decide which direction she should go. She thought she saw a speck of color in the trees at the back edge of the property, and she raced toward it, screaming his name so loudly the sound tore from her throat.

She'd hung his coat in the closet the night before. He didn't have a hat, gloves. He didn't know the area, knew nothing about the climate. He could get lost in the woods, be stranded all night without any way to keep warm.

She raced into the trees, and it was like her nightmare, branches snagging her shirt and poking at her legs, her heart pounding frantically. She fought through the foliage, searching the trees for signs that Samuel had been there.

"Raina!" someone shouted, but she didn't have time to stop. If she didn't catch up to Samuel now, he could be lost for good.

"Raina!" Jackson grabbed her arm, yanking her to a stop. "Where do you think you're going?"

"To find Samuel." She tried to jerk away, but he didn't release his hold. "He climbed out his window and—"

"He's in the house."

"No. He's not." She yanked harder, but his fingers were firm around her biceps, the grip tight without being painful.

"He is. He came out of the bathroom as I was heading down the hall."

"Are you sure? I could have sworn I saw him running through the trees."

"Positive." His hand slipped from her arm, burrowed under her coat and rested on her waist. She could feel its heat through her cotton shirt.

"I can't lose another child," she said, the words like shards of broken glass—hard and brittle.

"You won't," he responded, pulling her close, pressing her head against his chest. She could hear his heart beating beneath her ear, and she wanted to close her eyes, pretend she was in a place where she could believe forever existed, believe that love could last, believe that her heart would never be broken.

"I'm okay," she said, but she didn't move. Her legs were too shaky, her head still filled with memories of the nightmare and with fears of what might have been if Samuel really *had* wandered away.

She took a deep breath, inhaled masculinity, soap and some indefinable scent that reminded her of safety and of home.

Her eyes burned with tears, and she forced herself to step away. "I'm sorry," she said.

"Why?"

"Because I just had a major freak-out over nothing."

"His window was open. You thought he'd run away. That's not nothing." He glanced around the copse of trees, his jaw tight, his shoulders tense.

"Is something wrong?" she asked, a niggle of fear crawling up her spine.

"Probably not."

"That's not the same as *definitely* not."

It wasn't, because Jackson wasn't sure that there *was* nothing wrong Something felt off. He could feel it in the air—a hint of danger. Even in the middle of the day, light streaming through heavy branches and boughs, the trees were thick enough for someone to hide.

He didn't like that.

Didn't like it at all.

"How about we head back to your place?" he said, avoiding Raina's comment.

"What's going on, Jackson?"

"I don't know, but I'd rather try to figure it out after I get you back inside."

"In other words, you're going to escort me to the house and then come back and look around."

"Exactly."

"What if I don't like your plan?"

"I don't think I asked your opinion."

She shook her head, short blond hair fluttering around her face. "That's not the way this is going to work."

"The way *what* is going to work?" he asked, hurrying her back toward the house. The sooner he got her there, the happier he'd be.

"This." She waved her hand around as if that answered the question. "You going off and risking your life, and me cowering in the house, waiting for you to return. That's not the kind of person I am."

"Good to know." He opened the door, lifted her off her feet and deposited her inside.

"Hey!" she protested, but he was already closing the door and texting Stella to make sure she kept everyone inside.

He searched for thirty minutes and came up empty. He should have been relieved, but he wasn't. Someone had been in the woods with them. He was almost sure of it. He walked across the yard, stood near the back door and stared out into the gnarled orchards.

"Come on," he muttered. "Show yourself."

"You talking to yourself, Jackson?" Stella yelled through the kitchen window.

Was he?

He didn't think so.

He thought someone was out there.

He just needed a little more time to find the guy.

She opened the door, dragged him into the house. "What's going on?" she demanded.

"I don't know."

"But you're planning to stick around for a while to figure it out, right?" she responded, tapping her fingers on the counter impatiently. "Which means I'm stuck on the outskirts of some Podunk little town."

"I'm escorting Raina and Samuel to the doctor. After that, I'll bring you back to D.C."

"Sure you will," she said with a sigh.

"What's that supposed to mean?"

"You don't know how to keep your nose out of things, that's what it means. You see a kid and a woman in trouble, and you think you've got to drop everything to help."

"You're just annoyed because I won't bring you home now. If you really want to get back to the city immediately, you can call—"

"Don't say it!" she barked.

"—Chance." He said his brother's name just to irritate her, because that's the way they were together.

"You're a pain, you know that, Jackson?" Stella growled. "For your information, I have plans this evening, and if we don't get out of here, I'm going to miss them."

"What plans?"

"Plans that do not include babysitting a grown woman and a kid and that do not include getting a ride back home with your brother," she hissed.

"I'll try to get you back to D.C. before sundown."

"Which means I'm either going to be here for the foreseeable future or going to have to hitchhike home," she muttered, obviously annoyed.

"I think you need some coffee."

"I think I need a new job and new friends. Maybe even a new life."

"Really?"

"I don't know. Ever since I met your brother, I've been in one mess after another. A girl doesn't always want to be covered with dirt and sweat. Sometimes she wants to wear sequins and heels."

"Stella—"

"Forget it, Jack. I probably do just need some coffee." She grabbed a mug, filled it with coffee and took a sip. "It's not very hot, but it'll do." She marched from the kitchen with her head held high, but Jackson had a feeling the things she'd said weren't just the rantings of a caffeine-deprived person.

She was right, too, and that made him feel guiltier than he wanted. In the years since she'd been part of HEART, Stella had spent more time rescuing other people's families than she had building relationships of her own. That got tiring. He knew it as well as anyone.

It was one of the reasons why he'd finally conceded the point and allowed Chance to give him a couple of weeks off.

He loved his job, but he needed more.

He needed...

What?

That was the question he couldn't ever seem to answer. Not without taking a long hard look at what he'd built. He'd gone into hostage rescue work because of Charity. He continued because it fulfilled him.

But there were times when he wanted more than his empty apartment and the quiet evenings alone. There were long days of travel when he wondered what it would be like to have someone waiting for him at the airport when he returned home.

He frowned.

Maybe Stella wasn't the only one who needed a cup of coffee.

NINE

Life was spinning out of control.

That was the conclusion Raina came to as she sat in the exam room waiting for Kent to appear. Samuel sat on the exam table, stoic and silent, his eyes flashing with unhappiness. He didn't want to be there. He'd made it abundantly clear when she'd tried to get him into his coat, hat and gloves.

Jackson had finally managed to manhandle him into the coat, but the gloves and hat were still lying on the floor at the house.

She rubbed the back of her neck, trying to think of something to say. It used to be she had no problem with conversations. As a minister's wife, she knew how to talk to young people, old people, people in their prime and people near the end of their lives. There'd never been awkward silences or moments where she struggled to think of the right thing.

Back then, she'd thought she had the answers to lots of life's toughest questions.

She didn't think she had any answers at all anymore.

"Are you sorry you came to America, Samuel?" she finally asked.

He met her eyes, let his gaze drift away again. "No."

"You seem unhappy."

"No," he repeated, and she thought she heard a slight tremor in his voice.

"Are you scared?" She sat next to him, put an arm around his stiff shoulders. It felt uncomfortable, but somehow right, too.

"Yes," he whispered, his body sagging against hers. He probably weighed fifty pounds soaking wet. She felt every bone, every muscle.

Someone knocked on the door, the soft tap nothing like Kent's usual brisk rap.

"Come in," she called.

"Hey." Jackson stepped into the room. "You guys have been in here for a while. I thought you might be hungry." He reached into his coat pocket and pulled out two wrapped muffins.

She knew they'd come from a little diner that rented space in the basement of the building. She met Destiny there for lunch every few weeks. That was the thing about her friend. No matter how busy Destiny's schedule was, she always made time for Raina. Apparently, she didn't think Raina would return the favor.

Maybe she didn't think Raina *could* return it. After all, she'd seen Raina at her worst. Seen her huddled under blankets, sobbing into the mattress, hugging piles of clothes that belonged to her husband and son.

"I need to call her," Raina said as she took the muffin Jackson offered.

"Who?"

"Destiny."

"The friend who broke up with her boyfriend and

didn't tell you?" He unwrapped the second muffin and handed it to Samuel.

"That's the one."

"You want to ask her why she didn't tell you?"

"I know why she didn't tell me. She didn't want to overwhelm me."

"Then why bring it up to her?" he asked.

"Because I want her to know I'm here for her."

"She knows."

"You've never even met her."

"I don't have to." He snagged a piece of her muffin and popped it into his mouth. "I've met you."

"What does that have to do with anything?"

"It has everything to do with it. Look what you're doing right now. You're sitting in a doctor's office with a boy you barely know. That's not what someone who isn't there for her friends does."

She shrugged. "Maybe not."

"Definitely not." He took another piece of the muffin.

"I thought this was for me," she protested, and Samuel broke off a piece of his and shoved it into her mouth.

She was so surprised, she laughed, pieces of muffin falling onto the exam table and the floor.

"What's going on in here?" Kent peered into the room, a deep frown line etched in his forehead.

"Sorry. I guess we're getting a little silly from fatigue." She used a paper towel to wipe of the crumbs and tossed the mess into the trash can.

"You know you're not supposed to have food in here," he snapped as he walked into the room.

"My fault, Kent," Jackson offered, leaning his shoulder against the wall. "They were both hungry, and I wasn't thinking about rules."

"Maybe you should next time. This is a medical clinic. Not a diner." He shook his head disapprovingly. "You should probably wash your face, Raina. It's a mess."

"Why be rude, Doc?" Jackson said, straightening to his full height and taking a step toward him.

"I'm not rude. I'm honest. Right, Raina?"

She didn't plan to agree, so she just shrugged. She knew her boss. He snapped when things didn't go the way he planned. Obviously having people eating in one of the exam rooms wasn't part of his plan.

Samuel looked up from his half-eaten muffin, cocking his head to the side and studying Raina.

"You are wrong. She is not a mess. She is very beautiful," he said solemnly, his eyes the deep black of a moonless sky. He reached out, his fingers almost brushing her cheek before his hand dropped away, and her heart shuddered with the deep need to offer him comfort, security. Love.

"Like Sari," he mumbled, blinking rapidly and shoving a piece of muffin into his mouth.

"Who is Sari?" Jackson asked before Raina could get the words past the lump in her throat.

"My sister."

He had a sister? Raina had been told he was alone in the world, that everyone in his family had died.

"Is she in the refugee camp?" she asked, wondering if there was any way she could find the girl and bring her to the United States. Samuel might adjust better if he had someone familiar with him.

"She is dead."

"I'm…sorry." It was such a lame thing to say. Something she'd heard so many times after the accident that hearing it come out of her own mouth made her feel physically sick.

"I am sorry, too." Samuel slid off the exam table, tucking the remnant of the muffin into his coat pocket. "I think the doctor is not a good doctor if he thinks you are a mess. Let us return home."

"Wait a minute, young man," Kent said, closing the door before Samuel could escape. "I didn't mean a mess in the literal sense. I just meant she had muffin crumbs on her face. They're still there, by the way," he intoned with a frown in Raina's direction.

"You're right, Doc," Jackson responded, closing in on Raina and brushing his hand across her cheeks and then her lips. Her pulse jumped, a million butterflies dancing in her stomach.

"Better?" he asked, shooting a half smile in Kent's direction.

"Much," Kent said drily. "So how about we do what we're all here for. Take a look at that leg. Hop back up here, young man." He patted the exam table.

Jackson expected Samuel to balk, but the kid seemed to have finally accepted the inevitable. He clamored back onto the table, settling in a heap of bone and fabric. Kent frowned and brushed a stray crumb from the table before unpinning the pant leg that covered Samuel's stump.

Jackson found the guy supremely annoying, his facetious manners grating. If he'd known what a bottom-dweller the doctor was, he'd have brought some milk with the muffins. Maybe a piece of fruit or two and a few dozen saltine crackers. Just to get under the guy's skin.

Chance wouldn't approve, but he wasn't there to give a lecture on it.

Jackson backed up against a wall and watched as

Moreland rolled up the pant leg that covered Samuel's stump. There were two raw wounds there. Both looked infected.

Jackson winced as Moreland swabbed both with antiseptic.

Samuel didn't move a muscle. Not even a twitch.

Raina, on the other hand, had her hands fisted so tightly the knuckles were stark white.

"Relax," he whispered, lifting one of her hands and trying to rub some blood back into it.

Moreland shot a look in their direction and frowned. "Want to come take a look at this, Raina?" he asked.

"Sure." She hurried over.

"We've got two infection sites here," Moreland said, as if it weren't obvious to anyone with eyes in his head.

"I noticed," Raina responded.

She didn't seem any more impressed with Moreland than Jackson was.

"I doubt it ever healed properly after surgery. I'm going to give him an antibiotic shot and write you out a prescription. I want to see him Monday. If things don't look better, we may have to have him admitted to the hospital."

"No hospital," Samuel said, his chin wobbling, his eyes filling with tears that surprised Jackson.

"Don't worry, sport," he said. "It's not going to come to that."

"Says who?" Moreland scoffed. "You? Because from where I'm standing that leg is getting close to needing more surgery. The likelihood that he'll end up in the hospital is pretty high."

Jackson hadn't been all that keen on the doctor when they'd met earlier. Now he liked him even less. Scaring a child who was obviously becoming distraught didn't speak well of the guy's character. "You're forgetting something, Doc," he responded. "Samuel is a tough kid, and he doesn't want to have surgery or spend more time in the hospital. He's going to take really good care of the leg."

"He's a ten-year-old boy. He has no control over the situation," Moreland said, not bothering to look up from a chart he was writing in.

"He's a smart ten-year-old, and he and I are going to make sure that leg heals up just fine. Aren't we, Samuel?"

Samuel nodded, but Moreland was still too busy writing to notice.

"You're leaving town today, aren't you, Jackson?" Moreland asked, completely ignoring the comment and offering Samuel no reassurance.

Which annoyed Jackson even more than he already was.

"Yes," Raina said.

"Maybe," Jackson responded at the same time.

Raina frowned and swiped a strand of hair from her cheek. "You have to get back to D.C.," she reminded him. "You have a job and a house and—"

"My vacation starts Monday."

"Your house—"

"A one-bedroom apartment. I don't have a dog, cat or plant that needs to be taken care of." And he wasn't in all that big of a hurry to get back to D.C. Lately, he'd been missing the slow pace of rural life. He'd almost booked a flight back home, but his parents had taken their yearly pilgrimage to Cambodia to ask for information on Charity, and there was no one at their little place in North Carolina. He could have visited Grandma Ruth, but she was on a Disney Cruise with twenty of her closest friends.

"Whatever your plans," Moreland interrupted, "I don't think you can change the course of Samuel's treatment. I'll write out the scrip and send Molly in with the antibiotic injection. Give me five minutes, okay?" He smiled at Raina and stalked out of the room.

"I think I ticked him off," Jackson commented.

"That's not hard to do." Raina touched Samuel's shoulder. "You okay?"

"Yes."

"When the nurse comes in you're going to have to have a shot of medicine. Do you know what that means?" She looked into his eyes when she spoke, her voice gentle, her expression soft.

He imagined she'd been like that with her son, and he imagined that it must have nearly killed her when she'd had to make the decision to disconnect life support and let Joseph go. There'd been a photo in one of the local papers—Raina saying goodbye to her son. The article had been about a mother's heart and organ donation, but it hadn't been able to capture the pain she must have felt as she'd made the choice.

She must have sensed his gaze. She glanced his way, offering a tentative smile. "If you want to go back to the waiting room, you can."

"Is that what you want me to do?" he responded.

"I—" Her cell phone rang, and she frowned, pulling it from her pocket. "It's Andrew. I'd better take it."

She pressed the phone to her ear.

"Hello?" she said, her body tensing. "Yes." Her gaze

locked on Jackson, her face losing all color. "Okay. I'll be there. Yes. I'll let him know."

"What is it?" he asked as she shoved the phone back into her pocket.

"Butch didn't die of natural causes," she said, her gaze darting to Samuel. "He was murdered."

TEN

Murder.

Raina rolled the word around in her head while she waited in Andrew's cubicle. He'd already made it clear that she wasn't a suspect. She wasn't so sure about Jackson. Despite what Andrew had said earlier, he'd insisted on questioning Jackson behind closed doors.

They'd disappeared a half hour ago and hadn't returned. The way things were looking, Jackson might just be the prime suspect.

He might be the *only* suspect.

Thank goodness Stella had offered to stay at the house with Samuel. The last thing he needed was to sit in a police station for half a day.

"This is a mess," she muttered.

"What's that, dear?" Gretchen Sampson looked up from her computer screen. A gray-haired grandmother of ten, she'd been working as a receptionist for the River Valley Police Department for more years than Raina had been alive. Everyone in town seemed to know her, and she seemed to know everyone in town. If there was trouble, she knew it, and if someone was in need, she spearheaded the effort to help.

After Matt's and Joseph's deaths, she'd been the first on Raina's doorstep, offering a casserole and a hug. "Nothing. I'm just…worried about my friend."

"That good-looking guy Andrew is questioning?" She glanced at the interview room, her gray curls so short and tight they barely moved. "You've got nothing to worry about."

"Andrew seems to think he might have been involved in Butch's murder."

"Nah. He's just being cautious."

"I hope you're right."

"I know I'm right. I probably shouldn't say, but I heard Andrew talking to Garrison Smith. That young guy who just joined the force? Blond hair and brown eyes? Looks young enough to be in grade school?"

Raina knew who she was talking about. Garrison had transplanted from Miami a few months before the accident. He'd been on the scene when they'd pulled Matt and Joseph from the car, and he'd been with Andrew when he'd broken the news to her. "I know him."

"He found Butch facedown in a ditch beside the road. Pretty close to where you guys had that incident this morning. There didn't appear to be any trauma to the body, so Garrison assumed that Butch had died of natural causes." She paused, apparently waiting for some kind of reaction from Raina. When she didn't get one, she continued, "He did due diligence. Took pictures of the scene. Including a footprint in the mud near the body. After the coroner realized Butch had been strangled—"

"He was strangled?" That wasn't something Andrew had mentioned.

"Yes, and whoever did it wanted to make sure he was well and truly dead. His larynx was crushed. Poor guy."

Gretchen blinked rapidly, and Raina was sure she was fighting tears.

"I'm so sorry that happened to him, Gretchen. No one deserves that kind of death."

"You're right about that. Butch might have been a drunk, but he helped me around my house after my husband died. Painted my barn one year and fixed the fence when it was coming down. He never asked for anything but a hot meal." Gretchen sniffed and wiped at her eyes. "But I'm getting off the subject. That print Garrison took the picture of? It didn't belong to your young man."

"He's not—" *Mine,* she almost said, but stopped herself before she could voice the protest. "How do you know?"

"Easy. Your friend was wearing boots, right?"

"Yes."

"Garrison said the print came from a running shoe. Nike, maybe. They're looking into it."

"It might not belong to the murderer," she pointed out, and Gretchen shook her head.

"You're wrong there, dear." She leaned forward, snagged Raina's hand and pulled her a step closer. "Now, you didn't hear this from me, but there was another footprint found. It matched the other exactly."

"Where did they find the second print?" she asked, her stomach turning. She'd been hoping there was no connection between Butch's murder and the man who'd chased her through the woods. She had a feeling those hopes were in vain.

"Right near where they picked up that stuffed dog of your son's."

"We aren't sure it belonged to Joseph." She'd thought

it was his, but until she got a closer look, she couldn't be sure.

"It did. Andrew found a tag on it. Had your son's name written right on it in blue Sharpie. Joey Lowery. Looked like the little guy had written it himself."

He had.

The day he'd brought it to kindergarten for show-and-tell, he'd scrawled his name in uneven letters on the small tag. Since he hadn't been able to fit Joseph, Raina had helped him spell Joey.

She could remember it as if it was yesterday. The way he'd scrunched up his nose and stuck the tip of his tongue between his lips. The way the marker had slipped and left a trail of blue across the kitchen table. She'd scrubbed and scrubbed to get the mark off.

How she wished she'd just left it alone. That tiny little line that her son had made.

She blinked back hot tears, her chest so tight she couldn't breathe.

"Are you okay, Raina? You look pale." Gretchen stood and grabbed her arm, her chocolate-brown eyes filled with concern. "Sit down. Take a couple of deep breaths."

"No. I just need some air. Tell Andrew I took a walk. I'll be back."

"I don't think that's a good idea. He really wants to talk to you when he finishes with your friend," Gretchen called, but Raina wasn't in the mood for listening. She ran down a short corridor, slowed her pace as she walked into the lobby. A couple of people were sitting in chairs there, the late-afternoon sun filtering in through over-size windows.

She shoved open the door, the fall wreath someone had hung slapping against the glass.

The air had the cool, crisp feel of winter, and she pulled her coat closed, zipping it up against the breeze. Downtown River Valley bustled with activity this time of year, people coming from D.C. and Baltimore to shop for antiques or peruse the artisan shops that lined Main Street.

She headed away from the busy stores, turning onto Elm Street. Matt's parents had once owned a house there. They'd sold it five months after the accident and used the money to buy a place in Florida. As far as Raina knew, they still lived there. She sent them cards for every holiday and birthday, but they'd changed their phone number and hadn't bothered giving her the new one.

In their eyes, she'd been the reason their only son and grandchild had died. If she'd been the happy little homemaker she was supposed to be, she'd have been home when Matt decided to take Joseph for ice cream. She wasn't sure what difference that would have made, but her in-laws had made it very clear that she should have either saved their family or died with them.

Sometimes late at night, when the house was quiet and her thoughts were loud, she was sure they were right. That she'd been the reason for their deaths. That if she'd just been less selfish and more devoted, Matt and Joseph would still be alive.

Hot tears burned behind her eyes, but she didn't let them fall. She'd already cried an ocean of tears and it hadn't done her any good. Keeping busy, being active and crawling into bed so exhausted she fell asleep before her mind could wander into dangerous territory was way more effective than crying a million more.

She pulled out her cell phone, dialed Destiny's number.

Destiny picked up on the first ring, just the way she'd known she would.

"What in the world is going on, Raina?" she nearly screamed into the phone.

"What are you talking about?"

"Did you forget it's the Harvest dinner for the singles group at church tonight?"

"I told you I wouldn't be there. I can't leave—"

"Samuel alone. I know. You've said it about a million times. That's not what I'm talking about. I'm at the church, cooking for this shindig, and Doctor Moron—"

"He is not a moron."

"Then he's an imbecile."

"Destiny!"

"What?"

"Just because you don't like him—"

"Since when did I say I didn't like him?"

"Every time I mention his name."

"I have nothing against him. I have everything against the two of you getting together. He's not the kind of man you need in your life. You need one that—"

"I don't need one at all," she cut Destiny off before her friend could go on another one of her "you need a good man in your life" diatribes. "And apparently neither do you. Andrew told me you and Lucas broke up."

"We didn't break up. I did. He's too controlling."

"You never mentioned that before."

"Because he wasn't controlling until I decided I wanted to spend a weekend in River Valley instead of going to some stupid psychiatric convention in D.C.," she huffed.

"Was that the weekend you helped me clean out Samuel's room."

"It was. Best weekend of my life, because I realized what a loser Lucas was and freed myself up for Mr. Right."

"Destiny—"

"Don't tell me I made a mistake, Rain. I didn't. If Lucas was the right guy for me, he wouldn't have left a dozen messages threatening to end it all if I didn't get back together with him."

"Did he really do that?"

"Of course he did. Said it was a joke when I called the police and reported a possible suicidal psychiatrist, but I'm not buying it. The guy is sick in the head, and I'm better off without him. Now, can we please get back to Moron Moreland? He has called me sixteen thousand times trying to find out if I know what's going on with you."

"Are you sure it was that many times? Kent is a busy guy," Raina teased as she crossed Trent and continued along Elm. The houses were farther apart on this section of road, the lots at least five acres each. In the distance, the sun hung low over mountains cloaked in gold and red.

"You're missing the point, Rain," Destiny responded, not a hint of amusement in her voice.

"What *is* the point, then?"

"That something must be going on or he wouldn't be calling. So what is it and why did it take you this long to call me?"

"I was at the police station. I didn't want to call from there."

"At the police station?" Destiny nearly shouted. "Will you please tell me what's going on?"

Raina explained briefly. When she finished, Destiny

was silent. Surprising, because her friend was almost never without words.

"Are you still there?" Raina finally asked.

"Yeah. I'm just not sure what to say except…wow!"

"Yeah. Wow."

"What is Andrew doing to find the guy responsible?"

"He didn't tell you?"

"Tell me what?"

"He's contacting Lucas."

"Because he owns a blue Jeep? My brother has gone off the deep end." She sighed.

"Does he know that Lucas—"

"Threatened to kill himself? Of course he does. He's the first person I told, and he's the one who told me to call the D.C. police."

"Maybe that's why he suspects him."

"Could be. Andrew is a pretty smart guy. His theories are usually pretty spot-on. I'm just not sure Lucas would go to such lengths to get my attention. Are you at the station now?"

"No." And Andrew wasn't going to be very happy about that.

Neither was Jackson.

She glanced back the way she'd come. The street was quiet, the sinking sun casting long shadows along the pavement.

"You're at home?"

"I'm taking a walk."

"Are you crazy? Someone is after you, and you're on a leisurely stroll."

"I guess I didn't think things through very carefully."

"Well, you should have. You're my best friend, the

sister of my heart. Anything happens to you, and I don't know what I'd do."

"You'd go on." *Just like I have,* she almost said. She didn't.

"I need to call my brother and put a burner under his behind. Maybe that stuffed dog will be the clue he needs to find the guy responsible. Goodwill should know who bought it. I still have the donation receipt the clerk gave me the day I dropped everything off there. I thought I'd wait a while to give it to you." She didn't say that she'd been worried about Raina's mental health, but they both knew it was true.

The room had sat untouched for almost four years. Cleaning it out for Samuel's arrival had been one of the most difficult things Raina had ever done. "The police will probably want it. Do you mind if I stop by your place and pick it up tonight?"

"You know you can, sweetie. And don't be sad, okay?"

"I'm not sad." She stopped in front of a white picket fence, looked into a yard she knew almost as well as she knew her own. The grass wasn't nearly as lush as it had been when her in-laws had owned the property, and the wraparound front porch looked gray and dingy. There were no curtains in the windows. No furniture that she could see. Someone had hung a for-sale sign near the edge of the property. From the look of things, it had been there a while.

"Then what are you?"

"Terrified?"

"I don't blame you. This whole thing is creepy. Who would want to scare you like this?"

"I have no idea." She opened the gate and walked

into the yard. The old swing still hung from the porch ceiling, and she went straight to it, sitting down in her familiar spot, the old chains creaking a protest.

"Aside from us, who knew about Joseph's stuffed dog?"

"Andrew. My family. Probably a few friends."

"And anyone who read the local newspaper after the accident. Remember the picture they ran? The one with you standing near the wreck holding Joseph's dog?"

"Actually, I've been trying really hard to forget it." She'd been distraught. Her face had been streaked with tears, her hair a tangled mess. For weeks afterward, she couldn't walk through a grocery store or stop at a gas station without someone stopping to offer condolences.

"Well, you can't forget it now. That photo opens up a whole list of suspects. I'd say almost everyone in town saw it."

"I'll mention it to Andrew."

"You'd better, and you'd also better be careful. Someone killed Butch, and that same person could come after you next."

"I'll be careful," she responded, pushing against the porch floor, letting the swing rock back and forth.

A Jeep passed the house, moving so slowly it caught Raina's attention. Old and dark blue, it had seen better days, one backlight smashed, a dent in the back bumper, the license plate so covered by grime she couldn't read it. It couldn't have been the one that had nearly run Jackson down, but her pulse leaped anyway, her throat going dry with fear.

"Raina? What's going on?" Destiny asked.

"Nothing. It's just—"

The Jeep pulled into a driveway a few houses up, disappearing for a heartbeat and then reappearing. Pulling back out onto the road and heading back in her direction. She stood, backing up so that she was closer to the house and more hidden by its shadows.

"What?" Destiny nearly shouted. "Raina…seriously, you're freaking me out."

I'm freaking myself out, she wanted to say, but the words stuck in her throat as the Jeep slowly passed. It pulled into another driveway, and her heart nearly jumped from her chest as it reappeared, crawled toward her.

"Call the police," she managed to whisper through her terror. "I'm at Matt's parents' old house on Elm Street and there's—"

The Jeep stopped in front of the house, and she could see a figure in the driver's seat.

"And what? Raina! What's going on?"

She would have answered, but the door to the Jeep opened and the driver got out. Black pants, black shoes, a black coat that hid his build. He was tall, that was all she knew for sure, and he was wearing a hood, a mask, gloves.

She reached for the front doorknob, her heart slamming against her ribs, her blood pulsing with fear.

"Have you missed me?" he asked, his voice the soft raspy warning of a snake waiting to strike.

She yanked at the door handle.

Locked!

She pivoted, rounding the side of the house, jumping from the back edge of the porch, footsteps pounding behind her.

Something snagged her coat, and she was yanked backward.

"You shouldn't ignore me," he hissed in her ear, his forearm pressed around her throat. "You should never ignore me."

She struggled to breathe, to think, to free herself.

In the distance, sirens shrieked, but she could barely hear them over the pulse of blood in her ears.

She jabbed her elbow into soft flesh, slammed her foot on his instep.

He groaned, his grip loosening just enough for her to gulp air, just enough for her to scream.

He shoved her forward with so much force she nearly flew, her shoulder knocking into the old oak tree Joseph used to try to climb, her head smashing into bark Matt had once carved their names into.

She saw stars, and then she saw nothing at all.

ELEVEN

Jackson pulled up behind Officer Wallace's police car and jumped out of the SUV, bypassing an old blue Jeep as he followed Wallace across the yard. Thank the Lord he'd insisted on driving his own vehicle to the police station. Otherwise, he'd have had to find another way of getting to Raina.

He didn't think Wallace would have been amused if he'd hot-wired a car.

"Go back to your vehicle," Wallace yelled, but Jackson had no intention of obeying orders.

He'd played along, answered a million questions about a crime he'd had nothing to do with. He was done playing. Raina was in trouble, and he wasn't counting on anyone but himself to get her out of it.

"I said—"

"Let's split up. You take the left. I'll take the right," Jackson cut him off.

"I don't like this, Miller. You get hurt, it's on your head. You get Raina hurt, and I'll throw your butt in jail and let you rot there," Wallace muttered, but he headed to the left and eased around the corner of the house.

Jackson moved to the right. His Glock had been confiscated at the police station, but he'd faced worse situations without it. Not an ideal scenario, but he'd make it work.

A saggy wraparound porch butted up against faded wood siding, mature trees growing so close to the house that their branches touched the windows. He stepped out from their shadows, scanning the backyard, Officer Wallace in his periphery. Raina was somewhere nearby. She had to be. That she'd been kidnapped again, was being held against her will again, wasn't something he wanted to contemplate.

He stepped farther into the yard, spotted what looked like a pile of fabric near the trunk of an old tree. No. Not fabric. Jeans. A coat. White-blond hair.

"Raina!" he shouted, sprinting toward her.

She sat up slowly as he reached her side, her eyes glazed, blood dripping down her forehead. He pulled off his coat, pressing the sleeve against her forehead.

"Ouch!" She batted at his hand, but he held firm.

"You're bleeding."

"You're going to be bleeding, too, if you don't stop adding to my headache," she mumbled, some of the color returning to her face.

"Are you threatening me, Raina?" he asked, sliding his free arm around her waist, relief coursing through him.

"I might be," she muttered. "I get grumpy when I'm in pain."

"Good to know." He pulled his coat away from her forehead, eyed the shallow gash. "I don't think you're going to need stitches."

"Also good to know," she responded with a slight smile.

"You might have a scar, though."

"I'd rather have the kind that can be seen than the kind that can't be." Her eyes drifted closed, and his heart jerked with fear. He'd watched people die from wounds that seemed minor, and he wasn't going to let that happen to Raina.

"How is she?" Wallace crouched beside him, his jaw tight, his expression grim. "I've already called for an ambulance."

"I don't need an ambulance." Raina's head came up like a shot, all the color that had returned to her face gone.

"Yes, you do," Jackson told her, pressing the coat back to the wound on her head. "You're bleeding like a stuck pig."

"Head wounds always bleed a lot." She nudged his hand aside and held the coat sleeve herself. "I'll go home, slap a Band-Aid on it and be good to go."

She tried to get to her feet, but he tugged her back. "Whatever you're thinking, it's not going to happen."

"I'm thinking that I'm going home, and I'm thinking it *is* going to happen," she insisted, but she didn't try to stand again.

"Did you see the man who attacked you, Raina?" Andrew changed the subject, his voice hard and just a little sharp.

"Not his face. He was wearing a ski mask."

"How about his eyes?"

She shook her head. "He grabbed me from behind, and I was too busy fighting to notice much." Her voice shook, and Andrew patted her shoulder.

"It's okay. We'll talk more after the doctor takes a look at your head."

"I already told you, I'm not going to the hospital."

"You don't have a choice, Raina. We've got a victim's advocate waiting there."

"Tell him to meet me at my place or at the police station."

"Sorry," he responded. "It's not going to happen that way."

"I'm not—"

Sirens blasted through the afternoon quiet, and Andrew glanced over his shoulder. "I'll let the EMTs know you're back here. Sit tight."

"I don't think so," Raina mumbled, easing away from Jackson's arm and struggling to her feet.

He followed her up, setting his hands on her waist when she swayed. "You're not thinking clearly."

"I hate hospitals, and I don't want to be in one," she replied, her voice breaking.

"You worked in one for a few years," he pointed out, gently brushing strands of hair from her forehead. The wound had already stopped bleeding, but the skin looked raw and swollen, the flesh bruised. She'd hit her head hard.

"That was before."

"Before your husband and son died?"

"Yes."

"Just because they died doesn't mean you will. You know that, right?"

"It has nothing to do with that, Jackson. Nothing at all."

"Then what does it have to do with?"

"You want to know the truth?"

"That would be a lot better than a lie."

She didn't even crack a smile. As a matter of fact, he

wasn't sure she was really listening to his words or paying attention to her own. She seemed far away, her gaze fixed on some distant point. "I hate hospitals because they remind me of what a failure I am."

"A failure? What's that supposed to mean?"

"It means my son died right in front of me, and I couldn't do anything about it."

Her words speared straight into his heart.

He knew what it was like to live with guilt, to think there was something more that could have been done, some solution that could have been found that would have changed things for the better.

"Raina—"

"Don't, Jackson." A tear slid down her cheek, dripped onto the ground near their feet. "Nothing you say can change how I feel."

"I know." He tugged her into his arms, and she rested her cheek on his chest. "But nothing you feel can make what happened your fault, either."

She tensed, then relaxed against him, her arms sliding around his waist, her hands drifting to his back. Voices carried into the silence, the sounds of the ambulance crew mixing with Wallace's deep commands, but she didn't move, and Jackson didn't feel the need to make her. Standing there with her felt more like coming home than anything had in a very long time.

"Sir?" A young dark-haired woman appeared at his elbow. "We're going to need to take a look at the patient."

He released Raina reluctantly, stepping back as two men moved in.

"Did she say anything else to you?" Wallace asked, his tone grim.

"Nothing that will help."

"You know that I should arrest you for interfering with an investigation, right?" the older man growled, his gaze on the ambulance crew and Raina.

"I didn't interfere."

"You didn't stay out, either."

He had a point, but Jackson wasn't going to apologize. He'd done what he'd felt he had to do, and he'd do it again in a heartbeat. "Just so you know, I'm not planning to stay out of it."

Wallace sighed. "Just do me a favor, will you? Be careful. I'm already dealing with one homicide. I don't want to deal with another."

"I'll be careful." He glanced past the officer, watching as the ambulance crew helped Raina onto a gurney. She didn't protest, just lay back and closed her eyes.

"Since you're here anyway, you want to head to the hospital with her? I'm going to look around, see what kind of evidence I can find."

"He left his Jeep. That should contain plenty," Jackson responded, his attention still on Raina.

"I'm calling in a state team for that. This is the second blue Jeep the guy has used. Maybe there's some message in that that I'm not seeing."

Surprised, Jackson met Wallace's eyes. "I'm glad to hear that you're calling for backup."

"I figured you would be." He lifted his hat, ran his hand over his hair. "But you're not going to be happy to hear this. I'm going to say it anyway, because Raina is like a kid sister to me. You hurt her, and I will have to hurt you, and I'm really not going to care if I go to jail for doing it. Got it?"

He got it, all right.

He had a kid sister.

He'd do anything to protect her, would hurt anyone who hurt her. "I get it, but you should probably get this— I don't walk away from people I care about. And I care about Raina. As long as she's in danger, I'll be around, and I'll be sticking my nose places you probably don't want me to."

Wallace shoved his hat back on, nodded curtly. "I hear you. Just don't break the law, and we'll be just fine."

The ambulance crew maneuvered the gurney past them, and Wallace nodded in their direction. "You'd better go. The victim advocate will be at the hospital, but I want someone Raina feels comfortable with to be there, too."

"You want to ride with us?" the dark-haired woman asked as they wheeled the gurney onto the ambulance.

"Sure." He climbed aboard, took a seat on the bench the EMT indicated.

The ambulance doors closed, and Raina opened her eyes, looked straight into his. "I really don't want to go to the hospital."

"I know."

She scowled, but there was no real ire in her eyes. Just sadness mixed with fear. "I think you've got the story wrong, Jackson, because this is not how it's supposed to work out," she grumbled.

"How what is supposed to work out?"

"The epic adventure novel, Jackson. Get with the program," she huffed.

"And exactly how is the epic adventure supposed to work?

"The hero breaks down the door to the prison and carries the heroine to some safe hiding place."

"We've been there, remember? Now we're at the place

where the hero tells the heroine that everything is going to be just fine."

"Yeah? Then why aren't we in some cozy hideaway?" She reached out a hand, and he took it, held it gently as her eyes drifted shut again.

"Because you need to be seen by a doctor."

"Since you seem to have all the answers," she said so quietly he almost didn't hear, "what's the next part of the story?"

"I guess," he responded, "that depends on what kind of ending you want."

She nodded, but didn't open her eyes.

Didn't say another word as the ambulance engine roared to life and the driver sped toward the hospital.

TWELVE

Obviously she was going to live.

That being the case, Raina wanted out of the hospital.

Not in five or ten minutes, either.

Right at that moment.

The problem was, a victim's advocate had greeted her at the hospital and collected her clothes. Everything from the skin out had been taken, put in a bag and carried away.

Which left her sitting on the exam table wearing a cotton hospital gown and a bandage. Since the bandage was on her head, it wasn't covering much.

She glanced at the clock. She'd called Destiny twenty minutes ago, and her friend had promised to bring clothes. She hadn't arrived yet.

Or maybe she had and the police weren't letting her into the room.

Whatever the case, Raina was getting just desperate enough to take matters into her own hands. She jumped off the exam table, wincing as pain shot through her head. No concussion. No skull fracture. Nothing but a nice little goose egg and some scraped skin. It hurt plenty, though.

She walked to the door, thought about opening it and just…leaving. The problem was, she didn't think she'd get far dressed in a hospital gown. Especially not when she'd been brought to River Valley General, a place where just about everyone knew her. Not one of them would be willing to let her leave without telling the police that she was going.

The sound of a child crying drifted through the closed door, and she wanted to cover her head with the blanket one of the nurses had brought for her, do everything in her power to drown out the noise.

Joseph had been crying when they'd brought him in.

Calling for her, and she'd run to him.

He hadn't known she was there. No matter how many times she'd called his name, touched his battered head and bloody cheek, he hadn't known.

Her throat closed, and she opened the door. Not caring what she was or wasn't wearing. Not caring about anything but getting out of that room, away from that sound.

"Hey!" Warm hands wrapped around her waist, pulling her up short. "Where do you think you're going?"

She looked up into Jackson's dark blue eyes, and all the tears that had been clogging her throat burst out.

"I need some air," she managed, the words nearly choking her.

He took off his coat, dropped it around her shoulders. "Then let's get some for you."

She was in his arms before she realized what he planned to do, out the door of the hospital before she could think to protest. The tears were still pouring down her face, and her body was shaking, and she was really afraid that she would never breathe again.

"Shh," Jackson murmured, his breath ruffling the hair near her temple. "It's okay."

No. It wasn't.

It hadn't been okay for a long time, and if she hadn't been crying so hard, she would have told him that.

"Hey! You!" someone called. "Where do you think you're going with her? Put her down! I'm calling the police!"

Raina knew the voice.

Destiny.

She'd finally arrived, and from the sound of things, she was raring for a fight.

Jackson set Raina on the ground, shifting so that he was standing slightly in front of her. His shoulders and back blocked her view, but she knew they were in an alcove at the back of the hospital. She'd spent a lot of time there during the three days that Joseph had been in a coma, sitting on a bench, trying desperately to pray.

"Raina!" Destiny called. "I'll distract him. You run."

"No! Destiny!" But, of course, her friend was already barreling into Jackson.

To his credit, he didn't lose his balance and he didn't shove her back. He grabbed her flailing arms, holding them down as he sidestepped the foot she'd aimed at his shins. "Cool it, lady. I'm a friend."

"Friend? I know every one of Raina's friends, and you aren't one of them." Destiny ground the words out as she tried to loosen his grip. "Raina! Come on. I'll hold him for the police. You run."

"He's a friend, Destiny. Just like he said." She stepped out from behind Jackson, her legs a little wobbly, her heart a little wobbly, too. She hated the alcove, the hospital, all the memories that were there.

"How come I've never met him?" Destiny backed off, her curly black hair bobbing with the movement. At five-foot-nothing and less than a hundred pounds, she wouldn't have stood a chance if Jackson really had been a kidnapper.

Raina loved her too much to say that. "I met him in Africa."

"Oh." Destiny's brow furrowed, her dark eyes flashing. "That explains nothing."

"He brought Samuel to my place last night."

"I thought you'd hired a woman to do that."

"I did, but Jackson came along."

"And you didn't bother calling to tell me some good-looking, hunky guy was—"

"Tell you what, ladies," Jackson cut in, his arm sliding around Raina's waist, his fingers warm through the thin cotton of the hospital gown. "How about we get Raina back to the exam room? I'll step out, and *then* you can have a long discussion about me."

"Good plan." Destiny strode toward the hospital door and lifted a bag that was lying on the ground there. "These are the clothes you asked for, Rain. I just grabbed some of my stuff rather than driving out to your place. I figured that would save time."

"Thanks." She took the bag, thought about moving away from Jackson, but it felt good to have him there. She didn't want to think too much about what that meant. Not when she was so close to the place where she'd said her last goodbye to Matt, the place where she'd listened to her son call for her.

She swallowed back her tears, keeping her head down as Jackson urged her back to the exam room. Like every other room on the corridor, it was small. It felt even smaller with Jackson and Destiny there.

"I'll help her with her clothes," Destiny said, taking charge the way she always did. "You go wait in the hall." She tried to nudge Jackson to the door, but he held his ground.

"Is that what you want, Raina?" he asked, and she was tempted to tell him that being in the hospital had scrambled her brains and made her think that the only thing she wanted was to be in his arms again.

A silly thought. One that she'd be stupid to keep thinking. "Yes," she said, her mouth dry, her heart pounding, because she really didn't want him to leave.

"Okay." He touched her cheek, smiled gently. "I'll be right outside if you need me."

I need you, her brain whispered, but she shoved the words down and managed not to speak them.

"Wow!" Destiny breathed as soon as the door closed. "That is one fine specimen of a man."

"I guess." She shrugged nonchalantly, but she was feeling anything but nonchalant.

"You guess? *You guess?* Open your eyes and take a good look when he walks back in here. He is just about the finest-looking man I've seen around here in years."

Raina shrugged again and retrieved black skinny jeans and a fluffy pink sweater from the bag. "What in the world?"

"I was worried. I grabbed the first things I saw and ran with them. Hopefully, the jeans won't be too short."

"Too short? I don't think I can even get one leg in them!"

"Give me a break, Rain. You're skinny as a rail. So

just shut up and get the clothes on. I want to see your man again."

"He's not *my* man!"

"Then why was he carrying you out of the hospital?"

"Because… I was upset. I heard a little kid crying, and it brought back a lot of stuff that I wasn't ready to deal with."

"Oh, honey," Destiny said with a sigh. "I'm so sorry."

"Me, too." She pulled on the jeans, managed to button them and still breathe. The sweater was soft and just a little loose, and it was so much easier to think about that than to think about Matt and Joseph. "Okay. I'm set."

"You don't have any shoes," Destiny responded with a sly smile. "I guess I'm going to have to ask that hunk of burning love to give you a lift."

"Don't you dare," she responded, but Destiny already had the door open.

"Hey, Jackson! Raina needs you!" she called.

"I don't—"

Jackson stepped into the room, his hair a little mussed, his jaw dark with a beard. His gaze skimmed Raina's face, dropped to the pink sweater, the tight black jeans, settled on her feet.

"Shoe problems?" he asked with a half smile.

"I forgot to bring her some. Not that it would have done any good if I'd remembered. The girl has feet the size of—"

"I have perfectly normal-size feet, Destiny," Raina cut her friend off, her cheeks hot, her heart beating just a little too fast.

"You're right," Jackson said, moving so close Raina could see the fine lines at the corners of his eyes, smell the subtle scent of soap that clung to his skin. "They do appear to be just about perfect."

"That doesn't solve the problem," Destiny huffed.

"It's not a problem. Not yet. Raina can't leave until Officer Wallace speaks with her. He just called to tell me he's in the lobby and he wants us to wait here."

"Officer Wallace?" Destiny snorted. "My brother is a control freak. I never listen to him."

"He's your brother?" Jackson asked, looking as surprised as most people did when they found out the connection.

"Half, but we don't count that as any less than the whole thing." She tapped her finger against her lips and smirked. "Now that I think about it, I wouldn't want to annoy him. You two wait here. I'll go make sure he knows the way up here."

"You don't have to do that." Raina grabbed her friend's hand, but Destiny just smiled and pulled away.

"Of course I do. Sit tight. I'll be back in ten," she said with a wink that Raina was sure Jackson noticed.

She stepped out into the hall, offering a jaunty wave as she walked away.

"Well," Jackson said, that one word stretched out into so many syllables Raina couldn't help smiling.

"What?" he asked, taking her arm and leading her to the exam table.

"Your Southern accent is showing."

"Isn't it always? If not, my poor Southern grandmother will roll over in her grave." He smiled, lifting her onto the table.

"You really need to stop doing that."

"What?" He sat beside her, leg pressed to leg, arm to arm, and she wanted to smile again, because the room didn't feel so much like a triage room when he was in it. It felt more like...home?

She frowned. "Picking me up. You'll hurt yourself."

"You're kidding, right?" He laughed.

"No. I'm not kidding."

"I've carted two-hundred-pound men through enemy territory. I don't think picking you up is going to cause me any irreparable harm."

"That doesn't mean you should make a habit of it," she grumbled, and he laughed again, his arm settling around her shoulders, his palm resting on her upper arm.

"What if I want to?" he asked, all his amusement gone.

"Why would you?" She brushed lint from her jeans, her gaze on the floor, the wall, the ceiling. Anything but him.

"Because I think you're the kind of woman who'll understand what I do and why I do it," he said quietly, his fingers tracing a line along the inside of her arm.

She shuddered, a longing so deep, so undeniable filling her so that her heart ached with it. "Jackson—"

She wasn't sure what she planned to say, didn't know if she really had anything she could say. She'd never know, because Kent stuck his head in the open doorway, his gaze jumping from Raina to Jackson and back again. "Am I interrupting something?"

"No." Raina jumped off the table, her head throbbing with the movement. "What are you doing here?"

"I got a call that you'd been hurt, and I came to check on you."

"A call from whom?"

"One of the nurses. Are you okay?" He moved into the room as if he owned the place, washed his hands as if he planned to exam Raina. Jackson didn't know much about medicine, but he didn't think Kent was going to find anything more than the E.R. doctor had.

He stepped between Moreland and Raina, offering a smile that he didn't feel. "It's nice of you to come check on her, but she's already been examined."

"I'm sure she'd like my opinion." Moreland frowned, his gaze settling on Raina.

She looked tired, her skin pale against the bright pink of the sweater she was wearing. A blue bruise peeked out from under the bandage on her forehead, and dark bruises marred her neck. The guy hadn't just slammed her head into a tree—he'd choked her. Jackson's skin tightened, anger burning hot in his gut.

"Would you like his opinion, Raina?" he asked.

She bit her lip, obviously uncomfortable with the situation.

Why wouldn't she be?

The guy was her boss. If she said she didn't want his opinion, that could cause problems.

"Raina?" he prodded, and she shook her head.

"I think I've had enough of doctors for the day. I'm sorry, Kent. It's nothing to do with you. I just—"

"No need to explain," Moreland said, his voice sharp. "I get it. I'm going to check on a patient who was admitted last night. If you change your mind in the next hour or so, give me a call."

He stalked from the room, his back ramrod straight, his steps brisk.

Jackson met Raina's eyes. "Hopefully, he won't hold that against you."

"He won't. He's not that kind of guy."

"What kind of guy is he, then?"

"Very focused. He loves his job, and he wants to help people."

"And what kind of guy is he to you?" he asked, because Kent was giving off all the signs of a guy whose territory was being infringed on.

"I already told you, Jackson. He asked me out a few times. I wasn't interested."

"When did he ask you? Before or after you went on the mission trip together?"

"Before. Why?"

"Just curious." And just thinking that Kent Moreland was a little too interested in Raina's life, that he spent a little too much time hanging around a woman who said she wasn't interested in him.

Andrew had his sights set on Destiny's boyfriend. Jackson thought maybe he should turn his attention in another direction.

"What are you thinking?" Raina asked, shifting so that she was facing him. Her eyes were the oddest color. Not quite blue. Not quite purple. They hid nothing. Not her sorrow, her fear, her curiosity.

"He seems to be spending a lot of time chasing after a woman who said she's not interested."

She shook her head. "He has just about every unattached woman in town chasing after him. I doubt he's that concerned with the one who got away."

"And yet he showed up at your house early yesterday morning, came to the hospital this afternoon. He said a nurse called to tell him you were here. Why?"

"Because he's an on-call doctor here, Jackson. He probably spends as much time at the hospital as he does at the clinic."

"Is this where you met him?" he asked, not sure if it

mattered, but suddenly needing all the information he could get. Something was off about the doctor, and he planned to find out what it was.

"Actually, yes. He moved here from Wisconsin after his wife died. That was six or seven years ago. He started working as an E.R. doctor and opened the clinic a few years later. I met him my first day of work. We mostly just passed each other in the hallway, but after Matt and Joseph died…" She shook her head.

"What?"

"I guess he knew what it was like to lose someone. When I quit my job here, he offered to hire me at the clinic."

"And you've been working there ever since?"

"Actually, no. After the accident, I just wanted to hide away in my house with all my memories." She smiled, her eyes so sad Jackson touched her cheek, tucked a strand of hair behind her ear.

"You don't have to talk about this if you don't want to."

"I don't mind, and there's not much else to tell. One day, Destiny walked into the house and opened all the curtains and shades. She told me to take a shower and get ready, because she was bringing me to her church for a potluck. I was too tired to argue, so I went along with her. Kent attends the same church. He saw me, asked if I was ready to return to work."

"And were you?"

"I didn't think I was, but Destiny nagged me for a month, and I finally accepted the job."

"And went on a mission to Africa with Kent a few months later?"

"That was part of the church outreach program. I was

sick of feeling sorry for myself and thought it would be a great opportunity to do something for others. It turned into more of a nightmare."

"You made it through, though, and you've brought Samuel here."

"Yes." She frowned. "I hope it works out. The visa is only for a year. I'm hoping someone from church will step forward and offer to adopt him. So far, people seem a little…worried."

"Because of his background?" he asked, glad that she'd thought beyond the year. Samuel deserved permanence and stability. Not just a year of wonderful living.

"Yes."

"Maybe once they meet him, they'll change their minds."

"I hope so. There's nothing for him in Africa but hardship, and he deserves a lot more than that."

"You could do it," he suggested, knowing he was stepping into something that he probably shouldn't and not really caring.

"No, I couldn't," she said simply.

He wanted to ask why not, but she'd closed up tight, her expression blank.

Whatever she was feeling, whatever she thought about offering Samuel a home, he wasn't going to get it out of her.

Yet.

Eventually, he would. When the time was right. When she wasn't so exhausted and broken.

Voices drifted from the hallway, and Jackson turned to face the doorway, expecting Andrew Wallace to appear.

Instead, a tall, dark-haired guy with an attitude peered

in. The slightly shorter redheaded guy who stood behind him looked a little too amused for Jackson's liking.

A bad day had just gotten a lot worse.

"What are you doing here?" he asked, stepping back so his brother could enter the room. Daniel Boone Anderson sauntered in behind him, an annoying smirk still planted on his too-pretty face.

"Well, it's like this," Chance responded, his gaze settling on Raina. "Boone got a call from Stella. She said you were being questioned by the police. We left D.C. three hours ago and drove straight here."

"Because?" he asked, knowing it would annoy Chance and amuse Boone.

"HEART has a reputation to uphold, Jackson. You can't be dragged into the police department in every town you visit."

"And yet, he has been," Boone cut in, his grin spreading into a full-out smile. "How you doin', man?" he said, crossing the room and giving Jackson a smack on the back.

"I'd be better if you'd talked my brother out of coming."

"Hey, I just got back from Turkey. Been traveling three days. I can't be blamed for not thinking straight."

"Can we get back to the point," Chance interrupted. "How much damage has been done? Are you going to be arrested?"

"The officer in charge of the murder investigation will be here in a minute. Why don't you ask him?"

"Murder? Are you kidding me?" Chance looked as if he was about to blow a gasket, and Jackson decided to have pity on him.

"Don't worry, bro. I've already been cleared."

"Thank the good Lord for that."

Chance had barely gotten the words out when Wallace waltzed in as if he owned the place. Four grown men in a small triage area was about three too many.

Jackson would have volunteered to step out into the hall, but he wasn't going to leave Raina.

"Looks like you're having quite a party in here, Raina," Wallace said drily.

"I—"

Her response was cut off by a screech so loud it drilled its way straight into Jackson's skull.

"Fire alarm!" Boone shouted over the din. He glanced into the hall. "Smoke to the east. Let's move!"

No need for a plan. No need to discuss things. This was what the team did best, get people out of tough situations.

Jackson grabbed Raina, dumping her over his shoulder like a sack of potatoes as Chance ran into the hall. He followed, racing through acrid air and hazy smoke, heading west along the corridor, Chance a few yards in front, scooping up a little boy and clapping an arm around the kid's mother. Boone had taken up the rear. Jackson didn't have to look to know he was there. He could feel him like the air, the smoke, Raina's hands on his back.

He sprinted into the parking lot, set Raina down next to his brother.

"Keep an eye on her," he barked, and then he ran back inside.

THIRTEEN

The sun had set hours ago, the waning moon creeping above the trees and settling there. Raina had been watching its slow march across the sky, counting as the minutes ticked by on the grandfather clock that sat in a dark corner of the room. She'd tucked Samuel into bed an hour ago, kissed his cheek because it seemed as though he needed someone to do it. To her surprise, a tear had slipped down his face, dropping onto his dark blue pillowcase. When she'd tried to wipe it away, he'd turned onto his side and covered his head with the blanket.

She'd wanted so badly to pull it back and tell him everything was going to be okay. She just hadn't known how to say it. Not to a child who'd lost everything, who'd been taken from everything he'd known and dumped in a new country with nothing but an old backpack and a few tired pieces of clothes.

She'd put her hand on his shoulder and left it there, listening to his quiet sobs until he finally fell asleep.

Now she was at loose ends, waiting, wondering, worrying.

"Staring out the window isn't going to make any of them come back sooner," Stella commented. She'd stretched out on the couch, the quilt Matt's grandmother had made as a wedding present draped over her knees. A book in one hand, a bowl of popcorn in her lap, she looked completely relaxed and unconcerned.

"According to the news, three people were injured in the fire."

"Injured running out of the building. Not in the fire. There's a big difference."

"Either way, it could have been one of the men."

"Nah. I would have heard something if it had been." She stuffed a handful of popcorn into her mouth, held the bowl out. "Want some?"

"No. Thanks."

"Starving yourself isn't going to help, but suit yourself." Stella went back to her book, and Raina went back to the window. Across the street, Larry's lights were on, one glowing in the lower level of the house. Two in the upper level. That wasn't like Larry. He was a stickler for keeping lights off, eating at home rather than out and saving money any way possible. He might not have been the most neighborly guy, but he was more than happy to share his opinions about things. Before Matt's death, he'd come over a couple of times to warn about the folly of leaving an outside light burning in the middle of the night.

"I should probably go check on him," she said. Not that Larry would appreciate it, but she needed something to do, and she really did want to make sure he was okay.

"Jackson doesn't need checking on. He knows how to take care of himself," Stella responded without looking up from her book.

"I was talking about my neighbor. He's been having some memory lapses lately."

"That's too bad, but you're not leaving the house."

"Says who?"

"Me."

"It's been a long time since anyone has tried to keep me from going out at night."

"You're misunderstanding, Raina," Stella said, finally looking up from her book. "I'm not *trying* to keep you from going outside. I *am* keeping you from it."

You and what army? nearly slipped out of Raina's mouth, but she didn't want a fight. Even if she did, she had a feeling Stella could take her down easily. "Fine. How about you go over and check on him?"

"I'm not supposed to leave you here alone."

"Says who?"

"Says Jackson."

"When did you speak to him?"

"I didn't. He texted me while you were tucking the kid in. Said they should be back in a couple of hours."

"Why didn't you tell me?"

"You didn't ask."

"Are you always this irritating?" Raina finally snapped, frustrated with Stella and with herself because she'd been pacing around worrying about someone who apparently didn't need it.

"Yes," Stella responded. "As a matter of fact, I am."

Raina bit her lip and kept her thoughts to herself, grabbing the phone and dialing Larry's number.

He didn't answer. Not surprising. He never answered the phone after eight at night or before nine in the morning. That was another one of the things that he'd made sure Raina and Matt knew.

She slammed the phone back into the receiver, and

Stella scowled. "If I promise to go over there with you when the guys get back, will you relax?"

"That depends on whether you're any good at keeping promises," she responded, pacing back to the window and staring out at the dark yard, the trees, the house across the street.

"I helped get your butt out of Africa, just like I promised your folks I would. I got Samuel to you safely, just like I promised you that I would. So, from where I'm sitting, I'd say I'm pretty good at keeping promises. Now, how about you sit down and be still so I can finish my book. If I can't be on a hot date tonight, I might as well read about someone who is." She stuck her nose back in the book, and Raina forced herself to perch on the edge of the couch and do absolutely nothing. No fidgeting, no toe tapping, no getting up to wash out the coffeepot or sweep the kitchen floor.

It had been a long time since she'd done that. As a matter of fact, she'd been going full tilt since Destiny forced her to get out of the house and get on with her life. She'd accepted a job at the clinic, gone on mission to Africa, spent hundreds of hours working to bring Samuel to the United States. She'd attended church, volunteered at local soup kitchens, created things to fill her time so that she wouldn't have to do exactly what she *was* doing— sitting in the silence and listening to her own thoughts.

Maybe she should have, though.

Maybe somewhere in the hollowness of her grief, somewhere in the quiet loneliness of her new life, she'd find what she needed to move on and to heal.

Or maybe she'd just find a hundred reasons to crumble into a heap on the floor and cry until there weren't any tears left. That's what she'd been afraid of. That and the silence, because in it, she'd probably hear God gently nudging her soul, telling her that she couldn't waste her life because Matt and Joseph had lost theirs. She'd probably feel Him urging her back to the little church on the bluff, and the elderly congregation that hadn't been any more ready to let her go than she'd been ready to let go of her family.

Car lights splashed on the road, and Raina jumped up, watching as Jackson's SUV pulled into the driveway. A pickup truck and police cruiser were right behind it.

She opened the door, ran onto the front porch, waiting while the men got out of their vehicles. They all looked grim and tired. Even the redhead with the boy-next-door face and easy smile looked somber and serious.

Something was wrong. More wrong than a fire in a trash can at the hospital.

"What's going on?" she asked as Jackson jogged up the porch steps.

"Let's talk about it inside." He had a streak of soot on his cheek, and his eyes were shadowed with fatigue, but he still looked ready to do what was necessary to defend the people he cared about.

He also looked cold, his arms bare, his T-shirt no match for the chilly night air. She touched his arm, frowning at the icy feel of his skin.

"You're cold. I'll make some coffee for everyone," she said, leading the way back into the house and heading for the kitchen.

Jackson grabbed her hand, his fingers twining through hers. "We nearly drowned ourselves in coffee at the hospital."

"I could make—"

"Raina," he interrupted, his thumb skimming across

her wrist, heat sliding up her arm and straight into the cold empty place in her heart. The place she hadn't ever wanted filled again. The place she'd locked up tight and ignored for so long she'd nearly forgotten it was there. "Just be still, okay?"

"You're the second person who's said that to me today," she responded, easing her hand from his and walking to the fireplace. There was wood in the firebox, kindling in the newspaper box beside it. She hadn't lit a fire in years, but a book of matches remained in the small box on the mantel, a lone match clinging to the cardboard. She set up the starter, lit the match, her hand shaking so much it went out before it ever got close to the kindling. She'd have to get another book from the kitchen, but first she was going to have to hear what the men had to say.

She turned back to the group, bracing herself as Andrew stepped inside and closed the door. She'd known him for enough years to read the frustration on his face, the fear, the worry.

Stella hadn't budged from her spot on the couch, but she looked up as the door closed, her gaze skirting past the man who stood beside Andrew. Raina hadn't been introduced, but Chance Miller had made his relationship to Jackson obvious. An inch taller than Jackson with pitch-black hair and bright blue eyes, he had the kind of face that could have been on magazine covers or on a Most Wanted poster for the FBI.

"It's about time," Stella muttered, dropping her book onto the coffee table and stretching. "Since everyone is present and accounted for, I'm going to get some sleep. Hopefully, when I wake up in the morning, I'll discover that being stranded on the outskirts of Mayberry is nothing but a bad dream."

"You promised you'd walk me over to Larry's," Raina reminded her.

"Right. Well, we can't do it now. Knock on my door when the men are done with you, but by that time, I have a feeling it will be too late to bother." She sauntered from the room as if she didn't have a care in the world, but her shoulders were tense and tight, her movements stiff.

Once she was gone, it was just Raina and four men who were all staring at her as if she was a bug under a microscope. She met Andrew's eyes, bracing herself for whatever it was he had to say. "What's going on?"

"I don't know how to tell you this, Raina," Andrew said, taking off his uniform hat and smoothing his hair. He tapped the hat on his thigh, exhausted, worried, tense. She wanted to tell him to relax, wanted to say that no matter what, everything would be okay. The words caught in her throat, though, fear keeping them trapped there.

"How about you just tell me?" she finally managed to say.

"You've heard that someone started a fire in a trash can at the hospital?"

"Yes."

"After the fire department put it out, they found some things."

"What things?"

He hesitated, then pulled a plastic bag from his pocket, set it down on the coffee table. "Take a look at these. Tell me if they're familiar."

She moved closer, her legs leaden, her heart racing.

A photograph nearly filled the gallon-size bag. Face

up, its edges charred, dark smudges coating the glossy finish, it was a wedding photo. Not just any photo, either. The one Destiny had snapped minutes after Raina and Matt had said their vows. Unposed, they'd been captured smiling into each other's eyes, his hand on her cheek, her hand on his waist.

"I will love you for eternity," he'd whispered just before they'd kissed for the first time as husband and wife.

She shoved the memory away, leaned to take a closer look at the photo. Aside from the charring and the smudges, it looked...off, and she couldn't figure out why.

"Can I touch it?" she asked, her voice thick.

"If you don't take it out of the bag."

She nodded, lifting the plastic bag from the table, realizing another photo was inside. She turned the bag over, her heart nearly stopping when she saw the picture. It had been taken by a photographer friend on Joseph's first birthday. The friend had insisted on doing an outside shoot, despite the fact that it was the middle of February. They'd bundled up and gone to the church, spread a blanket out in the yard, the cold watery sunlight dusting their hair and skin with gold. Joseph had taken his first steps that day, and it had been captured in the photo—a laughing little boy, his arms outstretched, four-toothed grin on his chubby face.

Only there was no face in the photo.

Not on the chubby little boy or on the man who stood in the background, both hands stretched out as he urged the toddler on. Both had been scratched out. Only Raina's face remained untouched.

She turned the bag over again, trying to see Matt's face through the layer of soot.

Gone. Just like in the birthday photo.

She dropped the plastic bag onto the table, stepping back so quickly, she bumped into someone. Warm hands clasped her upper arms, and Jackson's breath ruffled her hair. "You okay?" he asked softly.

She nodded, but she wasn't sure she was.

Andrew cleared his throat. Seeing the photos had to be hard on him, too. He and Matt had been good friends. They'd gone fishing together every summer, took care of the churchyard together. They'd met for breakfast the first Monday of the month for years. Raina wasn't the only one who had been left with holes in her life when Matt died. "These are obviously yours, Raina," he said. "What I need to know is whether someone made a copy of existing photos or took ones you had."

"I…" She glanced at the plastic bag, but didn't want to touch it again. She could almost feel the vileness of the person who'd scratched the faces out. "Don't know. These are photos Matt kept on his desk at the church office. After he died, the office was cleaned out and his stuff was brought here. It's in boxes upstairs."

"You don't know if the photos were in the boxes?"

"I never looked. I can now, if you want."

"That's probably a good idea. I'm going to make a couple of calls. I'll be out on the porch if you find something."

"Okay." She didn't wait for him to go, just turned on her heels and ran from the room. She wanted to run outside, race through the trees the way she had in her dreams and in her waking nightmare. Maybe if she did, she'd somehow find a way to go back in time and return to the church while Matt's things were still in his office, those pictures sitting on his desk beckoning him to return home.

FOURTEEN

"I guess you're going to want to take care of that," Boone said to Jackson, settling onto the couch and picking up the book Stella had abandoned there.

"Not before he explains how he got himself into this mess," Chance growled, dropping onto a chair. He had soot on both cheeks, and his white button-down shirt was probably permanently stained.

Jackson decided not to point it out to him. "Since it was Stella's idea to drive Samuel here from Atlanta and since it was her decision to pick me up in D.C. and bring me along for the ride, I'd say she's the one you're going to want to talk to about that."

"She went to bed. That leaves you." Chance tried to stare him down, the bright blue eyes that he'd inherited from their mother's side of the family nearly glowing with irritation. Charity had had eyes just like that. Only her hair had been deep auburn, her lashes golden rather than pitch-black. Thinking about their sister stole some of Jackson's frustration. Family was family, and it mattered more than minor irritations.

Or major ones.

The floorboards above their heads groaned, and he

knew Raina was up there, digging through boxes that were covered with dust, looking for photos that she'd kept hidden away for years.

Boone was right. He *did* want to take care of it. "I'll explain the mess after I make sure that Raina is okay."

"Need any help?" Boone asked, grabbing a bowl of popcorn that had been left on the coffee table and shoving a handful into his mouth.

"No. Thanks."

He walked out of the room, half expecting Chance to follow him.

For once, his brother left well enough alone.

Maybe he was tired, or maybe he understood that what Jackson was doing had nothing to do with the case and everything to do with Raina.

He walked up the narrow stairs. There were only two rooms. The door to the one Stella was using was closed. Knowing her, it was also locked. The door to his room was wide open, light spilling out into the hallway.

Raina was sitting in front of the closet, an open box in front of her, a picture in her hands. She didn't look up as he entered the room, didn't acknowledge him as he sat down beside her.

"It's hard, isn't it?" he said, taking the framed photo she was holding and looking at the little boy who smiled out from it. "I remember when I had to go to Charity's classroom and clean it out. She was a teacher, and she had photos on her desk and a few emergency candy bars in her drawer. She loved chocolate."

"Matt loved his family and he loved God." She lifted a well-worn Bible from the box and wiped dust from its cover. "Nothing else really mattered to him."

"And your son?" Jackson said, looking at the photo

again. Joseph couldn't have been more than two when it was taken, his cheeks still chubby with baby fat. "What did he love?"

"Me." She offered a watery smile. "Matt. Everyone at church. He especially loved the older ladies who sat in the front pew. They always had butterscotch candy or gum for him in their purses."

She lifted a gold-wrapped butterscotch candy out of the box, tossed it back in. "I don't think I can do this."

"You don't have to," he said, wrapping an arm around her waist. "*We* will."

"It's been a long time since I've been part of a *we*," she murmured. "I'm not sure I remember how it works."

He chuckled, pulling the box closer. "It's probably like riding a bike. Once you learn, you never forget how."

He lifted a handful of books from the box, checked through them to be sure no photos were stuck between the pages. "Your husband liked philosophy," he commented as he set the books to the side and lifted a few more.

"He liked studying. There are probably books on everything in there." She reached into one of the other boxes, pulling out a pile of framed pictures. "This is what we want to look through."

She handed him half the stack, and he pretended not to notice that her hands were shaking. He doubted she'd want it pointed out, and it wouldn't change anything.

He looked through one picture after another, family shots and portraits, a few of church activities. He tried not to look too closely at Joseph or to study the pictures of Raina for too long. They'd had a happy life, a good life, and it had been snatched away from them. Looking at snapshots of their life felt voyeuristic.

By the time they finished with the third box, Raina's hands were steadier, her gaze a little less haunted.

"I guess they're not here," she said, setting a water-color of a butterfly on top of a pile of photos.

"It doesn't look like it." He stood, pulled her to her feet. "Do you know who packed the boxes?"

"Destiny and some people I worked with. I think Andrew was there. Maybe Lucas."

"Can you make a list of their names?"

"I have no idea who they were. Destiny brought the boxes to me and told me she'd had help," she responded, her hand still in his, her skin silky and soft and feminine enough to remind him of how much he missed having a woman in his life. "Andrew and Lucas were the only people she mentioned by name."

"Do you think she might remember who they were?"

"Destiny has a good memory, but it's been years." Her gaze dropped to the piles of things. "Funny how time passes and you don't even realize that it has." She sighed and tugged her hand from his. "I need to clean this mess up."

"I can take care of it."

"It's okay." She leaned over and grabbed a few of the books, dumping them into one of the boxes.

"Raina, it can wait."

He was right. It probably could wait, but Raina couldn't stomach the thought of leaving all of Matt's things strewn across the scuffed floor. She picked up a few more books and tossed them on top of the first batch. She knew Jackson was watching, and she didn't care, because all she wanted was to put the boxes back in the closet, close the door and forget about them again.

"Cleaning up isn't going to make your problems go away. You know that, right?"

"I'm not trying to make anything go away."

"Except the past, and that's not possible," he replied.

She met his eyes, saw compassion written clearly on his face. He knew what she felt. He'd loved his sister, lost her, had to live with that every day.

"How do you do it?" she whispered, because she wanted to know. Needed to know.

"Do what?"

"Live every day knowing that your sister isn't around?"

"By living every day hoping and praying that I can keep other people from living the same way. By telling myself every single morning that God means for something good to come out of what happened and that the best thing I can do to honor my sister, the *only* thing I can do, is be a part of that. Come on. We need to go tell Andrew what we found." His hand settled on her waist, his thumb resting on a sliver of exposed skin between her jeans and her sweater.

It felt good.

So good Raina could have turned in his arms, let her hands settle on his waist, her head drop to his chest. Let herself enjoy, just for a minute, the feeling of not being alone.

Jackson's eyes darkened, his gaze dropping to her lips, his thumb sliding across that tiny bit of skin. Her breath caught, and she wanted to lean in and taste his lips almost as much as she wanted to turn and run.

"You better go down the steps first. The stairway is narrow," he muttered, his hand dropping away.

She nodded, her throat too tight to speak.

She had loved Matt with her whole heart, but with him, she had never felt the quicksilver heat that raced through her when she looked into Jackson's eyes.

She shivered, hurrying downstairs and stopping short when she reached the kitchen. All three men were there. Andrew, Chance and the redhead Jackson had called Boone.

He smiled, held up a package of cookies that she'd left on the counter. "I hope you don't mind that I snagged a couple of these. I'm starving."

"I can make you something."

"No," Jackson said as he stepped into the room behind her, his arm brushing hers as he walked past. Her skin tightened, her body humming with an awareness she wasn't comfortable feeling. She'd closed herself off after the accident, locked herself in tight, because she hadn't wanted to risk her heart, hadn't wanted to ever again feel her soul shatter, her world shift, everything she'd understood be turned upside down.

"Boone is a food addict," Jackson continued. "If you start feeding him, you'll be feeding him from now until the cows come home."

"I resent that accusation, Jack. I might like to eat, but I can stop anytime I want to. The thing is, I don't want to." Boone pulled a cookie from the package and popped it into his mouth.

"I hate to interrupt the fun and games, folks," Andrew said. "But I think we have more important things to discuss than anyone's eating habits. Did you find the photos, Raina?"

"No." She opened the freezer and took out a plastic container of chicken noodle soup. It was so much easier to do that than to think about what those missing photos meant, to speculate on who took them and why.

"I helped Destiny pack the boxes, but most of the people there were your coworkers. Lucas was there. I remember that."

"I can ask Destiny who the other people were." She opened the container, dumped the frozen lump of soup into a pot. She'd made the chicken noodle for a church soup-and-sandwich meal, but she'd decided at the last minute not to go. She hadn't wanted to sit at a table filled with single men and women who all seemed to want nothing more than to find their soul mates.

All *she* wanted was to find some peace, but that was as elusive as mountain mist.

"I'll call her myself. See if we can get some answers for a change." Andrew sighed. "I'd better head out. I'm going to have to take the photos as evidence, Raina. I can't promise that you'll get them back."

"It's okay." But it wasn't really. Now that she'd seen the photographs, she wanted them desperately. Which was silly. She had plenty of pictures in her bedroom and tucked away in photo albums in her closet. She didn't need two more. Especially two with the faces scratched out of them. Still, sending them with Andrew felt like sending away a piece of her heart.

"I'll call as soon as I know something. In the meantime, stay safe. No more going for walks without an escort."

"I won't."

"Don't say it if you don't mean it, okay?" Andrew's gaze was sharp, his expression hard. "I don't like the way things are playing out, and if you're not careful, what happened to Butch will happen to you."

It sounded more like a threat than a warning, and Raina's skin crawled. She touched her throat. It didn't take much to crush a windpipe. A little more pressure and the guy who'd attacked her could have done it easily.

"I'm heading out." Andrew nodded curtly, no humor, no kindness, no compassion in his gaze, just that same implacable expression. "You have my cell phone number. Call immediately if anything happens."

"Do you want me to—"

"I want you to stay in this house behind closed doors until this is over. That's *all* I want you to do," he snapped.

He stalked from the room, brisk footsteps tapping on the floor, the front door opening and then shutting with a little too much force.

"Guy has a temper on him," Boone commented, pulling another cookie from the package.

"How well do you know him, Raina?" Jackson's brother asked.

"Really well. I've known him since we were kids. After I got married, he and my husband were good friends."

"I see." Chance crossed his arms over his chest, his expression unreadable.

Raina didn't know what he saw, but she had a feeling it wasn't anything good. "If you're thinking that Andrew has something to do with the trouble I've been having, you're thinking wrong."

"At the moment, I'm not thinking anything. Except that someone did a number on your head." His gaze dropped to her throat, and she resisted the urge to touch the bruises she knew were there. "And your throat. A little more pressure, and you'd be dead."

Exactly what she'd been thinking, but she wasn't going to admit it to Chance.

"Ignore my brother, Raina," Jackson cut in. "He gets grumpy when things are out of his control."

"I get grumpy," Chance ground out, "when my brother gets questioned by the police."

"I think we've covered this before," Boone said. "How about we skip the replay and have some of whatever is in that pot? It smells great."

He leaned in close, inhaled deeply.

Raina couldn't help smiling. He was good-looking, laid-back and a lot easier on the emotions than Jackson. "It's homemade chicken noodle soup."

"What kind of noodles?"

"Egg."

"You put carrots in it?"

"And celery. Roasted chicken and some seasoning. It's my grandmother's recipe. Passed down for three generations."

He whistled softly. "I think I'm in love with your grandmother."

"You haven't even tasted the soup yet." She laughed.

"But I will, and once I do, I'm going to be smitten. It's just the way it is."

"My grandmother will be flattered, but since she's been married for sixty years, your love is going to be unrequited."

"Maybe I can convince her to adopt me, then." He grabbed a spoon from the drying rack and dipped it into the stone-cold soup.

"It's still half-frozen!" she protested, but he scooped a spoonful into his mouth and sighed blissfully.

"Yep," he said. "Love. Just pour about half of that in a bowl for me. You and the brothers can share the rest."

"Selfish a little?" Chance asked, but even he seemed amused by Boone.

"Hungry a lot. Seeing as how that's mostly your fault for sending me off without enough cash to adequately nourish my body—"

"You had plenty of money," Chance protested.

Raina smiled, enjoying the banter and the obvious camaraderie between the men.

"The soup will be ready in a few minutes," she interrupted. "If you want to grab sheets and blankets in the linen closet in the hall while you're waiting, you can make up some beds on the couch. I'd offer beds, but I don't have any spares."

"There's no need for that," Chance said, his smooth baritone nothing like his brother's deep Southern drawl. Despite the soot that stained his dress shirt, he looked polished and put together, his black slacks pressed, his wool coat a deep black with no sign of fading or wear and tear. A shoulder holster peeked out from beneath the coat, but the gun remained hidden. He might look more polished, but Raina had a feeling he was just as tough as his brother. "Boone and I aren't planning to stay."

"We're not planning to drive all the way back to D.C., either," Boone mumbled through a mouthful of cookie.

Chance frowned. "You have a better idea?"

"Yeah. We take the lady up on her offer, make beds for ourselves and sleep until the sun comes up. I, for one, could use a little shut-eye."

"You can sleep in the car."

"You're not hearing me, Chance," Boone said. "I don't want to drive, fly or jog anywhere tonight. After all the travel I've been doing for the company the past few months, all I want to do is lie down. Doesn't matter if I'm lying down on a bed, rocks, a ledge or the floor, as long as I get to sleep and no one disturbs me." He closed the package of cookies and wiped crumbs from his shirt.

Raina stirred the soup and let the conversation wash over her. It felt nice, the words filling the room in a way nothing had in the past few months. It wasn't just the men's physical presence. It was their energy, their obvious connection and fondness for one another. They were family, and that made the house feel like a home.

She hadn't realized how much she'd missed that until it was there again—the warmth, the joy, the simple pleasure of being together.

She grabbed a spoon from the drainer near the sink, her eyes burning, her chest tight. Life was moving on. *She* was moving on. She felt that more than she ever had, felt the slow shifting of focus from the past to the future.

It was the way it should be, but it still hurt, because moving on meant letting go, and she didn't know how she could ever do that.

She turned on the water, rinsed the already clean spoon because she didn't want the men to see the tears in her eyes.

Something moved in the window above the sink. A face, pressing against the glass, skin white, eyes as black as the deepest darkness.

She screamed, stumbled back.

Screamed again as the lights went out and the kitchen plunged into darkness.

FIFTEEN

Jackson sprinted to the back door, adrenaline surging through him. Someone had been staring in the window. He'd seen the face, turned off the light to keep whoever it was from having a clear view of the interior.

"Boone, stay with the lady," Chance barked, coming up on Jackson's heels.

They hit the edge of the back deck at the same time, pausing in unison, a team, ready to work together, fight together, do whatever it took to succeed together. They had their differences, but when it came to the job, they were always absolutely in sync.

"Be careful, bro," Chance muttered. "I don't want you taken out by some small-town thug who has a crush on your lady friend."

"You be careful, too," Jackson responded. "Mom would ki…"

His voice trailed off as he caught sight of a dark figure moving slowly toward the corner of the house. *Very* slowly.

He touched his brother's arm, gestured to what looked to be an ancient man. White hair, white nightshirt tucked into baggy black sweats.

A disguise, Chance mouthed, but Jackson didn't think so. The guy moved as if every bone in his body hurt, his feet shuffling through dry grass as he picked his way across the yard. If he was trying to make an escape, he wasn't doing it very effectively.

"Sir!" Jackson called out, and the old guy paused, glancing over his shoulder and scowling.

"Go back to whatever shenanigans you were up to," he spat. "I'm going home to call the cops."

"I'd say the shenanigans are more on your part," Chance responded. "Peeking into other people's windows is a crime."

"She's not other people, son. She's my neighbor. I have an obligation to check on her when every light in the house is on and cars are filling up the driveway," the man snapped. "Too many people on this road lately. That's the problem, and you can rest assured, I'm going to let the police know about it."

"Larry?" Raina peered out the open door, her face a pale oval in the darkness. "Is that you?"

"Who else would it be? Now, like I said, you just go on back to what you were doing." He started shuffling away again, but Raina hurried onto the deck, probably would have gone after the guy if Jackson hadn't grabbed her belt loop and pulled her to a stop.

"I'm making chicken noodle soup, Larry. Come on in and have some before you go home."

"Come into your den of iniquity? I don't think so." But Larry stopped again, gnarled fists settling on his narrow hips. "What would Matt think? That's what I want to know? A Christian woman like you with three grown men in her house."

"There's a woman here, too," Raina responded, pulling at Jackson's fingers and trying to loosen his grip on her belt loop.

Wasn't going to happen. Larry might be old, but that didn't mean he wasn't responsible for Raina's troubles.

"And that makes it better?" Larry huffed, shuffling back toward them, his slow plodding movements almost painful to watch.

He made it to the steps, and Chance took his arm, helping him onto the deck. "Sir, I think you're misunderstanding the situation."

"What's to misunderstand? A beautiful young widow and three men who are taking advantage of her grief. I'd say I'm not misunderstanding a thing!"

"Actually, Larry," Raina said, "these men are from HEART. The organization that rescued me from—"

"I know where you were rescued from, Raina. It was all over the news," Larry snapped.

"If you're following the news, then you've probably seen the stories about my efforts to—"

"Bring a kid over here. Yeah. Yeah. I've seen it. What does that have to do with the price of tea in China?"

"Everything," Raina responded with a lot more patience than Jackson was feeling. "Samuel's flight got canceled because of the storm we had. Jackson and a coworker drove him here."

"And now they're all staying the night? You think that's appropriate?"

"Yes, actually," Raina said kindly. "I do. We aren't supposed to turn away strangers who are in need. Why would we turn away people that we know?" She took Larry's arm, led him into the kitchen.

The light was already on, and Boone was standing over the soup pot, several bowls on the counter beside him. "Looked like things were under control, so I thought I'd keep the food from burning."

"Good to see your priorities are right." Chance sighed, dropping into one of the kitchen chairs. He looked worn, the fine lines near his eyes deeper.

"Go ahead and have a seat, Larry." Raina pulled out another chair. "I made my grandmother's chicken noodle soup."

"Can't be better than Dora's," Larry muttered, but he eased into the chair, his bones creaking.

"Dora?" Boone asked, spooning soup into a bowl and setting it on the table in front of Larry.

"My late wife. May God rest her soul." Larry took the spoon that Raina handed him and dug into the soup with more gusto than Jackson expected. From the way he was eating, Jackson would say he hadn't had a meal in a while.

Raina must have been thinking the same thing. She frowned and opened an old-fashioned bread box that sat on the counter. "How about some bread with that, Larry?"

"I wouldn't want to impose," he said, but he took the slice she offered him, layering it with cold butter Raina took from the fridge.

"You want some?" Boone asked, pointing the serving spoon in Jackson's direction.

"No. Thanks."

"Suit yourself. Me? I'm going to eat seconds."

"When did you have firsts?" Chance looked up from the bowl Boone had set in front of him.

"While the ol—" He glanced at Larry. "While Larry was heading back across the yard. Took him a while and that was just enough time for me to eat soup."

"I've got old bones, kid. You don't understand because you're young and healthy, but just you wait. Your turn is coming, and you'll be the one shuffling across a yard you used to do backflips in."

"Good to know," Boone said without ire. He had the patience of a saint. "Want some more soup?"

"I think I will." Larry held out his bowl. "It's good soup, Raina. Not Dora good, but good enough to eat more."

"Thanks, Larry." She smiled, her eyes red-rimmed and deeply shadowed. "I'm making another batch tomorrow. I'll bring some over for you."

Jackson doubted that making soup had really been on her agenda for the day, but Larry's collarbone was prominent above the neckline of his nightshirt, his cheeks hollow. He either didn't have money for food or didn't bother eating. Either way, he needed to be fed.

He handed the guy another slice of bread. "You said there's been too many people on this road lately, Larry. What did you mean?"

"All kinds of cars driving up and down the road."

"You mean the cars that are in the driveway?" he pressed, because the guy might be thin and ornery, but his eyes seemed to be working just fine. If he'd seen something or someone skulking around the house, Jackson wanted to know it.

"Do you think I'm dense, son?" Larry retorted. "The police car drove away ten minutes ago. Five minutes after that, a car drove down to the end of the road, did a U-turn and left again. That's when I decided enough was enough."

"Did you see what the car looked like?"

"Black. A sporty little sedan. Not an American-made

car. Some foreign model." Larry sniffed. "You'd think people would want to support their own country's economy, but that's the kind of world we live in. Everyone for them—"

"Have you seen the car around here before?" Chance cut him off, obviously trying to keep the conversation on track.

"I can't say that I have." Larry frowned, dipping buttered bread into his soup and letting the broth drip down his chin as he ate it. "Of course—" he grabbed a napkin from a holder that sat in the middle of the table and wiped his chin "—I haven't seen the Jeep in a couple of nights, so maybe the guy got a new car."

"What Jeep?" Raina asked.

"How should I know what Jeep? All I know is that it's been coming around here for a few months."

Jackson's pulse jumped, and he met Raina's eyes. "Are you sure you don't know anyone besides Destiny's boyfriend who owns a Jeep?"

She bit her lip, shook her head. "No."

"Well, someone with a Jeep knows you," Larry replied. "Guy drives down this road once or twice a week. I almost called the cops a few times, but they threatened to haul me in for criminal mischief if I made any more false reports. Not that my reports were false. My church shoes didn't just disappear from my closet and reappear in my bedroom all by themselves, and someone *did* steal my lunch one day. I made that sandwich as sure as I'm sitting at this table eating pork roast."

No one pointed out that he was eating chicken noodle soup.

"What color was the Jeep?" Jackson asked, not sure

if Larry had really seen the Jeep or if he'd imagined it the way he'd imagined the pork in his bowl.

"Blue. Not one of those fancy Jeeps, either. An old one. Had a couple of dents in the fender. This guy is smart. Values his dollars." Larry nodded his head vigorously, his white hair flopping over his eyes.

"Is that the color of the Jeep they found abandoned earlier?" Chance asked.

"Yeah," Jackson responded, and it fit the description perfectly. If Larry was right about what he'd seen, someone had been stalking Raina for longer than a few days.

"Did you happen to see the driver, Larry?"

"Never got a good look at the guy. He did get out once. Walked up to Raina's front window and looked inside. The lights were on, but I knew she wasn't home, so I wasn't worried about him being some pervert. I thought maybe he was scoping the house out, trying to see if she had anything he could steal. Good thing Matt was a pastor and not a multimillionaire." He let out a bark of laughter that ended in a dry, raspy cough.

Raina set a glass of water near his elbow. "When was that, Larry? You never mentioned it to me before."

"A year or two ago?" Larry frowned, sopping up the last bit of soup with a third piece of bread. "And I didn't mention it because I didn't want to scare you. I've been watching, keeping old Bessie real close."

"Bessie?"

"My hunting rifle." He glanced around the room. "I guess I forgot to grab her on my way out the door."

"Thank the good Lord for that," Boone murmured.

"What's that?" Larry speared him with a hard look.

"You mentioned that you'd been seeing the Jeep for a few months," Boone said, sidestepping the question.

"Not a few years. So how is it possible you saw the guy a couple of years ago?"

"Did I say a couple of years?" Larry rubbed his forehead, his knuckles knotted with arthritis. "That was a mistake. The guy hasn't been coming out that long. You call the police. They'll tell you what day it was. I called them and left a message for that Eric guy. I knew he was your friend, Raina, so I thought he'd take it seriously."

"You mean Andrew Wallace?" Raina asked.

"Yes. Right. Andrew. I don't know what it is with me and names lately." He stood carefully, as if every movement hurt. "The thing is, I told Matt that if anything happened to him, I'd take care of you and the kid. I can't take care of the kid, but I can look out for you. Unfortunately, that dingbat cop didn't even bother to come out to investigate."

"Thanks for trying," Raina said.

"Don't thank me. Thank that husband of yours, when you see him on the other side." He paused with his hand on the front doorknob, his shoulders slumped beneath his baggy nightshirt. "Matt is the only person who ever understood about me and Dora, and I owe him big for that."

"What did he understand about her?" Raina asked gently, and Jackson braced himself for the answer, because he knew it was going to cut deep, make him think about all the things that were possible when two people loved each other enough to make things work.

"That when she died, she took a piece of me with her. I never did get that piece back. No matter how many years passed. Three decades, and she's still the only person I want to be around. Most people don't get that, but Matt did." He blinked rheumy eyes. "And you know, it was mighty nice having someone care about me for a while."

He opened the door, and Boone hurried after him, a heavy winter coat in his arms. "Hey, Pops! It's too cold to be outside without a coat."

"Who you calling Pops, boy?"

"It's what I call my grandfather."

Larry snorted, but he didn't shove away the coat Boone slung around his shoulders.

"Would you like it better if I called you 'old man'?" Boone put a hand on Larry's elbow and the two made their way down the stairs, whatever Larry said in reply was lost in the rustling of the trees.

"I should probably go with them," Raina said, more to herself than anyone else.

"Boone will take care of him." Jackson tugged her away from the open door and the chilly night air. "And I'm thinking it's not the best idea for you to be outside."

"He's right," Chance said. "If someone drove by the house after Officer Wallace left, we could be dealing with a stalker who's so deeply enmeshed in his fantasies, he doesn't care if he's seen. At the very least, we're dealing with someone who's keeping an eye on the house, who knows when Raina is home and when she's gone."

"The question is, what does he want?" Jackson asked the question that was floating around in Raina's head.

"Love? Attention?" Chance suggested. "He's a crackpot, so it's hard to say. I'm going to drive down the road, see if anyone is parked close by. I'll call Wallace on the way. Make sure he's updated on everything. Try not to get in any trouble while I'm gone, Jackson." He walked outside and shut the door, leaving a cool gust of wind and sudden silence in his wake.

"Do you think Chance is right about the person wanting love and affection? Do you actually think someone has been stalking me for months?" Raina finally asked, because she was hoping that he didn't.

"I don't know. Larry seems confused, but he was pretty clear on the details of that Jeep. It sounded just like the one that the police impounded at your in-laws' old house today. Which looked like the one that nearly ran me down. That's two vehicles. If Larry is right about the sedan, that's three. Could be our guy has multiple vehicles to keep from being noticed when he's following you."

"If he's following me."

"Don't bury your head in the sand, Raina. Something is going on here, and it all revolves around you."

"I know. That's what worries me."

"You don't have to worry, Raina. You have people who care about you and a God who's bigger than all your problems."

"I know, but it's still hard sometimes." She rubbed her arms, trying to chase away the chill that seemed to had sunk so deep into her bones that she didn't think it would ever leave.

"What's hard?" he asked, cupping her shoulders, looking into her face.

He was nothing like Matt. Not quiet or easy or bookish. If he had been, it would have been so much easier to explain what she felt when she looked into his eyes.

"This is hard," she breathed, her throat tight and hot from emotions she didn't want to feel. "Moving on. Letting go. It's hard."

"The other option is being like Larry. Bitter and lonely and angry at the world and at God."

"I'm not angry. I'm confused." She moved to the fireplace, putting some distance between Jackson and herself so she could think. "I thought I was doing it right, making good choices, following the path God wanted me on. Then the rug got pulled out from under me and—"

"You wondered if you'd made a mistake somewhere along the line. If maybe you were being punished for not being the Christian God wanted you to be?"

"Yes. I guess so," she admitted.

"It's a game our minds play, Raina, to help us make sense of the incomprehensible. But it doesn't speak to the truth." He touched her cheek, his fingers sliding to her nape, kneading the tense muscles there.

"What is the truth, then, Jackson?" she murmured. "That things just happen? That tragedy is all around us, and we just have to make the best of it?"

"That God's love prevails. Even in the darkest times. Even when we lose everything." He tugged her closer, his palm warm on her neck, his eyes midnight-blue and filled with sincerity and compassion. "That faith is something that grows during trials and that holding on to it leads us to the exact place where we belong."

Like here with you? she wanted to ask, but he leaned in, his lips brushing her temple, her cheek, her lips, and all the tears she hadn't wanted to cry were suddenly there, in her eyes, on her cheeks, dripping down her chin.

"Shh." He wrapped his arms around her. "It's going to be okay."

She could have moved away.

It should have been easy to, but she felt drugged by his touch, her muscles relaxing for the first time in what seemed like months. And instead of moving away, she stayed right where she was, her hands on his waist, her head resting against his chest while the clock ticked away the minutes and the wind began to howl beneath the eaves.

SIXTEEN

She woke to the sound of a child crying. Not the frantic cries of her nightmares. The quiet sniffles of someone who didn't want to be heard.

She sat up, cocked her head to the side. Rain splattered against the window, another round of icy storms moving in. The wind buffeted the glass and sent sheets of rain splattering against the siding, its quiet moan an eerie backdrop to the rain.

Was that what had woken her?

No. There it was again! Just below the sound of the storm. A quiet sob.

Samuel?

It had to be. She climbed out of bed, yanked a robe on over her flannel pajamas and crept into the hallway. Boone and Chance were sleeping in the living room, the soft glow of the fire she'd lit for them undulating on the floor at the head of the hall.

Samuel's door was open, his muffled sobs drifting into the hall.

"Samuel?" she whispered from the doorway.

The cries stopped, but he didn't respond.

She walked into the dark room, nearly tripping over

Samuel's backpack. He'd crumpled it up, spilled all the contents onto the floor. She flipped on the light, stepping over the mess and walking to the bed. He had the pillow over his head, one thin hand pressing it close to his ear.

"Samuel?" She touched his shoulder, felt him trembling.

She almost backed away, almost left him there because it seemed like what he wanted. But he was a child with wounds so deep, she wasn't sure they would ever heal. *Knew* they never would if someone didn't care enough to hold out a hand and pull him close, to tell him that things would get better.

She tugged on the pillow, and he released it, rolling onto his back and staring at the ceiling, his cheeks wet with tears. A picture was on the bed beside him, the grainy color photo smudged with dirt, one edge ripped off. She knew it was his family. Mother, father, a teenage sister, a toddler. He was there, too, much younger, but she recognized his wide brown eyes and thick lashes.

"It's hard when you miss someone, isn't it?" she asked quietly, and he opened his mouth, let out a mournful cry. It broke Raina's heart in a hundred ways it had never been broken before, and she reached for him. She pulled him onto her lap even though he wasn't a baby, wasn't her son, probably hadn't been held by anyone in so many years that he'd forgotten what it was like.

"I'm sorry, Samuel," she whispered against his ear. "I wish I could bring them back to you, but I can't. I can only give you what I have here."

"Until one year," he wailed. "And I will be alone again."

She winced at his words. That's the way it had been planned. A year of medical help, of therapy, of healing his body and mind. She'd been hoping and praying that someone would step forward before Samuel's visa expired, but there was no guarantee. She couldn't let him go back, though. She knew that now, had probably always known it. He deserved more, needed more, and if she didn't give it to him, she couldn't count on anyone else doing it.

"No. You won't," she said, because she couldn't tell him anything else. "We'll work things out, Samuel. I promise. We'll make sure you can stay."

He shook his head, eased off her lap, a little boy who looked like an old man, his eyes too filled with weariness.

"No," he said. "You have had your son, and he is gone. You do not need another son."

"I do not need another son like the one I had. There can only ever be one of him," she said honestly. "But I need someone. My house is too empty now that my family is gone."

"My heart is empty." He touched his chest, and Raina's heart shattered again.

"Maybe we both need help filling the empty places. Come on. Let's take your family photo and put it in a frame so that it won't be ruined." She offered a hand, and he took it.

"What is a frame?"

"Something to put photos in. With glass and plastic or wood around the edges. Like that." She pointed to a picture of a cartoon frog that she'd framed and hung on the wall.

Samuel nodded and reached for the family photo, holding it tenderly. She handed him a crutch and he positioned it under his arm, the picture so carefully held that it might have been the finest china or the most valuable jewel.

She had plenty of framed photos in her room, and she brought him there, lifting one off the dresser. Matt smiled out at her, his dark eyes filled with amusement. She remembered taking the picture. They'd been hiking on the Appalachian Trail a few months before Joseph's birth, the fall foliage thick and beautiful.

Her heart ached as she looked at it, but she slid it from the frame, placed it in a drawer that used to be filled with Matt's T-shirts, but had been empty for almost as long as he'd been gone. When she closed the drawer, it felt like saying another goodbye.

"Okay," she said, her voice just a little shaky. "Let's do this."

She helped Joseph slide the photo into place, showed him how to close the back, then flipped it over and handed it to him. "There. Now it will be protected. You can put it on the dresser in your room. After your infection is gone, we'll go to the store and have copies of it made."

"Thank you." He stared down at the photo, then set it on the dresser next to a picture that had been taken at the church picnic four months before the accident. She and Matt sitting in the shade of an elm tree, Joseph standing behind them, his arms around both of their shoulders. "There," Samuel said. "Now we are all family."

She nodded, because she couldn't speak, didn't even know what to say. She'd gone to Africa because she'd needed to escape her heartache and because she'd wanted to renew her faith. She'd thought she would give plenty and expected to get nothing in return.

She'd gotten Samuel, though. A boy who'd risked everything to save her life. The least she could do was risk her heart to give him what he needed the most. "Yes," she agreed. "We are all family. Now you need to get back in bed. Your infection won't heal if you don't get the rest you need."

He didn't argue, just hopped back to his room and climbed into bed. Raina pulled the covers over him, kissed his forehead, touched his cheek. "Sleep well, Samuel."

"Sleep well, Raina, and have the sweetest dreams," he replied. "Good night."

She turned off the light, left the door open and walked back to her room. It was nearly three in the morning, but she didn't think she could sleep. If she hadn't had guests, she'd have gone into the living room, sat in front of the fire, lost herself in a movie or a good book.

She paced to the window that overlooked the backyard. The wind whistled through the trees, scattering dead leaves across the ground. It gusted through the single pane glass, and she shivered. It looked bitterly cold out, but she'd rather be sitting on the back deck than be cooped up in her room. She touched the lock on the window, thought about how easy it would be to open it up and climb out into the whipping wind. Thought about just how foolish that would be.

"I thought I heard you moving around in here. You're not planning to make your escape, are you?" Jackson said quietly, his voice so surprising, she jumped.

"Good gravy!" she snapped. "You scared me."

"'Good gravy'?" He laughed, stepping farther into the room, his body silhouetted by the light filtering down the hall from the living room. Broad shoulders, slim hips, a laugh that made her want to smile. If she'd met him before Matt, she'd have been smitten from the first moment she'd looked into his eyes.

But she'd met him after, and she still couldn't seem to resist.

"You sound like my great-grandmother," he continued. "One of the most interesting Southern belles in all of Raleigh. The woman did have a way with words. She still does."

"I think I'd like your great-grandmother."

"Then you'll have to meet her. She's coming to D.C. for Thanksgiving. Might be hard to fit her and the rest of the Miller clan in my apartment, but I'll manage. If someone doesn't offer me a bigger space. Like a house. On some acreage."

"Is that a hint?" she asked with a smile.

"No hint, Raina. It's a blatant attempt to secure your premises for the occasion," he responded, his Southern drawl so thick, she laughed.

"Are you trying to charm me into it, Jackson?" Because it was working, and she didn't think she minded at all.

"Just trying to get what I need. Chance and I were supposed to host the meal at his place, but he burned his house down in an attempt to get out of it."

"He burned his own house down?"

"I should rephrase that. His faulty furnace exploded and burned the house down. He's homeless and living at the HEART offices for the next few months."

"Why not with you?"

"I live in a one-bedroom apartment the size of a postage stamp. He stayed three nights and decided he needed a little more room to breathe. His new house should be ready to move into by Christmas. In the meantime, I have the whole Thanksgiving dilemma to deal with. I need help, and I'm not afraid to ask for it."

She almost said no. She'd spent the past three Thanksgivings at her parents', having quiet meals where no mention was made of the people who were missing. It wasn't special or fun, but it was what she did, and it had become as comfortable as an old pair of shoes.

The thing was, she didn't really want comfort anymore. She wanted the little thrill of excitement that came from looking to the future, imagining new and wonderful things. If Matt were standing behind her, whispering in her ear, he'd tell her that was the way things should be. "You may not be afraid to ask," she said. "But I'm kind of afraid to give it. Your family sounds..."

"Intimidating? Scary? Overwhelming? Loud? Those are all apt descriptions. And the truth is, my family is a little nuts, but they're great people."

"You don't have to convince me. I'll help you out."

"Seriously?"

"Yes. I'll even make peach pie to go with the pumpkin and apple."

"You make the peach. We've got plenty of people in the family who will bring the others."

"How many are we talking about?" she asked.

"A dozen. Two. It's hard to tell. Lots of uncles and aunts and cousins. Stella usually comes, but I think that might not happen this time." He didn't explain why, and she didn't ask. She'd sensed tension between Stella and Chance, and she figured it had something to do with that.

"I should probably invite Larry."

"I think you should."

"And Destiny."

"And the good doctor Kent?" he asked, closing the

distance between them. She could see his face in the darkness, the hard angle of his jaw, the sharp edge of his cheekbone, the smooth firm line of his lips. He'd changed into a shirt that looked like a blue version of his brother's, only he hadn't tucked it into jeans that were a shade darker than the ones he'd been wearing earlier.

"I think he'll be busy working at the soup kitchen."

"What if he isn't?"

"I'm sure he'll have plenty of invitations to choose from. Even if he doesn't, I'm not planning to invite him. I wouldn't want to lead him on. He's not my type, and it wouldn't be fair to make him think he is."

"So, if he's not your type, who is?" He smoothed his palms up her arms, his hands settling on her shoulders.

She wasn't sure how to answer. Ten years ago, her type had been bookish and quiet, funny and smart, caring and just a little awkward. She was beginning to realize she had a soft spot for tall, dark-haired men with Southern accents.

It shouldn't have made her sad, but it did.

She swallowed down the lump of grief, tried to make herself smile. "I don't know. It's been a long time since I've thought about it."

"Maybe you could think about it," Jackson responded, his fingers playing in the ends of her hair. "And let me know after this is all over."

"*If* it's ever over."

"It will be. Trouble never lasts forever."

He was right. It didn't. Maybe heartache didn't, either. Maybe, after enough time passed, wounds healed and hearts mended and lives that were empty could be filled again.

A soft buzzing sound filled the room, and she frowned. "What's that?"

"My cell phone." He dug it from his pocket, glanced at the number. "It's Wallace. I'd better take it."

She switched on the light while he answered, perched on the bed while he listened. It wasn't good news. She could tell by the hardness in his eyes, the tightness in his jaw.

"Are you sure?" he finally asked. "Okay. Will do. Thanks."

He tucked the phone back in his pocket.

"What's going on?" she asked, following him as he walked into the hall.

"The evidence team found a scarf in the back of the Jeep that nearly ran me down. Fibers on it matched fibers that were clinging to Butch's coat when he was found."

The news was like a splash of ice water in the face, every thought of Thanksgiving and moving on fading in the wake of it. "So he was murdered by the person who's stalking me," she said.

"It looks that way."

He walked into the living room. She waited in the threshold, afraid to walk in on the men who were sleeping.

"Might as well come in," Boone called. "We're decent, and thanks to Jackson, we're awake."

She stepped into the living room, the firelight casting a warm glow over the room. She'd forgotten how nice it was to have the fire burning, the room toasty, the logs snapping.

Boone stood near the fireplace, his red hair fiery in the light. "I guess neither of you know the first thing about jet lag. If you did, you wouldn't wake a man who just got back from the Middle East."

"Sorry, Boone," Jackson said, and he didn't sound sorry at all. "But we've got a situation, and I need to fill you in on it."

"What situation?" Chance asked. At some point, he'd changed into a brick red T-shirt and faded jeans. Even in those, he looked polished.

"Hold on," Boone said. "If we're going to be briefed, we may as well get Stella involved. Otherwise, she'll show up right around the time I'm falling asleep again and want the information."

"Someone can fill her in in the morning," Chance said, stalking to the switch on the wall and turning it on. "Now, what's going on, Jackson?"

"Hold on, boss." Boone straightened to his full height and crossed his arms over his chest. For the first time since Raina had met him, he looked angry and just a little dangerous. "We don't break the rules for anyone. Not even for you, and the team rules are that everyone on a mission is present during the briefing."

"This isn't a mission," Chance growled.

"Yeah. It is. You set up the parameters of what a mission was way before the company executed its first rescue. Once we commit to helping someone, we're on mission together until the job is done. Doesn't matter if we're getting paid."

"Now you remember the rules?" Chance sighed. "Fine. Someone go get her. Then Jackson will brief us. Happy?"

"Does a whip-poor-will sing in the morning?" Boone responded.

"I don't know, Boone. How about you just go get Stella, so we can move on with things?" Chance growled.

"I will." He snagged Raina's hand as he walked by, pulling her toward the kitchen. "And maybe you can make some coffee for us, Raina?"

"Sure," she said, more worried about what else Jackson was going to say than coffee, missions or rules.

"And maybe an omelet? Some toast? Nothing fancy. Just something to keep the brain working."

"I can do that," she said, opening the fridge and pulling out what she needed.

"You're a good kid," he responded, ruffling her hair. "I like you. I think you and Jackson are going to do just fine together."

He disappeared upstairs, and she started the coffee-pot, cracked eggs into a bowl, put bread in the toaster. Went through all the motions of making breakfast for the team who was protecting her, and the whole time, his words were running through her head.

I think you and Jackson are going to do just fine to-gether.

A few days ago, she would have laughed at the idea that she could be fine with anyone.

She wasn't laughing anymore.

She was praying, hoping, believing that there was something good coming out of the bad, and that Jackson was right. That her troubles wouldn't last forever, that when they were over, she'd have Thanksgiving with his rowdy family and with Samuel, and all the things she'd believed about God and faith and hope, all the things she'd thought she'd lost when Joseph and Matt died, would finally be renewed.

SEVENTEEN

At ten-thirty in the morning, Raina had already run out of ideas for entertaining Samuel. Being stuck in the house wasn't fun, especially for a ten-year-old boy. Unfortunately, aside from a visit to the doctor, Raina and Samuel had been confined to the house. Thank goodness Samuel had another appointment scheduled for that afternoon. They both needed to get outside, get a little fresh air, try to move beyond the circumstances they were in.

Not easy to do when the circumstances never seemed to change. After nearly a week of investigating, the police were no closer to finding Butch's murderer. Which meant, of course, that they were no closer to finding Raina's stalker. Things had been so quiet for the past few days, Raina was beginning to wonder if there'd ever actually been a stalker. If not for the healing wound on her forehead and the fading bruises on her neck, she could almost believe there wasn't one.

Raina sighed, shoving her hands into soapy dishwater and pulling out a plate. She scrubbed it, rinsed it and handed it to Samuel.

"I can wash these," he offered. "You rest."

"It will be faster if we work together. When we're done, we can play chess." After nearly a week of spending almost all their time together, she'd learned a lot about Samuel. He loved learning. He loved games that made him think, television shows that taught him something. He could read quite a bit of English, and he loved books. He also liked to help, and he treated her like an elderly aunt who might expire at any moment if she didn't get enough rest. Sometimes that made her smile. Other times it made her wonder if she should slap on some foundation and blush and try to look a little younger.

The floorboards above her head creaked as she handed Samuel another plate to dry. Jackson was upstairs with Stella and Boone. Chance was in the living room on Skype with a team member who was in China. It seemed strange that a house that had been empty and lonely for years was suddenly full. That meant more dishes, more cooking, more cleaning. It also meant more companionship. Raina hadn't realized how much she'd missed that until she suddenly had it again.

"I was thinking," she said as she washed the last dish and pulled the plug. "After we go to the doctor today, we should stop at the library and get some books."

"Library?" Samuel wiped the last drop of water from the dish and carefully set it on the counter.

"It's a place where you can go and borrow books. Once you read the books, you return them and you can borrow more."

"Really?" His dark eyes lit up, a smile spreading across his face. "I think I will like a library."

"Who's going to the library?" Jackson walked into the room wearing what looked like another one of his brother's dress shirts. This one was a deep blue that matched his eyes, the fabric soft and well-worn. He'd rolled the sleeves up to his elbows and left the buttons undone, a dove-gray T-shirt beneath clinging to his chest and abdomen. His muscles were clearly defined, the holster he wore strapped to his chest emphasizing his masculinity.

Her heart jumped as he walked toward her, her stomach filling with a million butterflies. Being near him was like the first day of summer, warm and exciting and wonderful with just a hint of regret because spring was over.

"I thought I could take Samuel there after his doctor's appointment," she responded, hoping he didn't notice how flushed her skin was. She felt like a schoolgirl with a crush, awkward and unsure.

"Since when did he have a doctor's appointment today?" Jackson asked, snagging an apple from a basket of fruit Destiny had dropped off the day before.

"Since before he arrived. We're having X-rays done to see how the bone in his leg looks. The prosthesis can't be fitted until it's healed completely. I told Stella about it."

"Stella didn't tell me," he said with a frown. "This is going to be at the clinic?"

"No. We're going to River Valley Radiology. It's in the same building as the clinic, but not in the same offices."

"Good."

"What's good about it?"

"I don't like Kent," he said bluntly.

"Don't like whom?" Chance walked into the room, his shirt neatly pressed, a tie hanging loosely around his neck. He spent most of his time on the computer or on the phone, but when he wasn't occupied with work, he was kind to Samuel, offering to play board games and read books with him. That meant a lot to Raina, because she could tell it meant a lot to Samuel. He craved love and attention the way plants craved sunlight, needed it the way he needed to breathe.

"Kent Moreland. The guy makes my blood boil." And Jackson wasn't going to apologize for it. The guy called every day. He always had a reason. He wanted to check on Samuel or find out if Raina planned to return to work as scheduled or tell her that one of her coworkers had had a baby girl.

"Is he a person of interest in the case?" Leave it to Chance to get to the point and to the problem. No matter what Jackson's gut said, there was no evidence against Kent, nothing to make the police bring him in for questioning.

"No."

"Of course not!" Raina frowned. Her cheeks were flushed, her eyes glowing blue-purple, the small bandage that covered the wound on her forehead stark white. She looked young and pretty and too vulnerable for Jackson's peace of mind.

"I'm just asking," Chance responded, meeting Jackson's eyes. "I figured Jackson had some reason for not liking the guy. I thought it might have to do with the case."

"They butt heads," Raina responded, but that wasn't all there was to it, and Jackson thought she knew it.

"It's more than that," Jackson said. "The guy is pompous. He thinks he's better than the average Joe, and as far as he's concerned everyone but him is average."

"In other words," Chance replied, "he's interested in Raina and you don't like it?"

Raina blushed, but Jackson wasn't going to deny the truth. "There's that, too."

"What's Wallace have to say about the guy?"

"He's looking into Kent's background because I asked him to."

"What?" Raina frowned. "Why would you do that?"

"Because I don't trust him, and usually, I'm spot-on about people."

"It's true," Chance agreed. "But I think our better bet for a suspect is Lucas Raymond. I did a little research of my own, and he's been MIA for three days. Canceled his appointments, asked a neighbor to feed his cat."

Chance took a seat at the kitchen table, his gaze on Samuel. The kid had stacked clean plates on the counter and was putting dry silverware into a drawer, carefully arranging it by size and style. Jackson thought that probably amused his brother. Like Samuel, Chance loved organization and order.

"I can top the MIA psychiatrist," Jackson said. "Kent's wife committed suicide."

"Really?" Raina looked shocked. "He told me that she died in a car accident."

"She did. If you count sealing the car muffler, closing the car windows and running the engine until you succumb to carbon monoxide poisoning an accident." It had taken Jackson a couple of days to track down the information, but he'd finally managed to contact someone in Kent's Wisconsin hometown who was willing to talk about Cheryl Moreland's death.

"That's horrible," Raina said, her gaze jumping to Samuel. He'd finished with the silverware and was wiping off the counter. "And it may not be good subject matter for a ten-year-old boy."

She was right about that. Samuel didn't need any more sad stories in his life. He didn't need any more loss or heartache. Raina wasn't the only one Jackson was bent on protecting.

"Hey, buddy." Jackson touched the young boy's arm. "Why don't you go ask Boone to play chess with you?"

"It is okay?" Samuel asked, his dark gaze on Raina. He spent most of his waking hours shadowing her around the house, hopping from one room to another, doing everything he could to help her with chores.

"Of course it's okay," Raina said with a gentle smile. "But remember, we need to leave in less than an hour."

"I will remember." Samuel grabbed crutches that were resting upright against the wall and left the kitchen, his narrow shoulders already looking a little stronger and broader than they'd been when he'd arrived. It was amazing what a little good food and a lot of affection could do for a child.

"Okay. The kid's gone," Chance said impatiently. "So, spill. What's the deal on Kent's wife?"

"According to a neighbor, she took a handful of sleeping pills, locked herself in the car while Kent was at work and killed herself."

"Did she leave a note?" Chance pressed for more information, but Jackson didn't have much. He'd spoken to a neighbor and to Cheryl's sister. According to them, police hadn't found anything suspicious about the death and the coroner had ruled it a suicide. Cheryl's sister had questioned that, hinting that there might have been more to the story than the obvious. When Jackson had pressed her for clarification, she'd clammed up and told him she had to go.

He wasn't sure what that meant, and since she hadn't

taken any more of his calls, he didn't think he'd be getting an answer from her anytime soon. Hopefully, Wallace would have more luck. "No note. Apparently, not even a hint that she was suicidal. According to her sister, she was alive and happy one day and gone the next."

"That doesn't make sense," Raina said, grabbing the stack of plates Samuel had left and sliding them into the cupboard. "If she was happy, then why is she dead?"

"Her sister doesn't know. The neighbor speculated that she'd been depressed about not having kids. She'd been crying out on the front porch one day, and when the neighbor asked why, she'd said that she'd just found out she'd never have children."

"Sad," Chance interjected. "But not the end of the world."

"Maybe to her it was." Raina leaned a hip against the counter, her faded jeans clinging to long lean legs, her fingers tapping an impatient rhythm on her thigh. "I've known plenty of women who have gotten depressed about not being able to have biological children."

"How many of them took their own lives?" Chance intoned, his arms crossed over his chest, his expression neutral. Knowing him, he was calculating the odds, trying to figure out the statistics. As soon as they finished the conversation, he'd probably head to the computer and do the research, print out a bunch of information and then share it with the team later that night.

Jackson admired his brother's scientific approach to things, but he tended to work more on gut instinct and intuition. Right then, his intuition was telling him that a happily married woman with a good life and no sign of clinical depression didn't suddenly become suicidal because she couldn't get pregnant. "Wallace is looking into it. I was supposed to meet with him this afternoon, but I'll have to reschedule the meeting, though."

"Why would you do that?" Chance asked, glancing at his watch and frowning.

"Samuel has an appointment with the doctor."

"And?" His brother speared him with one of his famous you're-not-making-any-sense looks. Jackson ignored it.

"And Raina and Samuel need an escort."

"Boone and Stella can do it, and you and I can go to the meeting with Wallace. We need whatever information he has. The sooner we get it, the better."

"He's right," Raina interjected. "There's no need for you to reschedule, Jackson. Samuel and I will be fine."

Jackson ignored her comment, because he didn't want to leave her safety to someone else. Not even someone else who was part of the HEART family. "Boone and Stella can go to the meeting with Wallace. You and I can go to the medical appointment. That makes just as much sense as anything."

"Sure it does," Chance agreed. "Except Officer Wallace is expecting *you. You're* the one who's been gathering information, Jackson. *You're* the one who spoke to Cheryl Moreland's neighbor and sister. *You're* one of the last people to see Butch alive. You're also the one who nearly got run down by the Jeep, chased a guy through the woods—"

"All right," Jackson cut him off. "I get your point."

"Then stop letting your emotions rule and do what needs to be done," Chance said. "I've got a couple of calls to make, but I'll be ready to leave when you are. We'll go as teams of two and meet up here or at the doctor's office when we're done, depending on how long the meeting with the police takes."

Jackson scowled, but his brother was already on his way out of the room and missed his irritated glare.

"Jackson." Raina touched his hand, her fingers skimming over his knuckles, that simple touch shooting warmth straight into his heart. "Don't compromise your job for my sake."

"This has nothing to do with my job, Raina. I'm on vacation. I can do what I want." But, of course, he really couldn't. Even on vacation, he was part of the team, part of the family that had been knit tightly together by passion and mission and heart.

"You know you can't." She smiled gently. "Not unless you want to spend Thanksgiving listening to your brother complain about your poor choices."

"Chance isn't like that." He captured her hand, tugging her closer. She smelled like sunlight and flowers, and he thought that if he had to, he could live on that scent and on her smiles. "He'll respect whatever choice I make."

"But will you?" She rested her palm on his cheek, her skin smooth and warm, her expression soft. "You know if I were anyone else, you'd already have left for your meeting."

"And?"

"And that's what I want you to do."

"Too bad it's not what *I* want to do."

"But it's what you *should* do. Your job isn't just something you do, Jackson. It's who you are. I'd never want you to compromise that for me."

He wasn't surprised by her words, but he *was* touched by them. In the years that he'd dated Amanda, he'd spent too much time feeling torn between his job and their relationship. Her neediness had drained him, sapped his energy and made him question whether or not he could ever have a lasting relationship. Since they'd broken up, he'd come to terms with the strain a job like his put on a relationship. He'd told himself over and over again that he didn't have the time that was necessary to make forever work.

He'd been wrong.

"You're a special lady, you know that?" he murmured, his lips brushing the soft skin behind her ear.

She shivered, melting into him, her arms sliding around his waist, her head resting against his chest. "I'm not special. I'm tired and scared, and I want all this to be over, so I can move on with my life."

"When it *is* over, I hope that moving on means moving toward me," he responded, easing back so he could look into her face, read the truth in her eyes. "Because I'm moving toward you, Raina, and I don't know what direction I'm going to head if that's not what you want."

She hesitated, and he could see the sadness in her gaze, knew she was thinking of her husband and her son and all the things she thought she had to leave behind to move forward. "I am moving toward you, Jackson. But it might take me a little longer to get there. I have a lot of stuff to deal with."

"I know, and I'm willing to wait for as long as it takes."

She smiled, her lips trembling, her eyes filled with tears. He wanted to kiss them away, to make her forget the sadness of what had been and embrace the joy of what could be. He cupped her nape, brushed her lips with his. He only meant it to be comforting, easy, light, but they both leaned closer, and the kiss became more than a light touch, more than a gesture that said "It's going to be okay."

Her lips tasted of sunshine and flowers and tears, and he wanted more. He wanted everything, because with Raina, he knew that was exactly what he would get. Heart, soul, passion, none of it withheld, none of it hidden.

Her hands slid up his back, her palms hot through his shirt, and he didn't want to stop, didn't want to think, just wanted to take the gift that he'd been given, the chance at what he'd thought he would never have.

EIGHTEEN

"Hey, Raina! What time is that... Oh!" Stella's voice was like ice water in the veins, and Raina jumped back, slamming into the counter and stumbling forward again.

"Slow down," Jackson said, catching her waist and holding her steady. "You're going to hurt yourself."

"Man! Wow!" Stella stood in the threshold of the stairway, her eyes bright with amusement. "Didn't mean to interrupt. I wanted to check on the time for that appointment Samuel has."

"He has to be there at noon," Raina said, her voice a little rough, her breathing a little labored and, she was sure, her cheeks blazing red. "We should probably go."

"That's what I thought," Stella said, not even trying to hide her smile. "Of course, if you two want to hang out for a while longer, I can take the kid myself."

"No. He'll need me there."

"Okay. So, how about you go get him moving while I discuss the plan with Jackson?"

"Right. Sure." Raina met Jackson's eyes. "I guess I'll see you later?"

"You know you'll see me later," he promised, dropping a quick kiss on her lips. "But, as much as I hate to admit it, Chance is right. I need to be at that meeting with Wallace."

"You're meeting with that good-looking police officer?" Stella asked with a grin. "Maybe I should come along. Since I missed my date the other night, I'm in the market for a new guy."

"Sorry, Stella, but I need you to stay with Raina," Jackson said. "I'm counting on you to keep her safe. To keep them both safe."

All Stella's amusement fell away. Laughter left her voice and her eyes. She looked more serious than Raina had ever seen her. "I'll protect her and the kid with my life. You know that, Jackson."

He nodded, turning his attention back to Raina. "Make sure you stick close to Stella and Boone. I don't want anything to happen to you."

"I'll be fine," she assured him, but she felt anxious, worried, because he was worried and because she didn't think the calmness they'd had for the past few days was going to last.

"I'm counting on it." He dropped a quick kiss to her lips, gave her a gentle nudge toward the living room. "Go get Samuel. You don't want to be late."

She didn't, but she didn't really want to leave, either.

She felt right when she was with Jackson, complete in a way she hadn't been since the accident. The hole that her family's death had left was filling up, slowly flooding with new emotions, new people, new *hope*.

That's what had been missing from her life—hope in the future, belief that life still had wonderful things to offer, trust that God would take the bad and make good out of it.

Now that she had it, she wouldn't give it up.

She would have told Jackson that, but Samuel needed to be prodded away from the game of chess he was playing, and by the time she'd convinced him to brush his teeth and wash his face, Jackson and Chance had left.

There'd be time later.

Unless there wasn't.

That was the thing about life. Aside from the ones already lived, there were no moments guaranteed.

She shivered at the thought, hurrying Samuel out into the cold gray day. Muted sunlight filtered through the clouds but did nothing to warm the chilly air.

She unlocked the car, Stella and Boone hovering close by, gun holsters strapped to their chests and visible beneath their open coats. They looked tough and ready for trouble. For some reason, that didn't make Raina feel any less anxious.

The drive to the medical building took less than twenty minutes, the fall foliage vivid in the early-afternoon gloom. She parked close to the door, nearly tripping over her own feet as Stella hurried her inside and to the bank of elevators.

"We need to slow down," Raina panted. "Samuel can't keep up."

"He can when he's got a ride," Stella responded, gesturing toward the door. Boone strode in, Samuel in his arms. He set the boy down, handed him his crutches.

"I'm not liking this," he said, scanning the nearly empty lobby. "Things feel off."

"I was thinking the same." Stella punched the elevator button, her expression hard and unreadable. "Could be we're both just on edge. We're not used to being inactive for so long."

"Could be," Boone responded, but Raina didn't think he believed it.

She didn't believe it. Her skin felt tight, her hair standing on end as they got in the elevator and made their way to the third floor.

The radiology department was straight ahead, a few patients waiting for their turns. Raina walked to the check-in desk, smiling at the receptionist.

"Name?" the gray-haired woman asked with a smile.

"Samuel Niag."

The receptionist typed something into her computer and frowned. "I see him on the schedule, but there's a note here that says you need to see his regular physician for a recheck on infection before we run the X-ray series, and I've got no referral on file."

"We were in to see Dr. Moreland two days ago," Raina responded. "He cleared Samuel for the X-rays and was supposed to fax the referral over."

"We didn't receive the paperwork for the consult. I can call Dr. Moreland if you'd like. Maybe he can fax something over."

"Actually, I work in his office. I'll go see if I can grab what you need and bring it to you."

"Are you sure, dear? It really isn't a problem for me to do it."

"I'm sure." Mostly because she knew exactly how long it could take for a fax to be sent, and she didn't want to spend any more time at the medical center than necessary. She walked to the seat Boone had set Samuel in. "Hey, buddy. I need to run and get something from Dr. Moreland. Do you think you can stay here with Boone for a few minutes?"

"Yes," Samuel said, but he was obviously anxious,

his gaze darting around the room, his leg swinging with excess nerves.

"It's going to be fine," she said, crouching in front of him and looking into his eyes. "X-rays don't hurt a bit. You'll have them done, and when you come out, I'll be here waiting. Then we'll go to the library and get some books to bring home."

"No one said anything about a library," Stella said.

"We're going to the library," Boone responded. "The kid wants books, and he deserves them. He's a real trouper." He handed Samuel his phone, showed him a game he could play. "You two go ahead. I'll make sure the kid stays safe."

Raina hurried into the corridor, Stella at her side. "I don't understand why Kent didn't send the file over. He knows how important these X-rays are," she muttered.

"Because he's a self-centered jerk?" Stella offered.

"He's not self-centered." They rounded a corner, headed toward the east side of the building and the entrance to the clinic.

"Honey, trust me. I know self-centered when I see it. The guy is way more interested in what he can get from you than what he can give."

"He's always been very good to me, Stella," she said, feeling obligated to defend the man.

"Because he wants something from you. That's the way men are. They act like princes until they have what they want. Then they act like slugs."

Stella pushed open the clinic door, gesturing for Raina to step in ahead of her. "Now listen," she said, pulling Raina to her side. "We stick together, okay? If there's trouble, you do what I say. No questions asked. Got it?"

"Got it," Raina said absently. She was more interested in getting the file and getting back to Samuel than she was in Stella's warnings. They were on her home turf, standing in an office she'd spent a good portion of the past three years in. As far as she was concerned, the clinic was almost as safe as home.

"Hey, Raina!" the receptionist said as she approached the front desk. "What's up?"

"I brought Samuel over to radiology, but they haven't received the referral."

"Wish I could help you with that, but I'm clueless. Kent is on break, though. If you want to go back to his office, I'm sure he can get it for you."

"Thanks."

"I'll let him know you're heading back." The receptionist lifted the phone and punched a button. Seconds later, she hung up. "He said he'll be right up."

"Why not just let you go back there?" Stella muttered under her breath. "See what I mean? Self-centered. He wants to make a big show of being in control."

"I don't care what he's doing, as long as I get the referral."

"I care, and I might just tell him that when he finally shows his face. As a matter of fact—"

"Raina!" Kent appeared behind the receptionist, his white lab coat immaculate, an obviously fake smile on his face. "Sorry for forgetting to fax the referral. It's been hectic around here with you gone."

Raina didn't know how that could be, since people were filling her shifts, but she kept the thought to herself. "It's no problem, Kent, but Samuel's appointment is today, and I really need it."

"Come on back to my office. I'll get it for you." He

took her arm, his grip just a little tighter than she would have liked. Her skin crawled, and she would have pulled back and refused to go if Stella hadn't been following along behind.

"So," Kent said as they stepped into his office, "how have things been going?"

"I guess as well as can be expected. Samuel seems to be adjusting well and—"

"I didn't mean with Samuel. I meant with you." He gestured to the chairs that sat in front of his desk. "Go ahead and have a seat. I need to get the referral form."

"I think I'll stand," Stella responded coldly.

"Suit yourself," Kent said, shoving his hands deep into the pocket of his lab coat and shrugging. "I'll ask Mandy to help me find the forms. Unless you want to come and look for them, Raina. You probably know where they—"

"She's going to stay here with me," Stella cut him off, her eyes as hard and cold as ice.

"No problem." Kent shrugged and headed for the door.

Somehow, his feet tangled up, and he stumbled forward, knocking into Stella. She shoved him away, hissing softly and grabbing her upper thigh.

"What do you have in that pocket, Doc? A—" She went pale, every bit of color draining from her face.

Raina lunged toward her.

"Don't bother." Kent grabbed her arm, pulling her away as Stella crumbled to the floor.

"What happened? What did you do?"

"Shut up!" he snarled, pulling out a gun and aiming it straight at her heart. "Because if you don't, I will kill everyone in this building, including that little brat you seem to love so much."

"Kent—"

"I said shut up!" He waved the gun wildly, and she froze. "That's better. Now we're going to walk out of here together. If anyone asks where we're going, you say we're heading to radiology."

"Stella—"

"Don't worry about her. She'll be conscious in a couple hours with nothing more than a headache to deal with."

"But—"

"Do you want people to die, Raina? Is that what you want? Because it's not that hard to take someone's life. It's really not."

She went ice-cold at his words, and did what he said, walking out of the room and out of the building, her heart beating frantically.

She had to escape. Had to—

Something slammed into the back of her head, and she fell, every thought falling into darkness with her.

NINETEEN

"Open your eyes," a man said, the words seeping into her consciousness.

"Jackson?" she whispered, the word thick on her tongue, her head pounding.

"Hurry up. I don't have all day." A vicious slap stung her cheek, and she shot upright, her heart racing as memories flooded back.

Kent stood a few feet away, still in his lab coat, a cup of water in his hand.

"Where are we?" she asked, her throat clogged with fear.

"Don't you know?" He grinned, and everything evil she'd ever dreamed of was in that one little smile.

"No."

"Don't be obtuse, Raina. Look around."

She did. Saw old beige carpet and a baby grand piano that had been covered with a sheet. A fireplace. A small alcove that she knew had once contained a display table and tiny little angel figures.

Her in-laws' old house.

The knowledge shot through her. "What do you want, Kent?"

"What I wanted was you, but you didn't want me."

"I wasn't ready. I was still grieving Matt," she responded, easing toward the foyer. She made it to the threshold, the door just a few feet away. The dining room she'd eaten dozens of meals in just across the hall, the window allowing watery light to seep in. A shadow moved past. She blinked and it was gone.

Imagination or reality? She didn't know. Wasn't sure it mattered. Kent had a gun, and she was trapped inside with him. She reached for the door handle.

"There's no sense trying that door, Raina. I came in the back way. Broke the lock yesterday and set this all up." He gestured to dozens of rose petals that lay on the floor nearby. "I'm sure when they find you here, they'll figure it was your handiwork. Of course, they might not find you for a while. The house hasn't had many showings in the past few months."

"You're crazy," she spat, her voice trembling with fear.

"I'm not crazy. I'm angry. I don't like to be ignored, Raina," he said, his voice silky and soft and so terrifying Raina wanted to lie back down on the floor, close her eyes, pretend the nightmare away.

God, please, help me.

The prayer was as desperate as her prayers in Africa had been, the danger she was in just as real. Only there was no little boy with a water bottle in his hands, no helicopter flying in to rescue her. No Jackson, lifting her into his arms.

She blinked back tears, forced back fear.

A soft sound broke through the silence. Fingers on glass? She turned her head, looking at the window again.

Nothing. No face in the window there. No sign that help had arrived.

"Did you hear me?" he snapped. "I don't like to be ignored."

"I've never ignored you," she said, knowing that reasoning with him was futile, but hoping, praying, trusting that help was on the way.

"Drink this." He thrust the glass into her hands.

"What is it?"

"Death," he said, leaning toward her and inhaling deeply. "I'll miss you, Raina. I had high hopes that you were the one. After our time in Africa—"

"What time? We were trapped in separate cages. We never even spoke." She had to keep him talking, had to give herself more time. Give Jackson more time. He'd find her. She had to believe that. Had to believe that God hadn't brought her this far to let her die.

"We were the only survivors, because we were meant to be," he hissed. "I suspected you were mine after your husband died, and I knew it was true after Africa. God wanted us together, but you ruined it."

"I didn't know," she said, easing to the left, stepping farther into the foyer. She could see the kitchen from there, the back door beckoning.

"Because you ignored God!" he shouted so loudly the chandelier in the foyer rattled. "Worse, you ignored me! No one ignores me. Ever! Now drink or die with a bullet in your head." He pulled the gun from his pocket. "You choose."

"Okay." She lifted the glass, praying, trusting, hoping, even though she wasn't sure there was any hope left.

He smiled, the gun lowering a fraction of an inch.

That was her chance and she took it, throwing the

glass at his head, and taking off down the hall, running from him, running toward Samuel, toward Jackson—toward life.

Glass shattered, and the world exploded into chaos. Voices. Shouts. But she kept running.

Something slammed into her shoulder. She stumbled into the kitchen and out into watery sunlight. Ran across the yard, voices shouting behind her, feet pounding behind her. She kept going, because she'd finally found the strength to live again, and there was no way she was going to give that up.

"Raina." Someone grabbed her arm, and she swung around, fists flying, head pounding, fear giving her the adrenaline she needed to fight. To win.

"Stop! You've been shot. You're going to bleed to death if you don't hold still!" It was Jackson's voice, frantic and filled with fear.

She stilled, looked into his eyes, her head swimming, her body numb. "It's okay," she said, touching his face, her hand slipping away because she didn't have the strength to hold it there.

"No," he ground out. "It's not okay. Get me something to stop this bleeding!" he shouted, and Boone appeared at his side, his red hair mussed, his eyes blazing.

"If Moreland weren't already dead," he said softly as he leaned toward Raina and pressed a thick wad of cloth to her shoulder. "I would kill him."

She thought that he meant it, but her head was so fuzzy, her thinking so scattered, she couldn't be sure. "Where's Samuel?"

"With Stella." Jackson brushed hair from Raina's cheek with one hand, pressed down on her shoulder with the other. His hands shook, his heart racing so fast he thought it might fly out of his chest. The bullet had hit an artery, and if he didn't stop the bleeding, she'd die. Not in a shoddy little village in Africa. Right there in her hometown.

He gritted his teeth, angry with himself for letting her go to the clinic, angry with Wallace for not making his first shot a killing shot.

He glanced at Wallace. He stood a few feet away, his face almost as ashen as Raina's.

"I should have taken him out," Wallace mumbled.

That was the plan, Jackson wanted to say. They'd gone over it all, briefed everyone. Just like with every mission. Every team member had a job, a position, a common goal.

Only Wallace wasn't a team member, and he hadn't shot to kill. He'd given Moreland the time he'd needed to fire his weapon. It was Chance who'd taken Moreland down. He'd broken protocol by doing it, leaving his position and firing before the doctor could take another shot.

"It's not your fault," Raina said, her eyes drifting closed. "You didn't know Kent had a gun."

"Don't!" Jackson shouted, and she opened her eyes again, reached for his hand and squeezed it.

"I'm going to be okay."

"You're bleeding like a stuck pig!"

"Again?" She smiled, then grimaced. "This hurts more than my head ever did."

"Yeah. I bet. And it's about to hurt worse," Chance muttered, kneeling beside Jackson, covering his hand and adding pressure to the wound.

Raina winced, but she didn't complain. She knew how quickly a person could bleed out, and she knew she could easily be one of them. Jackson could see it in her eyes. Not fear. Acceptance and a hint of sadness.

"You'll take care of Samuel for me, won't you?" she asked, her lips colorless, her skin almost gray.

"I'm not going to have to," he ground out, his heart nearly pounding from his chest. She closed her eyes again, and he glanced over his shoulder. "Where's the ambulance?"

"Pulling up. I'll lead them back," Boone shouted, running to the front of the house.

The rest happened in minutes, the crew moving in, shoving him aside as they worked to stop the bleeding and to stabilize Raina. He could see the panic in the EMTs faces, knew they thought they were going to lose her. He moved toward them, wanting to tear them away, move in close, tell her that she had better not even think about leaving him.

"Stay out of the way, bro." Chance grabbed his shoulder. "Let them do their job."

"What if doing their job isn't enough?" He yanked away, took a step toward Raina.

"That's up to God to decide." Boone stepped in front of him. "But you getting in the way isn't going to help and it might hurt. Seeing as how the mission was to get her out alive, I'm not going to let you do that."

If anyone else had been saying it, Jackson would have barreled past, but it was Boone, and he knew exactly what it was like to watch someone he loved slip away. "I can't lose her."

"You're assuming you're going to, and that's no way to think. Not when she's lying right there, still breathing and fighting. So, how about you stop thinking about you, and start thinking about what she really needs? I can guarantee it isn't you pouncing on a bunch of people who are trying to help her."

The words cooled the fire that was burning in Jackson's stomach, stilled the panic that had filled his brain.

"You're right," he acknowledged, and Boone stepped aside, motioned for him to move past.

"Looks like they're ready to transport her. You go on with her. I'll go back to the clinic and get Stella and the kid."

Jackson barely heard. He was already moving toward the gurney that was being wheeled across the grass and onto the ambulance. An IV line had been placed, fluid already pumping into Raina's arm. She looked small and vulnerable and incredibly pale, but she opened her eyes when he touched her hand, smiled through the oxygen mask that had been placed over her mouth. "It's going to be okay," he said, his voice rough as sandpaper. "*You're* going to be okay."

She turned her hand and captured his, her grip stronger than he'd expected, her eyes staring straight into his.

He knew what she needed, what she probably wanted more than anything.

"I'll take care of Samuel," he said.

And she squeezed his hand, smiled again.

"I knew you would," she said, her voice weak and a little hollow.

He leaned close, speaking in her ear so she could hear over the sound of screaming sirens. "But just until you get out of the hospital and only if you promise to teach me how to make that peach pie you said we'd have for Thanksgiving. I want to impress Great-grandma when she's here."

"I promise," she said, and he knew that she meant it, prayed that she could keep it.

She closed her eyes, but her grip on his hand didn't loosen as the ambulance sped toward the hospital. He held on tight, as if doing so could keep her from drifting away, as if any amount of effort on his part could keep her with him.

When the ambulance finally pulled up to the emergency room, an EMT almost had to pry Jackson's hand from Raina's.

She opened her eyes, looked confused and scared and a little panicked. And Jackson leaned close, whispered into her ear, saying what he should have said before, saying what needed to be said just in case there wasn't another chance to say it. "I love you, Raina."

He wasn't sure, but he thought he heard her say, "I love you, too," as they wheeled her away.

TWENTY

Making pie crust one-handed wasn't easy.

Somehow, having extra help had only made it more difficult.

They'd managed, though, and Raina couldn't stop smiling as she looked at the broken crusts and misshapen pies she and Samuel had set out on the buffet table. Soon her less-than-beautiful pies would be joined by the food Jackson's family was bringing. According to Stella, they'd arrived in D.C. the day before, and had taken over Jackson's apartment. He'd driven back home after spending the day helping Raina make pies and had been forced to spend the night with Chance at the HEART office.

Raina smoothed a hand down her simple black dress. Jackson had told her to dress casually, but she wanted to impress his family. She hoped the black dress and lone strand of pearls would do it.

"You are beautiful," Samuel said. "This Thanksgiving is beautiful." He whirled around on his crutches, doing a fancy maneuver that made Raina laugh.

"It is, isn't it?"

"Jackson will be here soon?"

"I think so." She glanced at the clock. He'd said he'd

be there an hour before his family, but he hadn't called to say he was leaving D.C.

"I think we will get married," Samuel announced, hopping over to the table and looking longingly at the pie.

"You and the pie?"

"No!" Samuel laughed, the sound the most beautiful song Raina had ever heard. "You and Jackson and me."

"Well...actually..."

The doorbell rang.

Saved by the bell!

"We'll talk about it later." She ran to the door, ignoring the slight throbbing in her shoulder. It opened before she reached it, cold air sweeping in as Jackson stepped through the doorway.

He looked good.

So good she threw herself into his arms.

He lifted her carefully, kissed her squarely on the mouth, then set her down again. "I have bad news."

"What? Is your family not coming?" She wasn't sure if she'd be relieved or disappointed if that were the case.

"Worse. I overslept my alarm this morning and didn't wake up until Mom called and asked directions to your place. They were right behind me all the way here."

"What? I don't even have the silverware out." She darted toward the kitchen, but he snagged the back of her dress and pulled her to a stop.

"Great-grandma brought her silverware and her china."

"But—"

"And I suggested Chance take them on a scenic tour of the town. That should buy us about ten minutes. I don't think Mom and the grandmas will let Chance drive around for any longer than that."

"I'd better hurry, then. I still need to—"

He pressed a finger to her lips, sealing the words. "You need to relax. My family doesn't need fancy. They don't need perfect. They just need love, and I think you've got plenty of that to go around."

"You're right," she said. "But I still wish I had some extra time. I wanted everything to be ready when they got here." She glanced around the great room. The buffet table was out and the folding chairs that she'd borrowed from the church placed strategically around the room.

It looked nice, but she'd wanted to have a fire going and some music playing. "Maybe I should—"

"Stand right here with me and thank God that we have this day? It could have been a lot different."

"I know," she said, his words stealing away her nerves and insecurities. She'd almost died more than once in the past year, but she was here in her house with two people who she loved and who loved her. That couldn't take away the heartache of her loss, but it *could* fill the emptiness if she let it.

She wanted to let it.

"I was thinking," Jackson whispered in her ear. "That if we don't cut into that pie and eat a piece now, we might not get any. My family can put down some food. Not to mention Boone. He'll put away one of those pies all by himself."

"Is that why you really came early?" she asked with a laugh. "To steal a piece of pie before it's gone."

"I came early," he said, his expression suddenly serious, his eyes the deepest, darkest blue of the midnight sky, "because I love my family, but once they get here, they're going to steal you away from me."

"We'll have other days."

"We will, but they won't be like today." He glanced at Samuel, who was standing at the buffet table, his gaze locked on the pies. "A day when a boy gets to experience his first Thanksgiving and a man gets to watch the woman he loves meet his family. A day when the past is only the past and the future is something to hope and dream about." He touched her cheek, his fingers gentle and warm. "A day when everything I've ever hoped for is standing right in front of me."

"Jackson—"

"I love you, Raina, and I'm not afraid to let my family, my friends and the world know, but I wanted to come early to make sure *you* knew, because that's all that really matters to me."

Her heart swelled at his words, filling up with a million dreams she'd thought had died.

They were there in his eyes just waiting for her to believe in them again.

"I love you, too," she whispered, and he leaned in and kissed her with passion and longing and love.

When he broke away, she was breathless, joyful, ready for whatever the future would bring.

"See?" Samuel said from his place at the buffet table. "I told you we were going to get married."

"Samuel, he hasn't asked me to marry him."

"Yet," Jackson said with a smile, hooking his arm around her waist and tugging her across the room. "But only because my great-gran would withhold her sweet potato casserole if I didn't wait until she was here."

Her pulse jumped at his words, at the look in his eyes.

"Speaking of which," he continued, "I do believe I hear my father's old Cadillac coughing its way up the road. I think our time is up. Come on, Samuel. Let's open the door together."

He kept his arm around Raina's waist, put a hand on Samuel's shoulder, and they stood in the open doorway, autumn sun streaming through colorful foliage as a caravan of cars pulled into the driveway.

Larry crossed the road with a bag in his hand, joining the throng of people who were moving toward Raina. Her eyes burned with the joy of it, her empty house filling with people, her empty heart filling with love, all the trouble and sorrow of the past finally leading her to the place God wanted her to be.

A good place.

A *great* place.

A better place than she could ever have imagined.

She squeezed Jackson's hand, looking into his eyes and smiling as a dozen people ran up the porch stairs, their laughter and joy spilling into the house and straight into Raina's overflowing heart.

* * * * *

WE HOPE YOU
ENJOYED THIS

LOVE INSPIRED® SUSPENSE BOOK.

Discover more **heart-pounding** romances of **danger** and **faith** from the Love Inspired Suspense series.

Be sure to look for all six Love Inspired Suspense books every month.

Love Inspired SUSPENSE

www.LoveInspired.com

LISHALO2018

Toby Potter watched the flames shoot toward the sky as
he raced toward the building. "Robin!"

Sirens screamed closer. Toby had been on his way home
when he'd spotted Robin's car in the parking lot of the lab.
Ever since Robin had discovered his deception—orders
to get close to her and figure out what was going on in
the lab—she'd kept him at arm's length, her narrow-eyed
stare hot enough to singe his eyebrows if he dare try to
get too close.

Tonight, he'd planned to apologize profusely—again—
and ask if there was anything he could do to earn her trust
back. Only to pull into the parking lot, be greeted by the
loud boom and watch flames shoot out of the window near
the front door.

Heart pounding, Toby scanned the front door and rushed
forward only to be forced back by the intense heat. Smoke

billowed toward the dark night sky while the fire grew hotter and bigger. Mini explosions followed. Chemicals.

"Robin!"

Toby jumped into his truck and drove around to the back only to find it not much better, although it did seem to be more smoke than flames. Robin was in that building, and he was afraid he'd failed to protect her. Big-time.

Toby parked near the tree line in case more explosions were coming.

At the back door, he grasped the handle and pulled. Locked. Of course. Using both fists, he pounded on the glass-and-metal door. "Robin!"

Another explosion from inside rocked Toby back, but he was able to keep his feet under him. He figured the blast was on the other end of the building—where he knew Robin's station was. If she was anywhere near that station, there was no way she was still alive. "No, please no," he whispered. No one was around to hear him, but maybe God was listening.

Don't miss
Holiday Amnesia *by Lynette Eason,*
available December 2018 wherever
Love Inspired® *Suspense books and ebooks are sold.*

www.LoveInspired.com

Looking for inspiration in tales
of hope, faith and heartfelt romance?

Check out **Love Inspired**® and
Love Inspired® **Suspense** books!

New books available every month!

CONNECT WITH US AT:

Facebook.com/groups/HarlequinConnection

 Facebook.com/HarlequinBooks

Twitter.com/HarlequinBooks

 Instagram.com/HarlequinBooks

 Pinterest.com/HarlequinBooks

ReaderService.com

Love Inspired®

LIGENRE2018R2

Love Inspired®

Inspirational Romance to Warm Your Heart and Soul

Join our social communities to connect with other readers who share your love!

Sign up for the Love Inspired newsletter at **www.LoveInspired.com** to be the first to find out about upcoming titles, special promotions and exclusive content.

CONNECT WITH US AT:

Facebook.com/groups/HarlequinConnection

 Facebook.com/LoveInspiredBooks

 Twitter.com/LoveInspiredBks